SOLOMON'S CONCUBINE

ALSO BY S.A. JEWELL

A Christmas Dinosaur With Yellow Eyes

Visit from a Shepherd Boy

Blink

Of Friends and Followers

SOLOMON'S CONCUBINE

S.A. JEWELL

www.ambassador-international.com

SOLOMON'S CONCUBINE

ISBN: 978-1-64960-131-5
eISBN: 978-1-64960-181-0
Library of Congress Control Number: 2022930573

Cover Design by Hannah Linder Designs
Interior Typesetting by Dentelle Design
Edited by Katie Cruice Smith

AMBASSADOR INTERNATIONAL
Emerald House
411 University Ridge, Suite B14
Greenville, SC 29601, USA
www.ambassador-international.com

AMBASSADOR BOOKS
The Mount
2 Woodstock Link
Belfast, BT6 8DD, Northern Ireland, UK
www.ambassadormedia.co.uk

The colophon is a trademark of Ambassador, a Christian publishing company.

AUTHOR'S NOTE

As a woman and a Christian, I've always had a difficult time reconciling myself to Solomon's character. Here was a man who not only talked with God but also was given wealth, power, and wisdom from the Almighty. What was Solomon thinking in possessing nine hundred women? I realize they provided alliances--and no doubt land and material wealth--but hadn't God given him the wisdom to achieve extraordinary success without collecting a staggering number of women--and many idol worshippers at that? And what of these women? How were they used? I find it a bit disheartening that the Bible identifies only two--Naamah, Rehoboam's mother, and the Queen of Sheba.

So, to work through my negativity, I decided to imagine the heart and mind of one of Solomon's concubines who believes in the one, true God, and I created Nalussa. We know that as a concubine, she was there for one thing--and that is a part of her story, but not all of it. She has my questions about the famed king and many you might have, Christian or not. We are not only sexual beings, but we also possess heart, spirit, and intellect.

My desire for you, dear reader, is that this story will cause you to want to study the books of Solomon for yourself to learn more about the wisest man who ever lived. And perhaps in studying this wise-yet-foolish king, you will be able to understand a little bit better the grace that God gives to His children and have some of your own questions answered.

S.A. Jewell

CHAPTER ONE

The sun had been up at least an hour, and he had probably missed his opportunity of getting his animals and himself a drink from the village well. That is, he had missed the chance of asking the women and the bethulahs, or virgins, to draw water for him. They usually crowded around the well before sun-up to gossip as they filled their jars. He disliked hauling water and filling a trough for his horse and donkey. He had people, usually women, to do that for him.

He hadn't been riding long, but it was hot and humid, and he always made sure to fill or top off his flask and offer his animals a drink when he came across water. Who knew the next time he would find a brook, well, or stream in these parts? It was summer. Hot and dry. *I'll do it myself,* he grumbled to himself.

He dismounted, holding the reins loosely in his hand, and approached the cistern. From behind, he heard giggling. Ah, he was in luck! Turning, he saw two bedraggled girls struggling with their jars and laughing with one another as they crested the hill. He waited for them to see him, and when the taller of the two looked up in surprise, he held up his hand in peace.

They immediately went quiet, and the older one, whom he could now see, pulled her head-scarf close around her head. The closer they got, the more the man stared. Never had he seen such unusual beauty—even at a distance and with her face partially covered. Oh, he had seen beauty. In fact, he was an expert on beauty, sensuality, and women's intelligence. It was his job.

This work couldn't be entrusted to a eunuch. What did they really know? To some thinking, they had been rendered sexually useless, but he knew better. They were not totally useless. Most were still men in thoughts and actions. They could be counted on for protection, servitude, and loyalty to the king and his women. However, the king's advisors didn't trust them on finding the latest concubine for their ruler. That took a complete man, fully intact—one who could fantasize, going beyond visual and intellectual assessment to imagined activity. It was a pure physical reaction to intrinsic sensuality.

He watched the older one closely as she and the younger approached. He was truly stunned. Her face was tantalizing. It was difficult to assess her body due to her robes, and he would have to rely on the eunuchs to make that judgement; but once she was dressed in more revealing clothing, he would make the ultimate decision on her value if the eunuchs didn't find any tumors, sores, or deformities.

When they were within earshot, he called, "I'm thirsty," and nodded his head toward the animals. "And my horse and donkey need a drink, too."

The young women walked to the cistern and put down the jars. "Yes, sir, I'll get you and your animals a drink," the older girl said cautiously, avoiding his eyes. As she leaned over to untie the rope to let down the bucket, her scarf got in the way, and she hastily tied it behind her neck. He continued to gape. *I can't believe my good fortune. If her body turns out to be as stunning as her face, I'll be well-compensated by the king's advisors.*

"Can I help, Nalussa?" the younger one asked as she shyly scooted close to the older, who had dropped the bucket with a muted splash and was now pulling it up slowly.

"Yes, Noa. Fetch the cup over there on the ground." She pointed to a cup lying near the base of the well, and the younger girl, presumably her sister, plucked it up. Balancing the bucket on the edge of the stone wall of the well, she quickly dipped the cup into the bucket and handed it back to her sister to give to the man, who carefully reached for it, never taking his eyes off the elder. Casting him a quick glance, she stepped away to fill up the trough to the patiently waiting mare. The donkey nosed the weeds. He suspected she was surprised to see a horse and a donkey, for who in these parts normally saw horses? She would guess that he was important and wealthy because, indeed, he was.

"Thank you," he muttered to his surprise. He rarely expressed appreciation, particularly to women waiting on him. The cold water slid down his throat, and as he drank, he stared at the girl's back side as she bent to pour out water into the trough. A thrill shot through his belly to his loins, and he thought, *This is a treasure*. Finished, she stood up and looked back at him with those startling light amber eyes.

She was dark-skinned. Unusual for around here. Perhaps she had some blood of Cush or Ethiopia in her. What little he could see of her hair was densely thick and black, sprinkled with gray dust and bits of grass. It needed a washing. Tearing his eyes from her face, he quickly took in her hands, delicate-boned and overly dark from the sun. They were rough and dirty, and her nails, caked with black, were ragged and short. Her feet were in no better condition. Bare and dirty with bug bites around her ankles. But he was drawn back to her face and those exquisite, shining, amber eyes. So completely rare. They were like shining stars in the night of her face. So overcome with desire, he wanted to touch her. Instead, he spoke.

"Nalussa is your name?" She nodded, averting his eyes. He tried to get a better look at her face, but she wouldn't look directly at him. "I wish to speak to your parents. I have gifts for them." Before she could answer, he went into the bags strapped across the donkey's back and pulled out a large, gold cup. The girls gasped.

"Sir." The girl's voice trembled. "I can take you to my father; but we have no mother, and my father and brothers are in the fields."

"Send your sister for them. Now," he demanded. "We will meet at your house."

The little girl looked at her sister, who only nodded to her. Immediately, the little one took off like a rabbit hopping over clumps of grass and small rocks. She disappeared behind the small hill. The man pointed to the two jars on the ground. "Fill them, and I'll strap them to the donkey. Then take me to your home."

Nalussa quietly obeyed, keeping her beautiful eyes diverted to the ground, unsure of the situation. This was fine with him. He had no intentions of sharing any more information with her because she didn't need to know, and even her father would have little choice in his decision. This virgin was going with him. No debate.

Once she finished filling the jars, he hoisted them to each side of the donkey, securing them with rope. He marveled at how heavy the jars were and how slight the girls were, yet they must have trekked to this well to fill these heavy jars at least two times a day. Women's and girls' strength and endurance never ceased to amaze him.

"Sir, follow me." She pointed to the well-worn path leading to the way she and her sister arrived. The man hesitated, but sensing his question, she explained, "It's not far, but if you feel more comfortable on your horse, I can certainly keep up." She shot him a look of defiance.

This pleased him. She possessed boldness. She wasn't the timid, young thing he thought she might be. The king would like that. While he desired beautiful flesh, he appreciated self-esteem in his women. He was not interested in sex-slaves or women who prostrated themselves before him. No. When it came to concubines, he wanted engagement, discussion, laughter, and yes, of course, sex. In the case of a wife, of which he had many, his main criteria were that they were politically connected and wealthy women who would help bond his alliances and expand his kingdom. Beauty and sex weren't all that critical for those women.

"I'll walk. It was a long ride this morning, and I need to stretch my legs. Show the way." He grabbed the reins of his animals and tilted his head.

She moved quickly in front of the man and his animals, who followed her along a well-worn and wide path that led to the village and to the square. Neither spoke to one another, but the man imagined how the king's advisors would be thrilled with the beauty of this woman. And surely, the king would want her on the recommendation of the chief haram eunuch once the man looked into her startling eyes. He imagined what she was going to look like after she was cleaned up. Now, she was dirty and barefoot, covered in a well-worn mantel and robe. But the way she carried herself suggested innate royalty, a certain grace and confidence that few poor women possessed. And her beauty was truly mesmerizing: bronze skin that glowed, eyes like amber, and perfectly shaped lips! He had come across many women in his work, but this one was special.

He sighed. Every time he found a suitable woman—really, a young girl—it proved to be a dichotomy for him. On the one hand, he enjoyed the thrill of the hunt, so to speak. To find lovely, untouched women for the king's pleasure gave him a sense of success. On the other hand, how many women could a man have? He wondered more than once. This king was nearing three hundred concubines and hundreds of wives! Was the king even able to bed them all?

He wasn't even going to consider the vast treasury of gold and silver the king accumulated. So much that every year, the king received twenty-five tons of it! For that matter, silver was so abundant in the kingdom, it was nearly insignificant. Yet, he couldn't complain too much about the king's wealth. He and his fellow servants were certainly compensated very well. But sex was another matter.

Many of the women he found he could have wanted for himself, but he never acted on his desire because, for the most part, they were poor. They would bring nothing to a marriage, and in time, they would lose their looks and child-bearing abilities. And, he reasoned, the king took extremely good care of them in a manner they never would experience if they were left to marry a relative or villager. *But this one is different. She's definitely not afraid to snipe at a man.* "I can certainly keep up," she had pointed out to him. He smiled in appreciation. He liked her spark.

He closely watched Nalussa as she made her way toward the village. Such grace. Her movements were almost dance-like. He wondered if she would be a good contender for children, not that a concubine's child could compete with a wife's child. They came first, and usually the firstborn inherited the kingdom, although King David, with at least twenty sons, dispelled that notion. He had made

Solomon king, and he was definitely not even in David's first group of children.

Yet children were important on any level. While the harem had their share of the king's offspring, one would think there would be more. So, maybe the king wasn't bedding his hundreds and hundreds of women. That conjecture was certainly a part of the discussion whenever he and his companions got together. His thoughts went to her as she led the way, now silent. *What was she thinking?* he wondered. *Surely, she knew what this was all about.* His conscience momentarily pricked him. *Why should I deliver her to the king? Was it really all about the money? Don't I have plenty now? Couldn't I legitimately look for a wife of my own? I'm of prime age. And maybe, maybe, I'm just a bit lonely.* He fiercely rubbed his beard. *Don't think about it! Don't go down that path. You have a job to do! There'll be plenty of time to look for a wife!*

Off the square, Nalussa turned left and directed him to a small, well-kept dwelling. As he secured his horse to a post, a muscled man and two rugged, teenage boys arrived with rods and staffs in their hands. Trailing behind them was Noa, the younger sister, looking worried. Their father immediately took stock of the situation, taking in the rider's healthy looks, fine clothing, strong steed, and well-groomed donkey. By the look on their father's face, the man saw that he was not naïve and guessed why the rider was standing by his home with his elder daughter.

"You're one of Solomon's men," the father said simply. Turning to the younger boy, he ordered, "Go back to the flocks." The boy dashed away, and the older boy hesitated. "You stay, Son. Your brother needs to be with the animals; you stay with me and the girls." He looked back to the man. "I'm fairly sure I know why you're here and what you want. Come inside. Nalussa, Noa, get this man some milk, curds, and bread. Jasper, see to the man's animals. Your name, sir?"

He directed him through the door as the man replied, "Adriel, son of Shammah."

"Ah. Shammah." The father nodded. "One of David's mighty men of renown. And now, the son of a mighty warrior purveys for his king."

Adriel wasn't sure if he was being insulted or not, but he wasn't going to get into a personal discussion. He understood the man's distress. It happened more than he cared to admit. Some fathers were delighted to sell their daughters. Others, decidedly were not. This father was in the latter group. One moment, he had a daughter; the next, he didn't. No warning, no preparation, not even a few more hours.

He watched the father closely for signs of hostility as they settled on thin, drab rugs scattered over the packed dirt floor. The rising sun was streaming through a window, and the heat inside the small dwelling was intense. He accepted a cup from the eldest daughter, while the younger gave a cup to the father and her older brother, Jasper. Neither the father nor the brother took a drink.

"Solomon surrounds himself with only the best, true?" The father stared directly at Adriel and didn't smile. Nalussa bent to her knees to lay out bread and dipping curds on the rug between the men.

"Sir, with all due respect, that is *King* Solomon to you." Adriel lounged back and took a long drink from the cup, pointedly watching Nalussa as she gracefully stood up. The father narrowed his eyes but kept his peace. The older son gave Adriel a hard look but kept his mouth shut, too.

Turning back to the father, he gently set his empty cup down. "I'm here for your daughter. She is most beautiful, and her coloring and eyes are very unusual. Speaking for the king, he finds exotic women appealing and worth great wealth. I'm prepared to give you immense riches."

"Do I have a choice?" the father asked.

He leaned toward Adriel, who responded, "Of course not. But you will be well-compensated and likely never have to tend a herd again. Your sons will marry well because it will be known throughout the area that you are related to King Solomon. And your remaining daughter—I can see beauty in her, too—will have a dowry. So, my friend, let me get you your payment for your daughter. The day is still new. I'll take her back with me today."

The father opened his mouth to object or perhaps plea for one more day, but Adriel held up his hand. Noa began to cry and reached for Nalussa. Jasper put his cup of untouched goat's milk down and stormed out of the room, leaving a hot, angry silence in his wake.

The father watched his son leave, then turned to his eldest daughter, who stood still in shock and despair, holding tight to Noa's hand. "As you've witnessed, I have no choice, Nalussa. You'll become one of many in the king's harem." Sadly, he shook his head. "I should have given you in marriage sooner, but I loved you so much, I wanted to keep you for as long as I could. Now, my own selfishness has brought sorrow to me; my heart breaks." He roughly wiped his eye with the coarse sleeve of his tunic. "But I know, dearest daughter, even as a concubine, you'll want for nothing. They'll take good care of you. I have to let you go." He let out a breath of air. "You look so much like your mother. I'll miss the embodiment of her in you."

"Father, no!" Nalussa whispered in abject distress and sank to the ground, clasping his hands. Adriel abruptly stood, ignoring the tears and drama, shook out his robe, and went out of the dreadfully hot room. *This is the part I hate,* he acknowledged to himself.

At his donkey's side, he gathered three sets of silver utensils, three gold cups, gold and silver coins, spices, and three flasks of fine-pressed virgin olive oil. *How apt.* He smiled thinly. On this journey, he was prepared to find at least three *bethulahs* for the king; but in his experience, he knew this type of beauty presented itself once in a generation, and he didn't trust putting a reserve on the girl as he continued to look for more possible concubines. The father could easily marry her off, and the king's advisors would then have nothing to do with her.

Hmm. What if I made her mine? What if I courted her? He could conceivably work out a plan to win her and convince her father that he was worthy to be her husband. He had money, too. She would have a far better life with him as a legitimate wife than as a concubine. He could convince them both that he was a much better choice as a husband than Solomon, who probably didn't know half the concubines in his harem. Not only that, but she would also still be able to see her family; but if she's with the king, she'll never see them again.

The king would never know if I got to her first. No, that's a crazy thought. Adriel jammed the treasures in a large sack. *What am I thinking? My job is important. I can't just marry on a whim!* And he would lose out on a great bounty. No, he was taking Nalussa now. And hopefully, under those robes, she continued to be perfect. And he would just forget her.

CHAPTER TWO

Nalussa embraced her father, brother, and sister. "Please tell little brother Ziba I say goodbye." She swallowed a sob. "I'm going to miss you all so very much!" They, in turn, each hugged and kissed her, while silently crying.

Jasper clung to her. "I'll rescue you; just send word!" he whispered.

Her father stroked her shoulder, at a loss for words. There was nothing he could do. Noa began sobbing loudly, clawing at her older sister's hands. She never knew her mother, who had died when she was born. Nalussa was all she had.

Adriel helped her on the donkey; there was no need for baggage, for she didn't have anything to take with her. Nalussa looked back for the last time at her small family standing forlornly by their home. The chickens pecked about the dust, with a strutting rooster close behind; the scrabble of weeds was nosed by an orphan kid that she had been tending; and a lone blackbird called from the roof. She would likely never see them again. *How utterly tragic,* she thought. *A woman's life can be worth so much yet so little at the same time.*

As they moved through the village square, word was already out that Nalussa was chosen for the king's harem. Children ran alongside the horse and donkey, shouting for alms; vagrants in the square openly leered and hurled lewd comments; and the elders and teachers of the law pointedly turned their backs on the riders. The women, gathered in groups, looked upon her with envy; some shook their heads with pity, and some whispered with disgust at their king's appetite.

"Pray for children!" someone shouted.

Another added, "Be careful if you do have children! They'll be murdered!"

Still, another laughed. "Enjoy it while you can. Beauty fades like the grass, and new shoots will pop up."

"You've caused quite a stir in such a short period of time," Adriel commented as he looked over groups of gawkers. "And I can imagine how you'll be received once we get to the women's palace," he said under his breath.

"I heard you, sir," Nalussa replied indignantly, knowing her place was not to engage in conversation but continued anyway. "Tell me how I'll be received. It's the least you could do for me, since you purchased me like a goat or a ewe."

"Nalussa, you're more like a lamb." He gave her a kindly look and slowed the pace of his horse so they were riding side by side.

"A lamb to the slaughter?" she demanded.

"No!" he answered hotly. "You'll be brought privately to the head eunuch, who'll look you over and . . . " Here, he paused. In this position with the king, these men knew what would happen and were directed never to say any more about the matter. Admittedly, it made some men who sought women for the king very uncomfortable, and often it took just one encounter for even experienced men to grapple with the uneasy notion of how the women they found were treated.

"You should at least have the courage to tell me the truth, Son of Shammah. And I know who your father is. Everyone does. He was honorable, trustworthy, and one of King David's three 'mighty men.' He struck down the Philistines against impossible odds, but God was on his side. He was a godly man. Are you? Is God on your side, Adriel, son of Shammah?"

The man went quiet. They rode in silence for a while until Nalussa could bear it no longer. "Are you going to answer me or not?" she demanded.

He breathed in deeply. "You'll be asked to take off your clothes. The head eunuch will look you over for defects. He's pretty thorough, I warn you. He'll look in your mouth and ears, check your scalp and all your hair for lice, and will make sure you're a virgin. When he's satisfied you are and he doesn't find any defects, you'll be assigned your own servant, another eunuch who will then prepare you for the king. But this will take time. You'll be given new clothes; you'll bathe regularly; your hair will be washed and oiled, your fingernails trimmed and cleaned, your skin lathered and perfumed. From the looks of you now and the condition of your skin and hair, it will take a while before you will be ready for the king."

Nalussa pursed her lips and shook her head. How could he so blithely describe her humiliation without his own shame or remorse? "How many concubines does the king have? I've heard hundreds."

Adriel looked at her. "Yes. Hundreds. I don't even know the total count. But he has even more wives."

Her stomach knotted, and her heart lurched. *How dare this king?* was foremost in her mind. The wisest man in all the kingdoms, it was said, and yet he thought so little of the Lord his God that he went against the word of his Creator by acquiring so many women, like the stars in the sky. Distinctly against Moses' teaching.

She didn't hide her anger. "Does this not remotely bother you that he has so many women? And does he even manage to satisfy them all?"

Adriel stopped his mare for a moment. The donkey stopped, too. "Those are questions you should never ask. The king is the king. He can do what he wants, and it would serve you well to keep your comments and thoughts to yourself. If you are accepted as one of his concubines, he owns you. If you are rejected, you will be worse off than you can ever believe. You will never marry. No one will want you. You will be disgraced and cursed!" He clicked his heels to the mare's flanks and bolted ahead. "I'm not debating with you."

Nalussa fumed. She would lose, no matter the outcome. She would be surrounded by women vying for the king's attention, guarded by men, existing at the whim of a spoiled, exorbitantly wealthy, and so-called wise man, who viewed women through the cache of possession.

Everyone knew the story of Solomon. Beautiful Bathsheba was his mother. King David was intimate with her while she was still married to her first husband. She became pregnant, and David had her husband killed, so he could marry her. Their first child died from their illicit union. He married her, and she later had Solomon, whom she helped to the throne while one of David's other sons, Adonijah, was also vying for the throne. David anointed Solomon king, and shortly thereafter, Solomon had Adonijah executed.

The people of the kingdom knew Solomon was not only given the throne by David, but he was also anointed by God, Who gave him wisdom and knowledge to rule the people. The people were in awe of a king who directly communicated with God, Who blessed him richly with knowledge and wisdom and enabled him to amass fabulous wealth.

Thinking of what she knew about Solomon, Nalussa shook her head. *I'm not impressed.* Yes, she had heard that he certainly was wealthy beyond comprehension, but it also came at the expense of many people, both inside and outside the kingdom. A vast amount of people served him in all ways of existence throughout the empire and his enormous household.

I'm scared, if truth be told. I'm leaving my family forever and soon to be stripped naked and assessed like livestock! Nothing more than an adult's pet lamb that can be discarded and ignored. She trembled. Naked and probed. By a strange man. And so what if he was a eunuch? It didn't matter. He was still human.

Her bottom lip trembled. She refused to cry in front of her captor, who seemed so proud of himself for his find. The man turned around. "I didn't mean to scare you. Just preparing you for what to expect. Are you all right?" He looked at her with concern in his eyes. His anxiety was apparent, which surprised her. Did he realize that this was all wrong? Concubines were nothing new, but hundreds to one man?

She jutted her chin up and shook her head. Did he really care how she felt? He was so handsome, so sure of himself and his position, yet there seemed to be a softening. Maybe he had a heart after all. He asked her a question she could now answer. "I'm not all right. I've been separated from my family; I'm to be humiliated shortly for the way I look; and if I'm accepted, I'll be no better than a piece of fabric to be shaped into a drapery for the king." Devastated, she looked away. "I'm scared."

Adriel blew out a puff of air, clearly uncomfortable. "Look. I can't imagine how you feel, and I'm sorry for your fear, but look at it this way—you are going to be living in a safe, clean, opulent palace, surrounded by women and children—some who will become your friends. You'll eat and drink well. You'll have jewels and the best of the best. Because you are an exotic beauty, I'm sure you'll become a favorite of the king's, and he'll bless you with gifts beyond your imagination. Do you understand?"

She narrowed her eyes. "First of all, it's true, you can't imagine how I feel. Secondly, I liked where I lived, with a loving family. We always had enough to eat; I had friends; and I loved my life. Why would I want riches? Jewels won't buy happiness. And lastly, I've never known a man! Being purchased specifically for the purpose of pleasuring a man makes my stomach roil!"

"Enough! Nalussa, curb your tongue!" He couldn't listen to anymore. "From now on, I will not listen to your complaints or criticism." He glared at her.

She glared back, snapping, "As young as I am and even though I come from a shepherd's family, I still have a sense of self and human worth. I need to know what to expect. As I told you, I'm scared. Please have the kindness to tell me what to expect once inside the harem."

Adriel cleared his throat and sighed, shifting on his mount. "All right, listen. Watch your mouth around the harem, including the servant assigned to you. I tell you the truth. Although you will be very well-cared for, be prepared for gossip, jealousy, and yes, even treachery. The women and their eunuchs are conniving. They all want favor with the king, and they all want children. If you start complaining and stirring up controversy, you could easily be thrown out before the king ever sets eyes on you. If that happens, as I told you before, you will lose everything. Your family will have to give back the gifts. If they have been sold, your father will give up his flocks and sell his children. You will be worthless, except as a slave. Keep that in mind. Be obedient; be quiet; watch and pray." He paused, then said, "Look, I'm only doing my job. If I didn't find you, someone else would, and someone else might not have given you any information about what to expect." He let out a loud breath and said almost to himself, "You're at an age to be betrothed, and you're not. If you were . . . "

She could only look at him. *If I was, I wouldn't be in this situation.* What more was there to say? It was his job. If only her father had found her a good man as a husband, she wouldn't be riding on a donkey to a place she was likely ever to return from. It wasn't Adriel's fault. It really wasn't. Maybe if they had met under different circumstances . . .

Hours passed, and they spoke little, she sensing that he was troubled. When they stopped for water and a little food and rest, she noted his attitude had changed.

"Please, have a little wine and bread. You need to stay strong," he advised as he tore a piece of bread from a small loaf. If he hadn't just purchased her, she might find him to be pleasing.

She took the morsel and chewed slowly. "It's delicious."

"See? This is just a sample of what you'll be getting to eat. And that is just bread! Here, try a little wine. I've mixed it with water for you."

She slowly sipped and half-smiled. "This is wonderful. So sweet and light."

"Nalussa, the good will outweigh the bad . . . That is, when I say bad, I mean—"

"I know what you mean. I must make the best out of my circumstance."

After many hours, they came into Jerusalem and rode by the palace of Pharaoh's daughter, one of Solomon's wives. Nalussa gawked. Never had she seen a structure so immense and beautiful. What was the story behind this huge home?

As if reading her thoughts, Adriel turned to her. "Solomon made an alliance with Pharaoh, king of Egypt. When Pharaoh captured and destroyed the Canaanite city state of Geezer, he gave it as a dowry for his daughter to Solomon. She's a beauty, too," he added as an afterthought. "Wait till you see the king's palace and the harem buildings. It's out of a dream."

They did ride by Solomon's palace, which was, as expected, imposing and perfect. Far grander than Pharaoh's daughter's palace. Multi-storied, dotted with potted palms on ledges, and a different clump of dramatic, blooming flowers on each window and balcony. The sun reflected brightly off the white stone of the entire structure. It was dazzling to the eye.

The area around the palace was also breathtaking. Statues of rearing unicorns with wings, roaring lions with claws extended, and powerful bears on their hind legs bordered the promenade. The outer courts were lined with angels, cherubim, warriors, and imposing columns topped with gold chains, which were crowned with carvings of pomegranates and almond branches. Mosaic murals depicting peoples from foreign lands paying homage and giving gifts to the king were imbedded in the palace walls. Well-dressed groups of men and women walked the promenade and courts.

"Impressive, agreed? I never tire of young women's reaction when I take them into the city, particularly by the palaces." They passed palm trees and vibrant, dripping flowers hanging from baskets extend high on poles, interspersed with low, flowering shrubs.

For the second time, Nalussa smiled. "I would never guess a long day's ride from my humble village, this dreamlike city existed. I wish my family could see this."

Adriel laughed. "With the money they have from King Solomon's treasury, they'll have no problem coming and even staying in the city, although you won't be able to see them."

Nalussa breathed in roughly. "Don't go there," Adriel advised, guessing what she was thinking. "Once you're in the harem, you are totally protected from the outside world."

She let out a deep sigh. Wiping away tears with a trembling hand, she slightly shook her head. She was doomed.

The harem compound, adjacent to the palace, was constructed with a number of various-sized buildings of one and two stories in height protected by walls, hedges, and guards. What she could see of the buildings were also imposing. While elegant, the compound looked like what a fortress must look like. Impenetrable.

Adriel led them under an arch, past a guard who nodded to them, and into a small courtyard with high walls. He dismounted his horse and handed the reins to a servant, who also grabbed the reins of Nalussa's donkey while another man helped her dismount. Without a word, she followed Adriel into another small courtyard, under a covered walkway, and into a large, stone room with ornate doors trimmed in gold and silver on either side. An elaborately carved table and chair were placed at the far end of the room. A servant, waiting inside, immediately fetched Adriel and Nalussa cool water, handing them heavy gold goblets, while indicating they sit down. Two other servants silently entered through one of the doors with basins in their hands. Yet another servant followed, carrying a large clay jar to fill the basins. Carefully, each servant removed their guests' sandals and washed their feet.

Nalussa was blushing, clearly embarrassed. "Don't worry. They're accustomed to this," Adriel assured her. The water in her basin was black from her filth. The servant gently tried to rub a week's worth of dirt from her feet and wasn't successful, but in spite of her discomfort, Adriel knew she would be refreshed. They patted Adriel and Nalussa's feet dry with white linens, and the servant wiping her feet tactfully folded the cloth out of view and left.

Before Adriel could speak, the door opened again and a large, bald-headed man wearing fine linen and a purple sash entered with the look of pomp and authority until his eyes fell on the woman seated before him. All pretense of importance left him. He stopped and stared, cast a look to Adriel, then turned back to Nalussa. "Woman," he indicated with a wagging finger, "look at me." Frightened, she did as she was told.

After several moments, the man turned and exclaimed, "Adriel! You have done superbly! I know you are good, but this—this—is beyond anything I've ever seen in a while, and I've been here a very long time. She is stunningly striking! What unusual eyes! Her name?"

"Nalussa," Adriel answered proudly and protectively as he stepped closer to her. He introduced the man to her. "This is Jeriah. He is the king's chief eunuch over the entire harem." The man nodded and walked closely toward her. Adriel hesitated for a long moment, then made for the door. "I leave you in good hands."

She looked at him imploringly, but what could she hope for? He gently shook his head and left. Meekly, she ducked her head and stared at the floor as the door closed.

"Woman, look up. Don't ever cast those eyes down. They are a gift from God, and they show the power of His creation!" Obediently, she looked up and met his eyes.

Shooing the last servant from the room, the man said, "Take off your clothes." *So it begins.* She inwardly sighed but outwardly trembled. She was so tired, so beaten down. She did as she was told. What choice did she have? Slowly, she slipped the veil from her head and then slipped off her outer tunic and stepped out of her inner garment. Her feet were already bare. Jeriah's eyes went wide and brought his hand to his chin. Nalussa blushed deeply and felt her body flush with shame.

He twirled a finger in the air. "Turn around slowly." Self-consciously, she turned, then faced him, staring him straight in the eyes. Her entire body shook in fear and anger. He stepped close to her and ran his hands lightly over her body, feeling the tone of muscles and the condition of skin. He then thoroughly checked every portion of her body, looking for lice.

Standing, he commanded, "Open your mouth," and examined her teeth looking for any decay or looseness. Taking his finger out of her mouth, he next checked her ears. Pleased, he ordered her to sit on the end of the table. "I'm not going to hurt you." Satisfied, he told her to put her clothes on.

Nalussa thought she was going to retch and fought to keep the bile down. While she knew what to expect, she still didn't expect the violation, even if he was quick and gentle. She would never be the same again. Never. Quickly she slid off the table and snatched her clothes from the floor. She was panicked and sought to control her emotions with deep breaths, willing herself not to vomit.

"Nalussa. You are quite beautiful, an unusual-looking young woman with extraordinary coloring, both in skin, hair, and eyes. For all the women that have been brought here, you rank among the highest in looks, and that is out of hundreds. You'll eventually be housed with those young women of exceptional beauty. In the meanwhile, I'm putting you in the personal care of Adiah, who will get you an area to sleep, clean you, and feed you. Some women are special, and they have their own servant. Others are in groups with a servant over them. Each servant answers to me."

Nalussa said nothing. The head eunuch continued. "To give you a bit of understanding, the king has almost three hundred concubines and, at this time, twice as many wives and counting. The concubines are divided in a variety of groups mixing age, looks, personality, intelligence, and gods."

Nalussa gasped aloud. "Gods?"

"Yes," the man answered, smoothing his robe in irritation, betraying his feelings. "Gods. Some worship Chemosh, some Moab, others, the detestable Molek. The king indulges his foreign wives, who wish to worship the gods of their lands, and likewise to please his foreign concubines. I know you are a Jewess, but you must accept he does not discourage following Ashtoreth, the goddess of the Sidonians, either. Keep in mind, his wives represent important foreign alliances, so he supports their worship and their gods."

"But why? There is only one God!" Nalussa couldn't believe what she was hearing. These were detestable gods! Worshippers burned their children at those altars! Perhaps that was why the king had few offspring? "How can our king—who, it is told, has actually spoken with God our Creator—a king who has been given the gifts of wisdom and knowledge—worship foreign gods?" Horrified at speaking her thoughts out loud, she covered her mouth in fear and deep regret.

Jeriah angrily cleared his throat. "As I said, the king has many foreign women, and these women are more than wives or concubines in the physical sense of their descriptions. They are also politically connected. Thus, I order you, under the threat of expulsion from the harem, to never question the king's thoughts, behavior, policies, or taste. Never. Do you understand?"

Chastened, she nodded in submission. The head eunuch pulled a string that rang a bell outside the door. A small and very old man entered the room with surprising grace for his age. "Adiah, this is Nalussa, your new ward. She's not afraid to ask questions or speak her mind. I know that you will train her well." The head eunuch opened the door and left.

CHAPTER THREE

Adiah led her down a long passage to a tiny room with a low window, a pallet, two pitchers of water, and two small basins. One pitcher and basin were placed on an ornate, square rug with soft linens folded neatly to the side. Beside the other pitcher was a hole in the floor for waste that presumably was flushed down somewhere into the bowels of the building. She was so worn out mentally and physically, she flopped on the pallet, not caring of Adiah's reaction. She just wanted to close her eyes and escape.

He pointed to the hole in the floor. "Relieve yourself if you need. Use the pitcher and basin closest to the latrine. Use the pitcher and basin on the rug to wash your face and hands. I'll be back shortly with food. Then, you can rest. I'll be back later to check on you. Tomorrow morning, we begin anew."

He slipped out of the room as she laid back, closing her eyes. Although exhausted, her mind raced, going over all that had happened to her in such a short period of time. Never would she have guessed that morning as she saw her father and brothers off to the fields and readied her little sister for the day, that her life as she knew it would be over in a few short hours.

That night, after her evening meal and after the last check in with Adiah, she was finally allowed to rest. But as exhausted as she was, her sleep was fitful. She awoke continually throughout the night, reliving her conversations with Adriel, her subsequent humiliation, the longing for her family, and the sporadic worry for her future. She also questioned God. How could He condone the king's behavior of having so many wives and concubines? How could a blessed king pluck young *bethulahs* from their families? Pagan raiders did that!

When she was a little girl, she had overheard her older brother, Jasper, eagerly asking their father about King Solomon's hundreds of exotic and beautiful women and his immense treasure of gold and silver. It was all the young men out in the fields seemed to talk about. She remembered her father telling Jasper that yes, it seemed the king had everything he could ever want, but God had other ideas about women and wealth. He had said, "Jasper, God warned Moses a king should not take many wives because his heart would be led astray away from Him to other gods, and a king must not accumulate large amounts of silver and gold. Yes, my son, collecting women and accumulating wealth is not what God wanted in a king; it's a form of idolatry."

Jasper was dumbfounded. "Father, how can that be? We've heard that God has actually talked to Solomon! He gave him the wisdom and knowledge to rule the kingdom! Surely the king, with his knowledge, must know that God doesn't want him to have all those women and all that money? My friends and I thought he was being blessed! We envied him. I don't understand it."

"Son. I don't have an answer for you. I don't understand it either; the king has enormous blessings, yet he's clearly disobeying God. Just because he has untold wealth and a harem full of women doesn't make it right in God's eyes. So be careful what your desires are. You don't want to be on the wrong side of God. Don't be fooled."

She knew her father was on the lookout for a suitable husband for her. She accepted that. She was at the age when she would soon be betrothed to a man. Her father was very particular and was taking his time, although he couldn't hold out forever. A female *had* to have a husband and children, but her father was adamant whoever would take her for his wife would have only one wife and no others, including concubines. Her father believed God's intent from the beginning was one wife for one man. Her father promised her she would be the only wife in a household. If God said so, then it would be so. Until now.

She had been torn from her father's protection. It seemed unreal, and while it was not beyond her understanding—the king's lust for women was legendary—she never dreamed she would be thought of, let alone considered, to the point of being taken.

She was awake when Adiah knocked on her door at sunrise. "I know you didn't sleep well. No one does the first few days, but once you adjust to your new home, you'll be fine."

Nalussa said nothing as he set out food that was enticing and fresh. Fruit, curds, bread, goat's milk, and a sweet pastry of sorts. She discovered that even for all of her stress, she was famished.

"Eat, and I'll be back," he ordered. Before he closed the door, she stuffed the pastry in her mouth. She was shocked! What was this incredible delicacy? Some sort of fig, berry, and pastry mix, with a dusting of cinnamon and other spices she couldn't determine. Chewing, she realized how the flavors danced in her mouth like nothing she had ever tasted before. But it didn't matter. For as amazing as that small piece of paradise was, it couldn't take the place of simple curds and bread with her family. Satisfied and full in her belly but empty in her heart, she waited for his return.

A short walk down a wide, ornate hallway led them to an expansive room filled with pools of water, women laughing and splashing, and eunuchs passing out linens, soaps, and oils. Nalussa was wide-eyed taking in the scene as Adiah held her elbow and propelled her to a more private area.

The women in the main area fell quiet as she walked by, until one out of many said, "Hello, sister. Welcome!" After this, others spoke welcomes, too. Nalussa shyly smiled, pulling her robe tighter around her body, ashamed she was so dirty compared to the shiny white and brown women lounging and chatting in the pools.

Adiah pointed out an alcove and beckoned her to follow. "I'm going to take you to the baths for new arrivals. You'll wash your body and hair and scrub your nails and feet. I need clean. No evidence of dirt. Once you're ready, you'll go to another area, where you will begin your regiment of massage by an attendant who will use creams and oils. We want your skin soft and supple and your hair shining. Once you've been oiled, another servant will attend to your hands and feet, trimming nails and softening skin. When your time is concluded, I'll have clothes waiting for you, along with food and drink. We need some fat on you. The king doesn't want to hold bones."

The stone room was warm and scented with some sort of fragrance wafting through the air from incense burners. A servant was stoking a small fire beneath a tub elevated higher than the others. Conduits ran from the tub to others situated lower. Silently, the servant took Nalussa's robe and led her up three steps to one of the lower tubs. She was embarrassed by her nakedness, but the attendant barely looked at her as he helped her into the water. Once she settled in the basin, he sprinkled oil over her body, then went back to the elevated tub.

He opened a faucet, and pleasantly hot water cascaded over her. The oil foamed as the water crept up to her neck. She was given a sponge and began to bathe, while the attendant helped with her back and hair. Neither she nor the man spoke. She was soon getting used to her nakedness in front of men, who were seemingly uncaring. As eunuchs and servants of the harem, she marveled at their stoic indifference to nudity in a society where women were covered head to ankle.

Because of the condition of her skin and hair, she needed to wash and rinse a number of times. Once the servant was satisfied, he directed her to a lounge, where two more servants came in to work on her hands and feet. Olive oil was lightly applied to her hair and face. Next, they brought out butters, creams, and fragrant oils and slathered the rest of her body until she shined. Still, no one spoke. Finished, they wrapped her in linens and left the room.

I never thought this would ever happen. I never imagined anything about a concubine's life and how she was prepared for her duties. I never knew all these luxuries even existed. She smelled her arm. The smell was wonderful. *But I don't care. I've had amazing food and equally amazing body treatments, but I don't want to be here.* She closed her eyes, dozing off warm and clean.

She awoke to Adiah placing food and drink beside her. He looked at her appraisingly. "I'm sure you've been told a *number* of times how striking your looks are. This is beneficial to you and also to me. In my old age, I will be blessed with the king's gratitude when he comes to *know* you."

He fussed over helping her up and taking off the linens, and then he put her in a fresh tunic of pale blue and a robe of pink, dyed lightly in the juice of pomegranates. Again, she was amazed. Food, body treatments, and now clothes beyond her imagination. Feeling the quality of linen sliding over her shoulders, she was astounded. It was nothing like the tunics she made from the scratchy wool of the local vendors. This finely woven material breathed and fell loosely, yet gracefully, on her body. *If only little Noa could see this! If only . . .*

She pulled herself from the painful thought. "Adiah, tell me what is going to happen. I'm scared. I want my family. I'm . . . I'm . . . overcome." She waved her arm, taking in the room, the food, and stopping at him. In defeat, she dropped her arm to her side and bowed her head.

"Young one, it's understandable. I'm told you're a lowly shepherd's daughter. Your life has been limited to a one-room dwelling, a weekly trip to a small market place, the village cistern, and local fields. This is overwhelming, and I tell you, it is for nearly all of the concubines that come here. It's a change that is great, but you'll be amazed at how quickly you'll become accustomed to fine food, consistent hygiene and beauty regiments, perfume, clothing, servants, entertainment . . . the list goes on."

Seeing her eyes well in tears, he gently asked, "Tell me about your mother and father and if you have any brothers or sisters. I will better understand you and your ability to learn."

Nalussa sighed and sat down. "My mother died at my birth. She was the mother of my older brother, Jasper. She was from Cush. I don't know anything about her, and my father never spoke about her, other than to say she was loved and very beautiful. I think his heart broke when she died. My father remarried, and his second wife had my younger brother Ziba and then later died giving birth to my sister, Noa. She was a good woman, too. My father loves us all very much. The boys help out with the herds, and my sister and I look after the household.

"I love my father. He is so good. He took us to synagogue and made sure we were taught Moses' law. He can read and taught me a little. We prayed, sacrificed on the holy days, and joined in fellowship with our neighbors. Even without our mothers, we had a blessed and happy life. I miss them so much, and I've only been gone less than two days! I want to go home!"

Adiah was silent for a while. Finally, he said, "Nalussa, accept your new life. Yesterday is a closed door. The old is gone forever, whether you want to be here or not. You can never go back. The shame to your family would be insurmountable, and you would be on the streets, at best a prostitute or beggar. So, listen carefully. The life of a concubine can be either easy or hard. Comfortable or miserable. You make it what it is. If you choose to be accepting, you will enjoy friendships, extended families involving children—you might even have a child yourself, but we'll speak of that later—and you'll never be hungry, without shelter or clothing. In fact, you'll have the best foods, wine, delicacies, fine clothing, and maybe even jewels. If you choose to be miserable, you'll be caught up in jealousy, gossip, envy, vanity, and loneliness. The choice is yours because as long as the king is alive, you live here, and you belong to him."

"What happens if he dies? What happens to all of us?"

"We don't speak of the king's death, and do not ever mention it again."

But Nalussa wanted an answer if the king died. He wasn't young anymore, and certainly anything could happen. Would his successor inherit the harem, or would they be dispersed so new women could be brought in to fit the new king's tastes and alliances? Would the children of the wives and concubines be slaughtered because they were a threat to a new lineage? Certainly, the concubines had a right to be concerned for their future. And what was to become of them once they were old and no longer sexually active?

Frustrated, she ran through options of getting more information. Other women came to mind. As young as she was, she wasn't stupid. Getting caught up in gossip could be dangerous. She needed a discerning ear and careful tongue of her own. She'd have to be very careful about whom to ask, whom to trust. Kings come and go, and although Jerusalem had a long rule by Solomon's father, King David, even his reign was not without upheaval and challenges to his throne.

She recalled the story about Absalom, one of King David's sons and older half-brother of Solomon. He was banished from the kingdom for killing his half-brother, Amnon, who had raped his sister, Tamar. When he was finally allowed back to the kingdom, he led a rebellion against his father, who fled the city for his life. In front of all Jerusalem, Absalom set up a tent on the roof of his father's palace and had sex with the king's concubines. When the rebellion was quelled and Absalom killed, King David took those concubines and put them in a separate house under guard. He still provided for them, but they were ignored—and to Nalussa's mind, put away for life.

As a concubine, a woman's life was at the whim of a powerful man, but she wasn't going to let this be her story. She would figure it out with God's help, but for now, she needed to understand this new way of living. "Please, then, tell me about life in the harem."

"Yes. Let's move on," Adiah began. "We prepare all of our virgins socially and physically for an encounter with the king, which may or may not happen in their lifetime. Yet all the women must be prepared. We explain how to act in front of the king, offer suggestions of conversation, and dress them appropriately for the encounter. Is it during the day, in the afternoon, or late at night? Will it be for a meal or merely a tryst? The king favors loveliness, intelligence, spirit, sensuality, and whimsy."

Pursing her lips, she uttered sarcastically, "Whimsy?"

"Yes, Nalussa, whimsy. You must watch your tone of voice." Clearing his throat, he continued, "The king desires a sense of fun, humor, and appreciation of life's oddities. He's bored easily. He also loves beauty and sensuality. This isn't about goats or sheep rutting. It's about tenderness and intimacy with a mental connection."

Nalussa raised her eyebrows and twisted her lips. "Or not." Nalussa smiled.

Adiah had to smile, too. "You're right. Or not. If the king just wants to be satisfied, he won't bother with conversation, truly. But more often than not, he does want a conversation, a good one if possible. He's brilliant and an exceptional conversationalist.

"As for the sexual aspect of your responsibilities, I know that you have never been with a man, and I'll tell you the proper way of behaving in particular circumstances. The first time you are asked to come in to the king, do not initiate conversation or physical advance. Let him lead you. Trust me. He knows his way around a woman and her body."

Nalussa looked away from Adiah and gazed out the window. She didn't want him to see her indignation and fear. As young as she was, even though she didn't know a man, she did know herself. This wasn't the life she had hoped for. Not for all the money or food in the kingdom.

CHAPTER FOUR

After a week, when Adiah was satisfied that Nalussa was physically presentable and had adjusted to the behavior and attitude of a virgin concubine, he brought her to a larger area where young women her age were lounging and chatting on mats and couches or gazing out the windows. They stood at the doorway before fully entering the room. The women ignored them.

"I'm going to leave you here for the morning. I want you to become acquainted with the *bethulahs* in your group. Each have their own servant, who is training them. Once you have all completed your initial beauty treatments—remember, they are always on-going—and orientation, then it will be decided where you will be placed."

Nalussa looked at him in confusion. "I won't stay with these young women?"

"You remember what you were told by the chief eunuch? We divide our women in a variety of groups, mixing age, looks, personality, intelligence, and gods. Whatever group you end up in, they will be women of faith. We keep the pagan women separately, according to their gods. We don't want our women polluted by other gods and goddess. Only Yahweh is God."

She couldn't hold her tongue. "Adiah. How can the king couple with a pagan woman? God says the two will become one. The Rabbi teaches through Scripture, 'That is why a man leaves his father and mother and is united to his wife, and they become one flesh.'"[1]

Adiah pursed his lips. She cowered, fearing he would reach out and slap her for her insolence. Instead, he steered her back away from the door and into the hallway. "Nalussa, I feel connected to you. You could be my granddaughter if I was a complete man. I'll be leaving the service of the king soon because I am old. You are my last charge. As soon as you encounter the king, which I know you will, I will then pass you off to another, who will serve you, and I will retire. But I cannot, will not, allow you to question the king's behavior. It is a reflection on me and my training. I will not, at this stage of my life, have everything I have worked for, including my reputation, be destroyed because you question the king. No one does! We've been through this. No more. If I hear of another judgment critical of the king, you will be put out on the street. No matter how beautiful you are."

He led her back into the room.

The young women stopped their chatter and obediently stood for Adiah, who said as he entered, "Ladies, this is Nalussa, your new sister. I expect you to treat her well." With that, he left her.

For several moments, no one moved. Nalussa was smarting from Adiah's remarks, realizing she had stepped beyond her purview. She had to be very careful from now on, but the opulence of the room distracted her from further thought. She looked up. The room was spectacular. The high ceiling was covered in mosaics depicting women in various stages of dress, as eunuchs waited on them with platters of colorful fruits, or servants were combing the women's hair or draping huge pieces of jewelry around their necks. The women

1 Genesis 2:24

giggled at Nalussa's shock as she took in the designs, furnishings, tapestries, cushions, artwork, sculptures, greenery, and pools.

A small man, dressed in white linen, appeared by her side. "Look around. Embrace the magnificence of your new home." He pointed high to the heavy beams inlaid into the walls, where carved wainscoting was attached. Taking her arm, he led her about the huge room. "Laborers painted these walls using pinks and blues from crushed fruit and tiny berries. And see the touches of silver and gold inlay? These precious metals all came from King Solomon's mines. Each piece cut precisely to fit the design!" he proudly exclaimed and continued to walk her across finely woven rugs in deep purples and blues with touches of white that were scattered across the gleaming gray stone floors.

Stopping at one of the candles that were on gold stands of various heights placed throughout the room, he lit one from the coals in a bronze brasier. A sweet scent drifted from the flame.

"Please, sit." He indicated a couch by a window. She noted the couches placed in many different areas were constructed of precious materials. Her guide nodded toward her and said, "I see you appreciate fine craftmanship. All the furnishings are made of ivory, acacia wood, and ebony." She saw that these, too, were covered in colorful cushions and tapestries. He pulled back one of the rich, heavy drapes that framed the long, octagonal window. "Each window opens onto a small balcony overlooking the courtyard." From her vantage point she could see the potted plants and flowers adorning the sills.

Nalussa could only stare. Her home was one room with a dirt floor, shared by four people and the occasional goat and chicken who were always wandering in and out. A pang hit her heart. *Don't remember,* she warned herself.

As the man bowed to leave her, two girls who had been watching from across the room came forward with extended hands. "I'm Sachi, and this is Abra." They both laughed.

"Abra!" Nalussa said with a smile. "Your name means 'mother of multitude!'"

"I hope so—if I ever get in to be with the king!" She put a hand on her hips, swaying and laughing. She grabbed Nalussa's hand and pulled her, along with Sachi, to meet the other young women who were waiting in groups to be introduced. All asked where she was from, hoping she might have come from their own hometowns and villages; but to their disappointment, Nalussa could not offer any news or information. Disappointed, some walked away, but others remained to talk. All were assessing each other's faces, bodies, and grace. In a very short time, they would be competitors, but for now, they were on equal footing until they had been through their initial beauty treatments and royal education.

"Did a man named Adriel find you?" one tall young woman asked.

"Yes," Nalussa responded. "Considering his task, he was at least kind. But I didn't want to leave my family!"

"Oh, I did!" another lovely young girl interjected. "My father was going to marry me off to an old, distant relative! He was nearly thirty years older than me. Horrible, mean, dirty shepherd, of all people! I am blessed to be here and so grateful Adriel found me. We didn't talk much on our journey, but he was very good to look at and didn't smell like a goat." She rolled her eyes and giggled.

Sachi barely spoke above a whisper. "I didn't want to leave my family either, but Adriel gave them a lot of gold."

Abra tugged at her sleeve. "Oh, hush up. Adriel was a blessing. Stop your complaining! Look around you! See where we live? See the abundance of food and drink?"

The girls—some happy, some resigned—momentarily diverted from Sachi and Abra and took to the platters of fresh fruits placed in front of them, dropping the matter of Adriel.

As the weeks went by, the three young women began to trust one another more openly, growing closer. They had their treatments together but were separated for other training when they went off with their individual servants. Nalussa learned quickly to listen to Adiah and kept away from discussing the king's policies, preferences, and appetites—no matter her opinion. She would be subservient and watchful, keeping God's commands in mind, although it was proving to be a challenge.

After the initial grooming period was completed and the young women were healthy and plump, the group was divided. Nalussa, Sachi, and Abra were assigned together to an elite group of Hebrew women of stunning looks and intelligent and engaging personalities.

In all their time together, Nalussa was careful about not discussing her innermost thoughts with her two friends or anyone else because she soon discovered the women of her group were guarded and didn't share their fears or concerns—only their desire to be intimate with the king. Occasionally, she thought of Adriel. If only she hadn't fetched water that day with her sister, she wouldn't have been discovered by him. Yet, perversely, she recognized that he was an attractive man and well-spoken; and if they were in a different place and time, perhaps they could have been more than hunter and prize. *Now, why would I think that about him? We barely even spoke to each other! Besides, I can't think back because neither of us had any choice.*

Her only avenue to news about the social and political goings on in the palace was in listening and picking through gossip. Some of it was informative and some mean-spirited; but topically, it was all about the king's wives, his favorite concubines, and his unruly children. The young women got the information from the servants, who also liked to gossip. Except Adiah.

She spent every day with her mentor, Adiah, who taught her how to eat, drink, speak properly, and behave. "You'll be eating and drinking with the king, and it is important you do this with delicacy and grace." He picked up a goblet and took a tiny sip. Daintily, he picked up a piece of fruit and nibbled. "Always watch the king, no matter what he is doing and notice how he eats and drinks. Be a watcher. Be a good listener. Be grateful."

A part of her time was dedicated to enhancing her beauty, and the remainder of the day and night was with her friends, talking with the other women, whose main concern was being called into the king. She never got opinions or news from Adiah.

When the women did get loquacious over some piece of interesting gossip that was shared by their eunuch, she found herself shocked at the opulent description of the king's palace, the queen's palace, and the various buildings that housed his wives, other concubines, and staff. Who could imagine such magnificence? What was astounding was the amount of food and drink required to feed all the king's household—sixty-nine hundred liters of fine flour, 13,800 liters of meal, ten oxen, twenty cattle, one hundred sheep, and many deer, gazelles, roebucks, and fowl. Every day!

Very rarely, a new young woman would be brought in. After introducing herself, Nalussa would always ask how the woman was found. The sentence would usually begin with "A man named Adriel." They were either thrilled to have been found, or fearfully sad.

If the women weren't talking about how much food it took to feed the king's household, they admired their fine clothes and their attentive servants, who showered compliments on their vain souls. They spoke jealously of those going into the king and coming out with jewels and, of course, wondered and hoped when they would be next. Everyone wanted a child. It was foremost in each woman's minds. A king's child cemented their status in the harem and their status to the wives who did not have children.

This was also a concern due to the intrigue of ascension to the throne. Solomon was still robust, but although it was never discussed, a new king had to be identified at some point in time. Already, there were guesses—the foremost being his son, Rehoboam. Nalussa had heard whisperings about him for a while, but it was speculation, particularly since the king was still healthy.

One evening, the three friends were alone in a seating area, discussing if they would be called into the king, which none had yet.

"Our Abra is likely to be called in, I'm sure," Sachi commented as she looked around at the women in little clusters of camaraderie. "She, like all these others, is anxious to please the king. But . . . " She gave out a deep, sad sigh, smoothing out her tunic and looking downcast.

Nalussa raised her eyebrows. *But? You're not?* she wondered.

"Don't listen to her 'buts' or her dramatic sighs, Nalussa!" scolded Abra, breaking in. "Of course, I'm looking forward to being with the king. That's why I'm here! I'm beautiful and desirable. My life before the palace? I was living with a mother and father who wanted to sell me for my beauty to the highest bidder as either a primary or secondary wife! No, thank you. While they were looking for a husband for me, I took care of six brothers—some younger, some older."

She twisted her mouth in disgust. "My mother was sickly and couldn't help around the house, which was barely a booth, anyway. I did all the household work. My father only saw me as a fine possession to sell. I tell you, he was thrilled when Adriel showed up. He gladly handed me over, and I was thrilled! I don't regret leaving my poor, useless family behind. Now, I eat my fill; I dress exquisitely; and I'm incredibly cared for like a fine piece of sculpture or jewelry! And when I have relations with our king, I will be delighted. I can't wait!" She barely took a breath and continued, "Unlike our sweet Sachi, who mourns for her family and long-lost love. We are complete opposites!"

This was a surprise to Nalussa, who knew little about the relationship between Abra and Sachi. Sachi was always so quiet. Who was this "long lost love"?

Abra interrupted Nalussa's thoughts, looking accusingly at Sachi. "You are here for a reason, and that reason is King Solomon. So, stop being unhappy and enjoy the adventure!"

"I won't," whispered Sachi. "I don't care what you think, Abra. I don't want to be here. I miss my family!" She turned to Nalussa in desperation. "There was a man who wanted me, who actually loved me. But he was too late in letting my parents know his intentions, and he was poor. I was taken for the harem in exchange for much gold. How could my parents resist? He was brokenhearted."

"And Adriel found you." Nalussa stated.

Abra rolled her eyes answering for Sachi. "Yes, she told you before. The one who took you and me and almost everyone else here. Adriel. A fine-looking man, for certain. After the king, he might be my second choice."

Nalussa couldn't help but ask, "Do you think Adriel has a wife and family?"

Abra looked at her and scoffed. "You think a man who scours the countryside looking for beautiful women is married?" She smirked and leaned in close to Nalussa. "Why do you even ask? You find him attractive?"

"I was just curious what type of man he is with the position he has with the king, that's all." She turned from Abra to Sachi.

Sachi reached for Nalussa's hand. "I know we're not supposed to talk about this, and I don't with the others because they're gossipers and can be very jealous. But—"

Abra squeezed Sachi's arm, and she let out a yelp. A woman sitting close-by turned, staring disapprovingly. "That hurt, Abra!" She rubbed her arm vigorously.

"Sachi, how many times do I have to tell you to shut up? Someone," she tilted her head toward the small group of women now whispering and scowling at them, "is going to complain about you. And at the very least, they'll start spying on you to get you kicked out of the harem. You don't want that to happen. They already don't like you because you are prettier than they are, and they would love to see any competition ousted. So please, just keep quiet!"

Nalussa opened her mouth to speak, but Abra put up a hand. "And you are more beautiful than all of us. Your skin color is divine, and your eyes are startling. You will become a favorite, I'm sure, but you will also have enemies in the harem. Some—both seasoned and virginal—are going to be very envious of you. I warn you to be careful, too. How can you both be so naïve?" she asked as an afterthought.

"But I tell you, I don't want to be here either, Abra," Nalussa admitted in a whisper. Finally, her friends were being open and honest. Abra pursed her lips and tossed her head slightly in anger. "Please," implored Nalussa, "hear me. I don't fault you for what you want. You, too, are gorgeous and are sure to find favor with the king when your time comes. Honestly, I hope that you are happy and have many children. It's just that I don't want to be a possession. A sexual one, at that."

Sachi began to sniffle and covertly wiped her eyes. "I don't either, but Abra, I love you as a sister, and I want us to always be together if we have to live here forever. Please don't be angry with us."

"I'm not angry. I fear for you both. I have a different attitude about my position in life as a woman. We have no choice in how our lives will be lived. If I am to be Solomon's concubine, then I am delighted! But I warn you both. Be very careful what you say to the other women and especially to the servants. You can be replaced in the blink of an eye. And if you are thrown out of the harem, God be with you."

Their conversation was interrupted when they realized the room went oddly silent. The chatter and laughter stopped. A eunuch the friends had never seen before glided over to a servant who was combing out the hair of a delicate-looking young woman, whose features were fine and perfect. Her long, dark hair fell to her waist. Both were surprised as the man approached without a word and flicked his hand to bid them to follow. Without hesitation, the servant swept the woman's hair up with a clip and deftly covered her head with a saffron-colored scarf.

Immediately, the room broke out in whispered conversation. "Do you know what just happened?" Abra asked barely able to contain her excitement. Before either friend could answer, she smiled broadly. "Our sister is being taken into to the king."

"Like that?" Sachi grimaced. "She was clothed for hair dressing!" Even Nalussa would think his choice of the afternoon would be richly robed and bejeweled with a good dousing of perfume. At least, that's what she expected the king would want.

"Oh, my sisters." Abra kicked off her sandals and tucked her feet under. "The eunuch will bring her to the wardrobe room, where she will either pick out what she wants to wear or what the servants will suggest. She has already bathed this morning, so she's still fresh; and they'll fix her face, lips, and hair. Then, they'll drape her with his finest jewels, so he can be thrilled in taking them off." She giggled "He must be an extraordinary lover."

Nalussa looked over to Sachi, who was sitting rigid in stress, hardly sharing the excitement of Abra and the other women. Out of all the vast number of concubines who were rumored to exist, it was frightening to know that their small group was in the king's sights.

One of the servants wandered over with cool melon water and finely made date cakes. "My ladies, would you care for refreshment?" They all reached for a cup from his tray. "Please, take some sweets. The king likes his women healthy and plump."

"We are an elite group of virgins for the king's delight, are we not?" The servant nodded as Abra picked out a large date cake. "What can you tell us about our hopeful destiny for the king's pleasure?" Abra smiled coquettishly at the young slave.

What difference would flirting make, thought Nalussa. The young man was a eunuch with little sexual appetite. However, the man responded with enthusiasm. "Oh, indeed, you are ripe ones for the king's pleasure. This is the elite group of his Hebrew virgins. Once you have been with the king, you will then move on to another group. We keep the virgins separated from the active women. He, of course, loves his talented and experienced women, but he also craves untouched youth that only he is blessed to touch. You three are the finest *bethulahs* here." He smiled broadly and left to serve the others.

CHAPTER FIVE

That evening, Sachi dragged her mat close to Nalussa. Leaning on her elbow, she whispered desperately, "Nalussa. I want to run away. I don't want to go in to the king; I'm not like Abra and the others who are aching to be called. I'm so afraid. Even though he's the king, I've never been with a man before!"

"Of course, you haven't. That's why you're here with this group. None of us have been with a man before, and I'm sure many are scared, including myself. They just don't show it. We have to hide our emotions so as not to become the subject of gossip and ridicule," Nalussa soothed.

"But please, listen. I don't want to give my body to a man who will not be my husband! King or not. If I get pregnant, I will fear for the future of my child! And what happens when we lose desirability? I've heard we're confined to another part of the palace, cut off from everything except for our small world of older women and servants. I don't even know what happens when my child gets older. What happens if it's a girl? What happens when the king is no longer the king? This is not wonderful fantasy come true like Abra believes."

Nalussa agreed and held her hand. "Those are the same questions and fears I have, too. This I know: once we lose our virginity, we'll be put in the harem of Solomon's sexually active Hebrew women. My servant tells me that at least we three will be put in the highest group of the most beautiful women . . . " Here, she stopped. She couldn't well say, "But beauty fades." Was there a group for "old lovelies"?

"Sachi, if you run away, you and your family will be punished, ruined," Sachi interrupted. "I can't worry for my family anymore!" Nalussa squeezed her hand. "But who will have you if you could even escape? No one. You'll be on the street only good as a prostitute. Your only option, dearest Sachi is to stay here and be obedient."

Nalussa listened to Sachi, so young, cry herself to sleep. Disturbed and hurt for her friend, she couldn't get to sleep. Her mind and heart wouldn't let her.

I have some questions for you, Lord. I believe in You, and I know that you are not intimidated by questions. So, how can you bless a man like King Solomon, who is using women so blatantly? After all that You gave him, wisdom, knowledge, gold, silver, jewels, animals, possessions . . . Oh, the list is inexhaustible, and yet, that is not enough for him. He needs women as much as he needs gold; and he is sinning, and You're not doing anything about it!

She had heard all about Solomon's past and recent work for the Lord. One evening over supper, her father had told her about the king's temple. He had been up to Jerusalem for the dedication and was overwhelmed with what he saw.

"The king has built an astounding temple for the Lord!" he told his children. "I couldn't believe my eyes! Vast amounts of finished cedar, cypress, stone, and olive wood are used in the construction everywhere. The floors and walls are overlaid with massive amounts of gold. There are engraved figures of cherubim and palm trees and open flowers, all overlaid and spread with even more gold!"

He could barely contain himself. Nalussa and her siblings were mesmerized. She could visualize the huge, bronze pillars draped with bronze pomegranates that her father described were placed about the building and courtyard, along with lattices decorated with wreaths of extravagant chain work.

Her father continued, shaking his head in almost disbelief. "The king has an enormous, bronze basin forged for washing sacrifices that is placed in the southeast corner of the temple and supported by twelve bronze oxen, three each facing north, west, south, and east. The thickness of the basin is as wide as my hand," he exclaimed, holding up his hand. "And the brim is made like the flower of a lily."

Nalussa blinked and whispered, "And we live so differently." A plump hen pecked around her feet.

Her father, not hearing her, kept on with his story. "It's called the Sea, and it holds over eleven thousand gallons of water!"

Nalussa's little sister laughed and said, "It is a sea!"

"There was more to the courtyards and construction that I can't even remember. So much bronze has been used throughout the construction of the temple and its courtyards, it can not be weighed!"

The temple furnishings were equally extravagant, he explained. Almost every utensil and bit of furniture was made of gold or overlaid with it. What wasn't made of gold was made of silver or bronze. Utensils, pots, ladles, forks, candlestick holders, altars, incense burners . . . The list went on and on. Nalussa closed her eyes, visualizing the enormity of the building and the decorative wealth on display.

Her father sighed and turned to her older brother, Jasper. "I'm sorry I didn't bring you with me, but I needed you home with the family and animals."

Her brother had been deeply disappointed, and although he understood, he complained bitterly about it the entire time their father was gone.

Continuing with his descriptions, Father said, "And the abundance didn't stop there. At the temple dedication, Solomon offered to the Lord God peace offerings of twenty-two thousand oxen and 120,000 sheep, as well as so many other burnt offerings and grain offerings that no one knew the count!"

Her father spread his hands and shook his head. It was all so amazing. "All of it." He sighed loudly. "All King Solomon's construction, furnishings, decorations, and sacrifices are all beyond what any human could ever have imagined."

Indeed, Solomon's wealth and possessions were astounding. God had truly blessed him beyond precious metals and jewels, to garments, spices, animals, servants, and soldiers. He had fourteen hundred chariots and twelve thousand horsemen. And of course, Nalussa already knew, many, many women.

Nalussa finally drifted off into a fretful sleep only to be awakened a few hours later by rustling and urgent murmurs. "Awake! Awake!" Sachi was being gently shaken by her servant. Sachi raised her head in sleepy confusion. Groggy at first, she became wide awake and looked at Nalussa in abject fear. The man helped her up, and without getting her robe, he led her to the far doorway. Terrified speechless, she cast Nalussa a last look of desperation before she disappeared behind a door that led into the *bethulah's* private baths specifically set up for bathing before an encounter with the king.

Nalussa sat up. This couldn't be happening so soon, especially to dear, little Sachi! Abra, always on the alert to be called herself, got up, half-dressed, and hurried over. The other women had not stirred yet; it was still dark.

"Come quickly into the bath," Nalussa ordered Abra, looking about the room of sleeping women. Abra's eyes flew open in anticipation. "Come, quickly. Sachi's been chosen!"

Outside the doorway to the bath, Nalussa began before Abra could celebrate. "Sachi isn't ready for this, Abra." She was near tears. "Has her servant prepared her what to expect and what she should do? She's never talked to me about the sexual aspect of her training. She's terrified!"

"We all have to be ready. I'm sure her servant has told her all about what to expect and what she must do." But Abra brought her hand to her mouth, admitting, "I know she was scared, but I thought it was all about first-time fright . . . not terror!" As an afterthought, she asked, "Adiah has talked to you about what to expect with the king?"

Nalussa nodded her head vigorously. "Yes." Touching her friend's arm, she added, "We must pray for her." Silently, they bowed their heads.

By breakfast, word had spread quickly about Sachi's wonderful fortune, and several women came by to ask about Sachi.

"Was she excited?" one asked.

Another said, "I'm sorry I was still sleeping when they took her. I can imagine how beautiful she will be once presented and how thrilled the king will be with such a lovely virgin."

But others were jealous. "Sachi will be like a deer in front of a hunter's bow. She'll go still, eyes wide, not knowing if she should pretend she's invisible or bolt." Many laughed.

Abra and Nalussa went about their routine with their eunuchs. At lunch, they met up with each other, and after gathering fruit and cheese, they were handed sweet melon water. Finding a corner to sit without disruption or eavesdropping, they began to talk.

"She's been gone nearly seven hours. What can possibly be happening? Surely, he hasn't fallen in love with her and wants to take her for a wife?"

"Never a wife!" Abra scoffed. "The king's wives have to bring something to the table, so to speak. He looks to wives for wealth, political influence, alliances, land, territories, cities . . . whatever they can offer that is useful. Sachi has nothing but her virginal body. Now that it's not virginal anymore, what use will he have for a skittish fawn?"

"I'm going to ask Adiah what is going on. This is far too long for her to be away. I wonder if she's hurt."

Abra shook her head no. "Sister, neither your servant nor mine will ever break the code of silence. We both know they are of the few who don't gossip, unlike the others around here. And I'm glad some of these men do. At least, we get to hear what's going on in the palace and in the city. I have a lyre lesson this afternoon. I'll ask around if there's any news on Sachi." As an afterthought, she admitted, "I'm worried, too."

When Nalussa was met by Adiah to be taken to her etiquette lessons, she asked, "Adiah, I know that you don't gossip and that you stick to the king's business of grooming me, but I must ask, as your last charge, as one you said could be your granddaughter, what happened to Sachi? She should have been back by now, collecting her things and saying goodbye to us as she goes to the next group of women, now that she is no longer a virgin. And while some of us do gossip, I don't, and I need to understand what has happened to my friend!"

Adiah was silent for many moments, then whispered, "I can't—"

Nalussa interrupted. "You have told me many times your position—that the king is not to be questioned. I'm not questioning the king. I'm questioning you. I need to know, Adiah. I *must* know what happened to my sweet, young friend Sachi! She wasn't ready. Didn't her servant realize that?"

Adiah sighed and pointed her to a couch to sit on. He stood before her. "Some of us are friendly with each other, and some of us are not. It's much like how you form friendships and relationships within the harem. Some women you like; some you don't; some are friendly; some you have to watch out for. Some gossip; some keep to themselves. I am not friendly with Sachi's servant—not that I don't like him, I just don't have anything in common with him. He's young and inexperienced. Regardless, I wouldn't have talked about her with him, anyway, nor he with me. We are directed to keep our training and opinions to ourselves. We can't be the source of gossip. We only share information about our *bethulahs* with the chief eunuch of the Harem."

"I know that's how you are supposed to behave, but I've heard enough in this harem to make even you blush, Adiah. Certainly, the men talk and share the information with their charges, and they share information about their charges with the other eunuchs."

Adiah was stubbornly silent, busily looking for a scroll in his satchel. She reached for him. "Please, have pity on me! I'm human like you! We both have been sexually classified for use in the palace, but we are human! We have feelings, Adiah! We fear; we cry; we laugh; we sing. We worry about people we love! Even the concubines and eunuchs! Please help find out about Sachi."

He sat down, placing his hands on his knees. "I'm old. And, I've discovered, not well." As if speaking to himself, he said softly, "I have no fear anymore—only of God, and I know God is my Protector . . . I might add, my *only* Protector. King David sang, 'I love you, Lord, my strength. The Lord is my rock, my fortress and my deliverer; my God is my rock, in whom I take refuge; my shield and the horn of my salvation, my stronghold. I called to the Lord, who is worthy of praise, and I have been saved from mine enemies.'[2] I don't remember the rest; it was a long song."

She waited. Looking at her, he finally answered. "If she doesn't return by nightfall, I'll find out what happened to her."

---

2 Psalm 18:2-3

CHAPTER SIX

The next three days Adiah had no word on the whereabouts of Sachi. Rumor and gossip were rampant throughout the entire harem. By now, all groups had heard about a sweet, young virgin who was called into the king's chambers, then disappeared from sight, along with her servant. Was he so smitten that he married her? Or was she so inept that he banished her? Even if she was no longer a virgin and was probably designated to another group, she left all her belongings behind and never said goodbye to her closest friends. The eunuchs who gossiped denied seeing her or her servant since her pre-dawn tryst with the king.

"I can't stand listening to the speculation. It's disturbing. We're worried sick, and the rest are enjoying the drama." Nalussa could only cast a disgusted glance at her sisters chatting and laughing. They didn't know Sachi. They never bothered to find out anything about her. They were too busy primping and planning and hoping that they would be next for the king.

Abra was confused. "I've been pestering my servant, who is adamant about not knowing a thing of Sachi. How could he not know? Surely they talk among themselves!"

"If her servant is gone along with her, then there's no one, with the exception of the chief eunuch, who would have any knowledge. So, unless your man has a close relationship with the chief, he wouldn't know anything either." She didn't tell Abra that Adiah was going to try and find out. She needed to keep that a confidence. She owed it to Adiah. He was risking enough for her as it was.

Two days later, as Nalussa and Adiah were walking in the courtyard during a break from her lessons in the Psalms, Adiah said, "I have news on Sachi. Let's sit over here in the shade."

Nalussa's heart pounded. *Oh, please, God, let her be all right! Let her be in another wing of the harem.*

They settled under an arbor laden with heavy clumps of fat grapes. The shade was welcome. In another time, she would have plucked one of the luscious fruits and popped it in her mouth. Now, all she felt was burning in her stomach.

"I'll tell you the complete story, but you must promise not to say a word to anyone, including Abra. If it gets out, they will know where the information came from, and I will be eliminated. This information comes directly from the chief. I asked him. Because we are old friends, he unburdened himself and told me."

Nalussa nodded. "You can trust me."

Three concubines and their servants walked past. They smiled and waved and kept walking. Adiah began. "She was dressed beautifully in a pale pink linen gown that set off her hair and skin tones. Her servant put gold chains around her neck, one with a dazzling fiery opal the size of a fist. She was stunning in gold sandals and a gold veil crowned with fresh, deep pink flowers. I saw her from the hallway. She looked like an angel. A terrified angel. She was so frightened that it took two servants to help her walk into the king's chambers. They brought her in, left her, and closed the door. In less than twenty minutes, the king rang to remove her from his presence."

"What happened?" Nalussa gasped, putting a hand to her mouth.

"Don't interrupt. Let me finish," he admonished.

Nalussa nodded and gripped the bench.

"The story is, she began to sob uncontrollably, telling the king she was scared; she didn't want to be there; and she wanted to go home. I believe he tried to soothe her, but the servants could hear her begging him not to touch her. She was wailing like a little child."

Nalussa took a deep breath. Adiah continued. "He immediately called in servants. Cowering on the floor, she wouldn't get up, and they removed her on a pallet. She was inconsolable. They moved her and her servant to a small cell on the second level of a minor tower to the east of the palace.

"The same hour, the servant was brought back before the chief eunuch, who berated him for not telling him that she was not prepared to go into the king. He told him that the king should never have to experience anything like this. This kind of behavior is inexcusable. He called her a worthless concubine and banished both of them from the harem and the palace to be placed outside the grounds in a common abode.

"Naturally, the servant was distraught. He tried to defend himself. After all, he himself was so young and inexperienced. He had no idea she would have a breakdown. She was his first charge. The chief would have none of it. The behavior of the concubine and the lack of control of her eunuch all meant serious trouble for the chief under King Solomon's rule. He didn't banish them but ordered that they both be put under guard; they would be fed and clothed, but they were doomed to confinement forever. In time, probably forgotten, too," Adiah admitted.

Nalussa didn't have any words to utter. It was all so wrong. How could they harvest young virgins strictly for the king's pleasure? Oh, she heard the defense too often—first from Adriel. So many of them were delighted to be taken care of for the rest of their lives. Food, clothing, shelter. What fate could they have suffered if they weren't chosen for the king? Poverty? Abuse? Yet she wondered how they would feel in five to ten years—whether or not they got a turn with the king and were then forgotten? Lonely? Rejected? And what would happen to them if a new king came without a care for the old king's concubines? And the wives had another set of problems.

"I have a bit more to say, Nalussa." She came to attention. "Her young servant went back to the cell in the tower to tell Sachi their common fate: imprisonment for life." Here, Adiah stopped and gazed around the courtyard with rheumy eyes, seeing the young concubines laughing and chatting while their servants hovered by to be ready should they need them. They were happy and content. Pleased to be in the comfort of the king.

He turned back to Nalussa. "An hour later, when the guards came to take them away, they both had fallen to their deaths."

Nalussa jumped up. "No!"

***

Word had reached Adriel about Sachi and her servant. Her fear and misery deeply shocked the king, sending the servants scurrying in to calm the situation. Naturally, because of the nature of gossip, all sorts of tales were spun, but Adriel knew from the moment he placed her on the donkey to take her to the harem she was nearly spiritless in her desolation. He recalled thinking he should return her to her family, find someone else, but he was committed. She was lovely and young. Perfect for the king.

Had only I listened to my inner voice, she might be alive today! He numbered the many who didn't want to become a concubine. There were less than those who wanted to, but he should have moved on from those who didn't want to go. "It's a little late now," he said aloud and knocked on Adiah's door.

"You shouldn't be here!" Adiah admonished as he opened the door. Grabbing him by the arm he pulled him inside, firmly closing the door. "This is off-limits to you!"

"I know; I know. But I just heard about Sachi, and I'm torn over what happened!"

"It isn't your fault. It was your job." The old man sat down heavily.

"But if I hadn't taken her!"

"You can't go back to what you should have done," Adiah said as Adriel buried his head in his hands.

"But Nalussa! She didn't want to come here either! But I took her anyway! Is she okay?" Adriel looked up with fear in his eyes. "I couldn't bear being the one responsible for her hurt!"

"I'm watching out for her. Don't be troubled. She is a strong young woman and knows what will be expected of her."

"You mean, she hasn't been asked to go into the king yet?" Adiah shook his head. "Then please tell her that my prayers are with her, and I never meant to cause her or anyone else any harm. I . . . I care about her. Will you do that for me?"

The old man looked at Adriel for a long moment. "I will."

***

Back in the common room, there was little talk of Sachi and her servant's disappearance. For the most part, she was already forgotten. Most assumed that she was brought to another group within the harem now that she was no longer a virgin. Gossip was forbidden among the servants regarding Sachi. It was decreed punishable by death. Not one of the women's servants spoke a word, although by now, it was known throughout the palace.

The concubines just expected that she would have returned with a huge smile on her face, coyly boasting a little as she directed her servant to pack up her belongings. She would certainly kiss her friends goodbye before leaving for another group in the harem. But she didn't. So, what?

Who really cared other than me? questioned Nalussa. Her gaze went to Abra, who wouldn't forget her friend, but she didn't dwell on her either. The women all knew they were commodities to be moved around and enjoyed or forgotten according to the king's whim. Nalussa never told her friend the truth about Sachi.

Now that she and Adiah shared a secret, and Nalussa had proven herself trustworthy, the old man considered her more.

"I have something to tell you." Nalussa sat where he indicated beside him on the cushion. "Adriel came to see me when he learned of Sachi's death. He was quite shaken. He told me to tell you that he never meant anyone any harm, especially you. He cares for you."

Nalussa didn't blink. Her eyes went wide. This was a very important moment. The risk he took to go into an expressly forbidden area to seek out Adiah was dangerous. His need to tell Adiah that he was ashamed of the harm he had caused and, most importantly, that he cared for her! She stored this in her heart; it gave her courage to stay strong. At least she knew that not only Adiah cared about her, but also Adriel.

Adiah and Nalussa grew closer. Gone was the officious behavior of hammering perfection of behavior, conversation, attentiveness, and musical ability. Adiah recognized that Nalussa, on her own, had a level of achievement and intellect. She easily grasped the nuances of social behavior and clever conversation. She was also a natural for musical instruments, although having never had one in her hand before. She was a good singer—not great, but pleasant. She had wit and appreciated humor in others. She was a good listener. She had learned that from her father, she often pointed out to him; and when she did, he would always see her grow pensive and say, "Oh how I miss him!"

Although she hadn't been summoned yet to go into the king, she also accepted, with grace, her sexual role. Adiah was graphic in his explanations, yet always emphasized she must also possess sensuality, modesty, and tenderness. The king, for all of his excesses, appreciated diverse qualities in his women.

It wasn't long before it was her turn. Adiah appraised her as she waited for his suggestions. He selected a simple, saffron-dyed gown, coupled with a pale sage and saffron headdress so as not to compete with the opulent accessories of jewelry he planned to pick. Her bronze skin tone dazzled with the subtle application of gold-flecked cream and delicate perfume. Satisfied with her clothing, he called for the jewelry.

Two servants entered carrying a heavy chest on poles. Carefully, they set it down on a low table. Adiah bid them leave, and he opened the lid. Nalussa stepped back, awed.

One could never imagine a huge chest filled with wealth beyond calculation. The assortment was astounding in its flash and brilliance. Large and small precious stones and pearls mounted in intricate designs were of the highest quality, and the links of the chains were fashioned in all sorts of configurations. Nose rings sparkled with rubies and emeralds. Rings with huge stones were carelessly piled high. Ankle bracelets, with masses of silver bells that would tinkle with each step, were stacked in piles. Crowns of gold, embedded with colorful stones, were abundant, and curious amulets of forbidding designs were tucked in a corner of the chest.

"I was going to choose your jewelry, but I think you should choose whatever you would like to wear around your neck, wrists, arms, and ankles and choose whatever rings you want."

She sat staring for only a moment. "I choose nothing."

Shocked, Adiah couldn't say a word. Finding his voice, he asked, "With all of this, you don't want to adorn yourself with any of these accessories? They are stunning, valuable! Some of these pieces are irreplaceable."

When Nalussa didn't respond, Adiah shrugged his shoulders. He sat down to consider her. With a hand on his chin, he smiled. "It is your decision. The king enjoys seeing his lovely women draped with his wealth. You are intensely beautiful. We have many in the harem, but you surpass them all. The color of your skin, your lustrous hair, those eyes! You don't need jewelry. You will do well." With that, he rang a bell, and two of the king's servants entered the dressing room and took Nalussa away.

It was late afternoon. As she walked down the hallway to the king's apartments, the sun poured cleanly through the open windows and archways. It was hot outside, but inside, there was shade and a cross breeze, lightly rippling Nalussa's veil as she walked. Her heart pounded in dread. She hoped he would be kind and gentle. Adiah was quite clear with her as to what to expect, but knowing was different than doing. Hopefully, nature would take over, and her body would know what to do. She prayed, *Lord, please be with me. Guard my heart, oh God*!

The servant knocked on the door. Another servant opened it from the inside. She was ushered in, and the servants discreetly slipped out. She stood alone in an intimate, small room filled with lush greenery and flowers. The windows were open, catching a slight breeze. The white floors were covered in sumptuous, deep blue and purple rugs. Colors of royalty. The furnishings fit the room perfectly. A wide couch with cushions and throws faced a vaulted balcony that looked out to the sky. A smaller couch with a table was in the center of the room, and to the side of a window was a chair and a small desk with a golden lampstand, but the room was empty. She stood, nervously fingering her veil. *What should I do?*

A shadow came in from the side deck of the balcony. It was the king. The brightness at his back didn't allow for Nalussa to see his features until he turned and sat on the small couch. "I was told that you are one of the most beautiful women of the harem, and if that's true, you are one of the most beautiful women of the kingdom as well. Come closer."

She walked toward him until she was standing close enough to smell him. A subtle scent of spice filled the air around him, one finer than the scents in all the harem. He was good-looking and healthy, of average height and build. He had lovely, thick, dark hair with threads of silver, his beard the same. His eyes were a deep brown, almost black. His face unreadable.

She breathed in deeply, calming herself. Anger simmered in her heart. She was standing before a man who had been blessed by God, who had even had a conversation with God! How she wished just once that God would speak to her! To guide her! Explain His will! But no, it seemed all through time, God would speak to men, with few exceptions, according to the rabbis. *And here I am. To give my body to a man who has had as many bodies as he pleases.*

"Come. Sit. I'm told your name is Nalussa." Half-smiling and squinting his eyes, he breathed, "You truly are stunning."

She sat beside him as he tilted her chin to face him. He surveyed her face like an art appraiser and lightly took off her veil. Obviously pleased, he smiled and said, "You are incredible. I've never seen such beauty! I'm so pleased to have you here." He rang a bell, and a servant entered with delicacies, along with wine and fruit juice. After the man left, the king said, "Let's enjoy this beautiful afternoon."

She accepted a few sips of wine, but did not eat. He comfortably ate and drank while he spoke of his writings and his ongoing project of compiling proverbs. "Would you like me to read you something?"

Her interest piqued, she dared ask, "Your Majesty, yes, please. I would be most interested."

Pleased, he got up to the small writing table by the window. "I'm compiling wisdom to teach my sons and any other who might read my work. There is so much to learn, so much to understand, so little time." He rifled through pieces of parchment, and choosing one, he turned to her. "The Lord blessed me with wisdom and knowledge, as everyone in the kingdom knows. I am truly grateful that He granted my request. These qualities are needed to run such a vast and complicated kingdom. I couldn't do it without His help. So, I thought I would record important directives for success in life and success in a relationship with God. My sons need guidance. Particularly, Rehoboam," he added as confirmation.

He held up a slip of parchment and read, "Trust in the LORD with all your heart and lean not on your own understanding; in all your ways submit to him, and he will make your paths straight."[3]

She nodded. "Yes, Majesty. I agree. Do not be wise in your own eyes. Our understanding falls short of the Lord's ways, particularly when we don't know His will for us or understand His discipline. But I confess, I do question Him sometimes."

The king was annoyed and obviously surprised that she spoke without being given permission. He set his mouth in a thin line and asked, "Don't you have everything you need? You are treated well, aren't you? You are comfortable?"

"Of course, Your Majesty," she answered. He walked back to his desk and put the parchment down, stating, "Then God has been good to you."

She thought a moment. "Indeed, God has been good to me, but don't you think we always have questions for God? And many times, we don't seem to get an answer?"

He stopped and just looked at her. "My father, King David, wrote, 'Show me your ways, Lord, teach me your paths. Guide me in your truth and teach me.'"[4]

"If you are blessed to hear Him, my king." She met his stare.

---

3 Proverbs 3:5-6
4 Psalm 25:4

Coming back, he sat closer to her than he had before. She stiffened and willed her body to relax and her heart to slow down. He gently touched her face, tracing a finger down the side of her cheek to her neck. "You have a good mind. I find that appealing. No jewelry," he noted. "This is a first." His fingers traced her throat. She tried not to flinch.

So many thoughts were racing through her mind, including poor Sachi. She had no right to ask the king if he knew the fate of the concubine who was just not ready for him, but the consequence of the king's desires resulting in Sachi's death was lurking deep within her heart. He had to know. Surely, in the history of the harem, there had to be many women who didn't meet up to the king's expectations. Did he have any remorse regarding her fate?

"What are you thinking of, my sweet one? I assure you, I won't hurt you. I'm very careful with women their first time."

Taking her hand, he stood her up and gently kissed her on the cheek, then mouth. A deep kiss. His hand caressed her body as his other hand brought her in close. The smell of spice was intoxicating. As her anger and fear began to subside, her body took over, accepting the gentleness, yet excitement, of his touch.

CHAPTER SEVEN

They lay quietly afterward. Nalussa admitted that her body enjoyed the experience. Deftly, she removed the stained throw underneath her that proved her virginity and tossed it on the floor. The king lay dozing. She marveled how her body went contrary to her heart and mind, but that was all right. She might as well enjoy herself under the circumstances. He wasn't unpleasant. In fact, he was a capable and considerate lover—far more than what she expected from Adiah's discussions. But to give credit to her mentor, he wouldn't know the nuances of intimacy as the king would. For want of a better description, the king practiced on hundreds of women.

He stirred and rolled over, looking at her profile. "You are truly a treasure, Nalussa. An incredibly elegant, young woman. And although you came to me as a virgin, your eunuch taught you well. It is Adiah, isn't it?"

"*He* is Adiah, Your Majesty." Turning her head, she looked him in the eye. "He's not an 'it.'" She gasped at her own audacity and immediately said, "Forgive me, Your Majesty."

The king laughed, smoothing her cheek. "You are absolutely correct. Forgive me also." He got up—her cue to get up, too. She wrapped a sheet around her body as he pulled on a robe.

"You have confidence, my stunning one, but always think before you speak. Not all of us are so willing to be corrected. Here's another of my sayings: 'The words of the reckless pierce like swords, but the tongue of the wise brings healing.'"[5] She wanted to point out the saying applied to him, too, but she wisely kept quiet.

He smiled, appraising her. "The chief eunuch said I would be most pleased with you. I'm also most pleased with my scout, Adriel, for finding you and Adiah, who polished a rough gem. Both will be rewarded. You are unique, Nalussa. I'll call a servant to get you fresh clothes. Here, put on this robe." He handed her a finely woven garment of pastels and seed pearls he pulled from a basket on the floor. She dropped the sheet to put on the robe.

"I hope we get to know each other more," the king said, admiring her draped body. "You make me smile. I enjoyed myself, and I hope you did also."

Dismissing her, he walked to a cord embedded in the wall and pulled it. Immediately, there was a soft knock on the door, and two men came in. One to attend to the king, the other to escort Nalussa out.

So, the king was impressed with Adriel, she mused. She had heard several stories from the other concubines about how Adriel had found them, too, but the king never mentioned Adriel on their behalf—at least to her knowledge—and the women would have bragged about any tidbit from the king's mouth. In discussing Adriel, some said, "Oh, he is so good-looking, but a bit aloof." Some were distressed they were taken by him. "I didn't want to leave my family!" And others were grateful. "I would have died staying with my family.

5 Proverbs 12:18

There was no man available for a husband. I would have ended up a beggar or prostitute!"

And me? Nalussa padded silently behind the servant escorting her to the harem's baths. *I'm not better off. No. I would have had a husband chosen by my father, and he would have been a good man, I'm sure of it.* Yet in her mind's eye, she remembered Adriel looking at her with concern on their journey to the harem. Indeed, he was attractive and, she found out, kind. *I believe he cared then when he shot me that last look before he left me with the chief eunuch. It took the tragedy of Sachi to openly admit it to Adiah.*

In the private bath, she soaked in warm, scented water, thinking about her life, as a servant fussed about sponging her back. She was not so inexperienced as some of the others here in believing that the king was so impressed with her mind and beauty that she would be a love. No. She had nothing to offer him other than her body, and that would age, and another would be right behind her, more exotic, more willing to please.

His first wife was the daughter of the pharaoh. She remembered seeing the palatial building, the home Solomon built for her. Although she never gave it any thought until she came into the harem, the Israelites were forbidden by God to intermingle with the Egyptians. He also had a wife named Naamah, who was an Ammonite and the mother of Rehoboam, but Solomon took many other foreign wives of various Canaanite tribes. At home, she never considered Solomon and his wives, but here, the importance of who they were now did have impact. The Word of God through the writings of the prophets forbade intermarriage. She was discovering through gossip that many of his wives did, in fact, lead the king away from the one true God to their gods. He even built them temples and altars.

She shook her head in utter confusion. He was flaunting his desires over God's commandments. She couldn't reconcile herself to the situation. This was a place of jaw-dropping lavishness, but it wasn't a place that prioritized obedience to God's commands. And while it might be appealing to a lot of people because of the vast wealth that supported their lifestyle within the palace and kingdom, how could it go on? Would God allow it?

Maybe God wasn't allowing it. Although she was shielded and secure in the harem, Solomon's vast, well-run kingdom faced opposition. Jeroboam, an official of King Solomon who was in charge of the labor force, was prophesied to by the prophet Ahijah. The men met together when Jeroboam was leaving Jerusalem. She had heard that the prophet had on a new cloak, which he took off and tore it into twelve pieces before prophesying that God was going to tear the kingdom out of Solomon's hands and give ten tribes to Jeroboam and leave only one kingdom's current tribe to Solomon's heir.

Nalussa heard the gossip. Not all thought it was true, but the prophet was well-known. He said God wouldn't take the whole kingdom out of Solomon's hand, but it was enough of a threat that when King Solomon heard what the prophet had declared, he tried to kill Jeroboam, who wisely fled to Egypt.

She brought her thoughts back to herself. The reality was she was no longer a virgin. She was not married to the king, but she did have status as one of the more beautiful concubines. If she was with child, there would be more benefits, but she didn't want children. Now that she had been with the king, Adiah would retire. She had no idea who would be assigned to her, nor did she know where her new residence would be now that she was no longer housed with the virgins, or *bethulahs*. But her future was so uncertain. Was the kingdom uncertain as well?

Thinking about King David's prayer, she whispered, "Show me your ways, Lord; teach and guide me because I need a way to either reconcile myself to this situation or find a way out."

Nalussa was called into the king once a week for the next few months. Abra was finally brought into the king, too, and she, along with Nalussa moved into the elite group of beauties set aside specifically for not only their looks, but also their intelligence and personality. Abra was delighted. "I am hoping I'll have a baby, so pray that it will be so."

"It's possible, my friend," Nalussa offered. "You've been with him quite a bit now."

"Nalussa, tell me what he does to you, what he likes, and how you satisfy him. I know he likes to talk, too. What do you talk about?" She wanted to know everything about the king.

"No, Abra. What goes on behind closed doors is private, including the conversation. If it became known that you and I were talking about our relationship with the king, he would stop our visits."

"I certainly won't tell anyone! This is just between you and me. We're sisters, Nalussa! We can hold secrets. I just want to know how he is with you. I'll tell you how he is with me. If we can share what makes him happy, we can make it more interesting for him."

"No, Abra, no. Don't ask me again."

Angry, Abra stood up and flounced away to join her other sisters lounging in a shallow pool cooling off from the hot afternoon sun. They welcomed her, and soon, they were all talking about their hoped-for next visit with the king, but even they were cautious about what they discussed concerning the king. Their servants hovered nearby, eavesdropping, and if any of their chatter turned to gossip about the king, they would not only find themselves reprimanded but also likely not invited into his chambers again.

As time moved on, Abra remained aloof with Nalussa, as did the other concubines.

Nalussa asked, "Abra, please come sit with me. We haven't had a conversation in a long time! I miss talking with you."

Abra stopped and smiled. "Sorry, Nalussa. I have to meet the others at the pool. We can speak another time. I'm just very busy."

She was hurt that Abra had turned away from her. The other women were civil, but no one seemed to trust her. She watched Abra walk through the hallway out to the pool where the others were laughing and splashing. No one ever invited Nalussa to join in. Clearly, they were jealous with Nalussa's unusual frequency with the king because he still had many other women, including high-level wives, to whom he probably found himself obligated. Still, Nalussa was called more frequently than the others, even though the king had plenty of time to grow bored or find a new woman to titillate his mind and body. Nalussa was a favorite. Yet she was lonely. She would have been just as happy if the king didn't favor her.

Her status with the king meant nothing to her, other than the fact she had the opportunity to follow his writing project on wisdom, which was most interesting and, in some cases, disturbing, since he didn't always apply his nuggets of wisdom to himself. But she certainly was not his judge.

She often thought of the day Adriel found her and took her from her family. Sadly, she remembered them in their distress of her leaving and her father's resignation. *My only solace of that day was when Adriel began to be kind to me, as a friend. I remember his parting look. Would he remember how lost I was? Now, even my old servant Adiah is gone, as he said he would be.*

"Do you know where Adiah is? I would like to know if he is well." Nalussa needed a friend, not a servant to talk with; she needed her friend to share confidences with.

She was so lonely, but her new servant, preoccupied with getting her hair just so, answered in distraction, "I have heard that he is ill, but living with those servants somewhere on the palace grounds." He waved a free hand about. "He's with those who served the king well. He is cared for, don't worry." He placed his hand on his hip, stepping back and looking at the pins in her hair. Picking up another pin, he said, "I hope to end up there." He went back to pinning up her hair.

Aware her new servant was delighted he had inherited a successful concubine, he was throwing himself into his work to prove himself worthy. He was pleasant but limited in interesting conversation because his main focus was making sure she was always ready in case she was called. She missed even friendly banter. There was little opportunity for relaxing because of the ongoing baths, the lotion rubs, the massage of oils, the hair stylings—she never would have considered that her body, hair, and face would require so much maintenance.

As she was escorted to the king's apartments once again, she found herself puzzling over her dichotomy. She enjoyed her time with the king when discussing his writing projects, hearing about his latest acquisitions, or learning about the latest noble or king who came to pay him tribute. Yet she didn't look forward to the physical aspects of the encounter. Oftentimes, her body told her differently, but her mind was not engaged. If anything, she couldn't get it out of her mind how he gave his body to so many other women. It was unsettling.

Yet it was evident the act itself gave him solace and relief, and he found her attractive enough on an intellectual and physical level to call her frequently. But he certainly didn't have a loving, emotional connection to her that she could detect, nor she to him. Some of the concubines were in love, accepting they were not exclusive to him, and others viewed their role as part of their life and obligation. She rejected love and obligation, at least to the king. She was biding her time, and oddly, she seemed to have Adriel more and more in the deep recesses of her mind. Perhaps it was because she always heard the stories of the women he discovered for the king. Maybe it was the memory of the shared bread and wine or the fact that her life had so changed because of him. So, why would she think of him? Because Adiah said he cared about her? She was confused. *Am I attracted to him, or should I be angry at him? Nothing can come of my thinking about him,* she admonished herself.

This afternoon, the king was not as energetic. Perhaps she wasn't his first of the day. After satisfying himself, he sat up on a cushion, pouring wine for them both. "The Queen of Sheba has heard all about my kingdom and is coming to pay great tribute. She says she has many questions of me and hopes I'll indulge her! I'm planning a great feast to honor her visit."

He turned to Nalussa beside him and smiled, toying with her hair. "I'm inviting all my wives, children, staff, and favorite concubines. You'll be there. I want you all to see the power of this kingdom and how I am known far and wide." He fell back on the cushion and grinned. "The Queen of Sheba! I heard she is as beautiful as you, with the same coloring. It'll be interesting to see what transpires." Nalussa could only guess. Beauty and wealth. The combination would be irresistible to the king.

Abra met her at the archway of the harem. "Did you hear? The Queen of Sheba is coming, and we're invited to attended her welcoming feast! King Solomon told me this morning!"

"This morning?" That explained the king's energy level.

"Yes." Alba smiled broadly and tilted her head. "It's going to be so exciting. We haven't been out in public since we've been here, and we've never been to the king's reception hall. This is thrilling!" She grabbed Nalussa's hand and kissed her cheek. "I've missed you, Sister." She twirled and danced back to the young women, who were all talking excitedly and throwing sidelong glances at Nalussa.

Nalussa was heartened her old friend was back to normal, at least for now. And it would be fun to get out among other people, out of this building only for women. How long had it been? Even the servants were excited. They were going to make sure their women would be stunningly beautiful, enough to make all the king's wives look twice.

"You've heard!" her servant gushed. "I am going to make you more striking than you are now! Come, let's look at some new clothes!"

CHAPTER EIGHT

The women's servants labored diligently, seeing to it that their charges were perfect in every way from face, hair, veils, gowns, robes, jewelry—all the way down to their sandals. In the imagination, the gathering of the women on the rooftop of the harem was like a beautiful flock of excitable, exotic birds preening. Colorful robes and veils wafted in the breeze, setting off a kaleidoscope of color and texture as they waited excitedly to see the Queen of Sheba and her retinue pass by.

The crowds below were equally eager, craning their necks skyward to take in the astounding collection of beauty and sensuality. The concubines drew far more attention than the collection of wives at another level on the palace roof. While they were dressed equally, if not better than the concubines, with far more jewelry, they could not compete with the overall beauty of their second-place sisters.

Horns blared, and shouts came from the road. "The Queen of Sheba is coming!" The crowds lost interest in the women on the rooftops and directed their chatter and attention to the advancing parade.

It was a huge, long caravan. Nalussa couldn't believe her eyes as camel after camel passed laden with spices, precious stones, clothing, enormous amounts of gold, musical instruments, and mystery cargo. In the middle of the caravan was the queen herself. It was impossible for the concubines to get a glimpse of her, seated inside a covered and curtained chariot, but they would be in her presence at the banquet. They could barely contain themselves. Some had spent years in isolation, never glimpsing normal, everyday life. Nalussa herself had been separated from the outside world for over a year.

She drank it in. The crowds on the dusty road brought her to the reality of a vibrant and compelling way of everyday life of which she was no longer a part. It was not the first time she had thought of her family. There was no way she could reach out to them to find out how they were doing, since they were given such wealth in exchange for giving her up. Certainly, they moved on. She didn't fault her father in the least. He absolutely had no choice but to let her go. In her mind's eye, she saw her older brother, Jasper, hugging her, saying he would rescue her should she just say the word. Was there still hope?

"Isn't this wonderful? I never realized how alive the outside world is. I could look at the crowds milling about forever. Don't misunderstand me; I don't miss my past life and definitely not my family, but I miss the ability to walk the roads, go into shops, and see ordinary people." Abra wedged herself between Nalussa and another concubine and let out a sigh that was drowned out by the shouting below and the talk above.

"I do, too, but I miss my family, even the herd of goats!" Nalussa responded craning her neck to scan the crowds. "It was such a simple, uncomplicated way of life. As long as we had our house and food for all, we were happy. My father was so proud to get us clothing once a year. Now we get clothing whenever we go into the king."

"Yes, and amazing clothing at that. And don't forget how well we are fed. I'm not sure my family would recognize me with all this on my bones." Abra held up her bare arms as gold bracelets clanked about her wrists. "Look, smooth and plump!"

Nalussa admired Abra's healthy and glowing body. Every woman on the rooftops was in the same shape, whether wife or concubine. If they became sick, they were brought to a different place in the compound. When they died, they were given a simple burial, unless the woman was a wife. Only their close sisters mourned for them.

Nalussa turned her attention below. She wanted to run away and escape from the reach of the king and this way of life. She wanted to immerse herself into the crowds, the vendors, and the chaos. Although she adapted for survival, both mentally and physically, this was not where she was going to end up—isolated in a building, waiting on the whims of a man, even a king. She'd figure it out. She just didn't know how, but surely, God would give her wisdom.

Later that evening, the elite concubines were led into the tiered grand hall, where couches faced the front of the hall and were lined up beside low tables holding gold pitchers of wine and gold goblets. Placed in the front of the hall facing the couches was a long, low table with seating facing out to the main tiered dining area. The throne of the king and the throne of Pharaoh's daughter, his first wife, were situated there, and vast seating to the right and left of the head table held more tables and couches for the remainder of his wives and officials. The elite concubines were seated directly in front of the king. To the right of the king's throne was another throne of carved ivory and gold—much like the king's, only smaller—for the king's guest, the Queen of Sheba. The wives were arriving at the same time as the concubines, and once all were seated, a horn was blasted, a signal for all to stand as the king, his first wife, and his honored guest entered the great hall with much music and singing.

The multitude rose. Nalussa could only stare. The other concubines took one look at the Queen of Sheba as she walked beside the king, then stole quick, furtive glances at Nalussa. "I can't believe my eyes! You could be sisters, only you the younger and more attractive!" Abra exclaimed in a throaty whisper. She looked around the hall. It appeared many were making the same comparisons.

Nalussa shifted uncomfortably from one foot to the next. *This is astounding. We do look alike!*

Once the royalty stood in front of their thrones, there was a moment of silence as the king said an opening prayer. While the king was praying, the king's wife looked the concubines over. Her eyes opened wide as she rested on Nalussa. The king himself, finishing his prayer, extended his arms in thanks to the Lord his God. At the same time, he proudly looked over at the fraction of his harem sitting in front of him, looking directly at Nalussa with an amused smile on his lips.

Even the Queen of Sheba seated in front of the royal entourage subtly opened her beautiful mouth in surprise as she looked directly at Nalussa.

The king indicated they be seated. He continued to stand and gave an elegant speech of welcome and anticipation of strong alliances.

After he spoke, his guest stood up, gazing up at the king. She was exquisitely dressed. Her bare shoulders and arms glistened in shiny, bronze tones; and although petite and fragile, she exclaimed in a loud voice, "The report I heard in my own country about your achievements and your wisdom is true. But I did not believe these things until I came and saw with my own eyes. Indeed, not even half was told me; in wisdom and wealth you have far exceeded the report I heard. How happy your people must be! How happy your officials, who continually stand before you and hear your wisdom! Praise be to the Lord your God, who has delighted in you and placed you on the throne of Israel. Because of the Lord's eternal love for Israel, he has made you king to maintain justice and righteousness."[6]

She bowed to the king and said with a sweep of her arm, "Please, accept my gifts." In strode servant after servant with enormous amounts of gifts. Servants carried in so many chests of spices that never had been seen in one place. The sweet smell filled the hall as guests sniffed the air, smiling at the mixture of the unusual and aromatic scents.

Wooden caskets were brought in and presented to the king, each overflowing with precious stones and gold articles. Musical instruments of types that hadn't been seen in the kingdom were presented. Gorgeous woven bolts of cloth were draped around the servant's arms, and peacock feathers were flashed and waved. The guests were stunned. Even though they themselves had on occasion seen parts of the king's vast wealth, never had they seen so much in one place at one time.

After all the gifts had been presented, the king raised his arms to let the feast begin. "Now, my guests, enjoy!"

After one course was eaten, others followed until no one could eat anymore. Fish and game, poultry and vegetables. Luscious fruits none had seen before and pastries of all shapes and sizes. Wine in copious amounts. Everything served on enormous gold platters.

---

6 1 Kings 10:6-9

After more speeches by a variety of the king's staff, the final prayer was offered and the crowd dismissed. The concubines were giddy with fine food and wine. So many continually spoke of the similarity between the Queen of Sheba and Nalussa.

"Are you sure you're not related?" Abra teased.

"No," Nalussa answered.

"But do you remember your mother?" Abra asked.

Nalussa answered again, "No. She died at my birth."

Abra was stumped. "Well, I believe you and the queen are related."

Nalussa smiled and shook her head as Abra stumbled to the wash basin, allowing her servant to wash her face and help her out of her heavy jewelry and intricate clothing. It was surprising that she and the Queen of Sheba looked so much alike, but Nalussa's mother was from the same region as the queen was. And the women of Cush and Ethiopia were dark and stunning.

The queen stayed for six months, and there were many events, along with banquets and private meetings with the king and general meetings with the king, his artisans and musicians, and his officials. During that time, Nalussa was never called into the king nor was any concubine from her group.

For Abra, it was distressing. "I have got to conceive a child. It's the only way I can stay in a favored position. I've learned another group of virgins are being groomed, and as beautiful as we are, he'll soon want untouched flesh. I don't want him to forget me for a younger, riper woman."

"You aren't alone. All the others are wanting to bear him children, too." Nalussa tossed her head toward the women lounging by the pool. "Time isn't on anyone's side. And as long as the king has new women to enjoy, we'll eventually fade away."

"What about you?" Abra demanded. "You're called in more than any of us, except now that the Queen of Sheba is here, he has a double of you, but with the wealth and influence. While she's here, you'll be forgotten."

Nalussa shrugged her shoulders. This was no surprise to her. She expected she would soon be forgotten. He had other women and benefits on his mind.

Abra looked at her in accusation. "Aren't you the least bit jealous?"

Nalussa smiled. "Not in the least."

After a spectacular farewell banquet to which they were all invited, the king seemed more subdued than usual, at least to Nalussa. Perhaps he was saddened seeing his great admirer leave, for here was a woman as well-known as the king, with lands, people, and wealth, and who was not to be ordered about on his whim. He had met his match. He didn't own her. She was powerful in her own right.

Weeks after she left, the king did call for Nalussa, much to the chagrin of Abra, who was brutally honest with her friend. "If you conceive, I'll be overcome with jealousy! I won't know what to do. I will hardly forgive you!"

"Pray," Nalussa shot back. "Pray you do conceive and I don't because I don't want to." Abra was shocked into silence.

Inside the king's chambers, Nalussa was surprised at the king's change in personality. Gone was his sense of importance and vanity. "I've finished my sayings to my son and any of my other children who might be inclined to read them. The lovely and intelligent Makeda, the Queen of Sheba, was taken with my sayings and wisdom. She was most impressed with my writing. So, since she has gone, I've been working on another project." He got up and walked to his writing table. "My wisdom and knowledge are coming full circle."

Nalussa didn't respond. Was he different because Queen Makeda left him to go back to her kingdom, knowing that he had served her curiosity? Had she questioned his attitude toward women? She was, after all, powerful in her own right. If he read her his proverbs and his observations on women, particularly adulteress women, how did she react?

On one of the last times Nalussa was with the king, he had her read about his "warning on the adulteress": "Now then, my sons, listen to me; pay attention to what I say. Do not let your heart turn to her ways, or stray into her paths. Many are the victims she has brought down; her slain are a mighty throng. Her house is a highway to the grave, leading down to the chambers of death."[7]

She was still smarting from this written observation. What was the Queen of Sheba's reaction to this—if he read it to her? She no doubt would see the contradiction of a man with hundreds of women judging and pointing out the evil of an adulteress. Men had the upper hand, no matter the situation, and perhaps the queen saw this two-facedness and pointed it out to him. Surely, he couldn't apply the warning of an adulteress to himself or to his sons, men who could take on more wives and concubines at their whim.

Regardless of what Queen Makeda might think of King Solomon, his warning about an adulteress was meaningless and hypocritical.

---

7 Proverbs 7:24-27

But then again, perhaps he was not really referring to a woman who seduced and ruined a man, but maybe something else. Maybe it was a man's own sexual weakness.

She recalled that he had looked at her expectantly. Her response had been guarded. "Is this really about a woman? Or did you hide another meaning in this?" He had never responded.

Now, as he handed her this new parchment to read, something that most impressed him, she thought that power did indeed bring on myriad routes to destruction. Sex was only one.

CHAPTER NINE

She was shocked. His self-confident, practical teaching for seeking wisdom and avoiding foolish pitfalls in his earlier writing was dramatically different than what she was reading now. He wrote: "The words of the Teacher, son of David, king in Jerusalem: 'Meaningless! Meaningless!' says the Teacher. 'Utterly meaningless! Everything is meaningless.'"[8]

She couldn't help but snap a look at him as he was standing on the balcony looking out over the kingdom, his back to her. She turned back to the parchment. She read on, and again, she stopped, surprised at his change of heart. It was actually self-critical. Gone was the righteous authority, the desire to set things right, to warn against pitfalls. Here was an entirely different approach to life. He was proclaiming that the actions of man, no matter the action, was ultimately insubstantial and vain!

She read aloud, "I amassed silver and gold for myself, and the treasure of kings and provinces. I acquired male and female singers, and a harem as well—the delights of a man's heart. I became greater by far than anyone in Jerusalem before me."[9]

"Do you see where this is going, my lovely?" the king interrupted. "I denied myself nothing my eyes desired."[10]

---

8 Ecclesiastes 1:1-2
9 Ecclesiastes 2:8-9
10 Ecclesiastes 2:10

Solomon had turned to look at her, but she started reading aloud again. "Yet when I surveyed all that my hands had done and what I had toiled to achieve, everything was meaningless, a chasing after the wind; nothing was gained under the sun."[11]

She put the parchment down and looked up at him. He came to her. He looked old as he reached for her. "In my vain life, I have seen everything and had everything. When dreams increase and words grow many, there is vanity, but God is the one you must fear."

"God surpasses human wisdom and knowledge, and as we've discussed before, we don't always understand God's will or ways, which is why I agree—we must fear the Lord." Nalussa spoke clearly, with an edge to her voice. She always feared God. But He blessed her, too. Not in the way the king had been blessed, but he who was without love had nothing. She had her father and family's love, and even though they were not with her, they were in her heart. Did the king have love? Did a love leave him? Was that why he felt life "meaningless"?

He walked away and poured himself a large glass of wine before going back to the balcony. She spent the next hour reading while he continued to sip his wine, sigh, and look out over Jerusalem. She came to a troubling passage. She read it loudly, so he could hear:

> I find more bitter than death the woman who is a snare, whose heart is a trap and whose hands are chains. The man who pleases God will escape her, but the sinner she will ensnare. "Look," says the Teacher, "this is what I have discovered: 'Adding one thing to another to discover the scheme of things—while I was still searching but not

---

11 Ecclesiastes 2:11

> finding—I found one upright man among a thousand, but not one upright woman among them all.'"[12]

She put the parchment down. She was done reading.

"You find that harsh, my lovely?" He looked at her over his shoulder.

"Yes." She was guarding her words. "May I speak freely?" He nodded. "You say, 'I found one upright man among a thousand, but not one upright woman among them all.'"

She hid her disdain in her heart and calmly continued, "You have everything, Your Majesty. You have had more than your share of women. Yet I wonder, how many of them have *you* ever loved, and how many of them did you give the opportunity to love you back? How many have you given the opportunity to show to you their uprightness?"

"You sound like the Queen Makeda." He took a long drink. Wiping his mouth, he said, "She was surprised by your looks, by the way. She would never admit to any lineage, but I must say, the palace was quite humming with your similarities, including myself. I never would have thought it possible, yet you could be sisters. Even your minds are likewise. Both of you have open opinions. I think that's why I'm so attracted to you both."

Nalussa kept her peace, but the king continued, "Getting back to your comment, yes, I've loved—I'm capable of love. I've even composed a song about my love, but . . . " He sighed and took another drink. "I have many desires and needs. Many distractions." He shook his head mournfully.

Then how could you possibly expect to find a woman to give herself to you in absolute love and "uprightness" when you made it a point to collect

---

12 Ecclesiastes 7:26-28

as many women as possible? She didn't speak it. This was a time to keep silent, but she had no sympathy for this newfound sadness.

The king took a final draught from his cup and poured another. "I'm tired." He went to the wall where the cord was for the bell and pulled it to summon his servants. Immediately, two men entered.

As Nalussa got up, he turned to her and said, "Forgive me." She bowed and left.

On her way back to her rooms, she couldn't keep the thoughts out of her mind. She wrestled with forgiving him but ultimately concluded that his behavior or needs didn't reflect who she was. *This way of living is madness. For the king and his women. Is he just now discovering that possessions and total power do not equal happiness and fulfillment? What about his personal relationship with God? Was that "meaningless"?*

She turned to her escort. "Have you heard anything of my first servant, Adiah? Is he still alive?"

The man nodded. "Yes, he is alive but ill. The king thinks highly of him, and so he is well cared-for in his old age. We've been saying for months, we're not sure how much longer he will be with us or when he will go with his fathers, but he surprises us each day by opening his eyes."

Nalussa stopped. "Please, ask the king if I may see him before he . . . dies." She hesitated, then went on, "Please. Can you go to the king now and ask for permission?"

"Now? I don't think I can . . . but let me ask his personal servant to relay the message as soon as he is available."

A few hours later, the servant returned to Nalussa's eunuch with the message that the king had granted Nalussa's wish. Because of Adiah's favor and condition, she was granted immediate access.

The servant led her away from the concubines' halls and rooms along a wide hallway decorated with larger-than-life statues of men and, to Nalussa's dismay, the gods of the king's other women. It was well-known throughout the palace that children were sacrificed to those gods. It was beyond comprehension to Nalussa.

Crossing several courtyards, she came to a small, immaculate building flanked by tall palms; short, fat shrubs; and flowers bursting with color. Inside, she was greeted by her friend and first mentor, Adiah.

"You're surprised I'm walking and can greet you!" He smiled and took her arm, leaning heavily on it as he led her to a private chamber. "I'm actually feeling better, but I know overall, I'm not well. But God is good, and I'll be happy when it's my time. So, not to worry."

"I'm so relieved that you can get around. I was worried about you. I haven't heard from you in over a year and you . . . Adiah, you are my only true friend." She helped him to a couch and sat opposite him. "I wanted to see you."

"I hear that you're a favorite with the king, but I'm surprised you've not had a child yet." He coughed softly, covering his mouth. "I still hear what is going on in the harem."

"I've been blessed! I don't want to be with child, Adiah." Her emotions were getting the best of her, and she plucked the corner of her veil to wipe her eye.

The old man looked at her closely, knowingly nodding his head. "You're not happy, which is no surprise. Many of the women find themselves very unhappy, whether they go in to the king or not. Some, as I told you before, have adjusted and make the best of it and even like their station in life, and some . . . "

"Like Sachi," Nalussa whispered.

"Like Sachi," the old man agreed.

The two sat quietly together as a servant came in with hibiscus-flavored water and sweets.

After he left, Nalussa leaned forward and cast her fate at the feet of her mentor. "Is there any way out of here? I can't live this way. I can't fool the king anymore that I am happy to be in his presence. Although he is so intelligent, so full of wisdom and knowledge, I can't align myself to his self-serving paths. He's now writing that life is but vanity, including wisdom! Everything he claims is vanity!"

"The king is no longer young, although much younger than me. But it sounds like he is reflecting upon his excesses only to discover and record that all effort, work, and desires don't last forever. I found that out a long time ago."

"But, Adiah, his reflection doesn't absolve him from keeping women captive to his desires and not allowing them to lead normal lives! If he reflects that it is vanity, then why has nothing changed for us?"

Adiah interrupted, holding up a hand. "The king might speak of vanity, but it's not enough of an observation that he's willing to give up his possessions and power. Thus, as I've told you before, you must accept your place in life. Men are not equal to the king, and women are not equal to men. Never will be. Women are for childbearing, chores, and a man's pleasure. And as far as the king is concerned, you are there only for his pleasure, little else. If you happen to bring a life into this world, he will be happy; but as a concubine, your place in this palace is well beneath his six hundred wives. And as you age and are without a child, you fall behind the other concubines as well. You must accept that."

"I accept my place in society as I relate to men, but I don't accept my place in the palace. God never meant for women to be corralled as a flock of sheep, even if the shepherd is benevolent. And my God is bigger than any man, king or not."

Adiah sat back on a cushion tired. "Please, my dear one, keep all these thoughts to yourself. The king is still the king, and although he favors you now, his mind can change." They both took a drink of the sweet, rose-colored water and sat in silence. "I can only say again, be careful." He closed his eyes. "But please, come and visit again."

"Adiah, before I go, I must ask you a question. Do you know what has become of Adriel?"

The old man opened his eyes. "Child, I don't know. I never saw him since he visited me after Sachi's death. He was still working for the king. Put him out of your mind. Your life is sealed here . . . at least for now." He closed his eyes and reached out his hand to her. She clasped it and gently let it go.

Frustrated, she wondered what she was hoping from him. News of Adriel? What would it gain her? Validation of her observations of the king and her life? Rubbing her temple to quell her headache, she promised she would come back to visit and left for the concubines' rooms.

Little changed. She visited the old man as often as she could. She never asked about Adriel again. The old man was still the same and not willing to offer her any advice other than for her to bear it. She was called less often by the king, but when she was, he always asked to read his latest piece he was compiling for his book of wisdom.

She concluded that it was an interesting compilation of his thoughts that addressed vanity of self-indulgence and even the vanity of living wisely. It was still an unsettling conclusion to his way of life. She wasn't sure what to make of it.

The most remarkable of his observations was his piece on "A Time for Everything":

> There is a time for everything, and a season for every activity under the heavens: a time to be born and a time to die, a time to plant and a time to uproot, a time to kill and a time to heal, a time to tear down and a time to build, a time to weep and a time to laugh, a time to mourn and a time to dance, a time to scatter stones and a time to gather them, a time to embrace and a time to refrain from embracing, a time to search and a time to give up, a time to keep and a time to throw away, a time to tear and a time to mend, a time to be silent and a time to speak, a time to love and a time to hate, a time for war and a time for peace.[13]

She was softening her opinion of him. He was not the vibrant, controlling presence he had once been. He was a gentle lover now; gone was the exuberance of discovery. Many times when he asked her to come in, he merely poured himself a glass of wine and handed her a sheaf of parchments to read. She looked forward to the ability to gain insight on his innermost thoughts. She didn't miss the frequency of the bed. But even reading his reflections, his thoughts still didn't change the continued lavishness of his environment, the strife that was beginning to bubble to the surface of the kingdom due to the demand of royal upkeep and the evidence that he didn't practice what he preached.

For example, she read, "Enjoy life with your wife, whom you love, all the days of this meaningless life that God has given you under the

---

13 Ecclesiastes 3:1-8

sun—all your meaningless days. For this is your lot in life and in your toilsome labor under the sun."[14]

Who was he writing to? The reader? It couldn't be himself. He had too many wives, and the extent of his toil amounted to thinking up the next project that others would manage and build. He might have changed in his mind to some extent, but he was still the king.

14 Ecclesiastes 9:9

CHAPTER TEN

Adriel was called to Adiah's room. He last saw him when he visited him upon Sachi's death and told him how he felt about Nalussa. His heart thudded. Was she all right? Why else would he summon me?

He found the old man lying on his pallet, attended to by a servant equally as old, whom he quickly dismissed when Adriel entered. The room was sparse but beautifully appointed with a writing desk, a gold lampstand, and a well-cushioned pallet on which the old man was lying.

"Adriel, sit. I don't know how long I have." He gasped for air and continued, painfully slow, "And . . . I must get a message to Nalussa."

"Yes, of course. The most beautiful woman I have ever found." *And lost.*

"Good. I've known you since you've been in King Solomon's service, and I trust you." He paused and closed his eyes for several moments. Struggling to regain breath, he laughed. "And ha! If I can't, well, then, it doesn't matter because I'll be dead soon. There's little they can do to me now."

Adriel grabbed the chair and scraped it close to the old man. "I'm listening, Adiah. Speak. There's no one here but me." The eunuch had his interest, especially if it involved Nalussa.

"The king is dead," he whispered.

Adriel gasped aloud. "Dead?" Not what he expected!

Adiah raised a feeble hand. "Hush, time is short. Only a few know, but soon, word will spread." Again, he paused for a moment. Breathing in and out, he stated, "There is to be great upheaval. Rehoboam will be anointed king, and he is going to purge all the king's servants." He closed his eyes and struggled for breath. "I don't know what will happen with the wives because King Solomon made alliances with their families, so the new king will have to be careful how he deposes them."

Adriel held the old eunuch's hand as he struggled to speak. "As for the concubines . . . well, God be with them. I don't know if Rehoboam will flaunt his power by going into his father's concubines, as King David's son Absalom did, or if he'll open the doors of the harem to his men. I don't know, but you must get Nalussa out of the harem."

Adriel's first concern was selfishly for himself, then Nalussa. What would become of her if he couldn't get her out? If something happened to him, he could never help her. He was the king's procurer of women. He could be blamed for the king's excesses. As if reading his thoughts, Adiah pulled his hand away and pointed at him. "I don't know what will become of you. It's possible because you've done so well, Rehoboam might keep you on; but then again, he might not. He might not want any vestiges of his father's legacy left." He closed his eyes, leaning back on a cushion.

Adriel, trembling, didn't have to think it over. He was scared. He didn't like Rehoboam, and the man and his men didn't like him. There were undercurrents of discontent within the palace about the exorbitant cost of keeping the king's women. Nalussa was the king's favorite. Everyone, including Rehoboam knew this. Food, clothing, and jewels were all showered on the wives and concubines, especially the favorites. It was one thing taking care of horses and men who defended the kingdom, but it was another thing to support the king's women, who only took care of the king.

Rubbing his beard in distress, he whispered, "I'll do as you say." Once he got Nalussa out, he, too, would disappear. Perhaps with her. Could this be God's timing? For certain, Rehoboam was never to be trusted.

"See the scroll with the king's seal in red?" Adriel looked to where the old man was shakily pointing. A deep basket filled with parchments. "Take it and give it to Nalussa . . . it's from her king . . . she'll understand . . . " He drifted off.

Adriel popped off the chair to dig through the parchments, pulled out the right one, and fit it under his robe.

The old man opened his eyes. "Try and save her. I wish I was well enough to give you some ideas . . . but . . . " He gasped and coughed. "I'm so weak, I can barely think." Before closing his eyes, he gazed at Adriel dreamily. "She is the most beautiful in the harem. And she has asked after you. I believe she cares for you, too. So, quickly, go now, my son. Be safe."

Adriel touched Adiah's cheek and hurried out, making his way toward the harem quarters. Thoughts upon thoughts were colliding within his head. This morning, he was a carefree man. Now, his world had changed.

The problem at the moment was how he was going to get to Nalussa. How was he going to get her out? Where would they go? And she was asking after him? Perhaps to help her escape? Or could there be more on her mind? Never had he expected these events to happen so quickly. Ah, yes, he was toying with a plan in case the king died and Rehoboam turned threatening, but he didn't get very far in thinking where he would go. It depended on a lot of things. Like wars.

He had an idea and headed to the chief eunuch's office, rapping on his door and praying he would be there. A servant opened the door, and Adriel looked over his shoulder to the chief who was at his desk.

"Sir, you know that Adiah is very ill, and you allowed me to visit him as he requested. He's asked me to get Nalussa and bring her to him, so he can see her beauty and be uplifted," he lied.

The chief beckoned him in while sitting, distracted, making neat stacks of harem records. "I know he's been sick. I was with him yesterday. He did mention seeing you. I'll do as he asks, but make sure she doesn't touch him should he die while she's in there. It'll defile her, and she will have to go through the purification process and be unable to go into the king if he calls for her." He instructed his servant to take Adriel to the greeting hall of the concubines and for the man to bring Nalussa to him.

Adriel's mind was spinning as he followed the servant. He first needed to explain the situation to Nalussa. He was certain they couldn't escape now. He'd need a plan to get her out of the building, across the courtyards, and past the gathering places, the sentries, the staff, the servants . . . he shook his head. No, they couldn't just run now.

When she finally appeared, he rushed to her and hastily dismissed the servant.

"Adriel! I haven't seen you in a long time. Why are you here?" Confused, she looked beyond where he was standing to the empty doorway. "What's happening?"

"Nalussa, you must come with me. I have to speak with you . . . very serious news . . . "

Nalussa gasped and touched his arm. "Is it Adiah?"

Not answering, he ushered her through the doorway and hurried her down the hallway to an alcove used to store water jugs. Pushing her behind a wall, he got close to her face. "Adiah summoned me. He's very sick. He told me some news. The king is dead. No one is safe. Rehoboam will be anointed king; I've got to get you out of the harem. There's no telling what the new king will do!"

Nalussa put her hands to her mouth. "Abra is with child!"

"There's nothing I can do about that. God be with her. I'm here to get you out!"

"NO!" Nalussa shrank back against the wall, horrorstruck. "I can't leave Abra. They'll kill her and her baby!"

Adriel looked around the dividing wall, then roughly grabbed her arm and ordered, "Walk with me." She did as she was told, visibly shaking. He heaved a huge, anxious breath, trying to act normal as a few staffers walked by and nodded.

"I don't think word has leaked that the king is dead. Those two acted normal." She was referring to the two men that passed them.

Adriel looked back over his shoulder at the retreating men. "Yes. They're acting normal. So far, all is normal, but pandemonium will erupt as soon as the king's death is announced. King Solomon's old guard will be looking for favor and status quo, while his son's loyalists will be vying for their positions."

Adriel was stressed. He had to act soon. "It could be announced today; I don't know. There might or might not be a period of mourning, depending on if Rehoboam is threatened in any way. But with the changing of the reign, there will be a lot of people moving about, getting into position, or fearing for their lives. Rehoboam has a following, and he's been clever at keeping his plans secret, except for his inner circle. I honestly thought I had time before something like this happened. I fear for myself, too. No one is safe or secure. We've got to get away." Adriel pulled his lip in worry.

Nalussa said, "All along, I wanted to know what would happen to the harem should the king die, and no one would speak to me about it. And now I know. We're not safe, but I must bring Abra along. I can't leave her behind!"

"I'll work out a plan." Her friend Abra added complication to the situation, and he wasn't sure how to handle the problem of helping another concubine to escape who was expecting. That condition alone could be seen as huge problem for the new king. "You must be prepared to leave at any moment after the king has been pronounced dead and while Rehoboam is wrestling with the logistics of taking over leadership. It's not going to be smooth. Too many people and places to manage and he's not his father. He lacks wisdom and experience; plus, he's an aggressive, stubborn man."

He stopped and looked at her, so lovely, so frightened. "Be aware. He and his court will be distracted until they regain control of all the moving parts, but as long as there are women to be had, the harem will not be safe. That's something they can manage. I'll try to figure out something as fast as I can!"

Nalussa whimpered. "I knew this would happen." She put a hand to her heart. "What will become of us?"

"I'll try my best to take care of you!" The moment was fraught with fear and hope. For both of them.

Adriel looked around. In order to continue to talk without arousing suspicion or be accused of inappropriate socializing, he steered her out of the harem toward Adiah's building and apartment. Even though the old man didn't ask for Adriel to bring her to him, it was the only way he could legitimately keep talking to her. As to what would become of them all, Adriel hadn't an answer, but he could guess. With a man like Rehoboam and the men he chose to surrounded himself, it was more than possible that any heir to the king would be eliminated. It happened throughout the past, whether children of wives or of concubines; they had to be destroyed to ensure the new ruler had no other to rise up and claim the throne. It was also not unusual for the new king to enjoy the old king's women, humiliate them, and then get rid of them one way or another.

This time, she stopped and held his arm, insisting. Her eyes filled with tears. "Can't we work a way to get us all out?"

Adriel wanted to say no, but he held his peace. He'd worry about that later. Now, it was a matter of how the course of events would throw off the security and routine of the palace. In the upcoming chaos that he felt sure was going to happen, they'd make their break.

When they got to Adiah's apartment, Adriel rapped on the door. The old eunuch's servant opened it slightly, poked his head out, and said softly, "He's sleeping. I'll tell him you were here." He looked over at Nalussa and back to Adriel. "I'll tell him you brought another visitor."

Adriel spoke, peering into the room at the skeletal, sleeping man. "Yes. Tell him Nalussa came by to see him, and all will be well."

On the way back, Nalussa grabbed Adriel's tunic. "Do you have anyone you can trust in helping us escape?"

Adriel narrowed his lips admitting, "No."

Nalussa said, "I have an idea. Go find my brother Jasper. He'll be able to help you. Between the two of you, you'll come up with a plan, and I'll prepare Abra—"

Adriel held up a hand. He had to stand firm. This was getting too complicated. "Not Abra! They would surely track us down for a king's heir. It's going to be risky enough and—"

"Listen to me. We can do this. Have faith in God's protection. We have little time. Maybe we could use Adiah as an excuse to leave the harem?"

"Possible." Adriel's mind was sifting through ideas. "We could use him as a cover by saying he wants to see you again . . . and maybe we can say he wants to see Abra, too, now that she's with child." He shook his head in doubt. "Only, that escape can only happen between the morning hours and late afternoon. By evening, your servants would discover you both missing and raise an alarm. It gives us little time to get out of the buildings and find a safe hiding place in Jerusalem. Clearing the city gates at night would be a problem."

He mulled it over. "No, that won't work. We'll have to do it sometime during the mourning period for the king or Rehoboam's transition, whichever works best as a diversion."

Nalussa held up a finger. "If they have a funeral for the king, we'll have to be there. We could possibly leave then, while throngs of crowds will be moving about, paying their last respects."

Adriel nodded. "I could get the chief eunuch's permission to escort you, rather than your servants, to the service. I'm sure I can work that out." *How?* he wondered. "I'll have to allude somehow to your status with the king—and I guess Abra's."

He pulled his beard. "Hmmm. Maybe that's how I can work it. Because I'm the one who found you two to begin with, I could offer to escort the king's two favored concubines to the funeral. That might work."

He looked at Nalussa. "Does the king know Abra's with child . . . er, I mean, *did* he know?"

"Yes, along with the rest of the harem, servants, and the chief eunuch." She thought back to the moment Abra announced her pregnancy. "She was so proud, boasting in her newfound status. The other women were so jealous and envious! We all heard how angry some of King Solomon's wives were when they got the news, too, particularly if they hadn't conceived yet. The news spread as quickly as a rainy season river."

"What was the king's reaction to the news?" Adriel asked.

"I don't know. The king never spoke to me about any of the other concubines, except once in a while, he would speak fondly of the Queen of Sheba. I did ask Abra about the king's reaction. She said he was happy in a quiet way. 'Another heir down the line,' he said, but she didn't speak anymore of the king's reaction."

They reached the harem. "Nalussa, give me some time to work this out. And Nalussa? I do care about you, and I'm so sorry—"

She held his hand for a moment. "Shhh. Put that behind you. Now go to my brother. He'll help!" She turned to leave, her heart hammering in her chest. She had so wanted to hear news of Adriel and even glimpse him in the palace, but certainly not under these circumstances of fear and possible death!

"Wait!" He reached under his robe and pulled out the scroll. "Adiah wanted you to have this."

"What is it?" She held it up and saw the king's seal. Another of his writings, no doubt. She hid it under her own robes and turned to go. "Please, Adriel, find my brother. He'll help. I know he will."

CHAPTER ELEVEN

Adriel didn't waste any time. As soon as he left Nalussa, he dashed through the palace out to the grounds to get his horse that was enjoying dried grass in the servant's animal enclosure. He stopped off at his home and gathered a few items to include water, some dried fruit, and a knife and short sword. One never knew what to expect on the outskirts of Jerusalem. Or what to expect when he came back.

He didn't know if he would find Nalussa's brother. In all likelihood, with the gold they received for her purchase, the family was possibly long gone to another area far from flocks and herds.

After leaving the palace late, he spent the night in the hills thinking how unlikely these circumstances were for him and Nalussa to be thrown together. Maybe it would work out for them. He prayed it would. He arose early the next morning and crossed a small stream running through a lush valley, dotted with goats and sheep and a lone shepherd, who ignored him. When he came to the outskirts of Nalussa's village, he hesitated. He didn't want to go to the village well because the last thing he wanted was to start gossip. Likewise, he was concerned about the village square and sought to avoid the market and the old men sitting by the gate. If he didn't find Jasper at the family home, then he would have to go back to the village and ask where the family had gone. He prayed they had not moved on. Generation after generation usually held fast to their land. He would soon find out.

Trotting along the path he remembered, it was apparent it was still well-used, and when he came through a small copse of trees, there was the house with chickens wandering about. This was a good sign. Dismounting, he approached the open doorway to be greeted by Nalussa's little sister. He was surprised how she had grown, and although different in skin tone, she was equally as lovely.

"You're the man who took my sister!" The young girl pointed at him accusingly. "Why are you here? Is she . . . is she . . . still alive?"

"Yes, she is. I've come to see your brother, Jasper. Where is he?" His horse was stepping about nervously, sensing her master's urgency. He patted her neck in reassurance and started to speak when the young girl—*ah, Noa is her name,* he remembered—interrupted.

"You're not going to take him, too?" Her small hands flew to her mouth, and she began to cry.

Adriel held up his hand. "No, no! Just tell me where he is!" Frightened, she hesitated. "Tell me now!" Adriel demanded, scaring her to answer. He was not in the mood for drama.

"He's in the fields to the east of the village square with my other brother and father. Don't hurt him!" she yelled.

He took off in a trot. He had just passed that valley and only saw one shepherd. How could he have missed two other people? He prayed she was telling the truth. Coming near to where he had been, he realized he missed the two other herders, who were sitting down by the stream. He approached fast, and the two figures at the water abruptly stood up as the other shepherd drew close to them. They held their staffs in their hands, ready to defend themselves.

As Adriel approached, Nalussa's father, Jonah, and Jasper immediately recognized him. The younger, not remembering, stood behind his big brother as their father stepped quickly toward the advancing rider.

"What is your news, Adriel? Oh, yes, I remember you, Adriel! A man I'll never forget!" the man shouted, obviously bracing himself for bad news. Jasper stood rigid, and the young boy, Ziba, cowered.

Adriel dismounted, holding the reins, and beseeched them, "I'm trying to help Nalussa, and we have little time. I need your help, Jasper."

Jasper shouted, bounding toward him, "What? What's happening?"

Nalussa's father grabbed his sleeve, holding him back, and ordered, "Shush. Let him speak."

His words came rushing out as they gathered around him. "King Solomon is dead. By now, it will be known throughout the palace, if not Jerusalem. Rehoboam will take the throne. I don't know what turmoil will result, but all the women in the harem are at risk, especially Nalussa, one of the king's favorites. Rehoboam could rape her to make a point of his authority."

The men were silent, stunned. Jasper jabbed his staff in the air, and in anger, he said, "Of course, I'll help! Have you a plan?"

Jonah said calmly, "Come, let's sit. Over on that hill." He directed the younger son to keep an eye on their animals. Once seated, he nodded to Adriel to continue.

"This is going to be complicated or not. I think we make the escape at the funeral. The palace, the grounds, the harem, the outbuildings, the grottos—all provide ample areas to hide, but at the same time, all those areas are swarming with people. During or after the funeral, when people are not themselves, could be the time to get her out of there." Here, he took in a breath. "There's a slight problem, though."

Father and son exchanged worried glances.

"Wouldn't there be many? Isn't that a given?" Jasper asked sarcastically.

"Yes, of course, but Nalussa insists we take her expecting friend with us."

"By the king? A sister concubine is with child?" The father looked in disbelief first at Adriel, then his son. "It's one thing to take a favored concubine; it's another taking one whose child could be a threat to the throne, no matter how far down the line! Rehoboam might order all children and their mothers slaughtered."

"I suppose everyone knows she's with child?" Jasper leaned toward Adriel in hostility.

His father again placed a warning hand on his arm. "Let the man answer."

"Yes, it's known throughout the palace, but she, of course, isn't the only one."

There was no point in further argument. They loved Nalussa, and if she wanted to save her friend and the unborn child, then that's what they would do.

"I need some women's clothing. Once we get them out of the harem and off the palace grounds, they must appear like everyday women. We can't arouse any suspicion."

"Not a problem," Jonah replied. "We still have Nalussa's clothing stored at the house."

Adriel turned to the father, curious. "Why didn't you leave when you had all that gold?"

"I didn't want the wealth. I still have it. It's in a goats' shed buried in a corner. I would never give up my land. Where would we go?" He shook his head. "No, our life is here, and we didn't need the king's money. We are blessed."

Adriel thought a moment. "We may need it if we have to escape to another kingdom for a while. Come, let's get the clothing."

The men stood and walked with Adriel as Jonah shouted to his youngest son to come near. "Ziba! Tend the animals. I'll be back as soon as I can."

Inside the home, Jonah went to a small chest and pulled out Nalussa's old clothes. "Here. I believe I can get two sets of clothing for you. I don't know how far along her friend is, but this robe is forgiving." He tied the clothing together and handed it to Adriel, while Jasper put together a few provisions for the trip back. "Son, take the donkey and dig up the gold in case you need to buy another animal or two. I know you can't come back here. This will be the first place they'll look."

"Yes," Adriel agreed as Jasper hurried out the door. "The chief eunuch keeps records on all the concubines. It won't be difficult locating Nalussa's home. As soon as we get out of Jerusalem, if it's safe, we'll try and get word to you where we are going."

Jasper came out of the shed with a small chest of gold. "If we take the cups, people will know where they came from. They're too big and obvious. The utensils are easier to carry and barter with."

His father took the chest from him and pulled out the cups. "I'll smash them down. You'll need all the resources you can get. If you have to go out of the country, which will probably happen, you'll need a horse or donkey for each woman and maybe even a pack animal."

He disappeared into a lean-to and began hammering, returning a short while later with flattened and broken pieces of gold. "Here. This will make it easier to dole out for your needs."

They saddled up with the bundle of clothing, some provisions, and a satchel with gold hidden in the side packs of the horse. They bade goodbye to Jonah, who wept to see his son leave and in fear for his eldest daughter.

"I pray I see you again, Jasper. I pray for all of you. Safe travels and may God have mercy on you!"

"Father, I love you, and we will come back to you. We just don't know when. God will be with us. God is good!"

On their way, Jasper confessed, "When we were young, we thought, wouldn't it great to be King Solomon or, at the very least, one of his mighty men? We'd have the best food and drink, the fastest horses, and as many women as we wanted. It was all we talked about when we tended the herds and flocks. That is, until you took Nalussa." Jasper paused for a moment before continuing. "My father had a talk with me about the king's appetite for money and women. It was against God's commands, yet even though the king was actually blessed by hearing the word from God, he didn't take God's word to heart; he continued doing what he wanted to do and what he does best."

"What's that?" Adriel turned back to look at Jasper on the donkey.

"Getting and taking whatever he wanted. No matter the cost to his subjects. He worked them hard, took their daughters for pleasure, took their sons for soldiers. He got whatever he wanted—everything his heart and eyes desired."

Adriel turned back, keeping his eyes on the path. He didn't want to talk about the king. The king had been good to him and rewarded him handsomely for the acquisition of Nalussa and many of the other women he found. Yet he was conflicted. While he saw some excitement and gratitude from some of the women he found for the king, he mostly saw frightened young women with broken hearts and shattered families. And for what, really? So the king could bed a virgin? She was no different than a fine wine from the wine cellar or a piece of dear jewelry from a jewelry chest. A possession to be enjoyed and savored and ultimately used and forgotten.

He knew he wasn't the only one who raised an eyebrow over the king's excesses. Many others in the kingdom and among the staff had sensory overload—especially older folk, though few people spoke out loud about it out of fear, but he heard the odd snippet of distress within the palace and throughout his travels. King Solomon's great wealth, the running of his vast holdings, and his many women and complicated projects came at the dear expense of others supporting his needs.

Admittedly, there was prosperity in Jerusalem and even the outlying towns of Judah, but there was always a cost. Always. The people of the kingdom gave their lives and children to the king's empire. Nalussa's family was not the only one who grieved over a lost daughter, for wealth was not always the motivator for happiness.

On a final note of thought, he did have to give the king credit. He dealt with people fairly and, in some cases, extraordinarily. He recalled the time when two prostitutes came to the king with a complaint. They were arguing over a baby. The first said that she had a baby in the house in which the two women were living. The second woman had a baby three days later. During the night, the second woman rolled over on her baby and killed him. Seeing that her child was dead, she took the other woman's baby from her while she was sleeping and put her dead son at the sleeping woman's breast. When the woman woke, she realized the dead baby was not hers!

Both women claimed the living baby was theirs. With wisdom, Solomon offered to cut the baby in half in order to reveal which woman truly loved the child. The mother was more willing to allow another woman to have him than to kill her own child. The king then determined who the real mother was.

All the kingdom was in awe over the king's handling of the situation. And this was just one of many of the king's rulings and decisions. He was not a cruel, impetuous king; he had the wisdom to handle complicated circumstances with cleverness and creativity.

Adriel came back to the present, addressing Jasper. "You'll stay at my house. I'll tell anyone who asks that you're family, but not many people should ask. I'm often traveling. But I'll pass you off as my cousin to get into the palace grounds, particularly for the funeral."

There was so much to consider. Getting the women out, getting them out of their funeral finery and into peasant clothing, then finding a way out of the city. The big problem? Nalussa's coloring. She stood out in the crowd. Devastatingly beautiful and bronze. No one would forget her.

CHAPTER TWELVE

The harem was in upheaval. King Solomon was dead. Women were crying; some were seeking out their servants to find out what was to become of them; and others were continually going from woman to woman, imploring them for advice and updates.

"How can we know?" one woman snapped to a tearful, plump woman. "We're trapped in here like horses in a stable with fire around us. Who will save us? We see no one, except our servants, and they're as uncertain and fearful as we are!" The private quarters and the great room were a cacophony of weeping and cries of confusion.

The servants were in the same situation. They had a meeting with the chief eunuch, who told them, "I know nothing yet. Rehoboam's deputy assured me that everyone is safe, but my advice is to keep the women calm. Do not procure any perfumes, lotions, soaps, or clothing. Make do with what you have and use sparingly. I don't know what's going to happen with supplies. My main concern is keeping the food chain flowing."

He glared at the men. "If you are unable to take care of your wards and keep them calm and presentable, you will be thrown out of the palace! I will not tolerate gossip, fear-mongering, or any other such behavior. Lives could be at stake. Rehoboam has gone to Shechem to be anointed king. As soon as I hear anything, you will be the first to know!"

The servants were frightened—not only for the women many had grown fond of, but also for themselves. A harem this huge took a tremendous amount of supplies, food being the most important. All of them hoped to ingratiate themselves to the new regime, but purges were going to happen.

Nalussa was comforting Abra in a quiet area of the courtyard. She brought her outside away from the others so they could speak in private, but Abra was incoherent with fear. "What will they do to me and my baby? Will they kill us? How can we get away?"

"Hush and listen to me. And swear you will not speak of this to anyone!"

Abra stopped babbling and listened, wide-eyed with hope. "Yes, I swear!"

Nalussa spoke urgently. "Adriel and my brother are going to rescue us." Abra gasped aloud.

"Shhhh. Keep calm. We don't want anyone to think we are plotting anything!" Nalussa scolded, keeping an eye on the empty courtyard. "I don't know how they are going to do this, but sometime between while the new king is being ushered in and we pay our last respects to King Solomon, we will escape when there is a lot of confusion and activity."

"How will we know to be ready?" Abra breathed in and out slowly, willfully calming herself.

"We must be ready at any moment. Stay close to me at all times. We'll keep a look-out for Adriel. It's possible he'll be able to escort us to King's Solomon's funeral, but this could change. We only spoke of this plan once."

"Nalussa, if we escape the harem and get away from the palace grounds, where will we go?"

"We haven't gotten that far yet. I don't know. It will be dependent upon a lot of things. We don't know how smoothly the transition will be with Rehoboam. And do you recall Jeroboam?"

Abra looked worried, nodding. "A little."

Nalussa pursed her lips, explaining, "He was told by the prophet Ahija that the kingdom would be torn apart and he would be given ten tribes—effectively dividing the kingdom."

Abra shivered. The prophet's words were gossiped throughout the palace and harem, yet most didn't believe it. However, King Solomon thought it was enough of a threat that he went after Jeroboam to kill him, but the man escaped to Egypt.

"So, a lot of things can happen. I'm hoping we can find a small village to hide in, but it's possible we'll have to leave the kingdom. I just don't know. But we have to be ready. The king's burial service will be in a few days' time. Do you have any jewelry?"

"Yes, I have some the king gave me. You have some, too?"

"No. In hindsight, I should have collected it in the case I needed it for bribes. I was too self-righteous to take anything from him." She thought of the scroll he had given Adiah to give to her. She hadn't looked at it because she didn't have the privacy in the harem to read it yet. It could wait, but it wasn't of any value with which she could barter. No doubt it was more of his reflections about "vanity." Well, he didn't have to worry about "nothing new under the sun" now. Everyone dies, no matter how rich and powerful.

"From now on, keep your jewels with you under your robe. We don't want others to get desperate and steal your jewels. We aren't the only ones planning, I'm sure."

Abra reached out and hugged her friend. "I was so mean to you when I realized he preferred you over every one of us. Then I was so boastful when I got pregnant, thinking that I was in a much higher, exalted place! Now I could be killed with my baby. Please forgive my selfishness and my own vanity!"

"The past is behind us. Let's concentrate on the future. Keep your mind sharp, stay healthy, and stay close to me. We'll get through this."

As predicted, the court was in turmoil with Rehoboam in Shechem to take over as the new king and the king's body being argued over as to whether to embalm according to his Egyptian wife's desire or to wash the body according to Hebrew custom. Because of the argument, Rehoboam's absence, and the king's body disintegrating with the elements, they hastily smeared his body with spices: frankincense, aloes, myrrh, cinnamon, and sweet calamus cassia mixed with olive oil that was used as the holy anointing oil. They wrapped him in linens, placed him on a bier, and readied him to be carried to the sepulcher of his father, David. Although Rehoboam was not present, the ritual would be witnessed by all of the king's staff and household as the city of Jerusalem expected.

Not only was the harem in a state of fear and confusion, the court and the citizens of Jerusalem were as well. How the king died was being kept a secret, for if he was sick, no one spoke of it. Thus, the people were not expecting their great, all-powerful king would die. In war or sickness, yes, but so quickly? Without warning? It was unthinkable!

The day of burial, crowds jammed the streets and alleys, and those who couldn't find a foothold on the streets hung out of windows and balconies. The priests led the procession, along with the Levites, followed by musicians, the most important of advisors, the minor advisors, the wives, the concubines, and lastly, the servants according to rank. There were nearly two thousand from the household and staff.

Adriel arrived at the harem just before they were set to join their spot in the procession. Nalussa was frantic waiting along with Abra. The servant led Adriel to the foyer and went to bring the two women to him.

The women bowed, and Adriel stepped in front of them, "Follow me and stay close. Do not wander off to speak to your friends." He threw a look at Abra. "Always keep your eyes on me." The other concubines followed in step, and there was no more opportunity to speak until they left the harem, crossed the palace grounds, and made their way to the temple.

The crowds lined the streets, and many people walked along with the procession. He finally had his chance when a man cut in front of him and he had to push him to the side, allowing him to turn to the two women following close behind. He said, "When I wipe my brow, follow me. Immediately!"

The narrow streets were crowded with sightseers and mourners. The procession began to loosen up as people cut in and around the different groups of official mourners. Adriel positioned himself in such a way that there was space between him and the group ahead. People took advantage of the space, inserted themselves, and followed along an unencumbered path toward the wide esplanade leading to the courts of the temple.

The soldiers, arranged to escort and contain the procession and repel the crowds, were on foot, unable to ride their horses through the narrow streets due to the huge amount of people. Their disadvantage was that they couldn't stop everyone from following along and joining the procession. They could stop some, but not all. They would have more control once the path opened up to the grand esplanade. Here, they would meet up with horsemen who would have a better visual in controlling the crowds. The official mourners would be in the groups, and on the steps to the temple, the high priest would perform the burial prayers.

As the crowd surged forward to more open space, Adriel prayed, "God of my fathers, of Solomon, your great anointed king, and me, your humble servant, let this go according to plan."

People were milling about the plaza, intermingling in the vast procession, throwing off the efforts of the soldiers to keep a separation between citizens and the court. The crowds finally settled down to hear the priest speak. It was a long, drawn-out ritual ending in prayers and blessings. Once the priest was finished, he dismissed the crowds, except the wives and high officials, who were obligated to continue with the priests and Levites making their way to the tomb. The concubines were not invited.

Heedless of the priest's orders, a portion of the crowd broke up to follow the march to the kings' tombs. The soldiers on horseback closed in around the official mourners to protect them, trying to discourage those who wanted to follow using whips against them with little success. In turn, the foot soldiers tried to corral the lesser officials, the servants, and the concubines back to the palace and harem.

"Get back! Get back!" the soldiers ordered, drawing swords. The attempt to move them back in an orderly fashion was near impossible, for controlling three hundred women and nearly as many servants and officials was challenging, particularly along the narrow streets. People were hurt, ran in confusion, and even fought against one another.

"Don't touch me! Let go! Help me!" came cries from the women and even many palace officials as more disruption heated and bubbled up as groups of men from the city aggressively lunged at the beautiful women hoping to get a handful as they passed. It was chaos.

Nalussa kept a sharp eye on Adriel, who was walking toward the edge of the crowd, protecting her and Abra, who followed close behind, holding onto the back of his robe like children with their mother at market.

"Keep close, Abra!" Nalussa shouted above the din. "We can't get torn away from Adriel!" Abra was too petrified to speak. The surging crowd was like waves tossed about an angry sea. There was complete confusion and disorder.

As the concubines were jostled and manhandled by the male onlookers, the soldiers were concentrating on keeping them together and at the same time keeping the men from touching them. Too few soldiers for too many people. Abra tripped and lunged for Nalussa, who grabbed two handfuls of Adriel's cloak.

"Don't let go!" he yelled as he plunged through the crowds.

Many women were yelping in distress, but one concubine's scream topped the rest. The soldiers turned their attention to a man running through the crowds with a veil waved high like flag of victory. *It was Jasper!* Nalussa would know him from any distance.

The soldiers' and people's attentions diverted, Adriel wiped his brow at the same time he pushed hard against two men who were standing close together with their hands outstretched for a grab and were caught off-balance. A lucky break for Adriel, they fell down hard, causing others to trip over them.

As the crowds trampled over the screaming men, Nalussa whispered fiercely to Abra, and squeezed her arm. "Now, now! Let's move!"

Holding onto one another, they pushed and stepped over bodies and scurried after Adriel, who headed for a narrow alley. At the end of the alley, they crossed under a broken archway, made a quick left, and ducked through an open doorway. Jasper was waiting for them in a room no bigger than a closet.

Nalussa squealed and threw her arms around him. He hugged her but breathlessly ordered, "No time. Change now. We must get moving." He withdrew a bundle from his satchel and handed it to Nalussa, who quickly untied it and gave a set of clothing to Abra. "We don't have time for you to fully change. Just get under the robes and veils. Quickly. We have no time to waste."

Adriel and Jasper changed their tunics, too, and put on head dresses dirty and worn. Nalussa's robes worked for both women, and they dipped out through the doorway and made their way away from the direction of the palace and the harem to the outskirts of the city and opposite the tombs of the kings.

Nalussa kept her head down and drew her veil just under her nose. She secured it with a hairpin and pulled her veil over her forehead. Only eyes, hands, and sandaled feet were exposed. They followed smaller crowds that were making for the city gate and finally got beyond the city proper.

At a public stable outside of the gates, the two men retrieved Adriel's horse, and Jasper grabbed two horses for each woman and the family donkey.

No one glanced in their direction as they traveled the road leading away from the city of Jerusalem. Moving with the crowds, they spoke little. Both women were fearful and exhausted, and the men were still under the influence of adrenaline.

They took to a side road, and after an hour, they stopped at wooded area. "Let's rest here," Adriel advised as they dismounted near a stream, and Jasper dug in his packs for bread and fruit.

While the animals drank their fill at the stream, Jasper hugged his sister. "We have a short-term plan. We'll stop here briefly; then we have to ride another hour or so to get to the hills. I've scouted out a cave where we can hide the animals and spend the night."

"They've discovered we're gone by now," Abra said in worry and sat down wearily on a clump of grass.

"Perhaps, but it's also probable that they don't know what to do about it. The walk back to the harem was confusing; there were many people swarming all over the concubines, and the soldiers had little control over the situation. I'm sure a lot of women took the opportunity to escape. The big problem could be a pregnant concubine has gone missing," Adriel stated.

"And the king's favorite concubine," Jasper added, nodding toward Nalussa.

CHAPTER THIRTEEN

While Rehoboam was in Shechem, some sixty miles north of Jerusalem, word had not yet reached him that many of his father's concubines had escaped the harem, notably one pregnant Abra and one favored Nalussa, who had been escorted to the funeral by Adriel, the old king's procurer of women.

Once they were discovered missing, the palace authorities sent out pairs of men, each with a messenger to go north, south, east, and west to stop at all villages and towns to find the two concubines and their accomplice. The messenger was to get word back to the palace with updates and sightings. If there were any. If the escapees were found, they were not to harm them but to bring them back to the palace to await judgment from Rehoboam, who had planned to make an example of his power by taking them for himself.

At the administration office in the palace, a secret meeting of only high-level staff met. The chief of staff called the meeting to order. "We must speak of King Solomon's wives and concubines. Regarding the wives, Rehoboam likely will disperse the childless ones, although we do not know. Those wives with children are in special keeping, awaiting the new king's orders. Our lives could well depend upon our keeping them secure. As for the concubines with children, all are accounted for and are secure within the harem."

Someone asked, "What about those who escaped?"

"I was getting to that. About fifteen escaped and, fortunately for us, didn't have children," the man responded.

"Except a pregnant one," a man standing by the windows interrupted, looking worried. "And King Solomon's most favored one, Nalussa. I'm sure Rehoboam will be furious, having a possible future threat to the throne on the run, along with not being able to force himself on the old king's favored one. He publicly made it known he was looking forward to that conquest!"

"I understand that. We all do, and we have men looking for them as we speak."

In fear and anxiety, the men in the room talked among themselves. The women were lost under their watch. Certainly, the new king would mete out punishment for their lack of control.

"But so far, we've received no word of success," the chief of staff admitted. He continued, "So. We'll go to Shechem to inform the new king of the fracture of the harem, the disappearance of a possible future threat to the throne, and the loss of the old king's favored woman. We'll also tell him fifteen escaped. We have no choice but to be honest."

One of King Solomon's advisors piped up hopefully, "Perhaps he'll have more important things to attend to rather than finding missing women who have to be continually fed and clothed."

"I don't think he'll put too much value on the missing ones, but on the other two he will," the man at the window persisted.

"It seems this is possible. He might not care about the others, but the two that are important to him, he will. In addition to our friend's point, King Rehoboam might have more pressing concerns.

We've heard that some of our people have gone to Egypt to inform Jeroboam, King Solomon's competitor, that he is dead. You recall the prophet saying that Jeroboam would end up with a sizable portion of the kingdom?"

"Ten tribes," the man at the window said. "And already people from Jerusalem are on their way to Shechem to see what will happen when Jeroboam confronts Rehoboam. There will be a taking of sides, so we can't wait here for news. As the chief of staff says, our group must go to Shechem to glean favor from Rehoboam."

"Indeed," one man agreed. "We must be the ones to advise the king when Jeroboam confronts him, and we must also be the ones to inform the king of the problem with the harem and the disappearance of Abra and Nalussa. We don't want him to hear it from gossipers. I don't trust his young friends. Who knows what they might counsel him?"

The man at the window pushed away from the sill, walked to where the chief of staff was standing, and addressed the room. "You can also depend upon a discussion about the upkeep of the kingdom. King Solomon placed a heavy burden on his people to keep the supplies coming in, and I don't know how long we can keep up the momentum, particularly with an inexperienced king with few alliances of his own. So, there's a lot to be concerned about, particularly Jeroboam, the prophecy, and the people who support him."

There was more grumbling and worry. Another man spoke. "Indeed, we have a lot to be troubled over, as does the new king. However, what of the escort, Adriel? I've been informed that Nalussa's first eunuch, Adiah, has died, and the chief eunuch has killed himself, so we can't make examples of them over their poor security. We're left responsible. We must find Adriel, who will lead us to the women."

"As I've stated, we've already started the investigation," the chief of staff replied. "We've sent men to his house, empty—no surprise there—and the family of Nalussa have no idea where she is."

"What about the money King Solomon paid for her?" someone asked.

"Let's not worry about that now. It's probably gone."

"But—"

"Enough! We have enough uncertainties without trying to arrest Nalussa's family and throw them into debtor's prison!"

Another man stood. "We must make our way to Rehoboam now if we are to maintain any power. We can't take the chance of becoming inconsequential to him, for he'll certainly kill us, fearing opposition or believing we were complicit in the escape of the pregnant one."

The men in the room heartily agreed. This was the time to find a secure place. And if there wasn't any position for them, then it was time to plan either their own escape or retirement with good wishes. Good wishes were unlikely, most believed. It was well-known throughout the kingdom that Rehoboam was not like his father—in temperament or knowledge.

"Rehoboam chose to spend his time growing up in the kingdom a privileged and opinionated royal with little appetite to learn the art of ruling," the chief of staff confided to the man who had stood beside him as the men filed out of the room.

"Indeed. He is a disappointment, particularly when Solomon spent so much time teaching him words of wisdom. The king even painstakingly wrote it all down for him to refer to and learn from."

"Apparently, it didn't work. The man is headstrong and relies on his friends for conduct and advice. And count on a double-edged sword of problems he's ill-equipped to deal with: confrontation from Jeroboam and the escape of two very important concubines."

The men joined their peers to make haste to Shechem.

***

Adriel carefully led his small party along the road well away from Jerusalem, being careful to keep in front, while Jasper brought up the rear. "Women, please keep your faces covered. We don't want any one admiring your fine, healthy, and plump skin. We've got to be on alert at all times."

The night in the cave was but a brief respite. The fear of being followed or tracked was in each mind. It wouldn't have been important for a woman to escape the vast haram, but because two of the prominent concubines had escaped or were unaccounted for, this surely would bring the wrath of Rehoboam down on those responsible for his father's precious property and the property itself.

"We know that Rehoboam is in Shechem. It will be a while before the news is delivered to him that Nalussa and Abra are missing. They will guess I was the one who helped them escape, but they don't know a thing about you, Jasper. This at least gives us less recognition along the road being two couples," Adriel called back over his shoulder, trying to reassure the women and himself. "I suggest we pass ourselves off as married couples. We still need to keep off the main roads. People will remember Nalussa if they glimpse her face. They will likely see her hands and feet. Maybe they won't think anything of it—or maybe they will—but we can't take the chance. As for a pregnant couple, I don't see it as a challenge. At least for now, we're just two couples that are on our way south after paying respects to our dead king.

Jasper added, "It gives us some lead time, too. We best make haste."

***

Trekking south, they made campsites off the roads in wooded, hilly, or rocky terrain, keeping well out of sight of curious travelers—or worse yet, travelers who would want to join them, for safety was in numbers. Yet, they still had to take the risk of stopping at the various villages for supplies, but the men were tasked for that.

On the outskirts of a remote village, Adriel said, "While we're here, take an inventory of what we need, and I'll go into the square."

Jasper raised his brows. "Do you think that's wise? Maybe I should go with you."

"No. Stay with the women."

Nalussa dug around in her sacks and then wandered over to her pregnant friend. Looking into her supplies, she tilted her head to Adriel. "We need bread, as always, and any fruits or vegetables. Water—we have plenty." She pointed down to a gully at a trickling stream.

At a dried fruit stall, Adriel began taking handfuls of whatever was available, showing it to the vendor who named a price, then dumping the pieces in his satchel. As he made his way from one stall to another, he glanced over his shoulder. A man and woman seemed to be following him at a not-so-discreet distance. He continued on, anxiety mounting. Covering the lower part of his face, he abruptly stopped, swinging around to face them. He gaped behind the cloth.

"Adriel?" a short, rugged man asked with hesitation.

Adriel, so shocked, froze as a woman timidly whispered, "Adriel?" They were all nearly face to face.

He swung around to bolt, but the man grabbed at his sleeve. "No! You're safe. It's all right, I swear!"

Both men stopped as the woman cowered behind the man, clutching his dirty tunic. Adriel recognized who she was. One of his finds. One of Solomon's concubines.

"Come, come over here." The man quickly indicated to a group of large stones by short wood fence. Reluctantly, Adriel followed, his heart hammering.

"What's going on, Lev? What are you doing here with her?" Adriel couldn't believe he was seeing the man he worked with at the palace and a young woman he, Adriel, had purchased for Solomon!

"You think you were the only one to escape? And escape with a woman?" Lev barely contained his sarcasm. "Once the king died and Rehoboam took over, we were all doomed. He wasn't going to keep any of us on. And as for the women in the harem? They were at the new king's mercy, and trust me, there was never going to be any mercy."

"How and when did you escape, and how were you to take her?"

"She has a name, Adriel. It's Mahala. We escaped shortly after Rehoboam came back from Shechem."

"Tell me, what happened after the ceremonies for Solomon, and Rehoboam took the throne?" Lev squinted his eyes, shaking his head, remembering. "That's when you left with the two concubines. You took great advantage of the confusion. I should have planned our escape then, but I was too slow in taking any action. You have both women?" He looked directly at Adriel.

Adriel was careful in responding and evaded the direct question. "We will have safe haven soon." It seemed everyone had a price. If Lev was caught, he could bargain with knowledge of Adriel.

Lev waited, but Adriel prodded him. "Tell me about Rehoboam and how you came to escape." He dug in his satchel and gave him a trinket of gold.

Lev hefted it in his hand. Satisfied, he nodded and slipped it in his purse. "When Rehoboam came back, his plan was to oust many of Solomon's close circle and replace them with his own confidants. I tell you, he was in a dark, foul place. Jeroboam, the contender, challenged him at Shechem; and along with the other ten tribes, the people rebelled. Rehoboam was no match for Jeroboam and his followers. He had to plan his own escape from Shechem back to Jerusalem!

"Then, to add more bad news, he nearly went insane when he was told that two of Solomon's most important concubines had escaped. You, my friend, were the talk of the palace!"

Adriel could visualize it. It sent fear coursing through his body. They had to find safety soon. Lev interrupted his thoughts. "Let me tell you about your fame. I happened to be on the outer edge of advisors when Rehoboam held a meeting in the great hall to get status of the different issues of the palace. The old king's chief advisor came before Rehoboam and said, 'Please forgive me, Your Majesty. We have a situation.'" Lev pulled his feet up on the rock he was sitting on and leaned back against the fence. "A situation, indeed!" He laughed out loud. Mahala, sitting on the ground, scooted closer to the fence as if trying to hide. Adriel leaned forward.

"So, the king, already infuriated to have yet another problem handed to him, shouted, 'Speak! This better be important!' I tell you,

you could almost see the chief advisor's heart beating through his tunic. Hastily, the chief explained what had happened on the day of King Solomon's burial, embellishing the crush of crowds and predatory men and being short-handed of soldiers because the new king had brought a sizable contingent to Shechem, leaving the main palace short-handed and on and on. He finally he got to the point and said, 'King Solomon's favorite escaped, Your Majesty, and . . . ' He paused, very afraid. We all held our breath. This was going to be bad. But he garnered courage quickly and said, 'And a pregnant one.'

"The court broke out in chaos! Rehoboam was livid, his face purple. He knew immediately who Solomon's favorite was. 'Nalussa and who else?' he shouted. Then he threw down his staff and stood, pointing a shaking finger to the advisor. 'I want those women back! I don't care how you do it, but do it. I will expect weekly updates on progress. I will not tolerate this loss! Did anyone help them escape?'

"Here, my friend, is where you get your kingdom fame. The advisor said, 'Yes, Your Majesty. We believe it was Adriel.'"

Adriel let out a breath. This didn't surprise him, but it only emphasized how seriously in trouble they all were.

"Wait, it gets better." Lev grimaced. 'Adriel?' the king screamed. 'The very one who bought the women to begin with?' He was apoplectic with rage. I've never seen anyone so out of control. He continued to scream that you were a traitor and that if the advisors didn't find you, they would pay dearly. It was crazy. I don't have to advise you. They are after you. Be very careful."

The men sat in thought as Mahala wiped her eyes with her head scarf. They were all in danger. Adriel turned to Lev. "So, how did you two get out?"

"He began to talk about Solomon's other women, and he was inclined to let go the wives who did not have children. They were no threat to him, and because he would release them back to their own lands, he would have alliances with their families. The alliances were more important to him than their bodies."

Lev shifted on the uncomfortable rock, rubbing his hip. "Rehoboam then said that any wife or concubine with children were threats. He wanted his men to take care of them. As for the concubines who are still serviceable, he wanted to keep them. That's when I decided to get me and Mahala out. God was certainly with us."

CHAPTER FOURTEEN

"I can only say that we make our way to Egypt, out of the reach of Rehoboam," Adriel advised to the group. He recounted his meeting with Lev. "No question he will be after us if he isn't already. The king will be relentless because he has important prizes he'll want to show all his kingdom: the spectacle of my death, Abra's slaughter, the elimination of a threat to his throne when he murders Abra's baby, and Nalussa's rape. And you, my friend—should he find out about you—" referring to Jasper— "your death will be prominently displayed as well. He's not a man to be scorned."

"Do you think Lev will turn us in?" Jasper asked in worry.

"Unlikely. They are both on the run, too, and he told me that if they know he and Mahala are gone, it's unlikely they'll bother with resources to go after them. She is of no consequence, coming from a poor family. And as for Lev? He is nearly as unimportant. Anyway, should they catch them—which again, I think is unlikely, we will be long gone. And while they know about me, they don't really know where Nalussa and Abra are, other than in some 'safe place.'"

They made their way around villages by keeping to secondary, more difficult paths. In disguise, the men would venture into town as traders or merchants swapping small pieces of silver or gold for food and other provisions. They camped in areas away from traffic and curious eyes, finding caves or treed copses.

It didn't take long for both women to miss their privileged lifestyles, at least for food, drink, and protection from the elements.

"I miss my comfortable couch," Nalussa half-heartedly joked as she lay on a thin blanket on the ground. "But believe me, I am so grateful to be free."

Abra responded, "I admit I enjoyed being pampered, too, but I sadly realize it's all in the past. My main concern now, is to get as far away as possible from Rehoboam." Her fear for her baby and herself was crippling. "Our only hope for survival is to follow Adriel and Jasper wherever they decide to run."

Yet she handed only some of her jewels to Adriel. The rest she hid in her robes. She had dreams and plans.

Each evening when they settled into a spot, the women would prepare a meal, and they would chat among themselves about finding safety in Egypt. Many nights Nalussa and Adriel would find themselves alone as either Abra went to sleep and Jasper stood watch, or on occasion, Abra and Jasper would walk together to just stretch their legs.

"I think God put us together, Nalussa," Adriel said one evening as he threw a stick on their campfire. "I know that I should never have taken you from your family." Nalussa began to speak, but Adriel held up his hand. "Let me finish. But I think that I was meant to take you from your family. So maybe this could happen. Us. Being together."

Nalussa smiled and shook her head. "I was content with my family, but I knew there would come a time when my father would have to let me go. We just weren't prepared for it to happen so quickly. But, honestly, Adriel, I was treated very well in the palace, but I wasn't happy being in the harem. Yet I never blamed you."

"Do you know that I even thought of asking your father for you for myself?"

"We didn't even know each other!" Nalussa protested with an incredulous look.

"I know. But even then, I thought you were special . . . to me. I lost the courage, and I thought only of the reward."

"Ha! Reward being money and not me?"

"Yes," he answered sheepishly. "But I was also scared. It would mean a complete change for me, and besides, he might not have agreed—although I could certainly make a good argument for my cause." He reached out for her hand. "But I'm ready for that change now. Are you?"

She looked at him. How often had she thought about him in the palace? Many times. How could she not? He did, after all, forever change her life. Admittedly, she, too, had been attracted to him, even though she had been with him for a brief time; yet his imprint on her was indelible. But it was all so complicated. She was Solomon's concubine. She would never have her own husband, family, or life. She was owned. How could she daydream about something she could never have? Even now?

"You want me, knowing I've been with another man?"

"Yes. I was the one who put you in the arms of another man, and you didn't want to go!" he looked away in distress.

Gently, she touched his arm. "I need some time to think about what you've said." She shook her head sadly. "I'm just so unsure about my freedom." She hesitated. "Our freedom. What will become of us?" The truth was she was torn. *How do I feel about him? Adriel could easily be thought of as a good husband, but our situation is all so fragile. On the run. Being hunted. A former concubine. No father to discuss a possible union, and if we were to be married, it must be done in a godly manner.*

Adriel heaved a sigh. "I understand. Our existence is in the hands of God. But I'll wait for as long as it takes."

Nearly three weeks into their escape, they sat around a smoldering fire by the mouth of a cave. Jasper shifted uncomfortably, and Adriel nervously looked over at the two women who were serving them food.

"Nalussa, Abra, we have to talk." Adriel anxiously ran a hand through his coarse beard. The women set the plates of bread, cheese, and fruit in front of the men and sat down, waiting and wondering.

"Please, speak." Nalussa looked up at him in concern.

Abra nibbled her nails in expectation. Both women had talked to each other about their possible future in a new land, the ability to stay healthy enough to keep traveling, and the worry about the time when they might find themselves on their own without men to validate them and take care of them. And there was always the fear of being discovered. They figured they were days ahead of Rehoboam's men, but they traveled far more slowly than trackers would.

Abra, being pampered for so long, found it difficult riding for hours over rough terrain in keeping with the alternate routes. There was little Nalussa could do to help, other than encourage her and keep praying. Nalussa herself was weary from the arduous hours. Her only form of past exercise was walking to and from the king's rooms and her activities in his bed.

Both women realized they had to keep moving. Any lost time could mean discovery. Nalussa kept her faith in God, no matter what happened. Even if He didn't protect them against harm, her hope was in Him. God was faithful.

"We can keep bordering the villages, but at some time, we are going to be seen—either on the road, at a well, or in some other place." Adriel spoke quietly, poking the ashes.

"People have already seen us," replied Jasper in concern. "We've been fortunate so far that they've just passed us by."

"It won't last. Someone will be curious. How can they not notice two beautiful women?" Adriel shot Abra an accusatory look. "You must keep your faces covered. I know it's hot, but all it takes is once glance from a stranger, and that person will remember your beauty! They'll talk among themselves and ask questions. Travelers always pay attention to fellow travelers."

"Particularly when everyone is on the lookout for robbers," Jasper added.

"So, please, let's all of us be careful in keeping our faces and heads covered. People along the way will remember us, and by now, Rehoboam has sent out scouts to find us. All it takes is for one person to recall seeing us at the water or on a back road near some village."

"And I know how it works," Jasper said. "There'll be two, three scouts. Once we're spotted, they'll try to hold us on the king's orders. The third man will ride back to the palace guard to alert King Rehoboam, and more men will be sent to escort us back."

"Yes, you're right. And it will be very difficult to escape, especially if they pay the villagers to help, which they will."

"And it's very likely it will be the women who will be remembered, especially once word gets out about two escaped concubines. If anyone looks closely enough, they'll see Abra's pregnant. And Nalussa? Well, my sister, people just can't forget you." Jasper smiled but shook his head with concern.

Adriel cleared his throat. "The point is, we must pretend to be husbands and wives." He waited for his words to settle in. No reaction from the women. "If people think we're married, we can move about more easily. Right now, Rehoboam thinks it's me and two women. He doesn't know about Jasper. So, two couples traveling won't draw that much attention, and the closer we get to Egypt, the less noticeable will be the color of Nalussa's skin."

"This is the only logical and safe way to get through this journey. Once we reach Egypt, we'll be safe," Jasper added.

Both women continued to sit silently. Inwardly, all of them knew it was the only way to continue, particularly with a pregnant woman.

Abra piped up. "I'll go along with pretending. We have no choice. What do you think, Nalussa?"

Nalussa looked shyly at Adriel. "Yes, I agree. "It's the safest plan we have."

They sat in embarrassed silence until Nalussa said, "It is important that we agree to this and behave accordingly." She was looking at Abra, who was pursing her lips. *What are you thinking, Abra? Jasper is not good enough for you?* Nalussa immediately shook her head. It was not the way to think of Abra. *Please, God, forgive my unkind thought!*

Jasper laughed, relaxing that they agreed, and turned to Abra. Joking, he said, "I'll be a better husband than the king. You won't have to get dressed up for me!"

Abra sat back, obviously in thought. Without preamble, she said, "Yes, that is for certain. I won't have to dress up or even be nice to you if I don't want to."

Jasper stopped laughing, rebuffed. "Oh, Jasper. I was only joking," Abra said unconvincingly, adjusting her head scarf.

Jasper stiffly got up and lightly said, "Let's not have our first spat then!" and walked off.

Nalussa slightly shook her head. *I would never want my brother truly married to her. She is, without a doubt, self-centered.*

She looked over to Abra, staring at the fire, devoid of any emotions. She looked back to Adriel and Jasper. "We know you both have made a huge sacrifice in protecting us. Your normal way of living has changed forever. I can tell you, we're beyond grateful. We will do whatever you ask, and for my part, I am delighted to 'pretend' to be your wife."

"Starting tomorrow," Adriel said, "You are my wife, Nalussa. Abra, you are Jasper's wife. Blessings to us all."

They all held up cups of wine mixed with water. "Blessings!" they said in unison. Except Abra, who admonished them, "Remember, we're pretending!"

That night, Abra snuggled close to Nalussa near the rear of the cave as the men lay down by the mouth to keep alert for any curious wild animal. The fire was out, and the night was mild. Night birds could be heard trilling in the stillness. The moon was halved and the sky clear.

Abra touched Nalussa's arm. "I didn't mean to insult Jasper. He's willing to be coupled with me, and under the circumstances, it makes sense. I'm just amazed he didn't complain about being associated with a woman who is carrying another's child, especially one who threatens the new king. A child that could possibly vie for the throne. It could get complicated once we get to Egypt."

"The child will not be a threat to the king. You must change your way of thinking. From now on, the child is Jasper's, for as long as we are all together. We must keep up the façade. Any other thought to the contrary would be disaster to us all." Nalussa was amazed herself that Jasper was so willing to sacrifice his life for a woman he barely knew—and with a child, no less, who could topple a ruler.

"I'm serious, Abra. I hope you'll reconcile yourself to the fact that you must forget about any royal future for your child. Jasper is willing to protect you. My brother is risking his life for you. Keep that in mind."

"I didn't mean to offend," Abra snapped and moved closer with a hand on her belly. "I'm totally agreeable to being your brother's 'wife.' At least he's good-looking. If I lived at home, who knows who my father would have married me off to. And in the situation I'm in at the moment, no-one would ever want me. Yet he's willing to protect me, knowing everything about me. I never expected that of him. Even Solomon couldn't protect me." Nalussa said nothing.

"Indeed, I realize I'm worth nothing as I am now," she continued pensively. "Men don't want to take on another man's child, and the only way I would be able to explain a child without a father would be to say I'm widowed. Which I am, so to speak, since the king is dead. I suppose no one can know that the child is Solomon's. It's just that I think of what could be . . . "

Nalussa turned to her friend. "What could be is that Rehoboam will find you and slaughter you and your child. So, keep your imagination to yourself. Jasper is a good man. He's protecting you more than you will ever know. He deserves loyalty."

Abra, chastened, changed the subject. "What about you? What do you think about being paired with Adriel?"

Her heart fluttered in a combination of fear, gratefulness, and relief. "I've known for a long time, even in the harem, that I had thoughts about him, although I didn't know him that well. But he's a man you don't forget; and in traveling with him these weeks, being with him constantly, I've come to know him and realize what kind of man he really is."

She looked out to the mouth of the cave. "Our men are making an enormous sacrifice for us. They—we—could all be killed. Like you, escaping with him is my only option. Where would I go if unmarried? If I ever made my way back home, what would be the future of my family? Who would have me if it was ever found out I was King Solomon's concubine and the new king was out to find me? I can't change the color of my skin or my eyes. My coloring is known throughout the kingdom, and all it would take is just one person to become curious. As it is now, I cover myself whenever we pass anyone.

"So, I, too, have no choice but to go along with Adriel's plan. And considering our place in life, I think we've been blessed. God is looking out for us. Pray we get to Egypt safely."

"But he's the one who got us into this situation. Had he not found us, we wouldn't have been a part of the harem."

Nalussa looked at her friend in disappointment. How hypocritical. She loved being in the harem and was thrilled to be pregnant with Solomon's child. She let everyone know she was happy to leave her miserable home in that destitute village! Adriel was only doing his job. How many times had she repeated that? She and Abra were beautiful. It would have been a matter of time until some other man found them to be sold for the king's pleasure.

"Adriel is a trustworthy man. He's kind and protective. Truthfully? From the moment, he came across me by the village well, I knew he was different. And as for him getting us in this situation to begin with, I have no argument. He did find us for the king. Yet I'm honored to be rescued by him because I know that he will never desert me, and more importantly, he cares deeply for me."

"Did he tell you that? Or is that in your own imagination? Nalussa, don't be naïve. He was probably afraid of Rehoboam to begin with."

Nalussa couldn't believe what she was hearing from her friend. "Don't you understand? It was my first eunuch who asked Adriel to get me away from the harem when he found out the king had died. Adriel could have said no, could have exposed the old man as a traitor, gaining favor with Rehoboam. Yet he didn't. And certainly, if he was afraid of his own life, he could have disappeared at any time, yet he chose to rescue me. And, at my request, you!"

Nalussa lay awake for a long time feeling a stab of distrust for her friend. She understood Abra's mind. If Rehoboam were to die, it was possible that Abra's child, if a male, could be a competitor for the throne, but she could just as easily have a girl. Yet Abra enjoyed the royal environment. And her sights on being queen mother were not irrational, Nalussa thought, except that her brother was imperiling his own life and future to protect his new "family" from any royal involvement. Dead or alive.

She also pondered Adriel's conversation with her. He was willing to wait for her. He accepted her conflict. Who would have thought?

She flashed back to the time she lived her life as an ordinary daughter and sister, to the moment she was carried off by Adriel to live a cloistered existence among women and bedded by a king!

She never would have dreamed her only purpose in life was a king's desires. She resented this, but she hadn't a choice. She adapted. Then the king died, and Adriel—of all people—helped her escape. Her mind was a jumble of thoughts. She felt deeply connected to him. But was she ready for a commitment? How all unexpected!

Yet she would adapt to this, too. A woman without a man or family to take care of her was nothing. A beggar. A prostitute. Dead by the side of the road. The irony of it all? She was fascinated with Adriel. He took an enormous risk for her. And Abra? She could only keep an eye on her. She would not tolerate her brother getting hurt after all he had risked, too.

She looked over to her satchel and thought about the king's scroll stuffed inside. Adriel had handed it to her what seemed like so long ago. The only thing the wealthiest king in the land left her. She never had time to read it. More of the king's musings. She would read it one day when she wasn't so angry with a man who had it all. Women, money, and—it seemed to her—God, Who let him get his own way. But perhaps God was watching out for her. She was free, wasn't she?

Adriel and Jasper spoke quietly. They had discussed the marriage situation over the last few days as they came to realize that they must travel as couples. Once they had left Jerusalem, they were committed to their crime of rescue. Both men accepted their decisions to help the women and the possible ramifications.

Jasper spoke first. "I've been scared, to be truthful. From the day you took her, getting my sister away from King Solomon was on my mind day and night. I was obsessed with trying to figure out a way to get her back, but it was impossible. There was no way to communicate, to plan, or to coordinate. I told my father about it, but he said to accept what God has ordained. At the time, I had to. I had no one to help. Then when you showed up, I couldn't believe it. God sent you!"

"And you were ready," Adriel acknowledged. "Your sister said I could count on you. How do you feel about taking on the role of Abra's husband and continuing to protect her?"

"When I first saw her, I was startled by her beauty. She glowed. She didn't say much, but I knew she was petrified for herself and her baby. Initially, I was only intent in getting my sister to safety, but over these weeks, I've come to get closer to Abra. She's strong-willed, spoiled, admittedly, but I'd be lying to you if I didn't think her pleasing. I think over time, this might work out. I don't know what will happen when we get to Egypt. This journey gives us more time to get to know one another.

"It's ironic that I haven't any interest in a woman at home. In fact, I often thought I'd end up marrying someone I didn't want out of some kind of desperation. It would be intolerable. I remember my mother. How she and my father really loved each other. It's a rare occurrence."

He brushed his tunic. "If this charade works out, who knows?" Jasper lay back with his hands behind his head. "God is with us, I know."

Adriel turned on his side toward Jasper. "I often think if I hadn't been so set on scooping up Nalussa for the king's pleasure and my own reward, we wouldn't be in this situation now—"

"Don't blame yourself, Adriel. At that time, you had no choice. Someone from the palace would have found her eventually if my father hadn't already married her off, but he didn't have anyone in mind. He was hoping for that right man. So, for certain, she would have been discovered. All the people in the village spoke of her beauty, and there were plenty of men hoping to ask for her. My father wasn't going to be bought off by just anybody.

"My friend, you worked for the king in acquiring his women. I understand it, as did my father. Everyone throughout Israel knew of the king's appetite for women. So, it didn't come as a surprise when you found Nalussa. She's unusually beautiful. It's just that we didn't expect it. Like death. You know it's going to come, but you are just never ready."

"When I first saw your sister, I was so taken in by her looks. I've also found she has intelligence as well as beauty. Who would have thought I'd ever end up rescuing her?"

"God did," Jasper said simply. "We must put our trust in His ways, His will. We don't know what His plans are; we just need to have faith."

But whose side is God on? Will it work out for us or King Rehoboam? Adriel silently asked himself.

He couldn't sleep because his mind darted to the plan for the route to Egypt, what they would do when they got there, his hope Nalussa would turn to him, and the question of the future.

Stay in Egypt? Fortunately, they had some money and could invest in some kind of livelihood. They could never go back to Judah as long as Rehoboam was alive.

CHAPTER FIFTEEN

The next morning, they set off after a meal of bread, dried fruit, and water. Abra was very slow and in extreme discomfort; and Nalussa was anxious, but her main focus was keeping Abra in her sights for any sign of distress. The travel was taking a toll on all of them. Their aim was set on the border of Egypt, and without really knowing how far away it was—a day, a week?—until they reached the border town of Ra, they were in a state of constant stress.

Four hours and two breaks later, they continued on in the dry heat. Not a cloud was in the sky; the road had few travelers; and the road itself was in adequate condition. Nevertheless, they kept a moderately slow pace. Abra was becoming increasingly uncomfortable. A few travelers passed them with merely a nod; they, too, wanted to get to their next destination—probably Ra as well.

Adriel took advantage of one lonely traveler, who passed them with a wave. Pulling a tiny scroll from his pocket, Adriel hurried over to a man whose donkey was laden with goods. The two men conversed, then Adriel, thanking him, patted him on the shoulder. "Godspeed!" He trotted back to the group.

"That man said we're only a few hours from Ra!" Adriel held up his crude map from his days of looking for and traveling to lands that boasted lovely women. He looked closely, tracing his finger along the road they were on.

"Can we stop for a bit? I'm so uncomfortable. I don't think I can make the few hours to the city without getting off this horse and stretching," complained Abra.

The men agreed to the break. Nalussa was excited. "We are safe! Finally." Nalussa laughed as she hugged a grumbling Abra.

"I can't wait to just lie down on a cushion," sighed Abra slipping off her horse. "My body is aching all over!"

Even the men were looking forward to being out of the elements, for they had been spending days traveling and nights sleeping in the wilderness, avoiding any settlement, and eating whatever they were able to buy along the way. Soon, they would be in an inn with fresh food, blended wine, and comfortable bedding.

Back on the road, it was getting late. As they came around the bend in the road, a group of travelers, who seemingly were not aware of them, were traveling up ahead. Three men on horseback were keeping pace with three riderless donkeys. Flashes of purple and white fluttered against one man's shoulder.

"Get off the road, now!" Adriel ordered. He pulled his horse down a slightly rocky slope matted with dense brush and clumps of spindly trees. "Get out of sight from the turn! Hurry! Hurry!"

The party quickly followed and dipped out of sight from the travelers ahead as they trotted unaware of their quarry taking a detour. Safely protected by brush and trees, Adriel held his hand up to stop, his heart thudding in his chest.

"They're from the king, aren't they?" Jasper resisted the urge to go back and get a better look. The women were wide-eyed in terror.

"I'm certain. I saw the king's standard, and their animals are far too big and healthy-looking to belong to any ordinary traveler." Adriel was at a loss for what to do. They could turn back, find a place to hide, and plan another route to the border of Egypt, but he knew of no settlements in that direction. The only one he knew of was the one to which they were headed, and they badly needed supplies and rest for Abra, for she was barely holding onto her horse's reigns.

The women and Jasper were waiting for him to make a decision; they only had minutes. He thoughts collided between escaping or confronting. It was all happening too fast. No time to plan, to plot, or even to discuss. There was even a part of him thinking that he didn't want to attack anyone, but they had to be on the offensive. If they were captured, there would be no leniency, for every one of them would be slaughtered. Including a child.

Urgently turning to Jasper, he pointed to the women. "We've got to hide the women somewhere and face these men before they get to Ra. It's our only hope for stopping them before they get to the city gates. If they go there, we can't, and we need supplies and rest for Abra. It's our only way for getting over the border."

The women were in shock and extreme fear. "What do you intend to do? Fight them?" Nalussa looked from one man to the other. "How can you possibly take on three of the king's men, who are probably trained soldiers?"

"Oh, God, help us!" Abra whispered. "What happens to us if they kill or capture you?"

Jasper assured her, "They won't. Nalussa, take Abra back to the last place we stopped. There was a hill there with many large boulders. Get the horses and yourselves hidden from the road. I agree with Adriel. We've got to stop these men before they have the ability to hire people to help them find us. They must've gotten word we were coming this way."

Adriel thought aloud. "This is the fastest route to the border. They probably figured that's where we'd be headed, but it doesn't matter whether someone saw us going this way or they're covering all the logical routes away from Rehoboam. Egypt would make sense for our escape. So, they're going in the same direction we're going in, and we're in no shape to take off into the wilderness without supplies and to try and find another way into Egypt."

"But once we're in Egypt, they'll leave us alone, will they not?" Nalussa asked.

"It's a typical border city. Not exactly well-ruled. They would take their chances in capturing or killing us. We have to get to that town and get provisions. We've got to do it now before they get there first. We can't outwait them."

"I don't know how much longer I can travel!" Abra was crying now, rubbing her belly. "I've been having pains, and they're coming more often. I can't go any further! Nalussa, I can't. I just want to lie down. Now!"

"Nalussa," ordered Adriel, not wanting to get caught up in any more emotion. "Deal with her. We'll look for you somewhere along this road." He dug in his belt, pulled out a long knife, and then tossed her a small pouch of gold and silver. "Take this. You might need it." Looking to Jasper, he asked, "Are you as good a swordsman as you say you are?"

"I am. Practicing for the day I would rescue my sister. Let's go. We'll have the element of surprise."

The men took off and made their way up the slope to the road, which was clear of travelers as the day was getting later. Coming to the bend, the road straightened, and Adriel, hiding behind a group of trees, could see the men ahead were taking their time as they made their way south. There was a slight hill to the right of the road at the bend, and checking out the terrain once more, Adriel saw that it leveled off ahead of the riders. Adriel jerked his head, and Jasper followed, crossing the road and ducking to the backside of the hill. Their own horses were strong and still energetic as they picked up the pace following a clear deer run that paralleled but was hidden from the road.

Could they hear their horses' movements? Adriel hoped not. They needed, as Jasper said earlier, the element of surprise. Getting just ahead of the travelers, Adriel and Jasper stopped at the base of the backside of the hill, and as the travelers came abreast, they swooped out from behind a clump of bushes in the path of the three men with their swords raised. Startled, the king's horses shied and backed up at the suddenness of the attack, throwing the men off-balance and causing them difficulty pulling out their swords. One man fell off his mount, landing hard on his shoulder. The other two men finally pulled their swords, but they were at wrong angles as they tried to defend themselves.

For a moment, Adriel considered that these were not the king's men, because of their awkwardness, and that he was mistaken in seeing the king's colors earlier. But soon, he spotted the colorful flag jutting out from under the fallen man's body. In a moment, the downed rider's own frightened horse stomped that man, rendering him inert. Dead.

The other two men were not dispatched as easily, even though Jasper and Adriel made initial bloody contact, seriously wounding them as they struggled for position. Still, with resolve to defend themselves, the king's men lunged with what little strength they had to fend off the attack. Jasper was sliced superficially in the arm but was able to get off a jab that immobilized his man, who slumped to the side of his mount. Causing it distress with the uneven weight, it reared, jettisoning the man out of his stirrups and to the ground.

Adriel received a cut to his arm as he lunged in to immobilize the remaining man. The man was fading fast, losing blood from a major wound to his chest. Overcome with blood loss, he, too, slipped to the ground. The fight was over in minutes.

"How badly cut are you?" Adriel shouted to Jasper.

"I'm all right. Not deep." He was wrapping his arm with pieces of his headdress. "What about you?"

"It's not deep, but we've got to get these wounds cleaned and wrapped." He was thinking of what to do now. Someone was going to come across the bodies, and they needed to decide what to do about the horses and donkeys.

Jasper cut into his thoughts. "We could say we came across an attempted robbery and stopped it. We throw the men across their horses . . . No, wait, neither you nor I have the strength . . . We leave them here and take their horses and gear into town, leaving it all there. That way, no one can accuse us of robbery."

"We'll bury the flag. No can know they're the king's men; if so, the elders might send a messenger to the king to tell him his men were attacked and murdered."

Dismounting, he said to Jasper, "Quick, help me check their packs to make sure there's no identification with the king."

As they were routing through the pouches, Adriel thought about it some more. "My concern is the women. Should we travel the hour or so to town with the horses and men's possession, leaving the women behind and getting to them later? Or leave everything as is, go back to the women, get them, and go into town?"

"Suppose Abra can't make it?" Jasper cautioned.

Adriel decided. "Good point. All right. We can't go back to the women. We can't leave the horses and donkeys. They are our proof that we didn't commit the robbery. Time is running short. It's near the end of the day. Let's go to town, find the elders, tell them what happened, then leave to get our women."

"It'll be dark by the time we come back." Jasper recalled how dark it was the previous night. There was just a sliver of moon weakly shining through the drifting clouds.

"We've got to chance it."

The elders were just beginning to disperse the gates of the town when Adriel and Jasper arrived. Adriel shouted, "We came across a robbery! Men were killed! These are their animals."

The elders and some of the younger men came running up to Adriel asking what happened as they took the reins of the animals, openly admiring the health and beauty of the creatures.

Adriel, with little detail, told of three men attacking them and how they warded them off, further explaining they didn't have the strength to put the dead men on the horses due to their own wounds. The elders took it in stride; many traveled to Ra and had their encounters with dangerous men. Yet the elder insisted that they get their wounds cleaned and bandaged.

"Where are the dead men?" an elder asked. Adriel explained as best he could, and the man turned to his fellow citizens and offered, "If we don't get them now, they'll be devoured by animals if they haven't been already."

Another man argued, "Why don't we just leave them then? It will be dark by the time we get back."

"No, we must not leave them in the road," the elder advised. "Are they Israelites?"

"I . . . I think so. They were well-dressed, and as you can see, their animals are well cared for. They were probably well-to-do merchants. I don't really know." Let them think they were merchants. No cause to raise any other suppositions.

After they were bandaged up, Adriel said, "We must leave and get back to our women. Please, we can buy food, water, and wine."

"Why didn't you bring them with you to avoid having to go back when it's dark and dangerous? We have our share of robbers and wild animals." The elder was surprised. "Why would anyone leave women behind in the wilderness?"

"Our women were frightened badly, and we hid them. We must go back. We'll be here in the morning."

"God willing," a man mumbled as he led away one of the horses.

The elders bid them goodbye and directed some of their men to get a wagon ready to get the bodies. If they weren't Israelites, they would merely leave them for animals. But they dared not leave the bodies of their brethren on an open road, due to their beliefs.

Adriel and Jasper were exhausted, and their horses were as well. The animals had rested and taken water and fodder. And the men had eaten some bread themselves and drunk some wine, but they were tired from travel, the fight, the duplicity of telling lies to the elders, and the concern for their women. And they didn't know where they might find them, especially in the dark.

An hour or so later, they were at the spot where the attack took place. Sure enough, animals and birds had eaten significant parts of the men's bodies. Bloodied garments were torn, and pieces of skin and bone were exposed. Parts of faces were gone.

"We're fortunate most of the clothing has been ripped and bloodied," Adriel observed. "I don't want anything, like fine garments, pointing back to the palace." Jasper looked away. The sight was gruesome and the smell overwhelming.

They kept moving. Around the bend of the road, they slowed and looked down the slight slope, scanning the land. It was dusk, hard to make out any movement or image different than the scrub brush. Adriel was just about to call out when he heard a weak mewling.

Jasper turned to him. "Is that what I think that is?"

Adriel answered, "A baby crying?"

CHAPTER SIXTEEN

Nalussa held the infant boy in her arms. She barely had enough water to wipe him off, but thankfully, she had plenty of cloth to wrap him in and keep him warm. Abra was wet-eyed and relieved her ordeal was over, grateful she and the baby were well. Nalussa handed her the baby, who fussed and cried.

After the men had left to confront the trackers, Abra wailed, "I can't go on anymore! I have to get off this horse!"

"Let me help!" Nalussa answered, in her own state of distress, pulling her friend down, then desperately looked for a place they could rest and be not too far from the road. Blindly, she led Abra and the two horses down a rocky slope and through a grove of dense bushes, following a deer trail that she prayed would lead them to a site they could rest in.

Not too far from the road, Abra screamed in pain as her water broke, and she doubled over.

Nalussa coaxed, "Can you make it to that spot over there?"

Abra breathed in deeply, only able to give a weak nod.

Collapsing in the small clearing, Abra doubled up in pain again, drawing her knees up high and wide. "This baby is not waiting!" she grunted and pushed.

Nalussa tied off the horses and dropped to her own knees, encouraging Abra to breathe deeply and push. Not more than half an hour went by when into Nalussa's hands appeared a curly, little head, followed by a bloody, mucus-covered body, who wasted no time to squall. Nalussa held the little one's tiny body in her hands. "It's a boy!"

Quickly, she cleared his nostrils and mouth. As she placed the baby on Abra's breasts, she waited until the afterbirth was expelled and the umbilical cord stopped pumping, whereupon she cut it and placed it with the afterbirth aside to bury it. They would be staying here the night, with or without the men, and she didn't want to attract predators.

"I am so blessed you helped me, dear sister! Look at this tiny, sweet boy. He's so beautiful." She gently touched the baby's head; he fussed some, and she put him to her breast. It took him a moment, but he latched on, contented to nurse. "Look! My precious baby boy is hungry!" She smiled and cried at the same time.

Nalussa smiled, too. "We are all blessed." She sat back on her heels, watching Abra feed her baby, and prayed that the men would get back to them tonight, but she worried they had been captured, or worse, killed. She had to face reality. It was possible. She and Abra could be alone now. Her only option was to get Abra on her horse tomorrow if she could physically do so and get to town. If she couldn't make it, Nalussa wasn't sure what to do other than do the best she could to protect the three of them in the wild. They still had some water and a bit of food.

Even if they made it to town, her great fear was that they would be easily recognizable now if there were any scouts about looking for them or if Adriel and Jasper had been captured and tortured to tell where they were.

If they arrived to the town unencumbered, could they bribe someone to protect them and get them to Egypt? So many things to think about! And now, she had the responsibility of an infant and a convalescing woman. She moved close to Abra. She was so tired, she could hardly keep her eyes open, but she had to stay awake. *Please, God, let the men come back to us. I don't think I can take care of us alone,* she prayed to God for protection. Then remembering the afterbirth and cord, she quickly got up and trudged a distance away from Abra. Finding a sandy area, she dug a hole with her hands and the edge of the knife and buried the waste, covering it with rocks.

Without any means for a fire, she pulled her robe about her and made her way back to Abra, who was lying on her side with the baby to her breast, dozing on and off. Nalussa wanted to sleep, too, but her greatest fear at the moment was keeping awake and alert for prowling animals. They surely would be smelling blood, and with a weak woman and infant, only she would have the strength to defend.

Staying vigilant with as much attention as she could muster to listen for sounds in the still night, she forced herself to keep her eyes open. The darkness had settled in, and it was nearly complete with a moon that was weak and hiding. Twice, she caught herself nodding off. The third time, she snapped awake to the sound of large animals approaching.

Her heart raced in her chest, and she got to a crouching position, holding the knife in front of her. "Abra, wake up!" Abra stirred but didn't awaken. It was so hard to see through the gloomy night, and the low bushes would give any animal good cover. Posturing herself in a defensive stand with her knife wavering in her shaking hand, she heard animals—big animals—swishing through the brush, coming closer. Her hands sweated; her heart pounded; and her mouth went dry. How could she fight these creatures off?

A voice pierced the night. "Nalussa? Nalussa? It's Adriel. Where are you? We heard a baby cry!"

Great relief washed over her, and she cried out loudly, standing and waving her knife. "Here, Adriel, here we are!" Staring into the darkness, she took off her head scarf and waved it above the bushes.

Jasper pointed. "Over there."

In the dark, they saw a light flurry that looked like the wing of a white owl. Without hesitation, the men and horses stepped in the direction of the waving scarf, picking their way carefully around bushes, low rocks, and weather-bent trees.

Nalussa continued to wave as the two great horses slowly moved toward her. Placing her scarf atop a bush as a marker because it was so dark and she didn't want to get lost, she ran to them. Adriel jumped off his mount and hugged her tightly as she clung to him, crying in gratefulness they had returned. "I didn't think you would be back! I had thoughts of you captured or even dead! Oh, praise God, you are here! I was so afraid!"

Adriel, too tired to talk, was only able to breath out, "We're here. We're safe."

Jasper tugged Nalussa's robe. "Where's Abra? We heard a baby cry. She's given birth?

"Yes, and again, praise God. There are not enough praises for Him tonight. She and the baby are healthy. It's a boy."

Jasper took his horse's reins and went toward the scarf that marked the cluster of shrubbery where the women and baby had found shelter. Adriel took Nalussa's shoulder and followed with his own steed.

When they got to the hiding place, the women's horses whinnied softly as the men's mounts greeted them with quiet, tired grunts. Immediately, Jasper set about feeding and watering the animals from the provisions they had brought from town, and Adriel said, "I've got some provisions," and dug in his pack and produced a skin of wine and pouches of food to hand to Nalussa. Quickly, she gave Abra a sip of watered-down wine and a piece of raisin cake.

Abra took a sip and a nibble of cake, then smiled and hoarsely said, "See I produced the king a boy! A worthy boy! See how beautiful he is?"

Jasper sat down, leaning toward the baby. Abra bid him, "Come closer. See how lovely he is? And healthy!"

Jasper smiled in pleasure. "Praise God!"

Nalussa and Adriel divided up the food and set it out for them to eat. Nalussa quickly told them, "Abra is in no condition to travel any further, so we'll have to take our chances and stay here temporarily."

Adriel agreed. "Don't worry. Jasper and I will take turns standing watch. There's little protection here, and the animals who are hungry will smell blood. But we can fend for ourselves. We'll be safe."

Nalussa, nodded and said to Adriel, "I was caught up in the birthing process and had little time to worry about being attacked by animals. God was good. The baby arrived, albeit with extreme pain, but quickly. It was only after I wiped the baby down and put him to Abra's breast that an intense weariness came over me . . . well, both of us. Abra couldn't keep her eyes open, and I struggled to keep awake and to keep us safe. It was shortly after the third time I fell asleep that I heard our own horses snuffling and the sounds of beasts approaching our site." Nalussa breathed in deeply. Adriel put an arm around her trembling shoulders and held her tight. "And it was you!" Nalussa called triumphantly. "Back safe!" She took Adriel's arm, but he winced. "What's that? You're hurt!"

"Both of us were sliced, but again, praise God, the wounds are not deep. Let us tell you what happened."

Abra had drifted off to sleep again, but Nalussa was wide awake now, jolted by the account of the attack and extremely wary of their reception in Ra. She said, "Unfortunately, we won't be just two couples passing through on the way to Egypt now. The elders will remember us should anyone follow up looking for a man of your description, a dark-skinned woman, and a woman either pregnant or with a baby."

"Yes." Adriel wearily nodded. "Jasper and I discussed that on the way here, but there's nothing we can do about it. The only thing that might throw people off is that they don't know about Jasper. We have got to get to town quickly before anyone gets curious about us, due to your looks. So many in the kingdom know about you. Abra? Not so much."

"I don't know if Abra will be able to travel tomorrow. It's very unlikely." Nalussa looked over to Abra, who was sleeping with Jasper beside her. "I wish we still had our donkey. It might have been more comfortable for her."

Adriel wasn't listening. He was fast asleep, but Jasper was hovering over mother and child and, at the same time, scanning the landscape for any threats.

The next morning, Abra couldn't make the trip. So, they waited another day, talking little, napping, eating, and watching. That night, Adriel lay down a few blankets that he carried on the back of his horse, and the four of them, plus the baby, sat together on the hard ground. A breeze had kicked in just cool enough to need a fire.

Adriel laid back, took her hand, and promptly fell asleep. She was satisfied with that. The toll of the last two days was extreme on all of them. The men who fought for their lives were still hurting and mentally wrestling with the killing scene over and over again. Both of them spoke of it often during the day. Nalussa, for her part, was relived of the worry of helping Abra bring her baby into the world and protecting against wild animals. Yes, the last two days were grueling and exhausting. However, she was soon realizing that Adriel was a man God had blessed her with, and she was grateful. She now knew what true caring and comfort was.

Looking at Adriel, she whispered, "You are a man of courage. How blessed are we that we can actually be with each other, no matter the circumstances?" For the first time in many nights, she slept soundly.

Two days later, Abra said she could get on a horse. They fashioned a sling for the baby on her breast and took it very slowly, stopping when it was too uncomfortable for Abra. It was fortunate that the road was not too rutted, that the sky was clear, and that there were few travelers who only waved and kept on their way. Passing two slow-moving couples on the way to Ra was not unusual.

At the gate, the elders greeted Adriel. "Ha! We're happy you made it back, my friend, for we thought you lost your women to the night creatures. We expected you back yesterday. God has been good to you."

Adriel smiled and mumbled, "All is well. Can you direct us to an inn?" Jasper and Adriel blocked the women with their horses, so the men at the gate had to peer around them. Nalussa kept her head down, her hands covered with her robe, and her feet dusted in sand and dirt to hide her coloring. Abra wrapped her robe around the baby, keeping it quiet on her breast. She, too, kept her head down and covered with her head scarf.

Without further discussion, because a small caravan of camels was approaching laden with goods heading for other parts of Egypt, the elders lost interested, directed them toward the inn, and stood waiting for the next group of travelers to approach.

CHAPTER SEVENTEEN

At the inn, they registered under false names, and each couple took a room. Money-wise, they were well-positioned and able to rent two good rooms. While the women stayed behind, the men went out for travel information to Egypt, provisions, and local gossip. They planned on spending the night; then they would set out the next morning if Abra was up to it.

In Nalussa's room, Abra came in. "You will be alone with Adriel, and I'll be alone with your brother and my son. He'll find out soon enough not to expect more than a conversation. Keeping up with the appearance of husbands and wives isn't too terrible, as long as he knows his place."

"Abra, Jasper is a godly man. He would never do anything untoward. And I have every intention of keeping myself from Adriel, and he, too, would never do the unexpected or inappropriate."

"I'm only saying that we are going to be alone in rooms with the men who obviously find us desirable, and we have to be careful!"

Nalussa gave Abra a look. "Understand, if Adriel and I decide we should marry, we will do it in the sight of God."

"If you should marry? I see how you speak to one another and how you look at one another! For certain, it is possible. So rather than pretending, it might make sense to marry quickly and get over this charade!"

Nalussa changed the subject. "How do you feel about my brother?"

"Oh, Jasper is young and clever," she answered offhandedly, then, with thought, added, "And he's proven himself a warrior, very brave! And although I'm a woman with another man's son, I know he finds me attractive. But I'm in no position in marrying anytime soon, if that's what you mean. I have a thought that he's thinking about me in more than just a protective way, though."

"So, how do you feel about him seriously thinking of marrying you?"

"I'm not sure what to think, although there is an argument for each thought. On the one hand, I would be a fool not to because he would take care of me and the baby. On the other hand, I do have a *king's* baby." She shrugged her shoulders.

"Abra, how many times must I remind you how dangerous it is to speak of your child in that manner! You could get us all—including your baby—killed!"

"Oh, stop telling me what to do. I only speak like this to you. Let's stop talking about me and what I shouldn't be saying. Let's talk about your love, for I believe it is love. It's hard to believe King Solomon was never special to you, but Adriel, of all men is."

Nalussa replied. "It's odd. For all of Solomon's power, riches, and skill, I never once thought of loving him. He had far too much. Never lacked for anything. With Adriel, who has nothing, I find myself drawn to him more and more. He looks at me differently than Solomon. He looks at me with gentleness, kindness, and concern. Solomon? He only saw a beautiful woman, one whom he possessed, one who would listen to him, and one who would physically indulge him.

"Adriel is an entirely different man, and you will find that so is Jasper. He has a kind heart and loyalty, and I pray that you will soften your attitude toward him and, if he is growing attached to you, have the courtesy to be honest with him." As an afterthought, she said, "I know he is very attracted to you. And I wish he wasn't.

Abra shrugged off the last comment and looked down at her baby. "I was in love with Solomon," she confessed. "I really thought he would love me back, but he never did. He wasn't even interested in the child." She shook her head sadly, kissing the baby's head. "I, like every other woman in the harem, was used for my body; some were used for a combination of bodies and minds, but mostly, we were all there because of our physical beauty. But I can't complain. I was well-fed, clothed, bejeweled, and now have produced an heir to the most glorious kingdom in the world!"

"Abra! Enough! Don't dwell on these dreams. You need to not think that way about your son. It is too dangerous. Jasper must be thought of as the baby's father." Nalussa narrowed her lips in frustration. "At least for the time being!"

"That's all I hear about from you. 'Be careful!' I know that I have to be careful. But it's true. My son is royalty," she insisted.

Nalussa sighed and changed the subject back to Solomon. "Unlike you, I never expected to be loved by Solomon. In fact, I didn't want to be loved by him because I knew I could never love him back. With Adriel, as I have said, it's different. I feel a connection to him that I never had with Solomon, even with all the interesting conversations we had. Although he had so much wisdom, I couldn't align myself with his self-indulgence. I asked him once if he ever loved, and he said he did, but ambition and other things got in the way. What kind of love is that?"

"I'd like to know whom he really loved," Abra wondered. "She must have smitten him—whoever she was—but I never heard of a beloved wife other than Pharaoh's daughter, who was favored but not overly loved." Abra paused for a moment, then dryly said, "But to soothe your mind, I assure you, I find your brother handsome, kind, and thoughtful. I look forward to a cordial relationship."

Nalussa wasn't convinced of Abra's honorable feelings toward her brother. She didn't want him to be taken advantage of as she watched Abra leave to feed the baby and lie down. Nalussa, left alone in her room, went to her satchel. She had never read the scroll from King Solomon. She pulled it out and smoothed it. "Song of Solomon," she read. Interesting title. She began to read.

Solomon's Song of Songs

She

Let him kiss me with the kisses of his mouth—
for your love is more delightful than wine.

Pleasing is the fragrance of your perfumes;
your name is like perfume poured out.
No wonder the young women love you!
Take me away with you—let us hurry!
Let the king bring me into his chambers.

Nalussa continued to read.

He

How beautiful you are, my darling!
Oh, how beautiful!
Your eyes are doves.

She

How handsome you are, my beloved!
Oh, how charming!
And our bed is verdant.

The poem, or song, was quite long. Explicit in imagery. Was it a celebration of the intimacy of marriage? Whoever the intended loved one was that was identified as "she" in the song, Nalussa had a thought, but the male counterpart of the song sounded very much like Solomon himself. She had a difficult time reading its entirety. It was so intimate, so intense. She felt like an outsider spying on two lovers. It almost appeared as if Solomon and his lover wrote it together to immortalize their intimate love.

Carefully, she rolled up the scroll and put it back in her satchel just as Adriel came into the room. He smiled and stood awkwardly, rubbing his hand down his beard. His words came out in a rush. "Please believe me, since the first time I saw you, I was taken by you. Not only your beauty, but your very being. I . . . I know you were Solomon's. But I told you I don't care, and I really don't. I've been thinking of you for a long time. I told you I believe that God has put us together and . . . " He sat down on the pallet she was reclining on and reached out to her. "And I want to love you!" His eyes looked at her with longing and gentleness. "I've told you I would wait for you, and I will! But please, I implore you, don't make me wait forever!"

Nalussa put her hand to his scruffy beard and drew it up the side of his face. She sat for a moment, then said, "I admit, the time we've spent traveling together has opened up an entirely different world of feelings for me. I found out I am capable of . . . love. And, Adriel, I realize we been through a lot and have had little time to spend alone;

but please understand, as I told you earlier, I do believe we can be together, but it must be done in the sight of God. We can find the right time . . . together. I promise."

He hugged her, and she dropped her head down on his shoulder then looked up at him. "One of my innermost concerns was that I didn't know how you felt about me and King Solomon. I worried. Adriel, I never loved him."

"I know, Nalussa." Adriel took her hands in his. "I know you never loved him. Your life with Solomon has no bearing on what I feel for you now."

"I have something I want to show you." She reached into her satchel.

CHAPTER EIGHTEEN

"Is this about you?" Adriel said, putting down the parchment. He looked over to Nalussa lying on the cushion beside him. "I've never been one for poetry, but I get the intent of his words."

"No, it isn't about me."

"I'm grateful for that," Adriel answered. "I would have been jealous. But who do you think it's about? For Solomon to write this, he must have been seriously infatuated."

"I'm not sure. It could have been Pharaoh's daughter, or perhaps Naamah, the mother of his son, Rehoboam; but neither woman was very dark-skinned. Out of all his many wives, I never knew one to be overly special."

Adriel thought a moment. "I was in and out of the palace all the time, seeing Solomon frequently with women and, of course, hearing all the gossip. I, too, have not heard about anyone overly special, other than you. But you say he never loved you."

"Trust me, he didn't. Oh, he favored me. I was possibly a friend to him if a royal would consider a woman, let alone a concubine, a friend. No, this was written to someone special, and I'll tell you who I think it was: Makeda, Queen of Sheba."

Adriel let out a low whistle. "Hmmm . . . you could be right. She was at the palace for a very long time. They spent a good part of every day together. She was dark, beautiful, very intelligent, and wealthy and powerful in her own right."

"A woman who attained his standards."

"But why would your servant Adiah want you to have this?"

Nalussa had been thinking about that since she read the poem. She didn't know the circumstances surrounding the need to get the scroll to her in the first place because it wasn't written for her edification. Did King Solomon know he was dying and knew she would try her best to escape once Rehoboam came into rule? Did he think that she would recognize whom he was writing about—or even collaborating with—and want her to get the poem to its rightful owner, not trusting anyone in the palace to indulge his one last need? Was this a need for the king to get his poem to the Queen of Sheba, professing their love and at the same time provide a means of refuge for Nalussa?

Nalussa didn't verbalize her thoughts, not wanting to overthink or create intrigue. "I don't know, but I think the king wanted me to get this to Makeda."

Adriel was incredulous. "Why would he choose you for an 'errand' that was never requested? It's not like you could walk across the courtyard and hand the Queen of Sheba her love letter—assuming she co-wrote it. You weren't even allowed outside the harem! How could he possibly think you could help him, and the big question is why?"

"If he knew he was dying, who could he trust to get this to its rightful owner? To anyone reading it, they would think, 'Oh, what a lovely poem or song. It's a little embarrassing, all this love talk, but it's just another example of Solomon's creativity. Toss it out. He's dead. He needs no more women.'" They both sat quietly, each thinking that Rehoboam would do exactly that. Throw it out.

"Or maybe he wanted to get it to the queen and provide you a place of safety?" Adriel turned to Nalussa. "It makes sense, doesn't it? He was brilliant! He must have known he was dying, or in the event of his death, you would be in danger, and his treasured poem would be burned. What a perfect way to solve two problems. The queen gets a remembrance his deepest feelings for her and at the same time, he protects you, his favorite, with safe shelter!"

They both looked at each other. "I know what you're thinking, Adriel."

Later that morning, Jasper informed them that Abra really needed to rest at least another full day and night. She was getting stronger, feeling better, but still needed to heal. Adriel and Nalussa were anxious to get out of town before any more people came on the heels of their hunters.

"We'll wait one more day, but after that, we must leave this city and go deeper into Egypt to another town—Gia. We cannot continue to take risks as long as we're in Rehoboam's reach."

As the day languished, Nalussa sought out Adriel in the animals' shelter. He was alone, working on his horse's bridle. "Where's Jasper?" she asked.

Surprised to see Nalussa there, he stopped working and answered, "He's gone into the center to get some supplies because we're leaving tomorrow, regardless of Abra's complaining. He knows we can't take any chances of being seen and agrees that by now, it's possible Rehoboam's dead men have been discovered. We need to put distance between anyone coming out of Jerusalem." He stopped talking and looked at her. "Are you all right?"

"Yes, yes. Adriel, I am. But I've been thinking very deeply." She nervously twisted her head scarf. "We don't have to go on pretending anymore. I'm ready to make a commitment to you. We're going to be safe. I know we will. We can marry in Gia. Jasper can stand in for my father, and we can be wed."

Adriel reached for Nalussa. "Finally!"

The following day, they left, ignoring Abra's complaints. They were fully ready for the long trek ahead, being well-provisioned with water and food and being advised that there was plenty of grazing for their horses along the way. Traveling, they came across a few nomads with donkeys and camels laden with goods to sell in the towns and villages.

Neither Nalussa nor Adriel revisited Solomon's poem and the desire of Solomon to get it into the Queen of Sheba's hands. Abra was always within earshot, and Jasper was distracted with worries.

Well into Egypt, they breathed a collective sigh of relief, and the new town came into view. Entering the gates, the public square was a frenzy of activity. Soldiers swarmed the public places, and the markets were crammed with military and people from all regions buying, selling, eating, and drinking. Goats roamed; chickens scattered; and children played.

Yet fear pricked the party as they passed group after armed group of men who cast them hostile looks and made it obvious they were looking them over.

Adriel leaned into Jasper. "What's with all of these soldiers? I wonder what is going on? Surely, it's not us. These are Egyptians." He frowned.

As they stopped near a vendor's over-crowded drink stand, Jasper said, "Let me find out what's going on and get a skin of wine." He handed the reins of his horse to Adriel and elbowed his way through the noisy crowd to get refreshment but more importantly, information.

He spied a man in typical Hebrew dress waiting in line. "What's going on? Why so many soldiers?" He nodded toward a group of soldiers eating and drinking by a makeshift shelter.

The man looked him over. "You're Hebrew. Where are you from?"

Jasper hesitated because he didn't trust anyone, and even though they were in Egypt, it didn't mean they couldn't be kidnapped, or worse. "I'm from Judah." He didn't want to say the city of Jerusalem. Who knew of Rehoboam's reputation here because Egypt was where King Solomon's rival, Jeroboam, fled after the king sought his life?

"Ah, Judah. Did you hear? You remember Jeroboam?" Jasper nodded. "Well," the man continued, "he and his supporters went all the way to Shechem to confront the new king, Rehoboam."

"To challenge him for the rule?" Jasper wouldn't be surprised. It was a common thread in conversation that Jeroboam would be given ten of the twelve tribes of Israel. At least, that was the prophecy.

"Initially, no, I don't think. But word just got back that he tried to reason with the new king in lightening the people's loads for forced labor and conscript. We all know how hard King Solomon had everyone working to keep his households in food and drink, to keep his projects going, and to provide everything else that was needed in the kingdom. That's why I'm here. I had enough. Just got up and walked away. I'm glad I did." He took a bite out of a hunk of cheese.

"So, what happened?" Jasper wanted to know. This could mean a different course for them.

"Jeroboam asked the king, and the king, in his pompous, privileged way, said no. If anything, he was going to make it worse for the people! So, Jeroboam and the people rebelled!"

Jasper was aghast. He worried for his father, younger brother, and sister. "Please, tell me more."

"From what I've just heard, the kingdom is split. Jeroboam has the loyalty of ten tribes and set up his rule from old King Solomon's palace in Shechem, and Rehoboam has the remaining two tribes, Judah and Benjamin. Jerusalem isn't even the main place of worship anymore, I'm told. Can you believe it? The other ten tribes will soon be worshipping golden calves up north! Yes, indeed. The kingdom is divided. Israel up north, and Judea in the south."

Golden calves? That was an abomination, but Jasper relaxed a bit. At least, there was no war between the tribes, even though the kingdom was now, apparently, split. His family was south of Jerusalem, far, far away from the border near Shechem and Jeroboam.

"But what's with all the soldiers here?"

"Shishak, Pharaoh Shosenq I, is mobilizing his troops to cover here and Ra. He's going to build a fortress and armory here. Look who he's got: Libyans, Sukkiim, and Ethiopians." The man tilted his head toward the soldiers who were laughing and talking among themselves. "Rumor has it that Egypt might invade Judah, now that the kingdom has shrunk. There's still a lot of treasure in old King Solomon's temple, I'm told."

The man slid he eyes toward the soldiers. "They're laughing now, but don't let them fool you. They are not friendly. Keep your distance from them, especially if they know you are a Hebrew. They might come after you just for sport." The man turned to go.

"Wait. Is there any safe place my wife, baby, and my friends can stay?"

"Not in the center of this town. Every room, stable, and space is taken up. I suggest you go outside of town. You might find some shelter there. I'm staying with the goats, and there's no space there either."

When it was Jasper's turn for wine, the vendor had nothing left. "Sorry," was all he could say. Jasper dodged through the crowds to where he left Adriel and the women. He wasn't there. Frightened, he looked around among the crowd and didn't see his friends, and he didn't know where to begin to look. People and soldiers surged back and forth in the square. Spying a break in the crowds, he walked purposefully, keeping a look out for people on horses.

He was pushed hard from the back and nearly lost his footing. A belligerent soldier pushed into him. "Get out of our way!" he ordered and moved past him with six other men who were on a mission. Jasper followed in their wake but stopped as they abruptly halted before a man, lying dazed on the ground. Jasper looked around the backs of the men and saw that it was Adriel.

Pushing his way forward, he ducked around the soldiers and got to his friend before the soldiers made any decisions.

"Adriel, it's me." He shook his shoulder. "What happened? Are you all right? Where're the women?" His words came out in a rush. Adriel groaned and opened his eyes.

The soldiers came forward, but Jasper held up a hand. "I've got him. It's all right."

Adriel weakly sat up. "Attempted robbery, but I stopped him." He looked over at a man who was lying on the ground. "It's all right. I'm fine. Nothing taken."

"What happened?" the officer demanded, eyeing both men suspiciously. Adriel gave as little detail as possible because it wasn't wise to bring attention to the women. Jasper understood his not mentioning them. Not in this crowd. Not with their looks. Slowly, he pulled Adriel to his feet, who was clutching one of their money bags. Worried for his friend but relieved they still had their gold, he hastened them both away from the crowds and another possible attack.

"Is anything broken? Can you move? We got to get out of here. I don't like these crowds or soldiers," Jasper whispered in Adriel's ear.

Disgusted, the soldiers went toward the man knocked out on the ground and dragged him by an arm out of the way of horses, wagons, and pedestrians. Dropping the man by a wall, they walked away. Adriel leaned on Jasper and hobbled through the crowd of onlookers, who dispersed once the action was over.

"What happened?" Jasper looked Adriel over for wounds.

"I should never have taken the pouch. But I saw an inn, and I just hopped off my horse, grabbing the money to buy a place for us to stay. But I was attacked from behind. I threw my fists; he threw his, got me in the head, but I was able to knock him down before he grabbed the gold. It was a foolish thing to do to blatantly carry that pouch. This place is jammed with thieves, people looking for trouble, and soldiers. I was lucky I didn't lose it all!"

Jasper held his arm tight, guiding him through the throngs. Adriel wrapped the pouch inside his robes. "Where are the women?" Jasper was worried.

"This way." Adriel led them to a small space by a stable nestled in a side road. As he walked beside Jasper, he grabbed his sleeve. "Listen,

Nalussa and I are really going to get married. Here. Will you stand in for your father in giving her away?"

"Absolutely! This is great news! I know my sister was struggling with a lot of emotions, like fear and worry, but that's always been my sister. She feels things deeply. But we'll make this work!"

The women were sitting on the ground with Abra feeding the baby.

"Don't you think he should have a name by now?" Adriel asked Jasper as he approached the women and baby.

"She's going to call him Heber."

"Ah. Heber the Kenite. Remember? He was a descendant of Reuel the Midianite, the father-in-law of Moses. He was the one whose wife, Jael, hammered a tent peg into the temple of Sisera. Remember? The warrior who commanded nine hundred iron chariots and oppressed the Israelites for twenty years! Good name."

"Well, don't you know your history! I guess your brains haven't been addled that badly, then." Jasper laughed.

"You've been beaten!" Nalussa came over to Adriel, looking him over in concern and worry. His robe was dirty; he had blood on his sleeves; and his knuckles were scraped. The side of his face was bruised and bloody as well. Gently, she touched his face. He flinched.

Jasper answered, "He was, but he's okay, and praise God, we still have our money! And great news! Abra, Adriel here is going to marry Nalussa! And I will stand in for my father, being the eldest brother. Isn't this great?" Jasper put a brotherly arm around Adriel's shoulders.

"You really are going to get married?" She looked between Nalussa and Adriel who nodded. "Well. I'm not surprised. Its about time." She turned to Jasper. "What will his *mohar*—wedding gift—be?

Something worthy, I hope." She cast a look at Adriel. "After all, you're contracting for a very special concubine. Solomon's!"

"She is no longer Solomon's," Adriel retorted. "I really don't want to hear that word again. You will think of her as my betrothed, and then wife."

"Well, excuse me!" Pointing at Jasper she stated, "We're still pretending, my friend, but don't give up hope . . . yet!" Then snickering, she said, "If Adriel stood in for my father in giving me to you, I wonder what valuable gift he'd offer?" An awkward moment ticked. Jasper took a step back in embarrassment.

She fixed him with a cunning smile and changed the subject. "Did you find us accommodations?"

Adriel opened his mouth to explain his attack, but Abra cut him off as she hoisted Heber to her shoulder. "Is there no room at the inn?" Abra looked up, vexed. "I've been riding on a hard-backed horse and sleeping on equally hard ground for days! I want a bed!"

"Don't you care Adriel was almost killed looking for a bed for you?" Jasper admonished her as she sulkily tucked her head to her suckling baby and insisted, "All I'm saying is we need a safe place to stay. I can't have the baby out in this chaos!"

Jasper held up a hand. "Let me go see if I can find anything in town. I know it's overcrowded here with soldiers, merchants, and people in general, but I'll go back to look. I wasn't able to get any food or drink." Abra shot him an angry look. Jasper put a light hand on her shoulder. "Don't fret. I'll be back with good news and food."

Adriel slumped down on the ground as Nalussa fetched water to clean his wounds, and Abra turned to watch Jasper trot down the path to the square carrying pieces of gold in search of a room and food.

Arriving back to the public square, Jasper decided to walk up and down the side streets that connected to the square, hoping to find some type of lodging. He was conflicted about Abra. No question he was attracted to her, but she wasn't a nice person. Was he just lonely and willing to settle for what seemed to be available? Or was he just taken with her beauty and his growing attachment to Heber? Oh, he knew the baby could be a complication, but he loved the little fellow. But at the moment, not so with Abra. She could be sweet and thoughtful one moment, then mean as a cobra the next. Perhaps it was best he bide his time. He, too, could pretend for a while. *Besides, I still have my family at home to think about.* His father, younger sister and brother. These were fearful times. *Indeed, I can pretend for a while with Abra, but once they are all safe, I will make some decisions.*

On the third street he walked down, a commotion erupted in front of a two-story stone building. People were screaming and waving their arms as their possessions were being tossed out onto the street from a second-story window.

This is a good sign. This is an eviction, thought Jasper. In the doorway stood two burly men, with harsh, Egyptian haircuts, yelling and threatening the men in the street, who were scurrying to pick up their belongings before the vagrant children made off with their things to sell in the square.

Jasper gave space to the ejected men, who were yelling and threatening while stuffing their clothes and other articles in satchels.

Quickly, he approached the two men in the doorway. "I'm thinking you have space here." He hoped they understood his language.

"You're thinking right," a veiled woman responded, looking around the side of one of the men in the doorway. "What do you need? You must have money. No money, no room."

"Two rooms?" he asked hopefully. She said something to one of the men, who beckoned Jasper with a finger. Passing through the doorway, they entered a clean and open courtyard filled with chickens, two goats, and potted flowers. There was a stairway that led up to a second-floor balcony that overlooked the small courtyard.

In halting Hebrew, the man told Jasper that he had to pay up front for the length of his stay. The man was not inclined to be hospitable. "If you can't pay, you leave. Immediately. Like those men."

"No problem," Jasper assured him. "I can pay. Two rooms, two weeks to start."

As Jasper doled out the pieces of gold, the man's eyebrows raised. "You can be assured you will be safe here. You're the kind of tenant we like."

That night Jasper, Abra, and Heber had one room, and Nalussa and Adriel shared another. Abra complained about the size of the rooms, but Jasper countered with, "At least you have a soft bed." Behind the building, the horses were safely stabled, watered, and fed.

"But it can't compare to my cushions in the harem," she said under her breath.

The men met in the courtyard to discuss the day's events and what Jasper had heard from a fellow Hebrew, while the women prepared a simple meal in Nalussa and Adriel's room.

They talked of Rehoboam. Adriel was surprised. "I never thought that Jeroboam would confront Rehoboam. This is a kingdom-changer."

Jasper agreed. "Although Rehoboam has a smaller piece, according to word on the street, he is still as mean as a scorpion, and it's imperative to stay as far away from Rehoboam as possible."

Adriel declared, "If Rehoboam has his hands full with possible rebellion, I believe we're safe in this place for awhile," indicating the upper rooms with a wave of his hand. "But I'm not so sure about being out on the streets. That man who attacked me was in the public square. There were a lot of people around, and no one helped. They just watched. I might have even heard laughter. It was sport to them." He looked over at Jasper, who was tossing pieces of bread to the chickens.

"I feel the same way. I'm not happy about soldiers marching about. It's one thing if they are highly disciplined and focused, but I think this mix of soldiers are mercenaries. Anything goes. This is a prosperous town, but do we want our women here?"

"I don't know," Adriel answered honestly. "But we have some time to figure it out, and I have some ideas."

Jasper gave Adriel a quick, intense look but said nothing as Nalussa came down to tell them supper was ready. As she walked away, Jasper continued, "One other thing. I told you I heard that Pharaoh is planning on invading Judea, which is why a garrison is being set up here. I'm worried for my family back home. If Pharaoh's men march to attack Jerusalem, my family could well be in the way."

"So, what are you thinking?"

"I need to find out more. If this is true, I must go back for my family and bring them here."

Adriel opened his mouth to object, but Jasper said, "I'll be safe. I know the route back, and no one knows I'm with you and Solomon's concubines."

"I know you'll be safe. I'm being selfish. I don't like the idea of being left alone with . . . Abra and the baby. Nalussa is strong, but Abra . . . " He drifted off.

Upstairs, Nalussa was listening to Abra fuss over Heber and complain about lack of sleep, poor food, no wine in so long, and having to wear the same robes since they escaped.

"I was quite content in the harem. I loved the food, the clothes, the wine, the pampering. Now, I have less than I had when I lived with my family."

"Abra! What a cruel thing to say. Your life and your baby's life have been saved by two men with no allegiance to you! My own brother has committed to your safety and is willing to call Heber his son! To protect you both! What other man would ever take on a concubine who has a bounty on her and her child's head?" Nalussa was angry. "If anything, you should be grateful!"

"Oh, Nalussa, I'm sorry! It's just that I'm so tired. I haven't been sleeping since the baby was born. I'm having a hard time adjusting to my role as a mother, the loss of King Solomon—whom I so loved—and . . . and it's been difficult adjusting to a meager diet."

Nalussa closed her eyes and breathed in deeply. "Abra, please understand the seriousness of our situation. We've escaped. There's little question we're wanted by the king, who will rape and quite possibly kill us if he finds us. Adriel will be slaughtered, and if Jasper is found to be a part of the escape, he, too, will be killed. And for certain, he'll murder Heber. Your 'wonderful' life in the harem is over. There will be no more fine foods, wine, clothes, or jewels. Yesterday is a closing door. You've walked through it, and it has been locked behind you. You can't go back."

"Come now; it's time to eat. The men are ready."

CHAPTER NINETEEN

"You're what?" Abra nearly screamed, waking the baby who did scream. Adriel went quiet; Nalussa gaped.

"I've got to go back and get my family and bring them to Egypt. Pharaoh is planning an invasion to destroy Jerusalem, and I need to get them out before that happens. This army is nothing but mercenaries; and they will murder, rape, destroy, steal, pillage, and burn a path to Jerusalem.

"You can't leave me here alone. Who will take care of us? What about our safety?"

"Adriel will look out for you—"

"No, he won't! He can't. He's busy with Nalussa!"

"Woman, keep quiet. He risked his life for you, as did I. There is no more discussion. You will stay here until I come back . . . Do you understand?"

She glared at him and stormed out the door to the courtyard with the baby screaming on her shoulder.

Adriel looked up from his wine. "Well, that went well."

Jasper pursed his lips. "I've been trying to be a good 'husband,' taking care of her, being attentive, but she is just a spoiled king's concubine. And, as you know, she has shown little interest in truly marrying me. And honestly? If it wasn't for Heber, I'm not so sure about the interest I now have for her. In the beginning, I was smitten. She was beautiful, sharp, and strong. But now?" He shook his head in defeat. "I've got a lot to think about before I make any kind of decisions, and right now I need to be concerned about my family I've left behind."

"How long will you be gone?" Nalussa asked.

"I'm not sure; Father will want to get his animals and home organized. Our brother and sister—if she's not betrothed—will come, too. I just can't leave them to be killed. Mercenary soldiers will think nothing of raping and killing our little sister. I've got to bring them to safety!"

"I understand, Jasper. Please, don't worry about Abra. Between Nalussa and me, we'll take care of her," Adriel assured him.

"Truth be told? I'm not really worried about Abra. Oh, I care for her and the baby, but she still thinks she's the king's concubine and is depressed that she's not living as lavishly as she once had been. If she thought for a moment Rehoboam would desire her, she would have stayed. She actually told me that. Except for the baby, she would have remained in the harem."

Adriel said nothing. Nalussa had told him a few things about Abra as well, but they both decided that she was not used to being responsible for a child. For so long, she had servants waiting on her, dressing her, bringing her delicacies from around the kingdom, pleasing her in every way, so it was a difficult transition for her to be pleasing another human being—and a helpless one, at that.

Then Adriel spoke up. "This is what we'll do in the event something happens here and we've got to leave. We need a plan in place, especially since you don't know how long you'll be gone. If something happens, we'll leave word with the owners here. We're thinking Sheba. I doubt they'll be going anywhere soon, and I truly hope we don't get in a situation where we have to leave either. So, obviously, come here first to find us or get information on us."

"Sheba?" Jasper was surprised.

"Yes, but nothing is certain. Don't worry. We expect to be here when you return. Don't worry about the women."

"But I am," Jasper said. "You are just one man against we-don't-know-what."

Adriel put his hand on his friend's shoulder. "I can take care of them. We're not in any threat from Rehoboam. At least, he won't send soldiers here with all of Pharaoh's mercenaries wandering about, but that doesn't mean he wouldn't send out spies. Listen, as long as we stay away from the soldiers and don't wander around in public, bringing any kind of attention to the women, we should be all right. This is a tough town, no question, but we have the money to last a long time. I'm planning on getting some work, anyway. To be truthful, as much as I love Nalussa," he smiled at her, "I can't be with women all day and night without anything to do. When are you leaving?"

"In two days, at daybreak. So, we better get you two married tomorrow!"

The following day, the four of them, along with Heber walked out onto a field. A short, but godly ceremony was performed, and Jasper, on behalf of his father, received Adriel's gift of a few broken pieces of gold and a handful of silver. He laughed. "Are these pieces from my father, that King Solomon gave you to pay him for Nalussa?"

Adriel blushed. "Yes, in truth, they are! But look, I included some pieces of silver from my stash, too, so your father will receive at least some of my money!"

"Let's celebrate, though quietly. We don't want our landlords to think we have been cohabitating illegally." Adriel touched Nalussa's cheek tenderly while Abra with Heber on her shoulder walked off. Jasper shrugged and followed her.

They gathered in a small courtyard. Nalussa and Adriel were beaming, Abra was distracted; Jasper was drinking; and Heber was sleeping.

The next morning, Jasper was gone.

Adriel found work as a woodworker, and Nalussa began baking bread for the inn and tending the chickens. Abra took care of a growing Heber, who was looking very much like his father, King Solomon.

Because the town was rapidly growing, vendors thrived, and what was available in some of the larger towns and cities was now found here. Abra befriended the innkeeper's wife, and the two began going into town, leaving Heber with Nalussa. Abra would come back, always with food and often with bulky packages. It wasn't lost on Nalussa or Adriel that she began to dress extremely well, which definitely raised some concerns.

Adriel brought his thoughts to Nalussa. "She still has her cache of jewels; I've never asked her for them because we still have plenty of gold and silver. She must be using stones from her jewelry to buy these clothes. I must say, I was hoping we could hang onto the jewels because as time goes on, we might need them to barter with. As long as Rehoboam is alive, we can't go back. We can't predict our future needs. We must stay prepared."

Nalussa jostled Heber on her hip. "She apparently doesn't care anymore about living frugally and being cautious. I agree. She's obviously trading some of the stones in for these very expensive robes. I know they're expensive. We all used to wear that quality of clothing in the harem. This is indeed disturbing."

"And I'll tell you another thing. If she's in shops or vendor's booths flashing jewels, word will get out that she is a wealthy woman. People are going to want to do business with her or, worse, will want to rob her. She's been going out with just the innkeeper's wife, who can't protect her should she get attacked."

"That's another part of the problem. The innkeeper's wife. Naturally, she gossips. I can imagine what is being said throughout town."

When Abra came back with a bulky package of clothing that afternoon, Nalussa beckoned her to sit.

"Let me first go up to the room and put this package away, and I'll be back down." Abra turned to go.

"No, Abra. Sit. Now. Put the package down and take your son. We have to talk." She handed the little boy to his mother.

Adriel walked over, but Nalussa was the first one to speak. "It's one thing to get the occasional tunic, robe, or head scarf, but another thing in buying clothes like the ones you wore at court. Abra, you can't do this. For one thing, we need to hold onto the jewels, so we can take care of our future needs—"

"These are my jewels, Nalussa! You had the opportunity of being gifted, too, but you were too proud! Now, look at you! Once the most beautiful in the harem, you now look like an everyday woman. You dress ordinary, and with scarfs hiding your face, no one even sees you!"

"Abra," Adriel interjected. "Who do you think took care of you since your escape up until now? The gold that was given to Nalussa's family was for her purchase. Her father gave it back to us, so we all could escape! The rest of the money we're using is from my payments from Solomon. But that's only a part of the point. If you start walking around like you're royalty, people will start to wonder who you are. We can't have people paying attention to you and asking questions. Surely, by now, Rehoboam has sent soldiers to look for the men that we killed on the road. We can't have spies going back to Rehoboam with descriptions of you and your jewels. Sometimes, you've even taken Heber, who looks just like King Solomon, along on your shopping trips. Think of Heber, too!"

"I'm tired of hiding! I have nothing to do but care for a child! My husband is gone! I'm bored sitting around a courtyard overtaken by chickens and goats. Let me tell you, if I didn't have Heber, I would have been one of Rehoboam's concubines. I only left because I was frightened, not thinking clearly of my options."

"Options?" Nalussa exclaimed. "What about the safety of your son? You know what Rehoboam would do to him *and* you! You have no options!"

Abra angrily flicked her robes and stood. "My son is royalty. Should anything happen to Rehoboam, Heber would be considered next in line to be king, and I would be the queen mother. My son and I would be living in King Solomon's palace! We would be running Judea! Have you ever thought of that?" she demanded, glaring at them before turning and walking away.

Nalussa looked at Adriel. "There could well be more sons for her to contend with if they haven't been slaughtered by Rehoboam."

"I'm sure Rehoboam has ridden himself of any competition and got them out of the way," he answered as he watched Abra cross the courtyard and climb the stairs to the second floor with her son slung over her shoulder.

Abra's behavior worsened. She was now sullen, talked little, and would go off to town with the innkeeper's wife to shop, leaving Nalussa watching Heber while Adriel worked. Nalussa was growing increasingly concerned because Abra wasn't curbing her visibility in town. She wasn't making large purchases, but each day, she brought home something small as if to make a defiant statement. Triumphantly, she would hold up a comb, a bracelet, an anklet, an uncommon piece of fruit, or a sweet. Nothing to share, nothing for Heber.

After work one evening, Adriel came to Nalussa, who was sitting in the courtyard idly feeding the chickens and watching Heber sleeping in his basket. She looked up with a smile and was just about to stand and greet him when he put up his hand for her to stay seated. Her smile left when she saw the expression on his face.

"The innkeeper stopped me just now."

His tone set off a trumpet alert in Nalussa's mind. "What did he say?" she asked cautiously.

"A couple of men came nosing by and asked about 'that beautiful woman who walks and shops about town and who is so well-dressed.' The innkeeper answered he had a few women staying here who were well-dressed and beautiful. Then the men said, 'We understand that this one is trading in fine jewelry and is often seen with your wife. We would like to be introduced to her.'"

Nalussa let out a breath. "What did he do?"

"He took their names and said he would give them to the woman they might be speaking of. And he told them to come back late tomorrow, and he would give them her response."

"They never asked if she was with anyone or if there was a child?"

"No. I didn't want to ask that to make it a point of concern. The less the innkeeper thinks about us, the better off we are. He has no idea who we are, other than Hebrews with money and now with jewels, traveling out of Judea.

Nalussa panicked. "We must leave now!" She mindlessly picked up the startled Heber and held him so close to her breast that he squealed. "We'll go to Sheba. The queen will welcome all of us, I know. We'll have a reason to show up in her court. We'll present her with King Solomon's poem."

"But what if she says it's not about her?"

"Don't worry about it. Let her decide."

"Do you think we'll be taking a risk?"

"No, Adriel. We're no threat to her or her kingdom, and we have a commonality with her with Solomon. We have no other place to go." She stood and paced, thinking. Adriel looked at her expectantly. She stopped before him. "I know. Tell the innkeeper that Abra is taking a short trip to Heilo but will be back in three days and will meet the men who are asking about her by the town well after midday. Tell him that you'll be accompanying her to make sure she is safe. Only, we won't go to Heilo."

Adriel nodded. "We'll go to Sheba."

She thought a moment longer. "Yes, that would work. Heilo's about . . . what? A day from here? We're paid up for the week. If we leave at dawn tomorrow, we'll have three days on them; and if the men go to Heilo to look for her there, we'll be in the opposite direction on our way to Sheba."

"And Jasper? I told him if we ever had to move on, we'd leave word with the innkeeper."

Nalussa pursed her lips, then said, "Good. Leave a note with the innkeeper for Jasper. Write 'We left for a great banquet like Solomon once gave. Remember the spices.' Everyone in Judea talked about the great banquet Solomon gave for the Queen of Sheba and the enormous amount of spices she brought as a gift."

"Would he understand this?" Adriel asked doubtfully. "What if the note falls in the wrong hands? Would they get it?"

Nalussa shrugged. "We've got to take our chances. If someone reads it, they might logically think we're going to Pharaoh's palace. It would make the most sense. It's closer. The jewels brought trouble, but good comes out of it. People now think that she is wealthy, and it wouldn't necessarily be a surprise that she would be going to see Pharaoh if they saw the note."

When Abra returned from the center of town, Adriel sat her down and told her what the innkeeper had relayed to him. Abra was stunned. She couldn't speak.

"We have to leave," Adriel said simply. "I'm not sure if these men are legitimate traders in jewels, spies, kidnappers looking for ransom, or just plain thieves. It doesn't matter. We have to leave."

"When? Where are we going?" Abra demanded.

Nalussa answered, "Before dawn tomorrow. Once the city gates open."

"But where are we going?" she insisted.

"Once we're well on the way, away from people, we'll tell you," Adriel said.

"Tell me now! And what about Jasper? Who knows when he'll be back? And he'll find us gone!"

Adriel got close to Abra's face. "Be ready to leave tomorrow morning before dawn. Do not talk to anyone. Do you understand? Our lives could be at stake!"

That night, they shared a common meal, but little was spoken. Abra left to pack, and Nalussa began putting their meager belongings together as Adriel went out into the night to fill up on water and fodder for the journey. Nalussa and Abra had some food stores that would last a few days, but after that, they would need a food source.

When he came back, he said, "I told the innkeeper the story of Abra going to Heilo for three days. By the way, he thinks we're her servants. Abra told his wife as much." He laughed. "She really does think she's royalty."

He sat down. "I also gave him the note for Jasper. He just said, 'Yes, I'll tell the men about Abra and hold onto this for Jasper when he returns. You expect him back this soon?'"

"I answered that you never know what happens along the road. He could come back unexpectedly."

That morning, they were on their horses with packs, bundles, water, and food. Little Heber was strapped to his mother's chest, and she stroked his little head in fear, anger, and worry. They passed through the city gates past a handful of sleeping soldiers and two alert guards, who asked where they were going and if they were returning.

"Heilo. Three days," Adriel responded, and the party kept their heads down. Heber was hidden under his mother's robe, and Nalussa's head scarf covered her face; but it was dark still, and there were other travelers waiting to leave as well, so they were rushed through the gates.

Abra turned to Nalussa. "We're going to Heilo? Why on earth there?" Nalussa didn't answer.

Finally, about an hour into the journey, Abra shouted to Adriel. "Where are we *really* going? Even I know Heilo is in the opposite direction."

Nalussa turned to her and said, "Our first stop is in two more hours. We will go to the village of Phara, spend the night, then move on."

"To where? Where are we going?" Abra insisted coldly. "And you didn't tell me how Jasper is going to know where we've gone."

"Why do you care now about Jasper? He's not your husband. You were very clear about not wanting that," Nalussa sniped back at her.

Adriel dropped his steed back to pace with her horse. "We're going to Sheba, and I've left a note with the innkeeper for Jasper. He'll know where to find us."

Abra's eyes went wide in genuine surprise. "We're going to Sheba? Across the Red Sea?"

"Yes, we plan to go to the queen's court."

Abra immediately went quiet. Nalussa noted that her anger and sullenness evaporated. She sat up straighter on her horse and had a slight smile.

"What made you think to go to the Queen of Sheba?' Abra asked Nalussa in admiration.

"I believe the queen will welcome concubines of King Solomon. She seemed to understand Solomon and, probably, I hope, have some compassion for us, the other women he enjoyed. I pray she has kindness for our situation."

"She'll surely remember you," Abra retorted. "You could be her sister. Everyone at the banquets saw the similarity between the two of you, including the queen and King Solomon. I hope she's not the jealous type."

Nalussa highly doubted that. The king had hundreds of women at the time Makeda had visited. Thinking of Heber, she did wonder how she would respond to a child of a concubine, but again, she knew the king did have children. Surely, she must have heard about Rehoboam coming into power.

"Finally!" Abra sighed. "We're going to a court where we'll be treated with respect. I'm glad I have proper clothes. I could lend you a robe, if you want."

After a night spent in the village of Phara, Adriel was able to get a roughly drawn map of the route to Sheba, but more importantly, they were able to buy their way into a caravan owned by Ethiopians, who were well-acquainted with extensive travel and trade with the kingdom of Sheba. Traveling this way gave the party security in numbers from potential robbers, the treachery of the encroaching desert, and also news about Rehoboam and his kingdom, Judah. The caravan was out of Jerusalem, traveling the same route as they did to Gia.

One evening in camp, the drivers talked about Pharaoh and how he was amassing troops in Gia to invade Judah by recruiting Ethiopians, Libyans, and Sukkiims.

"It's hardly a kept secret, but it's going to take some time to assemble such a force," a driver said.

"Now that Rehoboam has fewer subjects to protect him and his treasures, Pharaoh wants to march to Jerusalem and rob Solomon's temple of its wealth," one man stated. "And there's untold wealth there, I'm told. More gold and jewels that can be counted. Silver is nothing there. It was just a common metal to King Solomon."

"Indeed," another agreed. "Gold and precious jewels fill the temple. But I'd take silver too!" The men laughed.

"How will he protect the temple?" someone asked.

"I've heard Rehoboam is planning on fortifying cities in Judah and Benjamin territories to hold them back. At least fifteen cities are going to be protected with commanders, soldiers, fortresses, and supplies."

"It's going to hurt our business," the caravan master complained.

Adriel lightly touched Nalussa, whispering, "I'm sure Jasper has plenty of time to get the family safely to Egypt."

"Let's pray that he gets there before the troops get restless and go out looking for trouble. Hebrews coming into the city could be at risk!"

Abra overheard. "Jasper can take care of himself and the family. But once he gets to the city, it might be wise for him to hide out there rather than coming to look for us."

Nalussa turned to her in surprise. "Why? Don't you want your 'husband' and your new family to be safe with you? Why would he stay there when the very soldiers that will invade Judah will think nothing of killing our people? My brother's and family's lives will be at risk in Gia, too! It will be far safer for them all to come to Sheba."

Nalussa now realized that it was a good plan to escape to Sheba. Certainly, it would be unsafe to stay on there knowing that the attack on the Hebrews would be launched from there. Any outsider would be in peril.

"I think that if he finds a safe place, he should stay," she insisted. "The inn there is safe. If he comes to Sheba, he has to contend with the danger of robbers, the desert, and scarcity of food and water, unless he finds fellow travelers or a caravan like we did."

Nalussa had enough. She snapped, "You might not want Jasper with you, but I want my brother and my family to be with Adriel and me."

"It's not that I don't want him to be with me," she angrily countered. "It's just that they will be traveling many miles to get to Gia. I can't imagine how tiring it would be to rest briefly, then come to Sheba, especially with your father, an old man."

"My father is strong." At least, Nalussa hoped he was. She kept silent pondering Abra's attitude. Not wanting Jasper to be with her and Heber only reinforced Nalussa's overall concern for where Abra's ambitions lay. She didn't trust her anymore.

CHAPTER TWENTY

One evening, the caravan master beckoned Adriel to sit by the fire with him. He handed Adriel warm spiced wine. "Tomorrow, we plan to stop in the town of Naj for two days to off-load some goods, replenish supplies, and rest the camels. Then, we'll travel two days to the port where we'll cross the Red Sea; we have barges reserved for travel to Sheba. As you know, we left from Jerusalem, and we've been spending nights in camp." He stretched and yawned mightily. "My animals and men need a rest. You're welcome to stay with us if you don't mind stopping for a few days, and I very much recommend it. The last leg of the journey can be dangerous. Finding a reputable boat for crossing, robbers on the look-out for goods coming into Sheba—they're everywhere waiting for the opportunity to pounce."

He paused, shooting Adriel an appraising look. "Even the roads to Ra and Gia are dangerous. I'm told three of the king's men were murdered on their way to Ra looking for runaway concubines."

Adriel nearly choked on his wine. The caravan master whacked him on the back. "You okay?"

Adriel coughed, nodded, then asked, "What did you say? The king's men? Rehoboam's men?"

"Who else is king of Judah? Yes, three men. Although, when they found them, there wasn't much left because the beasts had already enjoyed a feast, but they found an amulet on a chain imbedded on the side of one of the dead man's necks with an inscription of his rank and his king, Rehoboam."

Adriel kept silent as the man continued. "Jerusalem is abuzz with the story that two of Solomon's favorite concubines are on the run, one supposedly pregnant. It's known one man rescued them, but it's likely he had help. Rehoboam is crazed. He wants them back to abuse them, then no doubt kill them—including the child, if there is one. So, he sends out men to the north, south, east, and west to find them. 'Course they can't go north no more. Jeroboam has that territory now. Israel."

He sighed. "The split kingdom is going to hurt my business. Anyway, rumor has it there's been sightings of the women. One rumor in particular is that two couples were seen on the road to Ra. And one woman was spectacular with dark looks."

Adriel's heart nearly flew through his chest. "And?"

"And the story ends there. Along with three dead men. I guess Rehoboam sent some other men to follow up. That's all I know."

The fire crackled, and the man poked it with a stick. "Will you continue on with us?"

Adriel couldn't risk going on alone. Not with only himself to defend two women and a baby. He wasn't sure of the master's intentions, but he'd take a chance that even if the man suspected them, there were only three of them, not two couples as the rumor went. "We'll stay with you, and we appreciate your hospitality. This is all unknown territory to us, and I want to keep my wife and her sister safe."

"Your wife looks so much like the Queen of Sheba. She is very beautiful. Are they related?"

"No. Her mother was from Cush, so she's dark and beautiful like the queen." He let out a soft laugh as the wine relaxed his mind and accepted a refill from the master. "I confess, when I first saw the queen back when she visited King Solomon, I was amazed at the similarity, too. In fact, even the queen herself was surprised when she first saw my wife at a banquet King Solomon gave in the queen's honor. The palace was humming at their likeness!"

The master looked startled. Immediately, Adriel regretted his remarks. The master would surely wonder why he and Nalussa would ever be at a king's banquet. King Solomon's, no less. Unease began to fill his stomach, mixing with the wine.

The man looked over at Nalussa and Abra, who were talking near a fire while Abra nursed Heber.

"Your wife's sister is a beauty, too. Does she have a husband?" Adriel wasn't sure how to answer, so kept silent, and the master continued, "Dead, eh?" He took a long drink from his cup. Wiping his mouth, he asked, "Are you all from Judah?"

"Yes, we are." Adriel took his own deep drink of wine.

"Why travel all the way to Sheba?" the master wanted to know.

Thinking quickly, Adriel answered, "We heard rumors, too, about a possible Egyptian invasion, and we live far enough south in Judah to be dangerously close to the Egyptian border and the soldiers. We thought Gia might be safe because there are so many nationalities living there, but it turned out to be too dangerous with a garrison being set up to stage the invasion, so Sheba seemed to be the best place for us to go."

"Hmmm. Your accent sounds like you're from Jerusalem."

"Oh, we've traveled there for holy days." He got up, shaking out his robe. "I must get back to the women to tell them about our stopover. Thank you for the wine."

"I carry only the best!" The man laughed and poured himself another cup.

Nalussa agreed a rest would be good for a few days but was anxious about getting into see Queen Makeda, and equally anxious about crossing the Red Sea to the peninsula. "Can we send a messenger to the court telling her that we're on our way and would like an audience with her because we carry a gift from King Solomon?"

"That's a good idea because once in the queen's presence, we can petition her for extended protection," Adriel said.

"Not only for us, but for my brother and family, too," Nalussa added.

Adriel nodded in agreement. "Of course, but listen. I think the master might be on to us, and not only that, but I also think I've made a mistake." He told her about his discussion with the master and then about them being at a banquet with the queen and King Solomon.

"Oh." Nalussa sighed in worry. "Oh, no."

"It'll be all right, I'm sure." But he glanced around cautiously. "One other thing. The master said that Rehoboam sent men out to follow-up on how the first group of men were murdered. I'm thinking those men who wanted to meet with Abra for her jewels might be the king's men."

"We're weeks from Gia and even further from Heilo in the opposite direction." Nalussa lightly touched Adriel's hand. "I believe we have enough distance and time between us. Don't fret. God will provide and protect."

They stayed at a busy inn in Naj and kept to themselves as much as they could. Being so close to the kingdom of Sheba, many of the regular travelers who were traders knew what the queen looked like, and when Nalussa wasn't covered cautiously, several men did a double-take looking at her, forcing them to take their meals in their rooms to avoid controversy and curiosity.

Yet Abra insisted she go out to town with Adriel for supplies, complaining, "I need to walk, to get moving! I've been sitting on a horse for days. I need to get out among people! Let me help you shop for our provisions." Reluctantly, Adriel agreed, and Abra gave Heber to Nalussa to watch as she left to get her head scarf.

Meeting him in the courtyard, she smiled and took his arm. She had made herself up, put on an eye-caching scarf, added jewelry, and wore her fine clothing.

"Abra, what are you doing?" demanded Adriel glaring at her. "We still have to be careful! We don't want to draw attention. Already, people have taken notice of Nalussa's looks. And now people will be looking at you, too!"

"Well, of course, I'm going to be looked at. I wasn't chosen for King Solomon because I was ugly! I know I'm beautiful. But honestly, Adriel." She looked up at him with big brown flirtatious eyes. "Do you really think anyone cares about us anymore? Rehoboam has more important things to worry about."

Adriel shook his head, pursing his lips. "All I'm saying is that we still need to be cautious. It's now known—or at least rumored—that three of the king's men have been killed—"

"By you and Jasper," Abra interrupted with a smug look. "You murdered the king's men."

Adriel didn't like her attitude. "As I said, three of the king's men have been killed, and you have caught the interest of two more men because of your costly dress and the way you've been bartering with your jewels. They could also be Rehoboam's men. It's bad enough having people gawking at Nalussa for her likeness to the Queen of Sheba without them gawking at you over your expensive clothes."

"Stop worrying," she admonished. "You're taking the fun out of shopping."

"You just don't understand, Abra. It's not a question of idle worry. We're traveling with a caravan that goes back and forth to Jerusalem. These men meet hundreds of people throughout their travels. Men gossip as much as women, and everyone from Jerusalem knows of the runaway concubines. Seeing Nalussa and you as candidates for concubine escapees won't be a difficult conclusion to come to."

They shopped without incident, although Abra was looked at by many people.

On the appointed morning, they rejoined the caravan at the city gates, everyone being well-rested and fed, except Adriel, who was stressed and anxious. Diligently, he eyed the caravan drivers for any suspicious looks thrown their way. For the most part, his party was ignored, and this gave him some sense of relief. Seeking out the caravan master, he asked, "We need an audience with the Queen of Sheba—"

"You and everyone else," the master interrupted.

"But we have good reason. We have something for her from King Solomon." He wanted to avoid detail. He was still unsure of how the poem, or song, would be received by the queen, but he trusted

Nalussa's judgment and could only trust the caravan master to find someone to get the message to the queen.

The master waited for an explanation, but when Adriel wasn't forthcoming, he wisely let the matter drop. "It'll cost you. I can send one of my men ahead, but you'll have to pay him and the boat master, and I want a commission."

"No problem. All he needs to say is 'A woman from Judah who looks like the Queen of Sheba has something to give her from King Solomon.'"

"But he's dead!" the master objected.

"This is urgent," was all that Adriel would say.

The two men discussed the rate; Adriel paid; and the master found a man. "He's trustworthy."

As the caravan was readying to get underway, Adriel found Nalussa with her horse, waiting for him to return. Taking her aside outside of earshot from Abra, he said, "A runner is being sent out before us to get a message to the queen."

"How will we know she will see us?"

"The man will wait for us at the city gates with the answer; then, we'll just have to take it from there."

They crossed the Red Sea and continued on to the well-maintained trade road. The city of Sheba rose majestically from the horizon. Even from this distance, the city walls were huge, fortified by turrets, with clusters of flags waving in the breeze. As they got closer, the view was even more impressive and as beautiful and imposing as anything even Solomon had built.

Nalussa turned to Abra, who was wide-eyed and grinning as she took in the grandeur of Sheba's walls. "This is as lovely as Solomon's city!"

The caravan came to a halt with all the other travelers at the gates, and Adriel stopped his group, got off his horse, and headed for the messengers' portico. There he found his runner, who waved at him as he bounded down the steps.

"I delivered your message, and the Queen of Sheba will meet you tomorrow at ten midmorning. I will take you to your quarters inside the palace, where you will be attended to. Your animals will be taken to the royal stables."

Enormous relief swept over Adriel as the caravan master joined the messenger and clapped him on the back. "Well done, my friend. It has never happened that I had a traveler so easily get an audience with the queen, unless he was bringing invaluable gifts. You, sir, must have something of great worth."

The messenger chimed in, "Either that, or you must be a hero, for her advisors told me she was delighted you were in her country and that she looked forward to meeting the concubine who was similar in her likeness."

The caravan master swiveled his head, looking Adriel full in the face. "I thought as much." He nodded knowingly. "In all my travels, I have never encountered a more beautiful one than your wife, who is extraordinary. Rivaling the queen herself." He shook his head. "And to think what King Rehoboam would have done if he got his hands on her."

Adriel ran back to get the women and baby with the messenger at his heels, who was looking for more payment, which Adriel gave. They waited their turn as people, vendors, and animals queued through the gates that opened onto a huge, elaborately decorated, open square that boasted columns, flowering trees, statues, and pools. Spicy, exotic scents filled the air, along with music and singing. Vendor stalls were set up on the periphery of the square offering different fruits and vegetables, along with all sorts of products ranging from clothing to quivers of arrows.

Nalussa was overwhelmed as they approached by the beauty of the palace. "It brings back clear memories of my life in the harem," she said aloud.

"And oh, how I miss court life!" Abra sighed. "Finally, I'm back where I belong with the rich and powerful. I hope we'll be able to stay until King Rehoboam dies!"

Nalussa thought a moment, agreeing, "True, we can't safely go back until there's another king."

They followed the servants, who took their animals, unloaded the packs from the horses, and led Nalussa, Adriel, Abra, and baby to their rooms in the palace.

"How exquisite!" Nalussa sighed, as she sat down on a fat cushion and tucked her feet under her legs. "After all this time traveling staying in inns, at camps, or on the hard ground, we now get to be in a beautifully appointed room with open views of gardens and exotic birds. God has indeed blessed us."

Adriel plopped beside her and poured them both a sweet drink from a golden jug set on a low, carved, ebony table. "This is a beautiful room. I'm looking forward to a bath, then love, then a long sleep, and finally, a good evening meal!"

Nalussa held up her cup, laughing.

Shortly, two servants entered, taking each to a different bathing area. Adriel lightly kissed Nalussa on the lips. "And I'm sure Abra is finally satisfied with her lodging, too!"

"I hope so. This is far more beautiful than the harem rooms. Definitely decorated by a woman with excellent taste."

Lounging in the bath with a servant attending her, Nalussa gave thought to her journey from being Solomon's concubine to Adriel's wife, from living in King Solomon's palace to sleeping on the ground or crowded inns, to now staying in the Queen of Sheba's palace. It was no small thing to have a king desire her, but Rehoboam's desire would be for her humiliation, then, likely, death. Even Solomon realized she had no future in Jerusalem.

Sinking deep in the warm, scented water, she thought, *A new beginning*. She was not the sum of her past, however recognizable it was: a beautiful woman whose sole purpose in life was to satisfy the sexual desire of one powerful man.

From a concubine's standpoint, her status in the harem rested solely on her beauty and was elevated only by Solomon's physical desire. Yet what would have she had been if she was never discovered for Solomon? A happy and contented woman in an arranged marriage? Would she have been elevated only by how many children she birthed? She never did get pregnant with Solomon. What would have happened to her if she never had children with a husband? She shivered in the warm water.

Yet she did have a husband now, who coincidently never mentioned children nor her relationship with King Solomon. He certainly accepted her past, and he diligently listened to her, kept her safe, and made her feel loved.

That night, after a very satisfying meal, she lay beside her husband and prayed Jasper would get her father, her younger brother Ziba, and her sweet sister Noa safely to Gia, then on to Sheba. "Please, God, let him understand the note about where we went to."

She turned to a half-sleeping Adriel. "If I'm not allowed to speak to the queen directly tomorrow, will you ask on my behalf if you and I, my family, along with Abra and Heber, can stay under the queen's protection until it's safe to go back to Judah?"

"Hmm-mm," Adriel grunted and drifted off to sleep. She believed that Abra was right. They couldn't go back until King Rehoboam was dead. Which brought her to her next thought. *I wouldn't be surprised if Abra placed her son in line for kingship of Judah.* If all of Solomon's children were dead, including Rehoboam, would a son by Solomon usurp a son by Rehoboam? She wasn't sure. But it would be a dangerous game for Abra to play. She would be far better off passing Heber off as Jasper's son and turning ambition away from the throne, but she wasn't so sure Abra would.

CHAPTER TWENTY-ONE

The hall was jaw-droppingly spectacular. Nalussa was in awe of the intricate and unusual, colorful designs imbedded in the stark white stone work. "Look at these vast columns throughout the hall!"

Adriel craned his neck. "And the flying arches, yes, they support those fantastic panels."

Nalussa blinked at the vibrant mosaic work of scenes depicting grand gardens and collections of mysterious animals. Expertly woven tapestries were hung from golden rods along cream-colored plastered walls, and huge fans made of palm fronds dotted the ceiling and were worked by slaves pulling cords in various corners of the hall.

"The workmanship is amazing," breathed Adriel. "It's equally as spectacular as Solomon's palace. See and feel how the combination of fans and the cross-ventilation from the high, open windows provide a continuous, warm breeze?"

"Oh, my, yes. The flurry of air stirs up the still heat from outside the walls," Nalussa exclaimed.

Her Majesty herself was seated on an ivory carved raised throne, with slaves on either side fanning her while incense burned on either side of the throne giving off a sweet cinnamon smell that lightly filled the hall. She was petite, dark, and very beautiful, clothed in an almost sheer material that faintly exposed her breasts. On each arm was a golden band, and on her head was a golden crown flashing all the jewels of the rainbow. Her wrists were covered in gold and silver bangles, and her waist was girdled with a shimmering golden sash. A simple skirt of pure white linen fell to her ankles, which were wrapped in silver chains with tiny silver bells. Her brown feet were sandaled in fine leather, tied in silver and gold ribbons.

She was stunning. Her black hair was cut short on the sides, and atop her head was a woven crown of braided hair. Her amber eyes were trimmed in black kohl and lips stained with red berry juice. Her brown eyes flashed intelligence, and her mouth offered a warm smile.

Adriel stood in front, with Nalussa slightly behind him and Abra holding Heber in her arms behind Nalussa. They all bowed low as they were introduced to the queen by an advisor.

Her voice was like honey. "I welcome you to my palace and kingdom. I honestly never thought I would see any of Solomon's court here in my throne room. This is an extreme pleasure. I understand you have something from Solomon you wish to give me?"

Nalussa stepped forward, bowed low again, and went before the queen's throne. Bending on one knee, head down, she extended her hand with Solomon's scroll. The queen plucked it from her hand, and with a nod of her royal head, Nalussa went to stand behind Adriel again.

Slowly and carefully, the queen unrolled the scroll and began to read, eyes opening wide in amazement. After a few tense moments to Nalussa' way of thinking, she placed a hand on her breast, abruptly stood holding onto the scroll, and motioned her advisor to escort her quickly out of their presence.

All three exchanged alarmed looks. Another advisor approached them and said, "I'll take you back to your rooms."

Adriel stammered, "Is the queen all right?" He was frightened that perhaps the poem wasn't about the Queen of Sheba and she was insulted.

The advisor answered, "She wishes to read what you have given her and would like some time alone. She will get back with you."

Back in their rooms, Abra came forward in anger. "What have you done to distress the queen? If you have jeopardized my safety or my plans, I'll be furious. I have nothing to do with whatever it is you gave her. What was it, anyway?" she demanded rudely.

Adriel began to speak, but Nalussa held up her hand and spoke instead. "I gave her something that King Solomon wanted her to have, and it's nothing of your concern."

Abra's eyes nearly popped out of her head. "How dare you speak to me that way? I'm scheduling a private meeting with the queen to tell her who Heber really is: the next rightful heir to Solomon's throne once Rehoboam dies—and die he will! If you have in any way jeopardized my ability to talk to the queen, there will be consequences!"

"What consequences? You're here as a guest, as we are. Don't threaten Nalussa or me. No one can stop you from whatever you're planning. We have no intention of getting involved with your plans, but you are putting yourself and Heber in danger. You have no idea what you are getting into," Adriel heatedly broke in.

Abra pointed a shaking finger at him. "This is bigger than either of you can grasp. I'm talking about my son being a contender for the throne of Judah. I will fight for that right." She whipped around to Nalussa with her hands on her hips. "And I will not be the wife of Jasper. So, dash those thoughts, and I don't want him in the way of Heber's rightful ascension when the time comes. Heber is Solomon's son and will be recognized as such, and I don't want my ability to become queen mother endangered by a man who stole me away from the palace to begin with."

"You are, indeed, ambitious," Nalussa stated, angry that Adriel and Jasper had risked their lives for her and her baby at her misguided insistence.

Adriel added, "You do understand that in order to make any claim on the throne, you'll need an army. You just can't show up at the palace and announce Heber as rightful king."

"Do you think me stupid? Of course, I know that! That's why I'm meeting with the queen to ask her for her protection and support. Surely, she'll want to see a son of Solomon's on the throne and not one of Rehoboam's from who-knows-what lineage!"

Adriel was furious as Abra stormed out of their rooms. "You were right. You thought this was going to happen, and it did! Jasper. Poor Jasper. He's going to feel . . . "

"Betrayed," Nalussa answered simply. "But although betrayed, I'm not so sure he loved her. He was in lust, certainly, but he saw her selfishness. I'm certain he'll be fine. And look at it this way: if we didn't escape to Egypt, we wouldn't have known my family would be in danger."

"Yes, this is true, but I want the queen to know that neither you nor I support what Abra wants to do. We'll stay here for as long as she lets us. We still have money; I can work. If she keeps us under her protection, we'll be safe until Rehoboam dies, however long that takes, and we can get back to Jerusalem. But now my fear is Abra's grab for the kingdom. I want nothing to do with those efforts."

"Nor I! To think she would plan such a thing is beyond my comprehension." Nalussa walked over to Adriel and put her head on his chest. "I worry for Heber. He's just a child."

"Children grow, become ambitious as well. Yet Rehoboam might outlive all of us."

Nearly two weeks later, the queen called them back into her presence and formerly accepted them in her kingdom for as long as they wished to stay.

"Until Rehoboam dies," Abra interrupted. Then she bowed and said, "Please forgive me, Your Majesty, for my impertinence. It's just that I so fear for my son . . . "

The queen thought a moment, looking hard at Abra. "Your son, I assume, is one of Solomon's sons?"

Abra looked up, smiled, and nodded. "Yes, Your Majesty, and if you have time, I would like to speak with you about a matter in private. I had hoped to speak with you sooner about this." She glanced at Nalussa, who steadfastly kept her eyes downcast. She would not support Abra's plotting.

The queen took a breath and continued, "I'll house you in apartments in the palace and see to it that all your needs will be cared for." Turning back to Abra, she said, "I'll have arrangements made for our discussion. And this is the first I have heard of your request to speak with me."

Before they were dismissed, the queen asked to speak to Nalussa privately, which Nalussa was grateful for. She hadn't addressed her family coming to Sheba and needing protection also. Adriel raised an eyebrow and walked out ahead of Abra, who was scowling at the attention given to Nalussa first.

The servants led Nalussa, the queen, her men, guards, and attendants to another room off the main assembly hall. Settling on a settee by a vast, open balcony that overlooked the dramatic city of Sheba, the queen pointed to a couch. "Come, sit across from me." Nalussa sat facing the queen, who handed her a cup of sweet juice and said, "You were one of King Solomon's favorite concubines. I confess, when I first saw you, I was surprised at how much we looked alike. I was even a bit jealous, to be truthful; but the more I got to know the king, the more I understood his need to be surrounded by beauty, and your beauty complemented me." She took a sip of juice, looking over her cup at Nalussa.

Putting her drink down, the queen suddenly asked, "Did you love him?"

"I did not. We had a sort of . . . friendship. I enjoyed his company; he was a very interesting, but conflicted, man." She was careful with her speech, not knowing this woman who sat across from her, who was powerful in her own right. Nalussa had come to learn her position was to speak only when spoken to.

The queen was silent for a while, then said, "I'm surprised you didn't love him. You spent more time with him than most of his wives, and yet you didn't succumb to his charms, other than sexually? Tell me, why you didn't fall in love with him?"

Nalussa sat up straight and looked out over the city, thinking over her answer carefully. Turning to the queen, she said, "It was difficult for me to accept that the only reason I was before the king was to be a part of his harem. And the only reason I was in the harem was for my beauty and body. I was in existence only for his sexual needs. He came to admire my mind later, and so we developed a friendship; but my primary use, so to speak, was that of my body. And he never loved me. So, how could I love a man who had hundreds and hundreds of women he used for his own gains?" She cringed. *Oh, I shouldn't have said that.*

The queen took another small sip of sweet juice. "I often asked myself the same thing. Yet, I did fall in love with him, and paradoxically, even though he had so many women to enjoy, he fell in love me."

Nalussa wanted to say, *I know why he fell in love with you. You were the only woman he saw as his equal. You were a queen in your own right with wealth, intelligence, and fame, and great beauty. You, yourself, were independently powerful, proving you didn't need a man to make you who you are.*

The queen continued as if reading her mind. "I was a good match for him, I know. Although my kingdom wasn't as vast and wealthy as his, my kingdom is still powerful and prosperous. I didn't need him. I was, and am, self-sufficient. He couldn't buy me or use me for his own gain. He had to love me for who I was: beautiful, rich, and intelligent."

Nalussa kept silent but thought, *I wish I had a copy of Solomon's reflections on the meaning of life and his woeful conclusion that all is vanity! Would the queen be surprised if she read that scroll?*

The queen moved on. "I want to thank you for bringing me his poem." She leaned over and took the parchment from a basket by the side of the couch and held it up. "It means a great deal to me. I remember so much of our time together, and now, in reading this poem, it has brought it back to life again. I'm exceedingly grateful."

She paused again, lost in the past. She could only nod.

Nalussa found it difficult to embrace the king's emotions in the poem, simply because he wasn't capable of enduring love. She understood the drama involving his initial lust and young love for his beloved, his "bride," but were his words and sentiments lasting? She didn't think so. He as much as told her so.

Nalussa gazed at the beautiful woman before her, wondering about her capability of true love. She read the young woman in the poem adored her beloved, and both lovers in the poem were immersed in each other. But were the sentiments of the woman sitting opposite enduring as well?

"And your thoughts on the poem?" the queen prompted, wanting to know her reaction to Solomon's writing.

"It's lovely, Your Majesty, written by King Solomon and his bride, who were in the first throes of young love, both physically and emotionally. It's very . . . intimate." *That's all I dare say,* Nalussa thought.

With so many wives and concubines of the king, the queen sitting opposite her could easily have been considered a "secret" bride of Solomon's, hence the co-written poem. Yet, knowing Solomon, he could have easily written both parts, which wouldn't have surprised Nalussa. In any case, the queen was grateful for the poem, and that was all that mattered. She didn't need to know Nalussa's opinions.

"You're a cautious one." The queen smiled. She gently put the scroll back in the basket. Changing the subject, she said, "The other concubine, Abra, wishes to speak to me about Solomon's son. I'm certain she has some ideas about his birthright, is that so?"

Nalussa wanted to deflect the question. "Your Majesty, I don't know if you have been informed of the entire situation."

The queen interrupted. "I do know of the situation. I have many spies throughout all the kingdoms. Adriel, aided by an accomplice, helped you and the pregnant concubine escape because Rehoboam was seeking to defile you and eliminate Abra and her child, who could compete for his throne."

Nalussa blinked. Here was an opening. "That accomplice was my brother, Jasper, who has gone back to Judah to retrieve my father, brother, and sister and get them to safety, out of the way of the Egyptians, who are soon to march on Jerusalem to ransack the temple. And I humbly ask if you will graciously allow them to come here until it is safe for all of us to return to Judah."

"I can do that," the queen agreed. "When do you expect them?"

"I don't know, Your Majesty. It could be months."

"And it could be years before Egypt actually marches on Jerusalem." The queen sat a moment and nodded. "Is Jasper married to Abra? You escaped as two married couples."

"Yes, we did, but no, they are not married. In the beginning, we pretended to be in order to fool the authorities or others who might be interested in our escape, but later, Adriel and I did get married," Nalussa explained.

"You didn't answer my question about Abra's intentions for her son." The queen paused, then asked, "Is she hoping to put her son on the throne when Rehoboam dies?"

"She has said so, but we—Adriel and I and my family—have nothing to do with her ambitions. However, she will need to discuss her ideas with you. We have nothing to do with her plans." Nalussa wanted the queen to clearly know that Abra was on her own.

The queen nodded, then stood, and an attendant came quickly out of the shadows. She spoke to him as another man entered the chambers to escort Nalussa out. As she was leaving, the queen called, "I thank you again for coming all the way to Sheba to deliver this scroll, although I'm sure it was a circuitous route, due to these political times. And I appreciate your candor about King Solomon. He and I were meant for each other only for a brief a time, for we both had our ambitions as well." She laughed. "Yes, indeed. We both met our match."

Adriel was anxiously awaiting Nalussa's return. "Is all well with the queen reading King Solomon's poem?"

"Yes, it certainly seems that she was the woman in the poem. She didn't say anything on the content. We talked a bit about Solomon, but she didn't dwell on details. She also said my family could find protection here for as long as needed, and she seemed to think that the Egyptians wouldn't march on Jerusalem for years. I don't know if that was accurate or just a remark. As a cautionary note, she said she has spies in many kingdoms, so Abra's scheming is especially troubling if gossip gets back to Rehoboam."

"What did she say about Abra?" Adriel paced, pulling his beard in deep concern.

"The queen wanted to know if Abra was going to challenge the throne once Rehoboam dies. I said yes, but we have nothing to do with her scheming."

"Nalussa, we have truly got to distance ourselves from Abra," Adriel firmly advised. "I know you love Heber, but keep away from them both. No one can see any attachment of you to the child. This is a serious situation. We don't know who will support her and who will be against her. Now that the queen knows and once she meets with Abra, others will soon discern what is going on. After all, Abra hasn't made it a secret anymore that Heber is Solomon's son. We must be very careful to keep quiet on the matter, but stay alert and be aware of any palace intrigue."

CHAPTER TWENTY-TWO

Abra was excited. She dressed in her finest robes and jewels. Looking at herself in a polished, silver mirror, she was satisfied; even though she'd had long travels, slept on dirt, and ate poor food, she still looked royal and beautiful, as well as imposing. She might have been a concubine, but she was a royal concubine with a king's son—a son who had every right to claim the throne of Judah. She realized it would be a while for Rehoboam to die, but anything could happen. In order to gain power, she must convince the queen to back her by providing money and soldiers, and in turn, she would pay a handsome tribute to the queen from Solomon's treasures once Heber was installed as king.

She smiled. Why, she could even have Rehoboam assassinated and rule Judah as queen mother until Heber came of age, but she would need support inside and outside of Judah. Which led her to think of Pharaoh. He was planning an invasion on Jerusalem. Would he depose Rehoboam or just rob him? If the Queen of Sheba turned her down for an alliance, then perhaps Pharaoh might be of use. Except if he was going to plunder Judah, what would he gain by making an alliance with her? Her beauty? She would weigh the two options of support and plot how she could entice either ruler to back her plans.

Yet caution was in order. Maybe she shouldn't have told anyone Heber was Solomon's son, she thought. Well, it was too late now, and besides, she needed to groom supporters for her plan.

She was led to the queen's administrative rooms in the palace. She realized that a private audience with the queen was improbable. Indeed, as she entered, two advisors were in attendance, as well as several inconsequential slaves laboring away with large palm fronds to move the still air in a room with floor-to-ceiling windows on three sides. Two ivory and ebony carved couches faced each other with a low, golden table placed in between. As was customary, colorful cushions were placed to sit and lean back on. Incense burned on tall, golden stands placed strategically throughout the room so as not to be overpowering.

The advisors sat behind the queen on stools with parchment and pens in hand, eyeing Abra as she was led to the queen, who lounged on one of the couches where a contented cat lay on the royal lap. Two small dogs played with bones under the table, and a blue and gold parrot preened itself on a stand by the window. Other tables placed on either side of the couches held goblets and pitchers of refreshment, along with trays of fresh fruit.

The queen, dressed in sparkling white linen trimmed with gold and a band of gold around her head, indicated Abra sit across from her. The dogs, excited to see a new person, began to bark and tried to hop up on Abra's lap. Terrified, she pushed them away as the queen ordered, "Down!" Obediently, the animals, disappointed to lose attention, returned to their bones. The cat slept on.

Rattled by the dogs, all manner of pomp had disappeared from Abra. She was not expecting animals, who deeply frightened her. In

Jerusalem, cats kept rodents away, and dogs were wild scavengers, often eating the corpses of those unfortunate enough not to be claimed by anyone as they lay rotting on the streets.

One advisor stood and spoke. "The queen wishes to hear what you would like to speak with her about. If we find it important, we are obliged to take notes so that there is clear remembrance as to what is said. Are you agreeable?"

Sitting up straight, forgetting her fright, she crisply answered, "What I am about to speak of must be kept in extreme confidence. It could mean life and death. Do I have your assurances of confidence?"

The queen nodded, and the advisor spoke again. "Yes. Whatever you say in this room will stay in this room."

Abra looked around at the slaves mindlessly waving the palm fronds. "What about them?"

The advisor smiled. "They are chosen for just these types of meetings. They are deaf and dumb."

Abra sighed in relief and began, "Your Majesty, as you know, my son, Heber, is King Solomon's son. After Solomon died and Rehoboam became king, he planned to do away with any male child of Solomon's who could be a threat to the throne."

The queen nodded. "And that would have included your son."

"Yes. Undoubtedly, Rehoboam will anoint his own son as the king of Judah when the time comes. I want to preclude that because my son is the rightful heir."

"What is it that you want from me?"

"I am looking for support. I need soldiers and funding to challenge Rehoboam."

The queen petted her sleeping cat. "What would I gain for this support?"

Abra was ready for the question. "You would receive yearly tribute, and any female offspring that you have would be promised to my son. Your daughter would be a queen of Judah, and the alliance for Sheba would be supported by the armies of Judah in the face of any threat from Pharaoh or any other kingdoms."

"Hmmm." The queen turned to the men behind her. "Did you write that down?"

"Yes, Your Majesty," they answered in unison.

"Let me think about this. I'm intrigued. Have you talked about this to anyone else?"

"This is between you and me and your advisors," she lied. Although she had only been a guest in Makeda's palace for a short time, she already had the attention of a few senior courtiers. One powerful one in particular. She was, after all, very beautiful and well-versed in sexual favors, and she certainly did not hide the fact that Heber was King Solomon's son and, as pillow talk would go, a rightful heir to the throne of Judah.

"What about your husband, Jasper, Nalussa's brother? It was told to me that you were a married couple, and I was also told that you are not."

"I am not married to Jasper. He was a person of convenience as we made our way out of Judah to Egypt. We pretended to be married. Nothing more. He has no idea of my actions. He is not a part of this."

"Nalussa and Adriel? What of them? Would part do they play in this?"

"Nalussa?" Abra laughed scornfully. "She was Solomon's concubine. She's just a . . . " She thought a moment, rejecting the words "discarded concubine," and simply said, "She offers us nothing." She flipped her hand.

"Wouldn't Adriel be most interested in getting back to Judah's court again?" the queen insisted.

Abra let out an impertinent, exasperated breath that wasn't lost on the queen or her advisors. "Adriel is now a husband. He also has nothing to offer of value either. Yes, they are aware of Heber's right to the throne and have tried to dissuade me; but they haven't any grasp on what could be, and they are of little significance."

They sat in silence for a moment until the queen said, "Let me discuss this further, and we will get back with you." The queen continued to pet her cat as Abra was led out.

The queen turned to her men as Abra disappeared down the hallway. "She obviously doesn't know about Menelik, my own son by Solomon."

"Who, by the way, is older than her son and would, if you so desired, lay claim to Judah," her senior administrator said with a smirk. "She's delusional."

"She's ambitious but not delusional. Her thoughts have merit. Let us see how this plays out. I want to know if Nalussa and Adriel are a part of this or not."

"What about Nalussa's brother, Jasper, and her family?" asked the other man.

"We'll address that when they arrive," the queen answered. "My opinion is that Abra is smart enough to know that she needs power and strategy to move her plan forward. Her friends and Nalussa's family are of no importance to her. It's true. They lack power and influence. They are nothing to her."

"She's not to be trusted," one of the men complained.

The queen nodded in agreement. "However, I want to see how far this goes and if there are any conspirators with her. Word will get back to her about Menelik, and when that happens, we must be very careful. See to it that he is safe. Send him to my palace in Chloe."

"And then what?" her senior man asked.

"Then, we wait and see. If we detect a threat to Menelik, if there are conspirators within our own palace who might like to be influential with the throne of Judah, we throw them all in prison, at the very least." The queen put the cat off her lap, and the dogs, cat, and advisors followed her out of the room.

CHAPTER TWENTY-THREE

Being under the protection of the queen meant that there was little to do to actually survive for Nalussa, Adriel, Abra, and her son. The months passed pleasantly enough for all of them as they were introduced to the culture of Sheba, the various foods, and many arts. The people of the court were educated and keenly interested in the ways of the Hebrew people, but equally important, they were willing to listen to the concept of the Hebrew God. Yet the Shebanites were no newcomers to the concept of one god, for Queen Makeda their queen was a firm believer in the Lord God Almighty of King Solomon. While she didn't encourage the worship of other gods, she realized that all would not come to believe in the one, true God; but in her court, she made it a point of emphasizing the beauty and logic of the Hebrew God and His commandments.

This attitude of religious freedom was new to them. In Judah, pagans were looked down upon by the Hebrews, and in many cases, they had nothing to do with non-believers of the one, true God and spoke disdainfully of them, although they traded with them. Nalussa and Adriel enjoyed lively conversations on the subject, but Abra usually did not join in. She was frequently seen walking about the courtyards with one of the queen's courtiers named Ebel, a man King Solomon assigned to the queen to keep her fluent in the Hebrew language when she went back to her kingdom. He was a scholar and expert on the Law of Moses.

As time went on, Abra spent less time with her friends, leaving Heber with a servant and spending long days with Ebel and his other colleagues. When they did gather together for meals, she was unresponsive and usually locked in conversation with her new companions. It didn't bother Nalussa because Abra was playing with fire in thinking Heber could vie for Judah. This would be a huge undertaking, one that only another king—or queen—could finance. As far as she and Adriel were concerned, they were at the pleasure of the queen; and as long as they could stay in Sheba protected, they would.

As time passed, Nalussa had nearly given up on her family. "Kingdom crossing is dangerous, the travel treacherous, and there is always the specter of illness," Adriel said, knowing well she understood the challenges.

"I know, but I can't give up hope, and I'm so grateful they'll have a safe place to stay once they get here."

He added, "I pray that Jasper finds the note we left and understands its meaning, so they will move on from Gia to Sheba."

Nalussa could only nod. Every day, she hoped for the miracle of their arrival.

Now the queen met with her guests on many occasions, often at meal times, but she frequently sought out Nalussa alone in the afternoon to talk about Solomon. It was apparent that as Solomon's concubine, she was still loyal to the dead king and was guarded with her opinions. But on the occasion of a deeper question or observation, she would answer the queen truthfully. Still, she was a bit of an enigma to the queen.

One afternoon, she called Nalussa into her meeting chambers. After settling on a couch, she offered Nalussa some wine. As her servant handed the goblet to her guest, she shook her head in confusion. "I am continually surprised that you never had a deeper connection to Solomon." The queen sipped her wine, eyeing her critically. "After all, he was a brilliant conversationalist and writer, who excelled beyond all the kings of the earth in wisdom, knowledge, and riches!" Nalussa kept quiet.

"So, your attitude is very curious to me. I understand your feelings about his many women, but you must admire his relationship with God. I remember him telling me that after the temple dedication, the Lord appeared to him and said, 'If my people who are called by my name, will humble themselves and pray and seek my face and turn from their wicked ways, then I will hear from heaven, and I will forgive their sin and will heal their land.'[15] I found that to be profound. To think that the God of all gods would appear and speak to Solomon in such a way. Surely, you had to be in awe of God's desire to speak to Solomon?"

Nalussa put her goblet down and folded her hands in front of her chest. "Truly, I was, and even now, I am in awe to think that our Lord God spoke directly to King Solomon. What an amazing thing! How many of us would so pray that we could have that visual and audible relationship with our God? And Solomon had it! Never mind the wealth or the wisdom. God gave him that, too. Yet all that was not enough for him. He wantonly chose to disobey God! This is what I can't reconcile for myself.

"We rely on our faith in God, even though we don't see or hear Him. How many of us have had God speak to us the way He spoke

15 2 Chronicles 7:14

to Solomon? Only Moses and the prophets. But if we sin, do we not confess and turn away from our sin?"

Nalussa couldn't stop herself. "We admit our sin, sacrifice through our priests, and attempt to keep God's commands. We're not perfect or righteous, yet neither was he—you must remember that. Although he had the benefit of actually having a conversation with God, he continued to collect women, knowing that was not what God wanted. It was through this collection of his many pagan wives and concubines that he was led to abandon the Lord his God. He chose to worship and sacrifice even their children to their gods. I wonder whose children were they really? I shudder to think. Sacrificing children is abominable!"

Queen Makeda sat quietly, petting the cat in her lap, not speaking.

Nalussa tilted her head and added, "Did he also tell you that the Lord said to him, 'But if you turn away and forsake the decrees and commands I have given you and go off to serve other gods and worship them, then I will uproot Israel from my land . . . and will reject this temple I have consecrated for my Name'?"[16]

The queen put the cat to the side, stood up silently, and walked to the open window to look out into courtyard. Nalussa once again worried if she had misspoken, but the queen eventually turned to her with a question. "Suppose he asked to be forgiven? You wouldn't know. He could have asked for forgiveness before he closed his eyes for the last time. In our judgment, we readily recognize the sins of others and less frequently do we forgive them, even if God does. Yet more importantly, we don't know the conversation that the sinner might have had with God regarding his or her sin. Shouldn't we hope that the sinner, as well as all of us, would be humble enough to go to

16 2 Chronicles 7:19-20

God for forgiveness?" She stared at Nalussa. "Know this, the sacrifice of children or the sacrifice of animals will never wash our sins away. Only God can do that—regardless of the magnitude of the sin." She turned back to the window.

This subdued Nalussa and gave her pause. *What the queen says is true. I'm being judgmental. Just because King Solomon saw and heard God, then went ahead to blatantly sin, doesn't mean that God wouldn't forgive him if he had repented.*

The queen looked over her shoulder. "King Solomon gave me all that I desired, anything that I asked for. He gave me his love and a son called Menelik."

Nalussa swallowed a gasp, no longer thinking about the queen's gentle rebuke on her opinion of Solomon. Her attention snapped to Abra. *Abra has exposed her aspiration to take over Rehoboam's throne when the queen herself has a son by Solomon!*

The queen, ignoring Nalussa's stunned expression, continued, "But to your point, God has indeed plucked all that King Solomon worked for out of his hand. His kingdom has been divided between Jeroboam and Rehoboam, with Rehoboam having the smaller piece. The people are rebelling in the Northern kingdom, along the borders. His troops are always in a skirmish against Jeroboam's men. My spies tell me that Rehoboam has appointed Abijah, the son of his wife, Maacah, as the next king when the time comes."

"Maacah is the daughter of King David's son Absalom, who tried to take over the kingdom from his own father and was brutally killed for his efforts," Nalussa said knowingly.

"Yes. Even convoluted relationships are enduring. I understand that you and Adriel do not support Abra's quest for the throne?"

This was an easy answer. “We do not, Your Majesty. Our desire is to be able to stay under your protection until it is safe to go back to Judah. Neither Adriel nor I have any position of power, much less wealth, to back such a scheme, but regardless, we have no interest. And now that I know of your son . . . ” She wasn’t sure if she should continue her thought.

The queen spoke up. “Do not concern yourself with my son.”

“Indeed, Your Majesty. My concern is for my two brothers, father, and sister, who are in the path of an Egyptian invasion. I have no idea when, or even if, they will reach the city of Gia. And when they do, I don’t know if they will find our note that we wrote in a very guarded way to come here.”

“Guarded? In what way?” the queen asked.

Nalussa shook her head in a combination of anger and frustration. “We had to leave Gia because two men were curious about Abra’s behavior with the vendors in the city. She was buying expensive garments and trading her jewels that Solomon gave her, bringing their attention to her. We were protecting ourselves, as well as her and her son. We feared that they were Rehoboam’s men, trying to find us to take us back to his palace. So, we opted to leave and seek shelter with you, and at the same time, it gave me the opportunity to give you Solomon’s poem.”

“You were right about the men tracking Abra. After the three men who were tracking you were killed—presumably by Adriel and your brother, or so the gossip goes—word got back to Rehoboam, and he sent others out to find you.” She gave Nalussa a sharp look. “He’s not giving up, no matter the outside threats from Pharaoh for Solomon’s treasures or Jeroboam for his kingdom.”

Nalussa took this as a warning. Rehoboam was still interested in them.

Back in her apartments, Nalussa waited impatiently for Adriel, who was with a friend of the queen's touring her immense stables and riding magnificent horses purchased from the peninsula on the far side of the Red Sea. When he eventually returned, she waited until he was through telling her about his wonderful day to hand him a cup of wine and tell him about the conversation she'd had with the queen.

"She has a son by Solomon?" Adriel was stunned, shaking his head in near disbelief. "And Abra, in her stupidity, went to the queen to ask for help in gaining Judah from Rehoboam's heir!"

"The queen never said that she or her son was interested in Judah, but Abra must know by now about Menelik," Nalussa reasoned. "She's been spending a lot of time with the queen's scholar, Ebel."

"Spending time sleeping with him, too," he said sarcastically. "Hmm. It's all making sense now. It's common knowledge throughout the palace that Ebel had his eye on her since she arrived. She knew that but bade her time. She's calculating. She made her move on him shortly after speaking with the queen, thinking that if she could get close to one of the queen's confidantes, then he could influence the queen in helping her."

"Surely, the queen won't back her, do you think?"

"No. What would she gain but dead soldiers?" Adriel responded. "You did tell the queen that we have nothing to do with this madness?"

"Absolutely. She's not sharing anything with me, so I don't know if Abra is in danger or not."

"Nalussa, she is. Anyone connected with her will be as well. She's put herself and her son in an untenable situation. The queen might be 'godly,' but don't think for one minute she will tolerate an insurgence on Judah originating from her kingdom or a threat to her son, even if she's not interested in Judah."

After supper, Nalussa looked for Abra, finding her with her lover, Ebel. They were in an intense discussion, facing one another in a garden.

"Can we speak in private?" Nalussa asked as they turned on her in mutual annoyance.

"Whatever you want to say to me, you can say in front of Ebel," Abra promptly answered, smoothing her robes.

"Then I have nothing to say to you." Nalussa turned to walk away. She didn't want Ebel involved. She didn't know him to trust him.

"Wait! Ebel, will you give us a few minutes?" Ebel glowered openly at Nalussa but left.

"What is so important you have to interrupt me in an important discussion?" Abra demanded, hands on her hips.

Nalussa didn't waste time. "You do know that the queen has her own son by Solomon?"

"Yes. I just found that out. I know what you're thinking. Heber and I are in danger. We're not. I'm told that the queen won't help me, and I should have been more circumspect before speaking to her in confidence. But I wasn't, and there's no way to correct it, other than grovel at her feet, which I will do if I have to.

"Ebel was advising me on the matter when you interrupted. He will go before the queen and ask her to forgive me because I had no idea she, too, has a son by Solomon. No one ever mentioned him.

How was I to know? Anyway, he'll smooth it over for me, and I'll simply ask for forgiveness in my naiveté and ignorance. Surely, she can't punish me because I didn't know?"

"I don't know the queen's mind. If Ebel can help you, then by all means, rely on him. I have no sway with the queen, and less so, Adriel. As long as you're aware of the situation, I'll leave you to Ebel to work things out with the queen."

"This is really none of your concern, and I don't need or want your advice when it comes to my relationship with the queen. You're only of interest to her because you were Solomon's concubine. I, on the other hand, have far better standing being the mother of one of Solomon's sons. So, please, stay out of my way," Abra warned.

"I will stay out of your way. For truth, if the queen thinks that her son should be on the throne of Judah, there would be no contest." Nalussa left the courtyard.

The following evening, they all dined at the queen's table. Adriel was beside Nalussa, with Abra seated across from them. Ebel was to her right, a surprise because he usually sat in a better seat closer to the queen.

There was unconcealed strain between Abra and Ebel, who carefully spoke to one another. Adriel and Nalussa were also cautious among the guests, rendering polite answers to inconsequential questions. The entire gathering seemed off to Nalussa. Everyone appeared watchful as they waited for the queen and her entourage to seat themselves at the head of the banquet table.

The queen herself was stunning, once again clothed in sparkling white linen trimmed in gold cloth. She wore huge gold earrings studded with pearls, a thin gold band wrapped around her forehead, and bangles flashing rubies and emeralds on both of her wrists. Around her neck was a series of intricately woven gold chains dripping with pearls and chunks of lapis lazuli. Her dark eyes were rimmed with kohl, and her thick, black hair shimmered with gold dust.

Abra was also dressed beautifully in the Shebanite style of simple design but sporting her own jewels she still had that Solomon had given her. Nalussa didn't remember the assortment of necklaces she currently had hanging around her neck, but those dangling from her ears and embracing her wrists were from the kingdom of Judah.

Once all were seated and the opening prayers made, the guests were served, and chatter began. "Ebel gifted me with these lovely necklaces." Abra lightly stroked her neck. "He has wonderful taste." Ebel smiled slightly and ducked his head. "Look, he gave me these lovely gold bangles, too!" She held up her hands for the guests sitting close by to see.

"They are lovely." Nalussa, who never wore jewelry because she didn't have any, agreed. She more than once chastised herself for not accepting jewels from Solomon. Now, she and Adriel depended upon the gold and silver that Solomon had paid for her, and that was dwindling, albeit slowly. The good news was that as long as they were living under the queen's protection, they were free of any type of payments.

The evening passed without anything unusual happening, except that Nalussa detected a tension emanating from the queen as she spoke to her guests, ignoring any conversation or eye contact with Ebel and Abra.

As they walked back to their apartments after the meal, Ebel and Abra continued onto the garden without so much as a goodbye.

It hurt Nalussa that Abra had rejected her so these last few months. She was even denied the joy of being with Heber because he was always protected and governed by a servant, who made it clear that Heber could not be alone with her. He was protected as if he was the anointed king-to-be.

"What was your impression of the queen and Abra?" Adriel asked when they were alone in the hallway.

"The queen was polite and coolly engaging as a royal but not behaving as she usually does in her charming, warm way. It seemed she was distracted. As for Abra and Ebel, they seemed preoccupied, too. I don't know. I'm just conjecturing."

"That was my impression, too." Adriel put his hand lightly on her back, steering her through the archway to their main room. A light breeze was wafting in from the high, open windows, and the moon was a sliver in the sky.

Settling on a settee, Nalussa sighed. "I feel that something is amiss. It has to be. Tonight was too tense. The request by Abra to the queen to help her take over the throne of Judah for her son must be on the mind of the queen. The queen wouldn't want her son to be usurped, even if he was not eyeing the throne of Judah, but she has to see Abra as a threat—a threat to the kingdom of Sheba's relationship with Judah."

Adriel sat beside her. "Right now, the only worth of Judah is Solomon's treasures, which admittedly is huge; but if Pharaoh himself is going to invade, the queen wouldn't want her kingdom caught up in that contest either. I don't know the role Ebel is playing. He's one of Solomon's scholars given to the queen. At heart, he's a Hebrew, and

Judah is his home. Obviously, he is in sympathy with Abra, and the queen knows it."

"The queen is a smart woman. My guess is should Abra admit she misspoke, the queen will confine Abra, Heber, and Ebel, ensuring they both understand she won't tolerate their ideas. On the other hand, she could easily kill them, getting rid of the problem altogether."

"I don't think she'll do that. She loved Solomon and still honors him. She wouldn't resort to murdering his son or the mother of his son."

"I know enough about palace intrigue to understand that children at any age can be a threat. They grow up and become powerful in their own right."

The next morning brought chaos. Soldiers stormed into Nalussa and Adriel's apartment yelling threats and demands, barely giving them time to wake and get dress.

"Get up! Get dressed! Hurry. The queen is waiting!" Shocked and terrified, they hurriedly dressed and put on their sandals.

Two soldiers grabbed them roughly by the arms, pulling them down the long hallway and down a steep flight of stone stairs into the throne room and into the presence of the queen, who was sitting like a stone statue on her ivory-carved throne. An advisor was planted on each side of her. Lines of soldiers and administrators filled the hall.

"I gave you protection, and you do this to me?" she fumed, pointing at them as they were pushed on their knees before her. Guards with swords stood over them, ready for any order.

Nalussa and Adriel, trembling in confusion and disbelief, kept repeating, "What? What is wrong?"

"Your friend, her son, and lover have disappeared!" She pointed her scepter at them. Shaking it, she demanded, "Where did they go?"

"We know nothing of that! Please believe us!" Adriel pleaded.

"They left us to go into the garden last night, and we retired to our apartments," Nalussa cried out. "We don't know anything. They don't talk to us!"

The court broke out in argument, conversation, and disbelief.

"They are lying!" someone said.

Another shouted, "They are a part of the rebellion and conspiracy for Judah that will bring disaster upon Sheba!"

Another cried, "Kill the Hebrews!"

Nalussa pleaded above the din, "We don't know anything! We are not a part of any rebellion!"

The queen held up the scepter for quiet. "Clear the hall, except the imperial guards and my advisors." Slowly and begrudgingly, everyone emptied the hall.

"Get up!" she commanded.

Adriel and Nalussa struggled to their feet with the rough help of two of the guards.

The queen's chief advisor came around from the side of the throne, stepping close to Adriel and Nalussa. "Abra, Ebel, Heber, and assorted assistants—we don't know how many—have escaped. They've taken time to plan this. All the men who guard the horses and chariots at night were poisoned by a contaminate in their drinking water. They've stolen our fastest horses and chariots. We have sent soldiers out after them, but they are hours ahead of us. Likely, they crossed the Red Sea into Egypt. Save your lives and tell us where they went!"

Adriel fell to his knees again. "Your Majesty. We don't know. We've told you all along that Abra's plans for putting her son on Judah's throne has nothing to do with us."

In tears, Nalussa knelt down beside Adriel with her hand across his shoulders, both heads bowed. "Queen Makeda. You know me. We've spent hours, months together. You know I don't lie. We've never supported Abra, and we certainly did not aid her and Ebel in any way. And if we did, why are we still here and not with them?"

"You were betrayed," the advisor barked. "They left without you!"

A voice from the back of the hall spoke loudly. "Your Majesty, Adriel was with the chief trainer touring your stables and riding your horses. Surely, he knows something!"

"Where is the chief trainer?" demanded the advisor.

"He is dead. Poisoned, too."

"Put them in the dungeons. Separately!" the queen ordered, and the soldiers took them away.

CHAPTER TWENTY-FOUR

Abra was frightened, although Ebel had organized their escape beautifully. They had left immediately after the banquet with the queen, leaving Nalussa and Adriel in the hallway on the way to their rooms. She had prearranged for Heber, along with his nurse, to meet her and Ebel at the queen's stables. Arriving at the appointed entryway, they were greeted by a half-a-dozen men loyal to Ebel who were not Shebanites but Hebrews. When Solomon had given Ebel to the queen, he had also given Ebel six servants. These servants were more than agreeable to support Ebel, the consort to the queen mother and her young son, who would soon be king. For years, they had longed to return to Jerusalem in their homeland, Judah. They had no loyalty to the Queen of Sheba and certainly not to the spoiled, arrogant Rehoboam, who was so different than his father, Solomon. They were more than willing to support a new king, whose mother would grant them status, land, and riches.

Yet Abra was scared. The night was dark, but the shadows did not hide the many men who had died a painful and gruesome death by poison. They lay about the stable at odd angles with foamy grimaces. Flies buzzed around the open eyes and mouths, even in the dark. The horses were skittish and nervous smelling death, but Ebel's men smoothly took the needed horses out of their stables, soothing them as they hooked them up to their associated chariots. This was done quickly and cleanly.

Abra took Heber from his nurse in the attempt to quiet his crankiness at being awake at this late hour. Her heart pounding and head buzzing near panic, she nuzzled his warm head for her own comfort. "I ask we leave here swiftly and safely," she mumbled to any god who might hear her.

Abra gave Heber back to his nurse and scuttled alongside Ebel. "We must get moving! Anyone can come by and see us. We need a head start! If they capture us, they'll kill us and my son! Our plans will be dashed!"

"Woman. Enough! It is under control. Shefti, take Abra and put her in my chariot. Take the nurse and the boy and put them in your chariot. Get the men ready to leave now." The man did as he was told.

As they left the stables, they cantered along a trail parallel to the city wall. A young Egyptian slave met them at a hidden gate that opened up onto a deserted path used by soldiers to quickly exit the city grounds without having to go through the main city gate. The guards at the gate were dead and hidden in the shadows. Hopping in Ebel's chariot, the slave directed them away from the perimeter of the city wall and out into the night. The two watchmen on this side of the wall were dead, too.

Once beyond the city, Abra finally breathed in relief. "If we can get ahead of the queen's soldiers by five hours, we should be free!"

Ebel put his arm around her and sat back in the chariot as the young slave drove the horses. He looked behind him, and the others followed steadily. "By the time the guards and stable keepers are found, we'll be well ahead. They'll never catch up with us, nor will they readily figure out where we've gone. The queen will send some soldiers toward the Red Sea and others north to Dedan. Once they discover we're on our way to Egypt, it will be too late to find us."

"Won't they see the tracks made by the horses and the chariot wheels?" the Egyptian slave asked, concerned for his own life.

"We're on a well-traveled route. The caravans go back and forth. Who is to say whose tracks are whose?" Ebel answered confidently.

"You've made arrangements for our barge, Ebel?" Abra worried.

"Of course, I have! The barge master is waiting for us now. I told him I wasn't sure when we would arrive but to be ready. Enough of your foolish worry, Abra! This is why I am your advisor. When and if they discover where we've gone, we'll be under the protection of Pharaoh, and the queen will never go up against him."

Abra was comforted. This plan was going to work, particularly since Ebel had already worked out communication between Pharaoh and her by bribing messengers between the two kingdoms. The Queen of Sheba had no idea the duplicity that lay in the heart of her teacher. Abra played Ebel's ambition by promising him power behind the throne of a child-king.

She laid it out to him. "If you would help me form an alliance with Pharaoh, I will make you chief advisor to the throne. As queen mother, I will rule until Heber comes of age; but you would be my advisor, and I would guarantee you continued power even when Heber is king."

Her plan for Pharaoh wasn't as simple, and although both schemes for Pharaoh and Ebel had real risk, they were achievable. If Pharaoh's mercenaries would fight Rehoboam's diminished troops for Heber's rightful place in ruling Judah, then she would pledge Judah and Benjamin territories to pay tribute to him as well as to

King Heber. She would also agree to split the treasures of Solomon without further bloodshed of his soldiers. He'd argued, of course, that he would just invade Jerusalem and raid the temple, but she had demurred. "Why risk failure on a one-time raid when once my son is on the throne, you will have a life-time of tribute and I will willingly split Solomon's treasures with you without further strife?"

Of course, she was more cunning than that. Once Heber was on the throne, she would honor the tribute, but not evenly; and once she assessed the treasure, the split, too, would not be even. Pharaoh would never know.

Her worry dissipated. She smiled as they sped along through the night, Ebel dozing and the slave leading the way. She was skillful in making men happy. Pharaoh wanted her. Perhaps she could get pregnant with his child. In any case, she would play both men. There might be a lot more to gain, and this time, she would be smarter in managing her plans. She was young, healthy, beautiful, and ruthless.

***

There was little light. The air was fetid and stifling. Nalussa had cried so hard, her eyes were swollen nearly shut. Pushed into the cell, she fell and slumped on the damp floor amid rat droppings and dried human feces. She gagged and threw up. Scuttling away from her own vomit, she pulled herself close to the bars, where the air was clearer, and the smell lessened.

Oh, God, please have mercy on Adriel and me. I don't know what to say. This is all so wrong. We had nothing to do with Abra's escape or the deaths of those men. Please, please, Lord, help us! She hung her head and cried tears she thought were long dried up.

Time passed. Bread and water were placed through an open slot in the bars, and although in anguish with little appetite, it was imperative that she eat to sustain what little strength she had. She cleared a small area by the bars to sleep on the stone floor and used a far corner to relieve herself. The smell of the tiny, airless cell was overpowering. Never had she dreamed she would be in such dire circumstances, and she continually thought of Adriel. Drifting in and out of sleep, praying and crying was all she could do.

Whenever she was given food and water, which was infrequently, she begged her guard to speak with the queen. "Please, have mercy on me and my husband. We are innocent. We had nothing to do with the escape. Please, let me speak with the queen or one of her advisors!"

"You and every other prisoner. Pray to your God. He's your only hope!"

She had no idea of time. Was it morning, afternoon, or night? Food was given at odd times and sporadically. She was so hungry and thirsty, yet she was always grateful she hadn't been tortured. What they did to women was unimaginable. Time continued to pass.

She was awakened by keys jangling in the lock. The door swung open, screeching on its rusted hinges. Struggling to sit up, she outstretched her hand. In the gloom, a large, calloused hand hauled her to her feet. Swaying, faint from lack of food and water, she stared up at the guard, who grabbed her by her waist and threw her over his shoulder. She could stand but was far too weak to walk the distance from the dungeon to the palace. The sunlight burned her eyes, and she weakly pulled her head scarf over her eyes. The man placed her in a cart and pushed her across the prison grounds toward the palace.

Once they got to the steps leading up to one of the many entrances, servants appeared and helped her onto a litter and brought her back to her apartments, before making a side trip to the baths.

She trembled as she was gently placed in a warm bath. The servants cut her long, tangled hair short, then washed her matted and lice-infested hair with special soap. The smell was overpowering. Her body was tenderly bathed and lightly rubbed with healing oil covering the scabs and bites from insects and fleas. Her nails and toenails were trimmed, and her feet rubbed carefully with pumice. They tipped a cup of sweetened coconut water to her lips. She tried to swallow and not gag.

Back in her room, she was clothed in clean linens and fed small amounts of fresh bread, nuts, and fruit. It was astounding how the body had come back to life, for surely, she thought she was dying a slow death. Weeks of deprivation had its consequences. As the servants melted away, she looked up in surprise to see a man hobbling toward her with the sunlight from the windows at his back. He was cast in shadow, but she knew it was Adriel. Barely able to get up, she halting walked toward him, and they fell into each other's arms, crying.

"I never thought we'd get out alive!" Nalussa wept as he held her carefully.

Pulling away, he looked her in the eyes. "I never thought I'd see you again. Did they hurt you?"

"No. They ignored me. Fed and gave me water occasionally. You?"

"I've spent the last few hours drinking small amounts of coconut water and nibbling fruit and nuts. I'm feeling better."

"But did they hurt you?" Nalussa could see the pain in his eyes.

"I couldn't tell them what I didn't know." Pulling away from her, he led her to the couch, holding her hand. They said little to each other. What was there to say? She saw he was in pain but wasn't going to badger him about what happened. He'd tell her in due time. In the meantime, they were finally together, safe.

"I've got to lie down." Gingerly, he lay on his side with a grateful smile on his face. He reached for her and closed his eyes with a soft sigh. He fell fast asleep.

Thanking God for their blessing, she lay down by his side, looking at his worn, tired face. She, too, fell asleep.

In the evening, they were awakened with more food and now a little wine. Exhausted, both mentally and physically, they spoke little, each cataloging their experiences in their minds but not quite ready to share, as servants buzzed around them like bees. Exhausted after the small meal, they kissed each other and fell back asleep holding hands.

The next morning, both were feeling better but still worn, weary, and confused. They barely had the opportunity to speak with each other when the queen's chief advisor barged in and said, "As soon as you are stronger, the queen will see you. But now, our doctors will see to your wounds and health." Bowing, he quickly left.

Immediately, a servant entered, taking Nalussa and Adriel to separate rooms to be examined and attended to by the palace doctors. When they were back together again, Adriel was visibly wincing and sitting cautiously on cushions, careful to avoid contact with his back. In pain, he placed a small alabaster jar on the table and asked Nalussa to help him take off his robe.

Without his clothes on, she gasped, putting her hands to her mouth. "What did they do to you?" His torso was covered with round sores about his back, arms, chest, and stomach.

"They kept me from sleeping and burned me with coals. But I couldn't tell them anything because I didn't know anything! I'm amazed I slept last night for the pain, but I was so sleep-deprived that I just closed my eyes and was dead asleep."

Nalussa hid her tears and reached for the jar on the table. "Is this ointment?"

"Yes. It's to be lightly rubbed on the burns three times a day, and it was just done by the doctor, but I can't stand the feel of cloth against my wounds."

"Oh, Adriel. I'm so sorry all of this happened! If I hadn't insisted on taking Abra with us to begin with!"

"Don't. You cared about her and her baby. We can't go back in time. We have to think about now."

Nalussa sadly nodded. "Yes. We must wait for the queen's next move."

The days moved slowly as Adriel healed and Nalussa attended to him. Their routine was carefully watched. Meals were always at a particular hour; exercise in the courtyard was monitored; but in their apartments, they were left alone. They had the opportunity to speak in private without being watched or listened to but were still careful of their discussions.

Nalussa's concern was not only for their future under the queen's protection, but also of her brother and family. She hadn't given up on them, but she didn't hold out much hope either. She was angered by Abra's treachery, but there was little she could do about it.

"Nalussa, let it be. Abra has chosen a very dangerous path to take. While it's possible that Heber might have a possibility for the throne, it is very unlikely. Rehoboam has a strong army, contrary to what Abra and Ebel might think."

Nalussa put her hand to her forehead. "Yes, I'm trying to get her betrayal out of my mind, but we both could have died if we weren't taken from the dungeons when we were. Did she even think of what might become of us because of her foolhardy schemes?" She sighed and stood up. "The good from all of this is my brother is no longer involved with her. I only pray that he and my family are safe, wherever they may be."

Adriel tilted his head and shrugged his shoulders. "It's difficult to guess. If we are allowed out of our apartments, we could go to the city gates and ask the travelers if they have seen anyone meeting the description of your family. The caravans, in particular, might have some news."

"Yes, we should do that. If we can leave these rooms. I'm going to send word to the queen through our servants that we want an audience. I hope she finds it in her heart to see us and explain our future here. Surely, she must know by virtue of our release that we were not involved with Abra's deceitfulness."

"One could only hope," Adriel responded.

CHAPTER TWENTY-FIVE

Long after clearing the port and finding rest and refreshment in villages along the way, Ebel and Abra, along with the Egyptian and the other Hebrews, continued on toward Kleopolis, where Pharaoh would be waiting for them at one of his many residences.

They had easily evaded the soldiers of Sheba, for by the time the militias made it to the port, they were well on their way to Lower Egypt. Like all secrets that are never kept, it was now known in Sheba that they were likely headed to Pharaoh, along with a booty of stolen gold and jewels from the queen's treasury.

"This way is the same route we came by caravan nearly a year ago when we were making our way to Sheba," Abra commented as they passed a familiar spot where other caravans were resting before continuing on to the port.

"Yes," agreed Ebel. "This really is the only safe and quick way north to either Lower Egypt and Judah or south to Upper Egypt and Sheba. We'll stop ahead for rest as well. Off this road is a protected town where we can spend the night."

"I always found it strange that Lower Egypt was closer to Judah than Upper Egypt," Abra remarked.

"The Nile River flows from the south to the north, so the regions are named for their location on the Nile," Ebel patiently explained. Abra shrugged.

They stopped in Naj, a city, though small, that was bustling and obviously prosperous. Well-fed vendors were busy with customers trading for a variety of spices, including coriander, fennel, juniper, cumin, garlic, and thyme. The air was filled with a mixture of scents, not unpleasant. As Ebel's men arranged for stables and rooms, traders were bartering for the precious spices, planning to sell them in Egypt, or taking them as far as Sheba while other travelers were waiting to buy small amounts for personal use.

Satisfied Heber was fed by his nurse, Abra took the opportunity to look around at the many people milling about, eyeing their clothing and guessing their status. Some were obvious traders; others were wealthy with servants; and still others were worn and weary from travel. She was happy to be out of Sheba and looking forward to the future with relish. In her mind's eye, she pictured power over Judah. How ironic to be living in Solomon's palace as queen mother!

Her daydreaming was cut short. She gasped. Across the market place, looking directly at her with shock and utmost confusion, was Jasper. Her eyes went wide, and her heart seized as she met his stare. Her body trembled in fear. At the same moment, Ebel, looking elsewhere and talking with his Egyptian servant, absently took her arm. "Come, we need to get our rooms."

She allowed herself to be led away as Jasper, dumbfounded, could only stare at her. Her heart thudded. "Hurry, Ebel, I . . . I need to rest and make sure Heber is fed!"

Ebel looked down at her in surprise. “The nurse has already fed Heber. You saw her. He’s fine, but I, too, would like to rest. Come this way. Let’s get out of this crowd.” They followed the Egyptian servant down a congested alleyway.

By the time they reached their rooms, Abra’s shaking was subsiding. “Ebel! I saw Jasper. He saw me! How is it possible of all the places in Egypt and all the masses of people in a market place, we should come across each other?”

The man before her went tense in surprise. Regaining his composure, he held up a finger. “You are not his legal wife. The marriage was never consummated. He deserted you—and for how long now? You have no obligation to him.”

“But what if he finds out where we’re staying? What will I say to him?”

“Nothing. Should he even find you, it doesn’t matter. I’m your husband now. He’ll have to confront me. Rest assured, he’ll leave you alone.”

But he didn’t. As Abra’s party left first thing in the morning, Jasper was waiting at the city gate as travelers made their way out of the city toward their next stop.

“Abra! Abra! What is happening?” Jasper shouted, running alongside her chariot as the horses came up to the gates. “Who is this man?”

Ebel instructed the Egyptian to slow down and shouted, “She is no longer yours, Jasper! You deserted her for far too long. I’ve taken her as my wife.”

“No! Abra! Where are you going? Where is Nalussa?” Jasper pleaded in desperation. “What has happened?”

"She is not yours! And where we are going is not of your concern." Ebel nodded to his servant to forward the horses.

Defeated, Jasper stopped following. Pitying the young man now standing with a desperate look on his face, Abra called back to him, "Nalussa is in Sheba." She resolved not to look back again, nor think of him. He was buried in the past.

Arriving in the city of Keopolis, Abra was overwhelmed at the vast structures and pylons that lined the streets, the array of temples and chapels dedicated to the different gods, and the clamor of Egyptians worshipping openly in the gods' alcoves.

As they approached the palace, the heat became more intense as masses of people, crowding each other, swarmed the grounds actively selling and buying. The Egyptian driver plowed through the square as the throngs parted angrily, hopping out of the way of the sweating regal horses and overpowering chariots. He stopped at the palace gates and presented a parchment to the guard with Pharaoh's seal. Immediately, they were admitted. Once in the courtyard, servants and slaves met them to attend to the horses and usher them up the stairway and into the palace.

Abra noted that the courtyard and palace were radically different than that of Solomon's palace and grounds, which were orderly and stately, or the Queen of Sheba's, which were fanciful and lush. Pharaoh's buildings bespoke power in the vastness and complexity of the buildings, statues, and other structures. The ominous specter of birdlike gods peered down from architraves or moldings and frames displayed around the many doorways and windows. Perhaps the designs were to instill intimidation from visitors and dignitaries, she mused. Figures of animal-manlike deities lined the courtyard, each on an imposing pedestal and in their own alcove, while near-naked soldiers, girded with golden spears, lined the steps leading to the chambers of the palace.

Barely a word was spoken by Abra to Ebel, who was busy ordering his men to get their boxes of treasures off the chariots and onto litters provided by the Egyptian servants. Soldiers hungrily eyed Abra. She shrank back behind Ebel as he strode up the stairs led by an officer of the guard. The atmosphere was menacing. Quickly, she followed Ebel as Heber began to wail. She wanted to wail, too, but this was about power, and she was determined to behave regally and not in fear or trepidation. She had the whole of Judah and Benjamin territories potentially in her hands; and although much smaller than the original kingdom, Judah, as a whole, was very wealthy, since it included Solomon's temple and treasures. Jerusalem was the centerpiece.

Ebel met first with Pharaoh, while Abra dressed nervously in their appointed rooms. She wanted to make a strong impression and made certain she was dressed immaculately, made up in the Egyptian fashion with heavy kohl outlining her eyes and lips stained with potent berry juice. She wore simple, gold jewelry around her head, neck, wrists, and ankles. Her long, dark hair was exposed and gathered loosely down her back.

Before Ebel returned, a servant summoned her, and she followed into Pharaoh's presence. She bowed demurely as she entered Pharaoh's chamber. He was alone. Where was Ebel?

"Please, sit. I've had an interesting conversation with your chief advisor, Ebel. He's touring my palace while we meet. I'm intrigued with your desire to take over the throne of Judah for Solomon's son, Heber. Your thought process interests me, but I confess I'm not fully supportive yet. Ebel was helpful, but I believe I would like more from you." He looked away from her toward a servant, who brought forward refreshment and set drinks and delicacies on a low table that was between them. The servant left the room. They were alone.

Abra appreciated Pharaoh's looks. He was lean, brown, and very strong. His arms were muscled, and his legs were straight and sturdy. He, too, was dressed simply in only a linen wrap around his waist, gathered with a gold and ruby clasp, and a short robe draped across his shoulders, also clasped with gold. He was handsome and commanding.

Impressed with her quarry and feeling her own power, she asked, "How can I make you more supportive? Surely, you know all the details of my plan from Ebel. What more can I do to convince you?"

He smiled and popped a sweet in his mouth. He stood. He unclasped his robe from his shoulders and the wrap from his loins.

Afterward, Abra smiled. "Your Majesty, did I convince you, or do you need more convincing?"

Pharaoh laughed out loud. "Your reputation precedes you! I heard delightful things about you from servants in Solomon's bed chamber."

Abra pulled away in surprise.

"Oh, don't be surprised. Special concubines are always rated and gossiped about, no matter who is the king. But I'm very curious about Solomon's favored concubine, a woman named Nalussa. I understand she's more beautiful than you with intelligence and wit. Can you tell me about her? You escaped with her. She's still in Sheba?" Pharaoh fanned himself with a palm frond. "Yes, so many lovely women are scattered among many kingdoms. Even Makeda, Queen of Sheba, is a beauty. I hear Nalussa looks similar to her but is even more beautiful."

Abra barely concealed her jealousy and anger. How dare he speak of Nalussa in her presence! Ah, but she would play him. Turning to him, she lightly stroked his chest. "But is she as clever as I am?"

Later, Pharaoh offered her a smug smile. "I admire your talents and your ambition. My advisors are discussing your proposal proffered by Ebel, who is competent and thorough. But how will I know you will treat me fairly? I could stand to lose a great deal . . . "

"Pharaoh, how? Rehoboam has limited troops. More than half the kingdom was split in favor of your protégé, Jeroboam, who I'm sure could help you from the north if you needed it, which I doubt. After all, why would you want to reward him with our plunder when you know that your mercenaries are far stronger than Jeroboam's armies?"

"I wasn't concerned about Rehoboam's or Jeroboam's men; I'm concerned about you and how you'll divide the bounty of Solomon's treasures and the tribute from the territories of Judah and Benjamin."

She sighed. "I'm not stupid. To lie to you would only draw your wrath, and I need your support. So, look at it this way. I'm buying your favor."

Pharaoh nodded. "It's true. If you falsely deal with me, you will incur my wrath. I can be a force you don't want to test."

CHAPTER TWENTY-SIX

A loud rap against the door frame startled a dozing Adriel, who was half-listening to his wife struggle with a stringed instrument he never could pronounce. Both looked to the door as a servant entered and said, "The queen would like your presence in her chambers immediately. I'm here to escort you."

Knowing that the servant would not know what it was about—or even if he did, he would not tell them—Adriel and Nalussa plucked their robes and silently followed, both worrying what to expect. Since they had been released from prison, they had not been allowed to leave their apartments nor did they have any interaction with the queen or her staff. They cast meaningful looks at each other but kept silent. They would soon find out. No use in speculating.

As they entered the great chamber, the queen was on her throne, and as usual, she was flanked by her advisors and body guards, who stared at them without any expression, like stone statues. Before her, standing with uncertainty, was Nalussa's family, huddled together. Without permission or thinking, Nalussa ran to them crying and embracing her father, younger brother, and sister, and her champion, Jasper.

"I prayed you would come! Praise God!" she said through tears. The queen motioned her servants to bring in couches for all to sit, along with refreshments as Nalussa and Adriel spoke excitedly with her family. After several minutes, Nalussa turned to the queen, not knowing what she should say, but the queen stood and walked down the dais to the huddled group of weary, expectant travelers.

"I understand this is Jasper, your brother with your family. I told you I would give them safe shelter, and I will. He has also told us that he saw Abra and is confused why she was in Naj with another man, who claimed to be her husband." She stopped speaking and looked over to one of her female servants. "Please take these two young people to Nalussa and Adriel's quarters and see to it that they are fed, bathed, and given rest. Please make arrangements for the family to be set up in apartments next to Nalussa and Adriel."

Nalussa's younger brother and sister knew better than to protest and followed the servant out of the room. The queen sat down with her visitors and wasted no time airing her concerns. "If Abra and Ebel were in Naj, it is likely they are on their way to one of Pharaoh's palaces in Kleopolis. It is also probable that they were able to get word to him about Abra's desire for the throne for her son. I'm guessing he's willing to hear them out."

Jasper swung an incredulous look at his sister. "Abra is going after the throne of Judah? With Pharaoh's help?"

The queen cut in. "It appears that way. For Pharaoh, he gets a foothold in Judah, since Abra and Ebel have no supporters in Judah that I'm aware of. If Pharaoh can place Abra's son, Heber, on the throne, he'll have power in Judah, ongoing tribute, plus Solomon's treasures, regardless of any compensation or cooperation Abra might say she will give him."

Jasper shakily took a cup of wine from a servant. "I can't believe she would do something like this."

"Jasper. She's always wanted to claim the throne for Heber—" Nalussa began.

The queen interrupted. "I also have a son by Solomon, and my concern is that if she gets Pharaoh's support and if she is able to overthrow Rehoboam, what would stop her from coming after my son either by assassin or army, knowing that he, being older, would be a possible contender?"

Nalussa's father spoke up. "Are you and your son interested in the throne of Judah?"

"Absolutely not," the queen snapped. "But I will not place my kingdom, my son, or myself in jeopardy. So, I aim to put a stop to this. I don't care if Pharaoh raids Solomon's temple, as was his original plan, but I will not allow this evil woman to gain power and threaten my son."

The room went quiet, except for the soft swish of the palm fronds the servants waved to move the air. The queen looked directly at Nalussa. "I don't believe that either you or your husband had anything to do with Abra's plotting. We were able to corroborate your story with one of our spies. I'm not saying I'm sorry for your treatment because at the time, I had no idea what your involvement was. Now I know. You were both telling the truth.

"Enjoy your family while you can. Time and circumstances change our course. You have safe haven here, but I can't control God's will." The queen stood, dismissing them.

The family was shown out of the queen's chambers to the apartments of Nalussa and her husband until their lodging was readied. When they finally had a moment alone, Jasper went to Nalussa. "I can't believe all of this! She left the safety of Sheba to pursue the throne of Judah for her son? Is she crazy? After all we did for her? What about the child? His life is now in jeopardy!"

"I know, Jasper." She gently patted his sleeve. "You risked your life for her, as well as for me. But she was caught up in the lavish lifestyle of Solomon. I don't think she could ever move beyond not having jewels, servants, comforts, and now, even power."

"But I thought that she was finally putting those thoughts behind her. She led me to believe she was adapting to her situation. What made her change her mind?"

"She's calculating, my brother. She betrayed our friendship, seeking a higher glory than what you could give her."

Jasper sighed. "She's between two very influential rulers, who will not take her ambition lightly—especially since she herself has no soldiers or supporters."

"That's why she went to Pharaoh. I can understand why he might be a willing listener. But know this: Pharaoh will want his share and more."

Jasper ran a hand through his beard. "I'm also concerned with the queen's power. She'll protect her son at all costs, even if Abra or Pharaoh have armies."

Nalussa sat down and pulled her brother to sit beside her. "Abra is clever and, to a degree, very bold in her ambition, but she doesn't think things through. Don't forget, Ebel is also a great influencer. He sees power in this for him as well. It's a dangerous scheme they have laid out, but there is nothing we can do about it. And we're here. Together. Safe."

Jasper sat quietly thinking, then said, "I've spent all this time traveling and suffering for Abra and our family. She has betrayed me in the worst way."

"Jasper, my dear brother. Move on. It's in God's hands." Nalussa suddenly stood, burdened with worry for poor little Heber. Looking down at him, she said, as much for herself as for her brother, "God is kind. He's brought us all together, and we are safe now. We can stay here as long as we want, and hopefully, when Rehoboam is no longer on the throne, we can go back home. Trust God."

Jasper shook his head in hopelessness. "Go home? When we went through Gia, there were even more soldiers at the garrison than when I left. The talk is constantly of invading Judah in the upcoming months. Rehoboam—he will be in for a fight for his life. It will be years before we can go home, if at all. And as for Abra and Heber? Who knows what lies ahead for them? Certainly, manipulation if not death. No, Nalussa, I'm afraid we can't go home for some time."

Several days later, a servant and guard entered the apartments. "Nalussa. Please come with us," they said simply.

Adriel jumped up. "Where are you taking her?" They didn't answer. "I demand to know where you are taking her!" His voice rose in panic. Jasper came running from one of the adjacent rooms.

The guard stepped forward with a spear ready. "She is to come with us now. Step back, or you will all be in danger."

"Adriel, it's all right. I'll be back shortly." Nalussa got up from her lounge and hurried between the guard and her husband and brother. Reluctantly, the men stepped back, Adriel kissing her on the cheek, letting her go.

She was led to a different part of the palace she had never seen. Her anxiety increased with each step, having no idea what this was all about. She was shown into a room with the queen's familiar advisors, excepting one, but Queen Makeda was not present.

"Sit," ordered one man, plump and important. Obediently, she sat in front of four men, all of whom looked her over like a fine piece of jewelry. She could well imagine what was going on in their minds, but she was at their mercy and that of the queen. She waited.

The elder spoke first. "We must stop Abra and her son from aligning themselves with Pharaoh and making their way to Judah. It's been verified by one of our runners. Abra has indeed gone to Pharaoh, but we have a plan for this. You are to go to Kleopolis and be presented to Pharaoh as King Solomon's favorite concubine. You will be offered to him. This will be attractive to him on a number of levels. First, it will solidify his overreach to Solomon's throne, having it made known that he is in possession of Solomon's favorite concubine. Second, it will threaten Rehoboam, who will soon know that not only will Pharaoh have you, but he also has Abra, who is claiming Judah on behalf of her and Solomon's son."

Another advisor smiled broadly as he lightly fluffed his robe to hang more attractively. "Pharaoh would have two of Solomon's concubines that Rehoboam is so desperately after!" He then rubbed his hands together.

The fourth man simply scowled. Obviously, he was apart from the other three. He was not overfed, soft, or nattily dressed. He stood strong in simple, yet well-made garments and solid footwear. On his hip was a short sword that none of the other men carried.

Nalussa looked at them dumbfounded. *What are they thinking? Would Pharaoh ever entertain the idea of me voluntarily leaving the safety of Sheba to ask to be one of his concubines?*

"Why would I voluntarily leave the safety of Sheba?"

"You won't. You'll be 'abducted' by a mercenary." The advisor tilted his head toward the man with the sword who was standing detachedly but never taking his eyes off Nalussa. "You'll be offered to Pharaoh for a handsome price, of course, and we believe that Pharaoh will be delighted. Once you're ensconced in the palace, this will give you and our friend here the opportunity to find out where Abra and her son are."

She sat dumbfounded, not knowing what to say.

"You see, you'll be viewed as a highly valuable prize. You will have to play along with the ploy."

"What if Pharaoh doesn't want me or refuses to pay for me?"

One elder leered. "Oh, my. He will want you. Trust me. The benefits of him having you play so strongly against Rehoboam."

Annoyed at their confidence, she demanded, "What would stop him from just taking me?"

"He won't. He is Pharaoh. He would never force himself on a woman. Kill her maybe or throw her in a dungeon, but never rape," the man with the sword said quietly. "I know him. I've worked with him."

The room was eerily quiet, and even the others became uncomfortable with the talk of rape. Nalussa wiped the sweat from her brow with her head scarf. "So, I am just a decoy while we find out where Abra is and what her routine is, and then it seems your plan would be to abduct Abra and Heber?" She glared at the man. "This will be complicated. Even I know that. How will we all get out alive?"

"You'll know more of the plan when the time comes. We haven't been introduced. I'm Shallum." The strong man with the sword stepped forward.

The next advisor spoke up, clearing his voice. "You will travel with Shallum, who is already known by Pharaoh and Pithin, another highly qualified soldier who is not known by Pharaoh. Additionally, you'll be accompanied by a woman servant, Tamin, until you get to Kleopolis."

"Will I be coming back?" Her voice trembled, and her palms were sweaty. They didn't answer her question but said, "You are leaving now. Shallum will have further instructions for you once you get to Kleopolis."

Three of the men stood to leave as a formidable, muscled man entered the room. "I am Pithin." Shallum nodded, and Pithin directed Nalussa to follow between them.

As they wound their way through corridors and walkways, Nalussa's mind was traveling faster than they were walking. "Will I be coming back?" she asked again, looking at them both. "What about my husband? Will someone tell him what's going on?"

Shallum stopped abruptly. "You're married?"

"Yes, my husband is Adriel! Didn't the queen's men tell you?"

Shallum and Pithin exchanged glances, not saying anything. Nalussa repeated, "Will I be coming back?"

"If all goes according to plan, I hope the answer will be a yes, you'll be coming back, but you must do everything exactly as I command you if you want to see your family again. Your entire family is under house guard until this is over. We cannot risk any heroics from them!"

What more was there to say? No one spoke as they hurried her from the palace into the courtyard, where two chariots waited with tethered horses and provisions. Tamin was waiting patiently by one chariot. She was dressed simply in a light-weight robe and veil, with very sturdy sandals meant for running. She was tall, strong looking, and, in her own right, formidable. Nalussa sensed that these three were a team and knew exactly what they were doing as they quietly commandeered her into one of the chariots with Shallum at the reins. Quickly, they left the grounds.

Nalussa couldn't think straight. She worried for Adriel, her brother, and family. She realized why they were guarded. If they knew, they would come after her. All she could do was pray that whatever the plan was, they would be successful, and she could return to her husband and family. That's all she wanted. *Please, God, hear me!*

No one spoke as they loaded onto the boat to cross the Red Sea to Egypt. This was familiar territory to her and where the shortest distance could be traveled by boat between Egypt and Sheba. Depending upon wind, it could take seemingly forever or a handful of hours. She huddled on the port side with her captors. No one spoke to her, but the three carried on an intense conversation out of earshot throughout most of the trip until the men decided to sleep. Tamin kept an eye on her.

When they finally reached port and disembarked, Tamin asked her if she was hungry. Not caring for her answer of no, the woman produced raisin cakes and goat milk and insisted she eat and drink. "You'll not become weak or ill on this journey. Not as long as I'm looking after you," Tamin declared and took a huge bite out of her own raisin cake. After they all ate, they continued on their way. Silently. She couldn't stand it.

Hours later, they stopped for a rest. "Tamin. Please. What is going to happen to me?" Nalussa clung to the woman's sleeve.

"I don't know. I'm here to look after you until you are delivered to Pharaoh. Then, Shallum has other plans. I don't know what they are yet."

After their break, Nalussa climbed into the chariot with Shallum, and as she sat down, she boldly put a hand on his arm. "Please tell me what I am to do, what you are going to do, and how this is all going to work out."

Shallum ordered, "Quiet. We'll speak when we stop tonight."

That evening, as they sat by a fire in the camp, Nalussa spoke up to Shallum. Tamin and Pithin were sleeping. "You said you would speak to me about what is going to happen!"

"You need to be brave and strong. If this fails, it's likely your husband and family will be under house arrest for a long time. The queen is God-fearing. She won't kill them or throw them in prison; but she is a strong ruler, and there are consequences for failure. We can't fail her. If she thinks her son is at risk, then she will protect him like a lioness."

He stirred the embers, a man brooding and dark-featured. "Pharaoh knows me. I am a mercenary of some reputation. When I show up with you, I will say that I recognized who you were and abducted you while you were beyond the palace in the town square and were separated from your servants. My reasoning will be I thought I would get a reward bringing you to him rather than Rehoboam.

"We are counting on his ego. Having the favored concubine of Solomon is quite a feat, especially when Rehoboam is still after you." He chuckled, shaking his head. "What an insult to the memory of Solomon! The conquest will be delicious for Pharaoh, especially when he is out to attack Judah!"

Nalussa said softly, "I am a married woman. No longer a concubine."

Shallum nodded. "That information surprised me. I wasn't told by the queen's men. This might work out better than I planned. You will say nothing about being married—not immediately—nor will you say you know that Abra is under his protection. Put him off until we—you or me—find out where Abra and Heber are housed. Mind you, play him out. It could take days, but do not say a word about being married." He gave her a long, steady look. She met his gaze in defiance, not knowing exactly where he was going with his directions.

"Once you've located Abra and Heber? Then what?" she demanded.

"Not your problem. But I'll enlist the help of Pithin and Tamin."

"Surely, you wouldn't kill a child!"

"I was ordered not to. So, I won't."

"What about Abra and her man Ebel?" she insisted.

He sighed and cleared his throat. "We're not interested in Ebel—only Abra. And we'll try to bring her back to Sheba alive."

"How will I avoid intimacy with Pharaoh?" Nalussa was desperately worried.

"I'm sure you can figure that out." He shot her a meaningful gaze.

"One last question, Shallum." She held up a finger. "Again, what about me? How do you plan to get me out of Pharaoh's palace?"

"I believe I have a plan, but you don't need to know the details. Simply put, Tamin will snatch Heber, while Pithin grabs Abra. This palace, unlike Pharaoh's others, is an easy in-and-out."

"You didn't answer my question." She would have swallowed hard if she had any spit left in her mouth. It was dry as a bone. Fear had taken over.

"I will get you when we can. It has to be at the right moment. Now, go to sleep." He threw the stick into the fire and crawled to his blanket to sleep.

The day they arrived at Kleopolis, they found lodging with baths. Quickly, without credentials or bribes, Shallum sent word about his find to Pharaoh, who responded with enthusiasm. The following day, Tamin bathed Nalussa with scented soap, oiled her body, and dressed her in simple, yet exquisite, finery. Tamin draped Shebian gold jewelry around her neck and wrists, hung rubies from her ears, and slipped emeralds on her fingers. The woman then expertly rimmed her eyes with kohl, stained her lips with berries, but left her extraordinary dark, dewy complexion alone.

The entire time, she spoke only orders to Nalussa. "Sit down, stand still, close your eyes, purse your lips." Nalussa said nothing. She was too tense to engage in any conversation. "Hold still!" Tamin swept back and pinned her hair under a simple, yet finely embroidered, headdress. "Stretch out your legs." She slipped on and tied soft leather sandals trimmed in died purple leather on her feet. Satisfied that her ward was up to the standards of Pharaoh, Tamin merely nodded her satisfaction and left the room.

Dressed and perfumed, Shallum led Nalussa to the chariot, where the horses were prancing in expectation. Neither Tamin nor Pithin were in sight. Traveling through the streets, Nalussa could not concentrate on the unusual buildings, or the sculptured gods in alcoves and on pedestals, or the general chaos of the city. She had too much on her mind and in her heart. Entering the courtyard, servants ran to take the horses and help Nalussa out of the rig. After years of training as a royal concubine,

Nalussa quickly fell into the routine of walking with confidence and grace while hiding the terror in her heart. Shallum guided her through the palace gates, doors, and ornate halls to the main greeting room. She walked behind him with her head high and a pensive look on her face, thinking, *How am I ever going to get out of this alive?*

The hall was crowded with people talking loudly and guards stonily looking for anything out of the ordinary. When Shallum made his entrance with Nalussa, people made room for her passing; and once the crowd saw her, all talking ceased, and heads turned to the only woman in the room who held beauty beyond that of any Egyptian goddess.

Pharaoh smiled, beckoned them forward with a wave of his staff. Dutifully, Shallum came before Pharaoh, dropped on a knee, and slightly turned to Nalussa, who bowed her head in subordination to His Majesty as Shallum introduced her to Pharaoh and his court.

"So, this is Solomon's favorite concubine!" Pharaoh breathed out, amazed and pleased. "You have presented her well!" The hall erupted in a cacophony of surprised discussion and titters.

Pharaoh immediately rose, followed by guards and advisors, and directed Shallum and Nalussa to follow. She passed among whispers and raised eyebrows. The topic of conversation was not only her beauty and the question of why she was presented to Pharaoh, but also there was already gossip in the halls about the ambition of Solomon's other concubine, who showed up at Pharaoh's doorstep with an alliance in mind.

"Ah, the intrigue!" An old man laughed. Others joined in.

Safely and quietly in smaller chambers, Pharaoh set about the directives to house Shallum for as long as he wished. "Take my friend, Shallum, for some well-deserved refreshment. I will see him in a while." Pharaoh didn't need to quiz either Nalussa or Shallum as to why they were here. Pharaoh knew from Shallum's communication.

As the men dissolved from sight, the king turned his attention to Nalussa. "You are a beauty!" He smiled as he handed her wine. "Do you know how curious this is?" Without waiting for an answer, he said, "My sister was Solomon's first wife!" He threw his head back and laughed. "If my father could only know who was sitting here before me now!"

Nalussa spoke softly, not knowing where this was going. "King Solomon built her a lovely palace."

"He did indeed!" Pharaoh laughed again, scornfully. "She was one of the lucky wives. She actually had some status." He looked at her closely. With disdain in his voice, he said, "My father was furious to know that over time, Solomon accumulated so many wives and concubines, displacing my sister, but fortunately, he died before the final count was made. As did my sister. She never knew he eventually had an astounding six hundred wives!"

"And three hundred concubines," Nalussa added, barely above a whisper.

"How can that be? And a supposedly godly man at that? Ah, but he had the knack for building alliances and treaties. And you, my pretty, brought youth and looks. At least, he went for beautiful women as well." Stopping to swig some wine, he continued, "And there is nothing wrong with that." He put down his cup and reached out to touch her, but she shrank back. *He doesn't waste any time.*

Surprised, he said, "You are different than your sister concubine, Abra. Do you know she is here?" he asked arrogantly.

She said nothing, only looked surprised. She wouldn't lie as instructed. She would trust God to protect her instead.

CHAPTER TWENTY-SEVEN

"I'll make arrangements for you to see her. I'm sure she will be delighted that you are here. In the meantime, understand you are mine, yet I take care of my loyal subjects very well, providing they take care of me." He looked at her meaningfully. "I have rooms prepared for you, and I'll see to that you are shown there immediately, so you can get more comfortable in your new lodgings. I won't leave you alone long, but you might feel more at home—or at least relaxed—knowing that Abra is here also."

They took her to two large rooms with balconies on the second floor of the palace, overlooking a courtyard with man-made ponds stocked with fish and turtles. The rooms were sparsely furnished with a couple of couches, a table with candles, and chamber pots discreetly placed under one of the couches. In the far corner of one of the rooms was the bathing area that held several clay pots filled with water, scented soaps, and luxurious linens. Curious, she opened a painted chest set near a wall. It was filled with lovely clothing, fine jewelry, and extra sandals.

She wondered where Shallum was staying. *How will we communicate?* she thought. Not caring about looking through the finery, she dropped the lid on the chest. Turning her thoughts to Abra, she reasoned it would be easy enough to find out where Abra was housed. She'd ask her when she visited. Abra always had a penchant for bragging and would be sure to let her know that her rooms were far better than Nalussa's.

Three days passed, and still she had not been visited by either Abra or called into Pharaoh's chambers, for which she was grateful. She was relegated to her rooms and cared for by indifferent servants, who brought her food and drink, refreshed the water supply, and changed out her linens.

Weary from worry and not knowing what was to come, she tried to sleep, but the heat was stifling as the sun poured through the open windows and the air so still that even the slightest waft of air from a bird's wing would have been welcome, but none came. Unable to nap, she sat up when she heard a familiar voice in the hallway.

"Well! Look who is here! Greetings, my sister!" Abra breezed in with her hair cut short in the Egyptian style, simple and straight, wearing an elegant tunic that hung to her ankles, cinched at the waist with a purple sash. Of course, there was gold around her neck, wrists, and ears. Her make-up was dramatic but couldn't hide her worldly concerns. Ambition could do that.

She dramatically hurried to Nalussa and gave her a brief hug, pulling away from her sweaty body. "I heard about the unfortunate circumstances that brought you here." She carefully looked her over, taking in the damp, but very fine, clothing Nalussa was wearing. She extended her hand to feel her Shebian jewelry that was far more intricate and sophisticated in technique than the simple geometric pieces of Egypt. "Shebians are far better artisans than the Egyptians," she muttered, dropping her hand and smiling thinly. "And here you are."

"Not of my own decision," Nalussa stated coldly and walked over to a jug of water. Taking a linen, she wet it, wrung it out, and wiped her face and arms, gaining little relief from the heat.

"I never thought I'd see you again—and certainly not here," Abra said.

Turning, Nalussa snapped, "I was snatched by a mercenary, who sold me to Pharaoh."

Her anger wasn't an act. Because of her beauty, her sexuality was being exploited all over again and this time because of Abra! She had hoped that once she married Adriel, her life as a concubine offering sexual favors was well behind her. Now, she had to figure a way to put Pharaoh off without compromising Shallum's plan to get Abra and Heber back to Sheba. She looked at her deceitful friend with hostility.

Barely paying attention to Nalussa, Abra swept around the rooms, looking out the windows and inspecting the furnishings. Nalussa was lost in aversion. Here walked her nemesis, parading in importance, while she, Nalussa, was a prisoner, a sexual plaything for Pharaoh. If she ever made it out alive, would her husband ever take her back?

Abra interrupted her thoughts. "He gave you humble rooms," she said with a sniff, casually looking around without any concern for Nalussa. "Apparently, you need to prove yourself before you get anything from him, but at least you have the opportunity to redeem yourself. Solomon certainly taught us a lot. My suggestion is to put your talents to use. Pharaoh can be generous."

She sat down on a couch, critically pointing at the bare walls with the lack of wall hangings or mosaics. "What a boring, colorless, hot room. Didn't he even give you a servant? Surely, you need servants. At least, someone to move this hot, brutal air." She fanned herself with a small, painted palm frond she carried by her side.

With great effort, Nalussa breathed in to control herself. Containing her contempt, she answered, "Oh? Are these rooms too bland for you? What are your rooms like? I suppose you have many servants, too?"

"I have the most luxurious rooms you will ever see! They are on the east side of the palace, also on the second floor, but I get the prevailing breeze. I see the sun rise, but in the heat of the day, the sun is on the other side of the palace, keeping my rooms cooler. And of course, I have servants to fan me at all times."

She stood with a curious arch to her eyebrows and walked over to the painted chest. "I have twice the size of rooms you have and, of course, twice the furnishings." She sighed smugly. "One room alone is for the nurse and Heber, and I have the rest to myself. And the views are spectacular. I, too, have a private courtyard with private stairs from my rooms down to it." She stooped and lifted the lid of the chest without invitation or permission and let out a little gasp. She closed the lid with a thud and turned, clearly surprised at the finery.

"What about Ebel?" Nalussa ignored her reaction.

She flicked her hand and walked from the chest. "He has rooms adjacent to mine with a common door that I keep locked. If he wants me, he must knock or send a servant to inquire if I'm available." She leaned in close to Nalussa, dismissing him. "But I'm here for a reason. I never thought I would have to say what is obvious of why you were sold to Pharaoh because you are, after all, a concubine . . . " She paused, staring at Nalussa. She smirked, "Yet some people never change. You still think you're above it all?"

Nalussa interrupted, holding up her hand. "This isn't about me; forget about me. I know why you're here in Kleopolis. You are planning on getting Pharaoh's support to help you get the throne of Judah."

Abra narrowed her eyes. "Of course." She smirked. "I suppose everybody in the Queen of Sheba's palace knows by now. But I can't forget you. My plans have been thrown off-course because of you. You see, before you came, Pharaoh agreed to support me in my quest to overthrow Rehoboam. Naturally, the incentives I presented to him were and are very attractive, but now that you're here, he wants more than what I've offered him and expects me to sweeten the pot again."

Nalussa waited. Abra paced and turned, saying, "Quite simply, Pharaoh wants you, and only if he gets you will he fully support me. So, I'm telling you to let him have you—he's actually a very good lover—and once we leave to march on Judah, I'll make an escape happen so you can go back to Sheba and your precious Adriel. Pharaoh will be out of Egypt and won't know you've escaped. He'll be too far away to do anything, anyway, so you are almost guaranteed safety." Her searing glare only angered Nalussa more.

Nalussa wet her lips, reining in her growing fury. Abra tapped her foot impatiently, waiting for a response. None came. She shouted, "Do you understand? I will not have my plans put in jeopardy because you think you're above any kind of compromise. Relations with Pharaoh equals freedom for you!"

Nalussa kept her voice steady. "If I agree to lie with Pharaoh, Adriel will divorce me! And how can you guarantee me an escape and safety? Who's to say Pharaoh won't put a guard on me?"

"As far as Adriel is concerned, lie to him or don't say anything at all, you senseless ewe! He would never know you had lain with

Pharaoh unless you told him, and besides, what does he expect? You're a concubine. That's what you do. You give your body to men who buy you in one sense or another! You have no control over your life. You never have, and you never will. You're just a woman!"

"I am not a concubine anymore! I am a married woman!"

"Oh, please. Spare me. What choice do you have? You can't put the ruler of Egypt off without consequences. If he can't have you, he'll banish you, and then what? You'll be a captive in a strange land of strange gods. Your God will forget you. Everyone will. You'll be forgotten, rotting in some small, blistering hot room, eating rotted fruit and picking lice out of your hair! You'll never see Adriel again, and trust me, with all the young beauties in Sheba, they'll petition Queen Makeda for him. Don't fool yourself into thinking he won't find another woman! He's a man. That's what they do. They move on!" She fanned herself furiously.

Nalussa said nothing.

Abra threw her fan on the floor and closed in on Nalussa, whispering harshly, "I'm telling you, let Pharaoh have you, and when he leaves on his campaign, escape back to Adriel or lose him forever! I am your only way out!"

"How? How can I trust you? How can I believe you?"

"You have no other choice but to trust me if you ever want to see your husband and family again. Next time I'm with Pharaoh, I expect you've made it happen." She stormed out of the room.

Nalussa was completely drained and sat down hard on the couch. How could she put off what seemed like the inevitable? Not able to sit, she hopped up and went to the balcony to look out. To the side of the terrace was a narrow, stone staircase that led down to the courtyard by the fish ponds and potted palms. Distressed, she pulled off her headpiece—none of the women in this hot, forsaken country bothered with covering their heads—threw it on the floor, and slipped out of her rooms, traipsing carefully down the staircase, but keeping under the covered walkway encircling the courtyard and away from prying eyes.

But it was the middle of the day in Egypt with heat so intense that no one, not even the beloved cats of the Egyptians, were prowling around. Overheated from the sun's rays and Abra's rage, she found refuge in a small alcove housing a statue of a man-bird-god glowering at whomever sat on the stone bench placed in front of him. Wearily, she sat down, wiping her brow, barely looking at the creature supremely staring down at her. She really had no options but to indulge Pharaoh and hope that she could escape, if Abra didn't betray her. And if and when she got back to Sheba, she didn't know what would happen.

She realized she hadn't prayed to God in a long time. In Judah, Solomon's Hebrew women went to the temple weekly. She enjoyed the fellowship, teaching, preaching, and singing. Once she left Judah and in between Egypt and Sheba, she never listened to Scripture being read or taught. Oh, she and Adriel had some wonderful, interesting discussions at the Queen of Sheba's palace with the courtiers about their beliefs, but there was no praying, worshipping, or music. She sighed as tears filled her eyes. She had forgotten about her God and her utter reliance on Him. No wonder she was in a storm. It was time for a talk. He had to hear her . . .

A shadow fell before her. Frightened, she stopped praying and turned to see Shallum duck behind her to the corner of the alcove, out of eyesight from anyone who might happen to wander the courtyard or glance out of any second story windows. "I found where she is," he said quickly, leaning against the wall.

"Yes, I know, too, but aren't you taking a terrible chance being here?" She sat motionless with her back to the courtyard so as not to arouse any concerns if she appeared to be talking to anyone.

"This time of day?" He snickered, yet still looked around. Shaking his head, he said, "Even an uprising would wait in this heat." Before Nalussa could respond, he announced, "We're taking Abra and Heber tonight. I'm invited to supper with Pharaoh this evening, which will give Tamin the opportunity to slip into Abra's rooms and grab Heber."

"How will she do that?" Nalussa shuddered.

"Don't worry. And Pithin will take Abra."

"How? Shallum! They must be well-guarded or at least have many servants looking after them! And what about Ebel? Surely, he needs to be contended with!"

"Nalussa, this is none of your concern. You and I will have an alibi to prove that we are not involved, and no one will know that they have been taken until the next day. This palace is hardly a fortress."

"But . . . but . . . what about me? Abra told me that if I didn't give in to Pharaoh, he wouldn't help her, and I would likely be banished to prison somewhere. But if I did allow myself to be taken by Pharaoh, she would make an escape for me once he left on his campaign to Judah!"

"She can't help you if she's gone, and Pharaoh will go ahead as he originally planned: invade Judah and raid Solomon's temple."

"But, wait! How can I get home?" Nalussa pleaded.

"Tell him the truth. You are married. He won't want a married woman. He'll let you go. Remember the story of Abraham and Sarah from Scripture?"

"Yes," she answered slowly, remembering. "There was a famine in the land, and Abraham took his wife, Sarah, to Egypt to escape. And he worried that when the Egyptians saw that Sarah was very beautiful, they would kill him so that Pharaoh could take her for his wife. So, Abram claimed his wife, Sarah, was his sister, so they wouldn't kill him. And Pharaoh took her."

Shallum crossed his arms on his chest. "Until God afflicted Pharaoh and his household with great sickness, and Pharaoh found out that Sarah was, in fact, Abraham's wife. He was angry and gave her back to him. So, you see, Pharaoh will not take you because you are married. Don't think for one minute that this Pharaoh doesn't know his history."

"Is that what you planned once you found out I was married? And what of the gold that was given to you for me?"

"Yes, to your first question—hearing you were married was a wonderful revelation. Up until that moment, I worried how I would ever get you back to Sheba. And as for your second question, I'll give it all back."

"But," warned Nalussa, "He's bragged about having Abra. Now, if he loses her, he'll certainly make it a point to flaunt my capture and seduction to Rehoboam if word hasn't been sent out already. How do you think he's going to handle being foiled twice?"

"I have no idea." Shallum swept past her into the harsh sunlight, then into the dark shadows of the covered walkway.

Nalussa covered her face with her hands. "God, I'm back. And I really need Your help," she prayed.

CHAPTER TWENTY-EIGHT

Tamin walked with confidence and ease, holding a stack of folded linens in her arms as she made her way to the room that housed Heber, Abra's little boy, and his nurse. Fortuitously, she didn't pass anyone because she chose a time when the servants who cared for this part of the palace were finished cleaning up from the supper chores, and now, they were eating their own meals in the lower rooms below the first floor.

The twilight had begun to set in, and shadows were deepening to the advantage of the abductors. With grace and speed, she entered the room and spied the nurse asleep on her pallet, having finished her own meal that included drugged wine. A very simple matter for Tamin, who earlier had sneaked into the preparation rooms for Abra and her son. Once a servant brought up meals for Heber and his nurse, she was able to douse the drink with a sleeping potion. Her only fear was that the nurse would drink it before she finished feeding Heber, but it was a chance she had to take. It appeared that the nurse's care of Heber came before she relaxed with her own meal. She was soundly sleeping.

Heber was sleeping, too, in his cot away from the doorway that connected his room to his mother's, which was closed, to the relief of Tamin. Deftly, she crossed the room, put the linens down, and scooped up the little boy, who stirred, opened his eyes, and complained he wanted to sleep. But he was too sleepy to cry or whine, so he snuggled onto her shoulder. Tamin shushed him lovingly. She was incredulous that the little one didn't make a fuss, for she had brought the stack of linens for that very purpose—not to suffocate him, but to cover his mouth should he start to wail.

Without disturbing him, she picked up the fabric, draped it over his sleeping form, and stole out of the room, following the quiet hallway to the far end, where a staircase led to the first floor and then out to the side of a courtyard. There, an opening led to yet another small courtyard, where a little-used egress led to a side street. In a covered shed, a chariot was waiting. But the first courtyard was her rendezvous with Pithin, for while she was snatching Heber, he was grabbing Abra. Their synchronized timing was critical. The path they chose was not guarded for nearly ten minutes, while the guards changed out and would then begin their walk of the perimeter from the top of the palace walls. The security in this palace was lax, simply because Pharaoh rarely visited. But still, they had to be off of the palace grounds in minutes in order not to be detected.

Disguised as a servant, Pithin knocked on Abra's door, knowing that Ebel was not with her. Earlier, Shallum had successfully bribed a servant girl to seduce Ebel and to keep him busy for the time noted. He was an easy mark. Ebel was known for his philandering, even though he was now Abra's husband. Because of timing, Abra's own servants had recently left for their supper, leaving her alone. This was the window of opportunity for Pithin and Tamin to work their scheme.

Abra opened the door and smiled in surprise, not expecting an unknown servant. Pithin was a handsome, healthy man, and his smile could win over the most cautious woman. And Abra had already proven she was hardly cautious. In one hand, he held up a golden goblet and in the other, a colorful pitcher.

"This is a surprise," Abra chirped coquettishly. "You're new, and what is this?" She pointed to the goblet.

Pithin entered the room and said, "This is a gift from Pharaoh. His finest wine. He would like me to pour you some."

"Well, of course!" Abra said in delight, eyeing the man. As Pithin poured the wine, she pouted. "I'm lonesome. Pharaoh didn't call me tonight, and Ebel is away. Will you enjoy some wine with me?"

This was exactly what Pithin had hoped for. Some wine, some flirting, getting her tipsy—then when she thought she was going to be seduced, he would grab her, gag her, and tie her wrists.

The wine was not diluted with water and so was strong. She made a little face when she tasted it, but after one or two sips, it went down smoothly. Pithin made a show of drinking but took in very little. Abra, on the other hand, thoroughly enjoyed herself. She chatted and flirted and bragged. As she moved closer to him, a little unsteady, giggling suggestively, Pithin put his arm around her tenderly, playing with her hair; and as she leaned into him, eyes closed, he moved like a viper, putting a hand over her mouth and clasping her close to his body. She was too shocked and unstable to fight back. Quickly, he put a gag in her mouth, then tied up her hands. Weakly, she struggled and grunted, but he held a finger to his lips and said, "Keep calm. You will not be hurt. Just do as I say, and all will be well." Eyes wide in terror, she groaned as he turned her around and marched her to the balcony.

Trained to hear the slightest noise, Tamin perceived rustlings and footsteps above to her right. Breathing a sigh of relief, she looked up to the second-story level and saw Pithin hurry along a woman's figure on the balcony, surely gagged and secured at the wrists. Holding an arm, he directed her to the narrow, stone staircase that led from her rooms down to the courtyard. The woman looked wildly about, then down, and found her footing on the top stone step. As she descended, she tripped on her gown and pitched forward. Pithin could not hold her. What seemed like slow motion, she sailed through the air in a sickening fall, landing with a dull thump on the rock patio by a statue of an animal god. Horrified, Tamin backed against the wall in shock; Heber slept on her shoulder.

As quick as a deer, Pithin bounded back in the room, wiped out the second cup of wine, then came out on the balcony with her goblet filled with wine, ran down the steps, knelt by Abra, and pulled off her gag and untied her hands. Blood seeped from under her twisted body. He dropped the goblet a few feet from her. The wine was as red as her blood.

Running toward Tamin, he harshly whispered, "Go!" They both ran into the shadows, missing the guards, who now had come on duty and would soon see the wrecked body of the once desirable and beautiful concubine of Solomon and Pharaoh.

Without a word, they ran through the second courtyard, careful to keep under the walkways and in the shadows. Once outside the palace grounds, they continued their pace to the chariot, where they made haste to put as much distance as they could from Pharaoh.

"It was an accident!" Pithin nearly cried as he took the reins and urged the horses forward. "She just tripped!"

Tamin was still in shock but answered, "What's done is done. It's for the best, anyway. She would have been imprisoned in Sheba."

They trotted off into the night. Heber began to wail.

After the evening meal, when Pharaoh and Shallum were enjoying more wine, a servant spoke with one of His Majesty's guards, who, in turn, hurried over to Pharaoh, whispering in his ear. Color drained from his normally dark face, and in shock, he turned to Shallum and hoarsely uttered in complete surprise, "Abra fell from the stairs leading from her balcony. She's dead!"

Shallum blinked. "This was an accident?" This wasn't part of the plan.

"Undoubtedly. It's dark; those stairs can be slippery; and they found a spilled goblet of wine not far from her body! This is tragic." Shallum could see that Pharaoh was not so concerned over Abra's death as he was about Abra's plot to challenge Judah's throne. Pharaoh threw back the rest of his wine, put the cup on the table, and signaled for more. "This marks a change in plans."

"For Judah?" Shallum asked non-committedly, hoping that Tamin and Pithin at least got Heber.

Pharaoh rubbed his chest and burped. "I will not fight Rehoboam for the throne without leverage, and Abra and her son were leverage. Once I got her and her son in place, she would offer me ongoing tribute without a great deal of effort on my part; but without her, all I have is a child, and it's not worth the fight."

"What about her husband, or consort, Ebel?" Shallum asked carefully. "I've heard much about him." He hoped he would be with the servant girl for the night, for once he found out that Abra had fallen to her death, he could look in on Heber—or not. But his life was about to change, too, with the absence of Abra and Heber.

Pharaoh snorted. "He is merely an academic. A Hebrew scholar. He has no standing with the Hebrew people. So, there's little point in going after the throne with a child who would need advisors in place, protection, and a strong communication system between Egypt and Judah." He shook his head vigorously. "I'm not interested in setting up a kingdom in Judah."

He leaned back, thinking. "But I'm not sure what to do about the child. I don't want Ebel to have him and allow him to think that he can go after the throne of Judah. And I don't want a son of Solomon! I'm going to have to think about what to do about both of them."

Shallum leaned in, biting the tip of his thumb. "Without your support, I wouldn't think Ebel would ever make an attempt at the throne, so perhaps you could merely expel him from your kingdom and let him find his way elsewhere. The Queen of Sheba won't want him, and if Rehoboam learns that he was a part of the plot with Abra, he will be killed if goes back to Judah. He's a man without a country. No threat at all. As for Heber . . . he's a child without anything. No threat there either. Send him back to Sheba." Shallum wondered what Pharaoh would do once he found out Heber was gone. But he had a question for Pharaoh. "What about your plans for Solomon's treasures?"

Pharaoh laughed. "Oh, I still plan to invade Judah. I will go after Solomon's treasures. That I will do. But it will be a simple raid, and then we'll leave."

He sat back, shaking his head. "I will miss Abra. She was very entertaining and cunning. I admired her ambition, and I certainly didn't trust her, but she was lovely to look at and enjoy. It's amazing to me that one moment, one can be vibrant and alive, and the next . . . " He snapped his fingers. "Gone."

As an afterthought, Pharaoh said, "I could eliminate Heber or maybe keep him under house arrest, but that takes effort. I could use him as a threat to Rehoboam, hold him over his head, so to speak, to make him more cooperative. I don't know. I've got to think about it."

The next morning, Heber's nurse finally woke, nauseous and suffering from a terrible headache. Why was she feeling so ill? The wine must have been stronger than she thought. She looked over to Heber's little bed. It was empty. Sucking in a deep breath to settle her head and stomach, she looked wildly about. No sign of the little one. Her first thought was that Abra had taken him. Quickly but stealthily, she made for Abra's apartments. If Abra hadn't taken him, she did not want to alert the mother of Heber's disappearance. She leaned her ear against the door and heard nothing. Slowly, she opened the door and found a servant quietly packing away Abra's belongings, with another man taking inventory of each item on a piece of papyrus.

Puzzled, she asked, "Where is my mistress?"

The servant making the list said, "Didn't you hear the raucous in the courtyard last night? Abra fell from the stairs leading to the courtyard. She's dead!"

The nurse was stunned. None of this made sense. Abra dead, her son missing, and she . . . well, was she drugged last night? Not hearing the discovery of Abra's body when her room and balcony was right next to the stairs leading to the courtyard? All the windows were open. Even if they were covered, she should have heard something!

She turned from the men and certainly didn't want to ask about Heber. If he had died with her, surely, they would have said something, so she turned back to ask, "Was she alone?"

The man, not looking at her, answered, "Yes," and continued making his list.

Quickly, she turned back to her rooms, thinking that her life was in grave danger under these very suspicious circumstances. No one would believe she slept through an abduction and a grisly death. Not wasting any time, she gathered her belongings and left the palace, with plans to go as far south along the Nile as she could.

Pharaoh roared, "The child is gone? How can that be? Where is the nurse? Bring her to me at once! And where is Ebel? I want them both here to explain where this child is!"

When Ebel finally stumbled into the room, dragged in by two huge guards, he was frightened and confused, weeping, "Your Majesty, I just heard about Abra and the disappearance of Heber!" He was pushed to his knees before the throne. He hung his head, moaning.

"Where were you last night?" Pharaoh demanded, pointing his scepter at him.

He trembled. "I was with . . . Ashta . . . all night long!" he mumbled, looking around in desperation. "I don't know anything!"

Pharaoh demanded, "Who is Ashta?" An advisor leaned in to the king, explaining she was a servant who worked in the kitchens. "Bring her here now!" he ordered.

Time passed. No one spoke. Finally, guards came through the main entryway and bowed before him. "Neither can be found, Your Majesty."

Pharaoh was apoplectic with fury. "This all can't be a coincidence. What is going on? Bring me Shallum!"

Shallum came in immediately, bowed, and waited for Pharaoh to speak, which he did in almost incoherent sentences because he was so furious. "Abra dead! Heber missing! Two servants disappeared! Is this a plot of some kind?"

Shallum tilted his head in reverence. "Your Majesty, let us speak in private with just your advisors." For the court was full of guards, administrators, and servants.

Pharaoh bellowed, "Clear the court!"

CHAPTER TWENTY-NINE

Pharaoh finally calmed down, while his advisors brought him fruit juice, wiped down his face with a wet cloth, and placed his hands in cool water as his servants fanned him furiously. The heat of the day was creeping in to add misery to the already emotionally overcharged king. Flicking his hands from the water and taking in a calming breath, he glared at Shallum. "Speak."

Shallum had been using the time Pharaoh needed to calm down to think out a logical explanation. Pharaoh was not stupid and would take this state of affairs as an elaborate plot for something. He would reason these events were not merely coincidental. Shallum prayed that Nalussa had not taken advantage of the chaos in the palace and bolted as well.

"Pharaoh." Shallum brought his hands together and sat down as a servant brought him a chair. "It seems that Abra's death was, indeed, an accident—you said so yourself—and because of that accident, Heber's nurse, who undoubtedly has grown fond of the child, worried of the child's future. Without a powerful mother to protect him and with a weak father in Ebel, who wouldn't . . . And with a king—you, Your Majesty," he paused and pointed, "who might kill him, she might have well decided to take him for herself."

"That's far-fetched!" Pharaoh retorted in disgust.

"No, no, it's not. You remember the story of the ancient Hebrew, Moses, when he was a baby? The then-king of Egypt directed the midwives to kill all the baby boys birthed by Hebrew women by casting them into the Nile. They didn't do as the king demanded, but when one Hebrew woman gave birth to a boy, she couldn't hide him any longer without being discovered. So, she put him in a basket and placed it among the reeds at the river. When Pharaoh's daughter went to bathe, she found the child, took pity on him, and raised him as her own. So, you see, Egyptian women love children—even Hebrew children!"

Pharaoh squirmed in his chair, not quite convinced. "But what about the disappearance of Ashta, the servant woman who supposedly was with Ebel?"

"My king," Shallum said almost condescendingly, "the woman he was with was undoubtedly terrified to be found in adultery. If she admitted being with a married man, particularly Abra's husband, you would have killed her, no? She ran for her life. So, you see, that explanation is all part of the chain of events." He was sweating heavily under his lightweight robes, himself in dire hope of being believed.

Pharaoh fumed but gave it all some thought. "It sounds plausible. One last demand to see if your explanation holds truth." Pharaoh called in his guards. "Where is Nalussa?"

Oh, please, God. Let her still be here in the palace, Shallum prayed.

Nalussa had been awake since well before dawn. She had heard a commotion in the night and figured it was as Shallum had briefly told her—that Abra and Heber were to be snatched. It must have happened. She heard the guards calling from her side of the palace, people running below in the courtyard, and others running down the hall by her door. She poked her head out and caught a servant as he was hurrying by. "What is happening?"

"I don't know. We were told to go to the east courtyard," the man said over his shoulder. She closed the door and went to her pallet but couldn't sleep. Now, up and dressed, she waited for her morning meal to be served. Soon, she would hear what had happened last night.

Her servant explained. "Yes, indeed, it was a chaotic night. Abra—I'm sorry to tell you because I know she was your friend—fell to her death from the steps by her balcony . . . " Nalussa abruptly stood, mouth open, aghast. The servant continued, "It was an accident. She had been drinking very strong wine and probably lost her footing, but what's worse is that her son and nurse have disappeared."

Nalussa was in shock. *Abra dead? Shallum never said that was a part of the plan. And the nurse was gone, as well as Heber? What had transpired that Tamin didn't take the child? And what of Pithin taking Abra? Did he push her to her death? That wasn't how Shallum had explained things, as brief as they were.*

Before she could ask any more questions, another servant entered and said, "Pharaoh demands your presence now." Fortunately dressed, she hurried behind the man, frightened, distressed, and not knowing where any of this would lead.

When she entered the presence of Pharaoh, she detected a collective ease of tension. She found Shallum on a chair in front of Pharaoh, and his advisors and two guards seemed relieved to see her.

"Have you heard about your friend, Abra?" one of the advisors asked. Nalussa nodded.

"Do you also know that her son and his nurse have disappeared?" another asked.

"I was told briefly by my morning servant that Abra's death was a fall, an accident, but I have no understanding of why the nurse and Heber would be gone."

Shallum asked permission to speak. The king nodded. Shallum proceeded to give her the reasons, and Nalussa, still very confused, could only agree by saying, "I can understand why the nurse might be fearful for Heber's safety. He is a sweet child, but it is disheartening not to know where they might have gone." She kept it simple, having no thought as to what would be happening next. Nalussa bowed before Pharaoh and asked, "Please, Your Majesty. This is difficult for me. May I go into my courtyard for prayer?"

The advisors kept silent, waiting for Pharaoh's decision. "Yes, you may. I will have the guards escort you back to your rooms." With a slight harrumph, he advised, "But take care walking down the steps. They can be slippery, as your friend unfortunately found out." He nodded, and two uniformed men came out from the wall to stand beside her. She bowed her head, and as she turned, she sent a penetrating look to Shallum, who slightly widened his eyes in some kind of acknowledgment.

For at least two hours, she waited in the alcove with the foreboding bird-god, hoping that Shallum would appear and explain to her what was going on and what the plans were for her to get back to her husband. While waiting, she prayed but was diverted in thought to her life since leaving her family so many years ago, ending up as one of Solomon's concubines. *How extraordinary my life has been. And where is it going? Does it end here?*

As a woman, she was viewed by men as a sexual being. As a daughter, she was loved by her father, purely on the merits of being his child. As for her sister and brothers, they, too, loved her and saw her in relation to themselves. And then there was Adriel. She never thought that once a concubine, she would ever become someone's wife. Yet he loved her deeply, accepted her for what she once was without judgment or jealousy. He was even content that she had not produced a child. Now, that was extraordinary. Would she ever get back to him?

She thought about Solomon's writings. Reflecting on them, she was now more open to accepting, rather than criticizing, his behavior. She recalled his words: "There is a time for everything, and a season for every activity under the heavens."[17] How true. Just as God planned seasons in nature, so, too, did His human creatures have their seasons through aging, circumstance, and revelation. Neither of which was in parallel with each other. Solomon went through his—physically, contextually, and spiritually—for in the end, he came to understand his life "under the sun."

She was probably in the summer of her life from a physical standpoint, but emotionally, she was in winter. Heartache, fear, loneliness . . . "But," she said aloud, "God brings forth spring after every winter."

"And spring brings hope, new growth, and the promise of fruitfulness." Shallum lightly touched her shoulder and stood to her side in the shadows. "Abra's death was an accident. Tamin and Pithin got Heber without incident. They have a safe house in Egypt they will be staying in until I meet up with them."

She so wanted to ask, "Will I ever be able to leave?" But he continued, "I don't know what happened to the nurse. It's very likely

---

17 Ecclesiastes 3:1

she just left, fearing for her life in not protecting Heber. The woman who distracted Ebel while Pithin and Tamin were executing the plan ran away fearing for her life, too. As an adulteress, she would have been put to death. Now all that's left is to take care of you."

"What's your plan?" Nalussa asked with little enthusiasm. It seemed almost hopeless. Pharaoh losing Abra, then her? His bragging rights to Rehoboam would be shattered.

"He'll be calling you to come to him. You will tell him you are married—"

"What if he doesn't care?"

"We've been through this before," Shallum said in exasperation. "He will care. He won't take another man's wife."

CHAPTER THIRTY

He did care. His anger was explosive. "You are telling me now that you are married?" He picked up a pitcher and threw it against a pillar. Shards flew through the air. Nalussa flinched and cowered, holding her veil to her face.

"I was afraid, and I didn't know how to tell you!" She stood trembling and shaken. He lunged at her, stopped, and stood towering over her. His hands shot out, gripping her shoulders painfully tight. Surely, he would kill her. She was of no use to him now, and worse, he had been duped.

She had been called to him by two servants, who escorted her to the roof of the palace where an ornate, open room was set up high above all structures, overlooking the city below. The views were dramatic and far-reaching. High, wide, carved arches hung with lightweight drapes that billowed gently in the soft breeze, protecting the inner sanctum from the soon-to-be harsh sun, but it was still very early yet. The sun was just a spot on the horizon, and the city was only slowly awaking. One floor below were the rooms of Abra, now cleaned, emptied, and vacant. No wails of a child or laughter would ever be heard from there again.

Just as quickly as he erupted, he went deadly silent, let go of her, and abruptly walked back to a couch, sitting down hard. He looked around less with anger than disappointment. The room was obviously readied for the seduction for which he was longing. There was a wide, low couch framed in ivory and covered with fine, colorful linens and pillows of all sizes. Incense, carefully placed beside the bed, was drifting in the gentle breeze, filling the area with a light, exotic scent. Flower petals were strewn on the floor. She kept standing, shuddering, her head bowed. He put a fist to his mouth, thinking aloud. "Did Shallum know?"

"No, Pharaoh, he did not." She was afraid to look at him. She hoped he wouldn't ask if he knew now.

"Well, this is a fine state of affairs," he mumbled to himself, getting up to pace, hands on his narrow hips. She fingered her veil nervously, waiting. He spoke coldly, pointed a finger at her and wagging his head. "You have been here long enough to have told me the truth. Now, I will be laughed at for being so fortuitous in having women whom Rehoboam wanted but then losing them!" He turned his back on her and said over his shoulder, "You can leave. I can't stand to look at you. I'll have my secretary give you some money to get back to Sheba. Go now before I change my mind and throw you off the roof!"

Hastily, she made for the doorway leading to the stairs that would bring her to the guarded hallway she would follow to her rooms. Her heart was racing. She couldn't wait to see what Shallum's plan was. She would leave now, but she needed money. Would Pharaoh send someone with it to her? She scurried past the two guards, who gave her a surprised look but did not pursue. Safely reaching her rooms, she put on the clothes she had arrived in so long ago, it seemed, but her jewelry—the jewelry Shallum gave her when she was first presented to the king—she stuffed in a satchel. Not much, but she would use what she came with and would leave Pharaoh's gifts he gave her. She didn't want to be accused of stealing.

She took a long drink of water, thinking. It was best to wait and see if Pharaoh would, indeed, provide her with funds to leave. It all seemed so simple. Too easy. But she was on her guard. Going to the window, she thought about going down into the courtyard to the god's alcove in the hope of meeting up with Shallum, but she didn't dare. She needed to leave soon, before Pharaoh could change his mind, and didn't want to miss a servant who might have the funds she needed to get back to Sheba.

An hour passed. Not willing to wait any longer, she gathered her things when a man entered without knocking, holding a small but heavy-looking pouch. Not saying a word nor even looking at her, he dropped it on a table and left. Grabbing the pouch and putting it in her satchel, she dashed once more to the window. Seeing no one, not even a shadow, she, too, left.

She was not stopped as she exited the palace grounds. A short distance from the palace and near the square to where she was headed, she sought shelter in a stall selling hibiscus water and sat to think. There was no way to reach Shallum, and as far as knowing where the safe house was where Tamin, Pithin, and Heber were hiding, well, who knew? If she could safely get to Naj, she could spend a day in the marketplace asking vendors if they'd seen an odd couple with a small, male child, but that could be dangerous. A lone woman unescorted was a target. She had to be very careful. On the other hand, the market was busy. It was a stopping place to sell or buy before the port, and there were many men and women with children wandering around. She could stay within the crowds.

Sipping her drink, she thought it would be unlikely vendors would remember seeing Tamin and Pithin, even if they were somewhat identifiable. Physically unusual—strong, tall, and healthy. Especially Tamin. She let out a sigh. Even if she couldn't find them, once she got to Naj, she would track down a caravan in or outside the city gates that was going to Sheba. She had funds to pay for transit and protection; and her only course of action, if she didn't meet up with Shallum and his cohorts, was to get to Sheba.

Seeing the little children playing in the street, she couldn't get Heber out of her mind. The little one was doomed. If he made it to Sheba, he undoubtedly would be put under house arrest—for the rest of his life. Queen Makeda would never harm Solomon's child, but she would not want to put her own son in danger either if it meant Heber could grow into a threat. Could she help Heber? Unlikely. There was no way to get him from Tamin and Pithin, even if she did find them. And no matter what the course of events, she had to get back to Adriel in Sheba.

Leaving the drink vendor, she made her way to the city gates of Kleopolis. There, she looked for travelers aligned with other groups, for safety was in numbers. By a small group of people with baggage and animals, she stopped. "Do you know of anyone going to Naj?" she asked a woman holding an infant. The woman looked her over, taking in her expensive garments, and turned away. "Please, I'm not a prostitute. I just . . . " Nalussa didn't know how to explain her fine clothing without sounding mad. "I am a married woman trying to get back to my husband!"

The woman, taking pity on her, turned back. "You were taken?" Nalussa nodded. "Hmm," the woman responded. "It doesn't matter whether you are rich, poor, or a slave, if you are beautiful, you are always in danger." She tilted her head. "Follow me."

Nalussa was introduced to a small group of traders on their way to Naj. They were hesitant to take Nalussa under their protection because, as one man argued, "Whoever abducted her will want her back, especially a fine-looking woman like her!"

"You are not in danger." She dug in her pocket and pulled out gold coins. "This should cover my journey!" The men debated among themselves, then a little man snatched the coins out of Nalussa's hands and said, "We have an extra donkey. You can ride a donkey, eh? Cover your face!"

Appreciatively, she thanked the woman, gave her a coin, and mounted the beast.

Finally arriving in Naj, it was very late. Deeply aware of being alone, she tagged behind the woman and child and the others as they made their way to find lodging. Fortunately, there was a space for her. She was relegated to a room a little larger than a closet, but she was safe.

The next morning, she hurried to the town square. As shoppers were milling about, Nalussa kept close to the crowds, occasionally asking vendors about Tamin and Pithin. Surprisingly, a few remembered them and Heber. The only good news about this was that it was likely their safe house was here; but that was not a guarantee, and she was not going to waste time in the pursuit of a couple who might or might not be in town. Her plan was to get to Sheba, join a caravan, and leave as soon as possible. For a brief moment, she felt saddened about Heber's plight, but politics were always deadly, particularly when it came to dueling heirs.

As the day wore on, she was able to find a small caravan that was willing to let her travel with them. They were leaving in the morning and expected her to be on time, and she wasn't, they would leave without her. "Pay up front, but once you get to the port to cross over to Sheba, you make your own arrangements for passage. We're only bringing our loads as far as our barges."

"I'm agreeable to that." She would figure the next step of the journey once she got to the port, but as she dug in her satchel for the money, she stopped. Hearing her name called, she abruptly looked around and saw Shallum quickly dismounting from his mare. Holding the reins of his horse with another tethered behind, he pushed his way through the complaining crowds.

"Stop. I'll take you there! Put your money away. Come with me." He took her elbow, leading her away from the group of people bargaining their way with the chief of the caravan.

Surprised and relieved, she followed him as he began explaining, "I found out Pharaoh sent you away when he ordered me to see him. He was furious with me for bringing a married woman into him and demanded the money he paid for you back with interest! Naturally he brought up the past Pharaoh and the story of Abraham and Sarah. He was really afraid our God would punish him and his household for taking a married Hebrew woman, even if you *had* once been Solomon's concubine!"

Clearing the crowds, he stopped, breathing hard, looking around at the crowds. "I honestly thought he was going to either kill me then and there or throw me in his dungeons. I gave him back his money with interest, explaining I didn't know you were married—of course, I didn't tell him I subsequently found out, but by upholding my ignorance, he was satisfied enough to let me go after several lashings." He winced in pain.

Instantly, she looked at his back and could see blood staining his tunic in thin lines. "Oh, Shallum! We should clean the wounds. You've been sweating, and the fabric has been irritating the cuts. Let's find a well."

CHAPTER THIRTY-ONE

East of the town in a small valley was a large well. Although late in the day, women were there filling jars as children played with one another; riders filled the troughs for their beasts; and stable boys were replenishing water jars for their animals to carry back to the mangers.

They found a stone bench, where he gingerly took off his top while she took his goat skin to fill with water. Using her veil, she gently cleansed the wounds, which, while not deep, were nasty enough. Patting them dry, she suggested he leave his top off for a while until they could get some salve and bandages.

Sitting quietly as the sun dried off his back, she waited for him to speak. He sighed. "We'll go back to town and get bandages, spend the night—I'll find us a place—then we'll leave tomorrow morning. If all goes well, we should be at the port in a few days' time, and I'll get you on a boat to Sheba and back to your husband and family."

She cocked her head. *What about Heber? Where was he?* "You're not coming back to Sheba? Who is bringing Heber? Wasn't that the reason for this entire escapade? To bring Heber and Abra back to the queen?" She involuntarily put a hand to her heart. She prayed, *Dear God! Abra's dead, but let the child be alive!*

He snorted in derision, shaking his head and flexing his shoulders as the tightness set in the wounds. "She fell in love with the little goat!" Nalussa looked at him in confusion. *Who fell in love with whom?* Reading her mind, he snarled, "Heber! Tamin and Pithin told me they wouldn't take him back to Queen Makeda and wouldn't let me take him! Tamin wants to hide him in Egypt and raise him as her and Pithin's son!"

Nalussa was stunned and put a hand to her mouth. How could plans so well-made go so sideways? How could a hardened warrior, a mercenary like Shallum, simply let Heber stay with Tamin? In her heart, Nalussa was thrilled at this turn of events, but certainly, there were unknowns. Why didn't he forcefully take Heber from them? He had an agreement with the Queen of Sheba to bring Abra and Heber back. Abra was dead, so there was no fault there, but Heber? Why would he give up so easily? She touched his arm, never voicing her many questions, only to ask, "What happened?"

"A mother's instincts kicked in, I guess. Tamin is my sister. Pithin is my best friend. They fell in love and never told me. You think I would have guessed it, but they hid it pretty well, trying to think of a way to break the news. And when this child came to her arms, well that was it. They both love him and want him and don't want him to end up in Sheba, possibly in prison for the rest of his life." He stood up. "Come on; let's go."

As she followed him, she asked, "But now what? What do I tell the queen?"

"You tell her the truth. Exactly what happened from the time of Abra's accidental death to my taking you to the boat. I'm not going back to Sheba. I'm going to wait it out in Egypt, and once Pharaoh comes back from his invasion of Judah, I'm going back to Judah, where I belong."

"Do you think the queen will send soldiers to find and bring back Heber?"

He looked at her and replied, "No. She can't send her soldiers into Egypt, and even if she sent mercenaries to look for him, they probably wouldn't find him. There's no description of my sister, Pithin, or Heber. And there are many, many families with a young son. She'll be angry, but there's nothing she can do."

"Will she punish me? My family?"

"Why? Neither you nor your family betrayed her. Just the people she sent out to do the job. That's why I'm not going back." Shallum carefully draped his robe over his back and got up to leave. "Come. Let's go into the city. We'll find lodging and bandages."

The next morning, they took off, Shallum with his wounds cleaned and bandaged and Nalussa in a daze, thinking over the entire exploit. She was numb to Abra's death, relieved at Heber's good fortune, but vacant in mind over what the queen's reaction to the failed plan would be. As Shallum said, she could only tell the truth.

Along the way, she prayed. Just because she believed in one God didn't mean that she wasn't terrified of the queen's reaction to the plan's failure. She did come to realize, though, that when she did seek God out in prayer and help, a peace settled on her that she couldn't quite understand; mentally and even physically, her burdens were lifted as if God picked up the weight from her mind and body.

When they settled in for the night at a campsite, Nalussa impulsively asked, "Do you believe and trust in our God?"

"I'm a Hebrew!" Shallum responded indignantly, throwing a stick into the fire.

"Just because you're a Hebrew and even follow the law doesn't necessarily mean you believe in God," she quietly replied. "You could easily let the priests and Levites do all the work."

He poked the fire, watching the sparks rise up into the night. "Like making sacrifices for our sins? I personally don't believe that the sacrifice of animals blithely takes away one's sin. We are always sinning according to God's commandments He gave to Moses, never mind all the other hundreds of laws that were not directly given to Moses from God. How can we not sin? If sacrificing animals covered our sins, then we'd never have any animals left!" Smiling, she waited for him to continue.

"I do believe in God, but not the way our temple leaders would have us believe: they come before God to sacrifice animals on our behalf. So, they lead and pray, and we follow. Now, I know He is an awesome God, One to be feared and revered, and sin has consequences, but I also think He loves us on a personal level. It seems to me that He would rather have us showing mercy and kindness to others, rather than taking the lives of innocent animals and thinking that our sins are gone, and we can go back to the same behavior until the next sacrifice."

That was a surprising admission from a man Nalussa thought to be hardened and worldly. He further surprised her when he asked, "Have you read any of King David's psalms of thanksgiving? He knew God loved him and was thankful. Why wouldn't God love us individually as He loved King David?"

She agreed. "I think He does love us as much as He loved King David. He had mercy on David."

"Exactly. And I believe He wants us to practice mercy to others as well. That's why I couldn't take Heber from my sister."

She sighed. "I'm grateful you didn't."

Shallum let out a snort. "Speaking of kings, God sure did love King Solomon! And Solomon . . . well, you know more about Solomon than me."

"I've wrestled with that knowledge," Nalussa conceded. "But in the end, I think King Solomon realized his own folly. He wrote down many interesting bits of wisdom concerning our foolish and sinful ways, and he also wrote about our quest for all the things that life can offer. He reduced it all to our vanity, and I believe he included himself in that assessment."

They were quiet for a while, watching the glow from the cinders, when Shallum asked, "This is a bit personal, but what did you think of being Solomon's concubine?"

She pursed her lips. "It's complicated. I had no choice; I adapted; he treated me as well as he did his other women. He enjoyed my mind, but his first interest was my body, which in time became less of a desire for him. I was confused and angry with God at first because of His favor to Solomon, but I've come to understand that God gives us choices. Solomon made some wrong choices, but we all do. So, who am I to judge?"

"True," the big man agreed. "We don't know the intimate relationship a person has with God. We only see the surface."

Changing direction, he looked at her profile in the glow of the embers. "I heard about your and Abra's escape from Rehoboam. That was impressive," Shallum admitted. "I didn't know that you ultimately married Adriel." He laughed. "I knew Adriel in the days of him roaming the country looking for women for Solomon. I always liked him. He knew a beauty when he saw one. But he never touched them!" Shallum was quick to add.

Nalussa laughed. "He found me, didn't he? He's an amazing man. He accepted me for who I was. I've been blessed."

"Indeed," agreed Shallum.

When they reached the port, Shallum found a man he knew to escort Nalussa from port to port and then to the Queen of Sheba's palace. "Don't leave her until she gains entry to the palace; then you may come back." The man agreed, and Shallum paid out the man's fees.

Nalussa said, "I'm relieved to be escorted. I was fearful to be left alone."

"First of all, I would never leave you alone, and second, if I left you alone, you would disappear in a minute. Keep close to him. Never be separated. Here." He went to his pack and pulled out a purse. "Take this and hide it. Don't let anyone see this. It's the money Queen Makeda gave me for the job. I've failed, so here's her money back."

Nalussa took the pouch and hid it in her satchel slung under her arm. On the one hand, she dreaded facing the queen, but on the other, she would soon see Adriel and her family. Her emotions were jumbled between apprehension, fear, and elation.

There was no scream. Only a look of utter surprise. The man watching over Nalussa opened his mouth, but no sound was made. A red bloom erupted in his chest as the arrow's feathers quivered ever so slightly in his tunic. Shallum instinctively pushed Nalussa down; then grabbing her arm, he scrambled away with her into the milling crowd. Those who saw the arrow protruding from the man's chest screamed, sending off a chain of chaos. In the mayhem that ensued, Shallum dragged her through groups of animals and people, who scattered, screaming and running for their lives. Three men on horseback thundered toward the quay but were impeded as baggage, animals, and people, terrified and running, obstructed their way.

"Who are they after?" Nalussa breathed as she bumped into men and women attempting to flee.

"Me! It must be me!" Shallum shouted, as he bent low, blending with the crowd.

Running along with a group of men who inadvertently shielded them, he suddenly veered off by a dock, pulling her under it. They slogged through the calf-deep water to a small, beached scow laying bottom-up against a bulkhead.

Above, the pursuers had to maneuver their horses amidst people and animals in chaos and dropped baggage and chests. Shouts were heard as Egyptian soldiers finally made their presence known trying to calm the people and stop the attackers.

Sliding under the skiff with her, he put a finger to his lips, listening. "It sounds like the soldiers are going after the men. Stay here. If I don't come back in an hour, God be with you. Bribe a fisherman or trader to take you to Sheba, if you can."

She looked at him wild-eyed as he said, "Now is the time to pray to our God."

He skirted the small beach and walked back to the main docks as people were returning after the excitement had died down and the soldiers had contained the attackers, who were loudly arguing with them by a small garrison.

Business as usual, Shallum noted, as the laborers and slaves continued loading boats and barges and people bartered for transit.

He saw four men carrying the dead man off. Each had a leg or arm. It was no time for sentiment, though he was distressed his acquaintance was killed. He darted toward a vendor, discarded his head-covering identifying him as a Hebrew, and bought one that Egyptian men wore. He walked swiftly toward a paddock, where he had put his two horses. Untroubled by any turmoil, they were casually nibbling on hay, waiting for his return. Only now, he couldn't return. He had to get Nalussa to Sheba. He grabbed a pack and a water skin and paid off the stable boy to look after the horses for a week, instructing him to hold them for at least another. He would be back to settle up his bill.

"I've heard that before. If you're not back in two weeks, they get sold," the young man retorted.

Buying a hunk of bread, he asked a vendor what was going on. The man nodded toward the three men still arguing with the soldiers. "You know the king of Judah? From what I hear, he has men wandering everywhere, even Egypt, for his runaway concubines. One's dead, but there's quite a reward for the one who's still above ground." The man chuckled. "Word is she is very desirable.

"But the story gets better. Pharaoh had her but let her go because he found out she was married," he crowed. "And Pharaoh himself is in on getting her captured to be brought back to Judah's king. Pharaoh's not happy about being fooled. So, he gave the okay for the men from Judah to track her down and to kill the man who brought her to him in the first place!"

"You hear all the news." Shallum was amazed that just days out from Pharaoh's palace, the word was already spreading about Nalussa and him. At least, there was no gossip about his sister, Pithin, and that little goat, Heber.

Making his way back to the docks, he kept his distance from the garrison, hoping the soldiers would detain the men for a bit longer. They wouldn't take kindly to Hebrews storming their port, killing a man, and causing damage and disrupting trade. Hopefully, they would send a runner to Pharaoh for verification, but it was possible they already had his seal and documents in the event something like this happened and they had to explain themselves.

He had to get them to Sheba. Slipping his way between the traders and travelers, he walked along the docks, trying to figure a way to cross the divide. Not wanting to get on a barge of a transit boat, he spotted a couple of decrepit-looking boats with sails lashed to their booms. He would steal one.

The three men were let go by the Egyptian soldiers and were now scouring the quay, checking passenger boats. He hurried to Nalussa.

Ducking under the boat, there was barely room for the two of them, but because it was lying against a bulkhead, there was at least a little space. He handed her water and bread. "We stay here until dusk, then pray the wind kicks up and we can cross. I've found a boat.

"They'll take us across?" Nalussa sounded doubtful.

"No, I'm taking us across."

CHAPTER THIRTY-TWO

Cold and wet, she huddled in the stern while Shallum, midship, used a pole, then oar, to get them as far away from the docks as possible. The night was misty with black clouds scuttling across the sky with the weather intermittently covering a weak sliver of a moon. There was wind.

Thankfully, with the activity going on at dusk, no one was paying any attention to the smaller boats that were either coming in or going out to fish. The men looking for Shallum and Nalussa were not evident, but Shallum ordered Nalussa to keep below the gunnels, so it would appear that he was merely a lone fisherman going out in the evening with his nets.

Finally, he raised the tattered sail and realized it was a pathetic excuse for a working boat. "No wonder it looked abandoned," he muttered. The sail had holes and pieces of fabric, along with grass and twigs that fell out as he hoisted the sail. "A nest that even the rats abandoned."

Nalussa struggled up, seeing that they were too far away for anyone to raise an alarm. "Do you know the way?" They could land anywhere if they followed the wind.

"I have an idea of direction. We'll have to tack, and it might take a while, but let's hope we don't run into any surprise squalls. The weather is iffy as it is."

It started to rain, but lightly. The wind was blustery and the waves choppy, but the little boat held its own as the weather conditions maintained. Hours later, cold and shivering, they came upon a dark expanse of what appeared to be land ahead.

"I pray this is the other side," Nalussa whispered. They had tacked so many times that she lost all sense of direction. Her exhaustion added to her dulled senses. All she wanted to do was put her feet on solid land. And sleep in a warm, dry place.

Shallum strained, looking for a sense of where they might be, but he had no idea. "I think that's land ahead, and I hope it's Sheba. Sovereign God, I want to get out of this boat!" Just as he spoke, the boat banged hard against a submerged rock. He fell forward, and Nalussa slipped backward. The boat screeched as the bow scraped and wedged itself hard; listing to the starboard side, waves began pouring in. "We've got to get out! Follow me. Hold onto my tunic!"

She sloshed through water to his side as he angled himself to get over the gunnels and into the water. With a splash, he jumped in. "Come! I'll catch you!" Nalussa jumped in. The water was freezing.

"Grab my tunic and don't let go! Hurry!" he shouted as the boat banged continuously against the rocky shoal. "We have to get away, or it will crush us!"

Nalussa's veil was washed off, and her robe over her tunic was dragging her down. She pulled it off and lunged for Shallum. He caught her arm and pulled her away from the boat that was soon to break up.

He was a strong swimmer. She was helpless, panicking, gulping water, and coughing. "Close your mouth, or you'll drown!" he demanded, pulling her through the water.

The water beyond the shoal deepened but eventually became shallower as they neared land. Nearly exhausted, Shallum touched bottom. Hauling her up, he walked with her under his arm until she, too, could stand on the bottom. Carefully, he let go, and together, they lurched their way to the shore. It was pitch black; but the wind had lessened, and solid ground was a relief. Shivering from cold, they sat on the beach, holding onto each other for warmth.

"Can you walk? We've got to find shelter off the beach, even if it's in the scrub brush."

Nalussa, who didn't have the energy to speak, only nodded. They made their way up a dune and in the dim, on-again, off-again moonlight found a path. "I don't think I can make it," Nalussa lamented.

"Stay strong. We've come too far for you to give up. We'll find a place to rest; let's just follow this path a little more."

Shortly, they came to a darkened hut, which was a relief, considering it was well into the night. Shallum walked ahead and, smelling a spent fire, knocked on the door. Again, he knocked, and soon, a small man opened the door with a dagger in his hand.

"I'm no foe!" said Shallum. "We've been shipwrecked!" He held his hands wide and empty.

The man looked at his wet and sandy clothes; then he looked beyond Shallum and saw Nalussa sitting on the ground. Opening the door wide, he came out and went directly to Nalussa, who could not get up on her own. Taking her arms, he pulled her up; and leaning on him, she stumbled her way to the door of the shelter.

Inside, she collapsed once again on the floor, and the man covered her over with a blanket.

Shallum began to explain, but the man held up his hand. He didn't understand a word of what was being said and so merely pointed to the floor. Once the big man sat down, the owner covered him with a blanket, gave him a drink, and offered him bread; but Shallum put a hand up. He was too tired to eat. He, too, lay down from exhaustion. The man watched them until morning.

Both awoke mid-morning to the smell of hot flatbread cooking on heated rocks outside the shelter. A cat nosed around them, then went to the corner to chew on a dried piece of fish. The man came through the door holding a straw basket and placed it before them.

They readily accepted bread, dried fish, and water the man offered. Although there was a language problem, the man understood they wanted to get to the city and palace after Shallum drew pictures in the dirt. The man walked them to a wider dirt road and pointed. Then, holding up three fingers, he nodded. Shallum and Nalussa understood it would be a three-hour walk.

Nalussa was still tired; but with a little food in her stomach and a dry piece of fabric the man gave her for her head and shoulders, she felt ready for the final stage of the journey. They walked slowly, speaking little. Fortunately, both had their satchels that carried the coins from Pharaoh, Nalussa's jewelry, the payment from the queen to Shallum, and an extra pair of wet sandals.

For his part, Shallum had his own pouch with money, presumably, and other travel gear. Nalussa looked his back over for signs of fresh blood. "Once you deliver me to the palace, you'll leave to go back to Egypt?" she asked.

"Yes, that's the plan. I've got to get far away from the queen. I have places to hide until I can make safe passage. Don't tell her that, but at least try to placate her. She'll ask how you found your way to Sheba. Again, be honest. Let her know that you are still being sought—as I am—by Pharaoh and King Rehoboam." He chuckled to himself. "I guess I can add her to the list of people wanting me."

"She might not care. At least, you'll be returning her money. The reality is, Abra's dead and no threat, and she might understand your sister's feelings for Heber. Hopefully, she won't be angry or vengeful."

"You never know. Royalty is unpredictable," Shallum explained.

"Yes. I thought getting away from Pharaoh was too easy. Little did I expect he would help Rehoboam's men to take you and me down. Will you be safe?" She looked at him with concern. Although their history was short, it was powerful.

"I'll be fine. I just hope at some point, I can go back to Judah." He smiled wistfully. "And I hope you and your family make it back, too."

"When Rehoboam dies," Nalussa said simply.

Coming through the city gates, Shallum walked Nalussa as far as the palace walls. "You're safe now. I'm leaving you, and I wish God's blessings." She stood, watching him go. He stopped and turned with a smile. "Adriel is a blessed man. And Solomon? He didn't know the true treasure he had in you." He made a brief salute and quickly walked away.

She felt a sadness watching him disappear around a corner. He had never once made crass or crude remarks or gestures toward her. He treated her with fairness as one would with a colleague or friend. Yes, she considered him a friend. He risked his life for her without asking anything from her.

She stood for a long time outside the palace walls, contemplating her filth and raggedness. Cautiously, she approached the gate. A guard appeared and confronted her, shouting, "No vagrants, no alms, no begging!"

With raw emotion, she explained who she was, and with a strength she didn't know she had, she demanded, "Take me to Queen Makeda. Now!"

The guard trotted away and soon came back with two official men, who peered at her and, in haste, ushered her through the gate. They began to question her as fast as arrows flying through the air.

"I will not speak until I see the queen." The officials corralled a young guard with instructions to alert the queen.

As soon as she entered the palace, more advisors showed up and hustled her to a smaller meeting room to meet with the queen. Sitting on a stool, she trembled with exhaustion and emotion. She wanted to see her husband and family. She was tired of the drama of kings and queens. She longed to be outside in the sun, away from the power of the anointed.

CHAPTER THIRTY-THREE

The queen entered with ceremony and security. Two aides were by her side, two soldiers in front, and two at her back. She was beautifully coifed, eyes outlined in kohl, and dressed eloquently, but there was a frailness about her. Everyone bowed as she entered, but Nalussa, standing on ceremony, did not bow but merely turned to look her full in the face. They had once talked together as friends. This woman before her was different. The queen's eyes went wide, taking in Nalussa's dirty and torn clothes, dusty feet, and tangled hair.

"Sit," the queen ordered and went to her throne. Once everyone was settled and a slave fanned the throne, the queen quietly asked why she was here alone and where Abra and Heber were.

Nalussa's first thoughts were for the welfare of her husband and family, and she had planned to proceed cautiously, but she was angry. She had been used by people for too long. She was not a sexual object, but a legitimately married Hebrew woman, a human being. She was not bait, not a plaything. Mustering her courage, she responded coldly to the queen and her court and told the story from start to finish. When a few tried to interrupt, the queen held her hand up. There would be no interruptions.

Nalussa concluded, "I know I have nowhere to go but to stay here until King Rehoboam dies. It could be a long time. I only ask that because of your relationship with King Solomon, you would treat me and my family with compassion. I did my part in trying to help you capture Abra and her son. While they have not been brought back to you, Abra, dead, is no threat to you, and Heber as a child with new parents without agenda has no governmental aspirations. As you know, King Rehoboam plans for his own son to take the throne of Judah when he dies."

Remembering the money the queen had given Shallum for his efforts, she held out the pouch filled with gold. "This is from Shallum."

The silent court looked to the queen for reaction. On her face was a look of resignation. The queen looked oddly at Nalussa and said, "Keep it. What is done is done. You may stay here with your family until it is safe for you to leave." An aide helped her up. With a regal sweep of her skirts, she stood for a moment, looking wearily at Nalussa, as if wanting to say something; but her soldiers and advisors surrounded her, and she slowly left the room.

Squeals of delight filled her family's apartments. Her younger brother and sister ran to her as her father, bent with age, tottered to her side. Hugging, kissing, crying, Nalussa looked about. "Where's Adriel? Where's Jasper?"

"In prison. When they found out that you were gone, and none of the officials would tell them anything, they became suspicious, so they set out looking for you themselves. They thought that somehow you went to Egypt after Abra because Jasper had seen her there with Ebel."

Her younger brother, Ziba, piped up. "But none of us could understand why you would ever go after them—especially if you were alone. You wouldn't take Heber from his mother!"

Her father nodded and added, "None of it made sense, and once they got to the port and started asking questions, they were detained and arrested by the queen's men."

Her brother stood tall and pointed to himself. "But I found out the real reason you disappeared. I'm friends with a chamber slave. These officials think that the slaves don't hear a thing!"

Her father led her to a couch. She covered her eyes, crying. "Is he here?" she asked.

"Yes," her brother answered. "He's in the dungeons with Jasper. I know where they are. I bring them food from our table every day. I've bribed the guards with our allotment of wine."

"Please, take me to them." Renewed in energy and determination, she stood.

Ziba had grown so tall, she barely recognized the youth from the child. Together, they followed a path of servant and slave hallways and wound their way under the palace. When the guard saw her brother, he smiled but grimaced at seeing Nalussa. "I can't let you bring her here!" The burly man complained. "If anyone gets a prostitute, it's me!" He laughed and got closer to Nalussa.

Her brother put out a hand on the man's chest. "Don't. She's my sister, and I'm taking her to see her husband."

"Sister? Dressed like that? She smells!"

"You want to keep getting wine?" The man stepped back and nodded. "Then let us pass. We're not freeing the prisoners, only visiting."

"Next time, my young friend, it's double portion, or you'll never see your friend and brother again!" the man hollered after them.

"How does he let you get away with this?" asked Nalussa, referring to the guard allowing them to see the prisoners. They hurried down the stifling, dusty hallway past empty cells.

"I'd say it's too bad, and I'm sorry—but he's addicted to wine, and it works to my advantage. Come."

Around a corner, the smell of human excrement, urine, and sweat became apparent in the dark hallway. Nalussa crept forward and let out a small cry. There were Adriel and Jasper, sitting in rank straw, quietly talking with each other. Both looked up. In surprise, as if not believing what they were seeing, they slowly stood. Coming close to the bars, Adriel reached out. At the same time, they shouted, "Nalussa!"

The visit was joyous and, at the same time, desperate. Nalussa told them the entire story. When she explained about Abra's accident, Jasper heaved a sigh. "You know, I loved her in an immature way. We really had little time to know each other, and the same is true for my relationship with little Heber. He was a good baby. I'm saddened Abra is dead, truly. But she didn't love me. I was just a convenience. As for Heber, I can only say I'm glad he's with a family who will love him and keep him out of palaces."

The two men then told their story of searching for Nalussa and trying to find out what had happened to her. In both instances, they not only came to a dead end on information and location, but they were arrested by the queen's men for treason.

"For whatever reasoning the queen might have had," Adriel said with a shrug, "that's what they accused us of. We never did see the queen but were hauled off and thrown in prison." Finally, at a loss for more words, Adriel rubbed his beard. "We have got to get out of here. We must figure a way out!"

"We'll work on it," Ziba assured him. "God will make a way!"

Nalussa kissed Adriel fervently and clasped Jasper's hand, whispering, "We will be back!"

On the way to the apartments, the siblings talked over how they could manage getting the queen to just let them go.

"Just ask?" her brother suggested.

"I will," said Nalussa, wondering if the queen would find compassion.

But Nalussa couldn't get a response from the queen. In fact, no one in the court would speak with her or her family members. Only one servant appeared and told her, "The queen's advisors say never to ask about freeing the prisoners again." Either the queen wasn't getting the requests because they were blocked by her advisors, or she really was not going to give her husband and brother clemency.

Days turned into weeks, and she always accompanied her younger brother to the dungeon. The guard was content with the plan as long as he got his drink. Adriel and Jasper were despondent, but Ziba insisted, "We will get you out!"

True to his word, Pharaoh took twelve hundred chariots and sixty thousand horsemen, along with a huge number of mercenaries, to invade Judah. He successfully overtook fortified cities and ultimately made his way to Jerusalem.

Invading Jerusalem, they stripped Solomon's glorious and astoundingly wealthy temple of gold shields, jewel-encrusted vessels, and gold and silver objects of art and decoration. Ten golden lampstands, one hundred gold basins, and all the golden tongs, cups, and firepans were taken. Prized storerooms of fantastic treasure rarely seen in any kingdom were emptied. Even King Rehoboam's house was ransacked.

It was mortifying for Judah; but God was with the kingdom, and King Shishak mercifully left, sparing Rehoboam's life.

After Pharaoh returned with great fanfare, his victory quickly spread throughout his kingdom. Nalussa and her family decided now was the time to go back to their country. It wasn't as risky now that Rehoboam had been humiliated and was too preoccupied defending his borders from Jeroboam, who, like a stinging wasp, was not about to stop his ongoing attacks anytime soon. Since his defeat at the hands of Pharaoh and his need to keep the kingdom secure for his son, Abijah, who would be appointed king in his place, Rehoboam became cautious.

Fortunately for King Rehoboam, Pharaoh did not want to overtake the kingdom. Upon hearing this, Nalussa brought her family together and asked if they were willing to take their chances in going back to Judah.

"What if we get permission to leave? Tell the queen that since Rehoboam has been plundered, Judah is in a weakened state, and Pharaoh has marched back to Egypt, we feel safe to return home."

"When the time came, she said she'd let us go and would fund our travel," Nalussa's sister, Noa, remembered.

"If you agree," Nalussa said anxiously, "I'll petition the queen for safe passage to the port. We have enough money to get us to Judah even if the queen doesn't fund us. I'll also ask to free Adriel and Jasper!"

The response from the queen's advisors was that they would be granted safe passage to the port and funded travel expenses to Egypt and then to Judah, but there would be no release of Adriel and Jasper.

The family was crushed. "What would be the reason to hold them? Surely, she must understand they're no threat. The failed capture of Abra and Heber had nothing to do with them!" her father lamented.

"I don't believe she is receiving the full message. I think the advisors are filtering what she hears," Nalussa mused. "They possibly have an agenda, although I can't think what."

Ziba shook his head. "We'll have to stay because we can't leave them behind. The queen seems to have forgotten about them and won't talk to us personally; and if we don't continue to bring them food and drink, they'll die. And how could you forget that Rehoboam is still on the throne and could be a threat to you, Nalussa?"

She answered, "Gossip has it that Rehoboam has more to worry about now that he has been robbed by Pharaoh. He's also continually at war with Jeroboam, since Pharaoh's attack. He's trying to hold his kingdom together for his son; he has little money. It's doubtful he would still want an older, married concubine. What would it prove now?"

They all went silent, each thinking of what to do. "Think of this." Nalussa stood up, energized. "What's to stop us from just breaking them out of prison? Right now, the advisors think they are rotting in prison, and the queen seems to have forgotten about them. By the time they're remembered, they'll be gone." Her father and brother exchanged doubtful looks.

Nalussa insisted, "The guard gets drunk every night. So, we give him a double portion of drink when we bring the men their supper. Then Ziba can sneak back later in the night and, while he's passed out, take the key, unlock the door . . . Then they can keep the door closed like it's locked. The guard rarely goes back there because we're bringing them their food and drink daily."

"Maybe that would work if we get the guard drunk enough," Ziba acquiesced. "The keys are on a long rope around his neck." Her brother scratched his head in thought. "It could be tricky getting it off him, but if he's really passed out . . . "

Nalussa continued. "Depending on wind, sailing from Sheba to Egypt can be as little as three hours. They could get to port and sail away. And I still have a little bit of money left from Pharaoh, my jewelry I've held onto, and the payment the queen gave to Shallum for the failed abductions. When we hire a boat for ourselves, we could hire a boat to be ready to take Adriel and Jasper across at night."

"Whoa, wait! Timing is critical," her father stated. "They'll have to leave at night when the guard is passed out. We can't have them escape before us. It has to be after we are gone."

"If their escape is after we leave, how do we get wine to the guard if we're gone?" Noa asked.

"This is how," Ziba spoke confidently. "My friend, the slave of the chamber? I'll have him bring the prisoners their meal because he'll tell the guard we've left the palace and from now on will be taking care of them and providing him nightly wine. He'll give the guard a double portion as my thanks to him for allowing us to feed the prisoners and letting my friend continue."

"This is going to work, Family! God is with us. Now is the time for a prayer of thanksgiving." Nalussa smiled.

"It hasn't happened yet," Noa cautioned.

"I believe it has."

CHAPTER THIRTY-FOUR

An official showed up at their apartments the following morning and said, "Your petition to leave has been accepted. You may go. The queen is not in residence, but I have been given authority to agree. Plan first light tomorrow. Chariots will be waiting to take you to the port, but you will have to make your own arrangements for transit to Egypt." He dug in his cloak and took out a small pouch. "This will provide you with the necessities of getting to the border of Judah. After that, you are on your own."

Ziba opened his mouth to complain, but Nalussa held him back with a slight look. "We are grateful." She bowed. "Please tell Queen Makeda I'm so sorry I didn't get the opportunity to thank her in person for her kindness in taking care of my family. I pray many blessings for her and a long reign."

The man barely acknowledged her remarks and left.

"Something's not right here," Nalussa observed as the man walked away. "The queen would never have kept Adriel and Jasper locked up for this length of time under these conditions, and she would not have ignored us for these many weeks."

"We can't worry about her. We need to pack and be ready for our trip. Tonight is critical," her father said. "You and Ziba will tell Adriel and Jasper the plan. Keep alert. The young friend of Ziba's has gladly accepted taking care of Adriel and Jasper. We've paid him well."

That night, Ziba procured two jugs of wine from the kitchen, and he and Nalussa went to the dungeons. By now, the guard, eager for his rations and delighted he got extra, happily waved them on, settling on his pallet for a satisfying night.

Arriving at the cell, Nalussa reached out to Adriel and held his hand, whispering, "We and the family leave at first light tomorrow . . . "

Adriel pulled his hand away as if he was burned. The men were horrified. "You're leaving?" Adriel demanded. Jasper grabbed the bars in distress.

Nalussa held a finger up to her lips. "Shhh. We have a plan. Tonight, while the guard is incapacitated, Ziba will get the key and unlock your door. Tomorrow night, his friend will take our place and give the guard a double ration of wine, then come to you with food. You'll have to gauge from the guard's snores if he is out. Then, while he is sleeping, make a break."

Surprised and euphoric it was going to happen so quickly, they hugged and danced in joy. "I was dashed to bits when you first said you were leaving, never expecting this amazing, simple plan. It will work!" Adriel clapped Jasper on his back.

Jasper put his head to the bars and said, "Thank God!"

"Here is the route to take." Ziba detailed exiting the dungeon corridors and finding the way out of the palace grounds. "What was the inn you stayed at in Naj?" Ziba asked Jasper.

Jasper put a hand to his temple, thinking. "I don't remember the name, but it was a medium-sized place that also sold goats and had a manger out back that was connected to a small field. If the inn was full, you could sleep in the hay in the manger." He thought a moment longer. "Yes, it was outside the city square to the west."

"We'll find it and wait for you there; and if we can't get room there, we will leave you a message as to where we went. If all goes well, you shouldn't be more than one or two days behind us." Ziba patted his brother on the arm in assurance.

"We originally planned to have a boat waiting for you, but I think it's wiser if you get the boat yourselves," Nalussa added, and they readily agreed. "Here, take this." She handed him a small satchel that contained an extra pair of sandals, head scarf, and knives for each man, and, most importantly, gold.

No one could sleep that night. Ziba stealthily left the apartments and made his way below the palace. Because the queen did not want criminals near her, she had a separate prison off palace grounds, so the old dungeon below was usually used as temporary incarceration and only for infractions made by palace workers who had to be disciplined. For months now, only Adriel and Jasper languished behind its bars. It was in poor repair and only guarded by the man who loved his wine and who lived in the hallway, rarely seeing the light of day. His space smelled of feces and urine. Even though his waste jars were set against the far wall, they were overflowing more than usual. Ziba pulled his head scarf to his nose and noted the wine jugs were empty.

Slinking carefully toward the fat guard slumbering noisily on a stained straw pallet, he nearly shrieked and narrowly missed on stepping on a rat the size of a kitten. Rats scurried in all directions, carrying leftover pieces of bread in their teeth from the man's meal.

Breathing through his mouth, Ziba cautiously moved again, keeping an eye out for darting rodents. *Oh, no!* He didn't take into consideration the man would be lying down, and he had to get the rope over the man's head, which meant he had to slide in between his head and mattress. Ever so gently, he pushed the stuffed pallet down, creating an indentation, and maneuvered the rope up and over the guard's short, matted hair, his heart pounding wildly. He prayed, *Please, God, don't let my heart wake him!* The guard, so deeply asleep, never stirred.

Straightening up, he tiptoed around the pallet. Even at night, down here, the mosquitoes were ferocious. He resisted the urge to swat them as they mercilessly whined around his head. *How could anyone sleep without a net over their body?* Ziba wondered and wasn't surprised to see bites all over the man's arms and legs. He truly was deep in slumber.

Quietly running down the hallway, he tripped over another rat, who squealed, but got to the cell without further incident. Adriel and Jasper had been tensely waiting for hours and were pressing their faces against the bars peering down the dark hallway. Even in the night, the heat was intense. Adriel and Jasper glistened with sweat as they slapped the mosquitoes with little effect. There were just too many.

Ignoring his own bug attacks, Ziba worked rapidly once getting to their door. Using pig fat, he stuffed the lock, shoved the key in, and turned. The fat lubricated the rusty metal, and only a slight scraping sound was made as the lock disengaged. He greased the hinges, too. Unlocked, he opened the door to small, squeaking sounds to hug Jasper, then Adriel. Gently, he closed the door, noting it wouldn't lock without the turn of the key. It was safe to keep closed, and no one would know it was unlocked. He ran back to the sleeping man, gently slipping the rope with the key over his head, and bounded away from the stench and bugs.

Back in the apartments, his family was waiting. As Nalussa went to him, he simply told them, "It's done. Let's get some sleep."

Before he turned in, he touched Nalussa's shoulder. "It's good we're getting them out now. If they're left any longer, they will die of fever or rat bites. The filth, the mosquitoes, the stench. It's horrendous!"

The next morning, with the help of some servants, they carried their belongings to the waiting chariots. Nervous and riddled with anxiety over Adriel and Jasper, they spoke little as they exited the palace grounds. No one met them to see them off and say good-bye. It all seemed so strange to Nalussa, but they were finally free, and soon, her husband and brother would be also. The streets were just awakening as vendors set up their stalls, and early buyers, hoping to avoid the heat, walked about inspecting the goods.

Nalussa couldn't help thinking that the queen was unwell. Although she looked beautiful, it was a fragile beauty, and her bearing, though regal, lacked vigor. Nalussa was saddened at the queen's bearing, but selfishly, she was also disappointed. She had hoped to have a private word with the woman whom King Solomon had truly loved and to whom he had written such a wonderful love poem. Queen Makeda was not only special to him but also to Nalussa. It wasn't just her beauty and queenly standing, but also the history she and Nalussa shared.

She had hoped there would have been more reaction from her about the failed plan, more questions about Abra, and perhaps empathy or sympathy for young Heber. *It's as if all of this drama that had caused so much anguish, worry, and even death is no longer important,* she marveled. *And the queen never expressed any concern or explanation about Adriel and Jasper being imprisoned? For treason? That was absurd! Maybe she didn't know?*

Well, it was all behind her now. The queen was left to her country; Nalussa would soon be reunited with her husband; and the entire family would be home in Judah soon.

How could she not think of King Solomon at a time like this? She remembered his words he had written: "When I surveyed all that my hands had done and what I had toiled to achieve, everything was meaningless, a chasing after the wind; nothing was gained under the sun."[18]

She smiled. *How true. Vanity. Kings and queens plan; nations rise and fall; people of all social levels come and go . . . Our tribulations will be but a forgotten story, for what is it all but human vanity? Yet all are under the will of God.*

---

18 Ecclesiastes 2:11

CHAPTER THIRTY-FIVE

The following night, Adriel and Jasper tensely waited for their moment of freedom. They heard the guard bellowing, "Who are you, and what do you want?"

A young man answered, approaching the towering man, "I'm Anat, and I'm taking Ziba's place because he's gone back to Judah. I've been directed to give you as much wine as you want, providing you allow me to continue to feed the prisoners."

The guard hungrily noted the two large jugs in the young man's hands. "This better be good wine and not watered down, for if it is, you'll not see to the prisoners again!"

"You'll like it. It comes from the queen's own casks." The guard grabbed the jugs out of his hands and tilted one to his mouth. Overpouring, he cursed as wine drizzled down his already stained and torn tunic. Swallowing, then wiping his soddened chest, he grunted, "Go."

The young man hurried to the dungeon and slipped Adriel and Jasper a satchel of bread. "When will you leave?" he asked anxiously.

"It will be late, but as soon as we hear him snoring, we'll make our way out."

"May your God protect you. I understand He's a real god. Unlike ours." He paused as if he wanted to say more but scampered away.

Hours passed, when finally, they heard the guard relieve himself, groaning. Scraping feet echoed down the stone tunnel, then came a grunted "oof." Then silence. Soon, his snores roared against the rock walls.

"Now!" Adriel ordered. Jasper slowly opened the door wide enough for them to squeeze through, and as Jasper closed it, scrapes and squeaks of the hinges sounded only like quarreling rats.

Getting past the guard was no problem; dodging the rats was. For they were everywhere, along with clouds of mosquitoes hovering over the sleeping man, who halfheartedly attempted to cover his face and head with a dirty rag. Desperately wanting to swat and slap, they refrained from moving their arms and hands while keeping a close eye on dodging scampering black bodies. With relief, they cleared the main door of the prison and jogged across a small courtyard, keeping to the wall where they found the doorway that led out into the city.

"Hey!" came a hoarse whisper. Adriel and Jasper froze. A shadow moved forward. "It's me! Anat, your friend, the one who saved you!"

"What are you doing here?" demanded Adriel, looking around for others. The young man exclaimed, "If I stay, they'll torture and kill me once they find out you're gone!"

Without waiting for more conversation, Jasper grabbed Anat's cloak and dragged him along as they made haste to dissolve into the shadows. As they ran, Anat breathed, "It's bad enough they'll kill the guard, but once they get the information they want from him, I'm done!"

"What you say is true. Come, follow us." Together, they made their way to the docks, which at this time of night was quiet, save for a few travelers looking for a safe place to sleep among the stacked chests waiting to be loaded in the morning.

Scoping out possibilities for escape across the water, there were few options short of stealing a boat, which they didn't want to do.

"If we wait until dawn," Anat advised, "we can find someone to take us across to Egypt. There's always someone looking to take a fare. Do you have money?"

Adriel answered, "Don't worry about that."

They found a pile of rocks and debris, sat, and waited.

Just before dawn, the docks came alive with caravans and travelers arriving along with boat captains and crews. The three men kept together as they approached various men for hire. Anat was right. There were many small boatmen, who were waiting at the port specifically to grab a traveler.

Arriving at a price, Adriel paid the man, and they climbed aboard. Because of the winds, they tacked back and forth, resulting in a longer trip, but the waters were reasonably tame. And once they got to the other side, they would trade in some of Nalussa's jewels for donkeys. Horses would be too expensive, and although they were away from Sheba, they wanted to blend in with crowds making their way into Egypt.

As Jasper bargained for beasts, Anat pulled Adriel aside and implored, "Let me stay with you until we reach Naj; then I'll be on my way. I can't pay you for a donkey, but if you get me one, you can easily sell it in the city." He thought a moment, then continued, "I can easily find work there, and I want to go home, too. I can earn some money to get to Lower Egypt. I'm Egyptian, and I've been blessed by your God because if I stayed, my life would be over. Even as gracious as the queen is, her advisors aren't. Now, because I took the risk to help you, I'm a free man and can go home again."

Adriel smiled, putting a hand on his shoulder. "You helped save us. You're welcome to continue with us." He hurried over to Jasper; they talked; then Adriel came back to Anat. "We'll get you a donkey. We might need an extra one, anyway, once we meet up with my family."

Anat was relieved. "Thanks, my brother."

"How did you end up in Sheba?" Adriel asked Anat as they followed Jasper winding his way through the people to the stables to pick up the animals.

"There was a famine in the land, and every able-bodied son or daughter got sold in exchange for food," Anat explained over the din of the crowds and hawkers milling about. "Not unusual, my family had to sell me because they needed to buy grain. Fortunately, the Queen of Sheba's entourage was getting ready for a crossing, and she bought a number of us desperate for money to buy food. She paid a premium for me because I could read and write, so my sister was able to stay behind with my parents."

Adriel remembered the famine that spared Judah and Sheba. So many starving people in Egypt either came into Judah to seek food or were sold to various traders so their families could buy grain from Pharaoh's enormous storehouses. Many died.

It wasn't the first time severe famine hit the nations. He recalled the ancient Hebrew patriarch Joseph, who was sold into slavery by his brothers and ended up in an exalted administrative position under the Pharaoh of those days. His father, Jacob, was told by his sons that their brother, Joseph, of whom they were jealous, had been killed by wild animals. In reality, while they wanted to kill him, they sold him instead to slave traders.

After a serious setback of landing in prison because Pharaoh's wife lied and accused him of trying to rape her, he was released and became number two in power in Egypt because he interpreted Pharaoh's dream of impending famine. Knowing it would happen, Joseph saw to it that Pharaoh's storehouses would be filled with grain. When the famine hit Judah, Jacob sent Joseph's brothers to buy grain. Through twists and turns, the brothers were forgiven, and Joseph and his father reunited when the family moved to Egypt. Egypt and Judah had a long history intertwined with famine.

The travel to Naj was uneventful. It took them two days, and they cleared the city gates late in the evening. "I'm thankful this worked out and that your God is so good in granting us friendship and peace. Please, let me spend the night with you, and then I'll leave first thing in the morning."

Adriel and Jasper were eager to find Nalussa and the rest of the family, even though it was late. Adriel explained, "I need to find my wife and family. You are welcome to come along, but if we find them where we think they'll be, I don't know about space."

"Not to worry," remarked Anat. "I'll sleep in a stable, but I want to see my friend Ziba one last time. His friendship changed my life!"

On the night she believed her husband and brother would make it to Naj, if all went according to plan, Nalussa waited by the small, gated wall that led into the inn, where they were staying. If, as she calculated, Adriel didn't run into any trouble, he could arrive from the early evening well into the night.

Ziba sat in the dirt by her feet. Barely keeping her eyes open, Nalussa perched on a stool with her head resting against the wall when, unexpectedly, Ziba tugged hard the hem of her robe, snapping her out of her sleepiness. Slipping off the stool, she nearly collided with him as he jumped up, squinting into the night.

"Do you hear?" He touched her elbow.

Straining to listen, she whispered, "Yes. I think so."

In the dark, lumpy shadows made their way up the narrow road. "Adriel?" Nalussa called cautiously.

"Yes! YES!" came the response, and a figure dismounted and bounded toward her.

EPILOGUE

Nalussa sat quietly, kneading flour for the evening meal. Adriel, Jasper, Ziba, and her father were with the herds. She missed her little sister, Noa, who had been recently wed and already pregnant, living with her new husband's family a village away. Yet, she had been blessed by a new sister in-law, who was Jasper's young wife. She sighed. Her brother finally found another, who, while not as beautiful as Abra had been, was a fun, loving, young woman, who had blessed her brother with a child he adored.

She herself was barren. It only bothered her when she thought that Adriel was disappointed that he hadn't an heir, but he never complained nor talked about it. He enjoyed life and his in-laws, and most importantly, he loved her, no matter her infertility.

She looked up from her chore and spied a man on a horse coming directly to their home along the narrow path. She squinted her eyes and smiled broadly. She would recognize that build anywhere. It was Shallum! Dousing her hands in a bowl of water and wiping them on a towel at her waist, she ran out to greet him.

"Oh, my! It's been so long!" she called as she looked up at him advancing. "Shallum! Welcome!" Behind him at his back was a small figure. She called again, tilting her head to get a better look at the person behind him.

Coming closer, she saw that it was a little boy, whose face had the shape of Abra's and whose eyes sparkled with an eagerness and brightness that was King Solomon's. She breathed out. "Can this be?"

Shallum dismounted and slid the little boy off the large horse. "It is." He smiled proudly. "Heber, meet Nalussa."

The little boy shyly clung to Shallum's leg, but the big man gently pried his hands off and moved him toward Nalussa, who knelt on one knee and held out her hands. "Come, Heber," she whispered.

Unsure, he moved toward her. She clasped him to her breast as a kaleidoscope of sounds and images flashed through her mind—hearing Abra crowing she was pregnant, Abra parading around big with child, seeing the tiny infant crowning between his mother's legs in the wilderness, watching him be cared for by an Egyptian nurse. And maybe seeing him—just for a flash—sitting on the throne of Judah. She held him close, breathing in his musty body. He squirmed.

As they walked back to the garden, Shallum explained, "You are all very easy to find. I was concerned Rehoboam might come after you, but I've heard he's not well and that his son will soon take over the throne."

Nalussa nodded in agreement. "I'm not worried about him anymore."

Shallum looked around the home and garden. "How is my friend Adriel and the rest of the family?"

Nalussa quickly told him but inquired as to why he was here with the child that Tamin and Pithin took to raise.

"They died," he said simply. "I was with them when we were caught in a tribal war in Egypt. No point in going into details, but little Heber was left an orphan again, and I took care of him as best I could. But I can't do it anymore." He looked at her imploringly. "I know your heart, Nalussa. Will you care for this child?"

She didn't have to think twice. "Of course!" She grabbed the confused little boy again and hugged him. Adriel would not question bringing in Solomon's son, and the rest of the family would welcome him. They would treat him as their own. Nalussa smiled. Adriel would get an heir after all!

Settling into the garden, Nalussa slapped some unleavened bread on the hot stones heating in the fire and poured out goat's milk for the two travelers. She produced dried fruit and cheese. The little boy ate hungrily, staring at her and Shallum not saying a word. When the bread was ready, he ate that, too. Sleepy now, he lay on the ground by Shallum's feet and fell fast asleep.

As the day's shadows begin to lengthen, Adriel, her father, Jasper, and his wife and baby came in from fields. Jasper's wife had insisted she go out with them to catch grasshoppers for snacks. By this time, Heber was awake, playing with the chickens and teasing the nursing kids.

One after another, the family stopped short with wide eyes and open mouths. Shallum stood and greeted the men as Nalussa took the pouch of grasshoppers from Jasper's wife. By now, Heber was no longer shy and allowed himself to be hugged and tousled as introductions and brief explanations were made.

The supper was a joyous one. Adriel looked over at his beloved wife and said, "Who would have thought we would be the parents of the last of Solomon's children?" He laughed aloud, slapping his knee.

"But, my husband, he is now our son and your heir. Praise be to God!"

For more information about

S.A. Jewell

and

Solomon's Concubine

please visit:

www.teamofGod.org

www.SaraJewell.com

teamofGod@earthlink.net

www.facebook.com/sarasantosjewell

www.facebook.com/teamofGod

Ambassador International's mission is to magnify the Lord Jesus Christ and promote His Gospel through the written word.

We believe through the publication of Christian literature, Jesus Christ and His Word will be exalted, believers will be strengthened in their walk with Him, and the lost will be directed to Jesus Christ as the only way of salvation.

For more information about

AMBASSADOR INTERNATIONAL

please visit:

www.ambassador-international.com

Thank you for reading this book. Please consider leaving us a review on your social media, favorite retailer's website, Goodreads or Bookbub, or our website.

More Biblically-Based Fiction from Ambassador International

During his lifetime, Daniel saw the fulfillment of God's promises, prophesied of the Israelites future as well as ours, and led pagan kings to God. From slave to the highest position in the king's court, Daniel shows how God can use an ordinary person to do extraordinary things.

In this creatively thought-provoking and gripping novel by debut author Andrew Stone, readers will discover a much deeper meaning as the lives of Barabbas and Jesus intertwine between the pages and weave a story of love and sacrifice.

Miriam, a widow in Judea, has only one hope for survival: she must go to Capernaum and live as a beggar. Meeting unlikely friends along the way, Miriam's path winds from Capernaum to the Sea of Galilee to Jerusalem. As she searches for friends and security, she eventually meets a man named Jesus of Nazareth. By His miracles and teaching, Miriam and her friends finally find something to believe in. But can they overcome the doubt and treachery that lurks in Jerusalem?

Made in United States
North Haven, CT
30 August 2024

56759421R00186